DEATH & September

DREW BRYENTON

Death and September
Drew Bryenton

This edition copyright © 2025 by Oxford eBooks Ltd.
Published under the sci-fi-cafe.com imprint.

www.oxford-ebooks.com

Story copyright © 2025 Drew Bryenton
Cover Illustration by Catrina Parton

The right of the author to be identified as the author of this work
has been asserted in accordance with the
Copyright, Designs and Patents Act 1988.

ISBN 978-1-910779-48-4

sci-fi-cafe.com

Also by
Drew Bryenton
from sci-fi-cafe.com

The Alter Inferno Complex
Elysium Burning
The Chains of Tartarus
Soulcrusher

Chain of Shadows
Halo of Thorns
On Black Wings of Vengeance

Fullchrome Afterburn
Gad's Army
Rotten Company

Prologue
Florence, Italy, The Year of our Lord 1314

IT BEGAN – as some say the entire universe did – with a quill pen scrittering across a creamy swath of parchment.

'Midway upon the journey of our life, I found myself within a foreste darke, for the straightforward pathway had been loste', wrote the pen, describing tight-formation curlicues of ink.

'Ah me! How hard a thing it is to say what was this foreste savage, rough, and stern, which in the very thought renews the feet!'

There was a silence, after the pen rasped right off the page, and then a voice was raised in anguish.

"The bloody *feet*? The feet! Oh, Saint Bartholemew's sacred bum-cheeks, pardon my Genoese! Where's the blotting paper? And could you two nincompoops keep this bloody cart steady?"

The cart in question rumbled along a narrow, rutted path, under the light of a sickle moon. It was a covered wagon, long past its prime, made of wood so warped (and canvas so moth-eaten) that even the highly motivated thieves of Florence had not been the least bit interested in stealing it.

It had taken a while to achieve the perfect pitch of filth and poverty. The owner of the wagon (who was a bit of a pedantic perfectionist) thought the smell alone was quite off-putting. He was right.

Some of this repulsiveness may also have had something to do with the woodcut of a jolly, beak-masked plague doctor stencilled on both sides, with a motto in the vulgar tongue beneath.

Pietro's Pus-Busters
Ulcers leeched while-u-wait!

Once again, the wagon's owner had been smugly self-satisfied with the results.

Light burst out in rays from holes in its canvas, piercing the mist which flowed thick and treacle-slow all around. It was a good night for mist, all murking and slithering between the trees. For this was on old forest, knurled and moss-bearded, left uncut by the Romans and sundry other ancients, who had known trouble when it put the wind up their togas. Forests like this knew how to *brood*. The trees slouched, glowering from knotholes.

The effect, as an oil lamp swung on chains inside the wagon, was one that a two-penny horror playwright would have given his velvet breeches to capture. Shifting shadows made the woodcut pox-doctor leer knowingly.

Of course, neither of the men perched up on the driver's seat was Pietro; he was a fiction, though both had enough splinters in their arses to wish for the steady hand of a barber-surgeon tonight.

Brother Martin and Brother Jacques were used to long rides and arduous conditions. They called themselves 'poor fellows', but what this meant, in the argot of the time, was that they were disbanded, utterly illegal, probably heretical Knights Templar.

This also meant that the crew of merry bandits who had tried to waylay this particular wagon, some way back down the forest road, were very, vehemently dead. Jacques and Martin had both seen action in the Holy Land, where anyone greasing out of the shadows and saying *'well well well'* with malice aforethought was likely to be an angry Saracen. Possibly dosed to the nipples on hashish, and clanking with poisoned cutlery, too.

The story about a prancing outlaw in green tights got

copied by a feller from England, or so they heard later.

The Templar brothers were killers, through and through. Which was why it was even worse that, presently, they both felt breeches-wettingly terrified.

"God's nostrils, Martin! This really is a bit of a forest darke, is it not?" asked the one on the left, knuckles tight on the reins. The horse, who had no name (except, of course, in the language of horses) did a little sidestepping dance as a twist of mist slithered across the ground toward it. "I figure we have lost the straightforward pathway some time ago, and no mistake."

Martin rolled his eyes.

"I'd go so far as to call it savage, rough and stern," said the squat little knight, rubbing at his bristled beard. "But darke with an 'e'? Next you'll be saying there be witches in it."

"What have you heard?" asked Jacques, trying to sound insouciant. There was a little quaver in his voice, though. "No such thing as witches. It's just old ladies what like to make herbal soaps and such. Magic's a peasant superstition!"

Martin had been part of a cadre of all-male soldiers, living in a roasting hot desert, for so long that it was physically impossible for him not to try to prank his Brother.

"But that's what we got disbanded for! Didn't they get you to kiss the mummified head of John the Baptist when you joined up? Swear to worship an idol of Baphomet at the Inverted Sabbath, and all that?"

"They jus' gave me a shilling and said 'yore in the army now my son it'll make a man ofyer'," muttered Jacques, who seemed to feel a little bit left out. "They never taught me any witchcraft! Typical! It's all about who you know. Bet you gave Sergeant Quency some kind of secret handshake, did you? Went to the right monastic battle seminary?"

He puffed out a long sigh. "Anyway, I heard we got disbanded because the King of France owed us lots of money."

The wagon rumbled on in silence for a moment, the sound of its wobbly wheels muffled by the mist.

"Aaaand..." added Jacques. "I heard they accused us all of umm. *Funny business.* You know." He made a vague, but suggestive gesture. "If you get my meaning."

Martin nodded, like the man of the world he wanted very much to seem to be.

"Ohh, *right*. Right. Like Brother Manfred and Brother Roger? Naaawww. Each to their own, so long as they're having fun, I say! Anyhow, it was the king of *France*, like you said. You'd have to arrest the whole... wait a minute! Did you hear that?"

Jacques had also been a Templar for several long years, and was used to the merry japes and mirthful shenanigans which his fellow Knights of Christ liked to play on each other, when they'd been besieged for weeks and there was only one woodcut of a saucy nun to pass around. He narrowed his eyes.

But then he heard it, too. A gurgling, hissing sound, like the sleeping breath of some great titan. A gust of wind went capering through the treetops, curdling the mist into wisps. The cart rolled, creaking, to a stop.

The noise came again, this time closer. Like phlegm being snorted through twisted tunnels underground.

"Do you have any idea what that was?" asked Martin, his face ashen. His hand went to his sword.

"No! Do *you* have any idea what that was?" asked Jacques.

The first knight rapped on the partition of the covered wagon, summoning the attention of the man who they were escorting through this forest darke. For a fair amount of money, it must be added.

"'Ere! Master Alighieri! Do *you* have any idea what that was?"

The muffled answer, when it came back, was more than a little tetchy. There was a certain insinuation of spilled ink, and a lot of swearing in Florentine. The sound came again, fairly rattling the leaves on the boughs above them. Jacques and Martin forgot most of their training and grabbed each other by the shoulders, looking into each others' bulging, terrified eyes. And...

"Well, don't bother asking *me* then. I only bloody live here!" said the witch.

Both of the knights' heads came around slowly, as if on little gimbals. The double look of dread writ across their features would have made a gargoyle-maker jealous.

"What the matter, Brothers?" asked the witch. "Suddenly re-animated severed head of John the Baptist got yer tongue?" She gave the kind of cackle which only comes with serious practice, and a copy of Dame Edith Gristlechurch's *'Advaunced Evyll Laughter for Funne and Profitte'*.

The Templars said nothing; confirmation of every witchy legend they had ever heard was staring them right in the face, in quite a confrontational way.

She wasn't of the old and hunch-backed variety, this one. Instead, the woman who blocked their path (with a personality ten sizes bigger than her body) was young, tall and spare, as if someone had sharpened a normal person down to a collection of edges. She wore copper-coiled braids in her hair, and a black cloak clattering with occult jewellery, most of it involving spiders. The obligatory pointy hat was there, along with a stare which suggested that a career in amphibian fly-catching was yours for the taking, if you came over all religious.

Martin and Jacques were pleased that she wasn't actually green. While both men had seen people go that colour, it was usually only a few days after a pretty unsuccessful battle, and they tended to smell horrendous.

"Bloody hell! It's a real one! Come on, Martin, hit her with some of that sorcery we're apparently in trouble for!"

Martin (whose knowledge of magic began and ended with nailing a horseshoe to your enemy's face for good luck)[1] decided to go with the classics. After all, they *were* working for a poet.

"Well met, upon this midnight dank and vile! Oh foul and ancient crone..." he began.

"Doris," said the witch.

"What?"

"It's Doris. And I'm not a crone. Still got to earn three more merit badges, including goose magic and advanced swearing. I'm a level nine dark enchantress till then."

Martin's mind tried to catch up, but his brain had become a little hamster wheel of horror.

This is how it ends, he thought. *Pop! Just like that, and it's trying to get a kiss from amphibiophile princesses for the next few decades...*

"Oh foul and ancient... *Doris*, then. We abjure thee to get out the way, right? The master's got to meet someone tonight about his new book, and it'd be a shame if he was late."

Doris rolled her eyes.

"Don't be a berk, son. I'm the only one who lives out here. He's here to see me, about these."

With a deft conjurer's flick-of-the-wrist the witch fanned out a brightly coloured pack of tarot cards. They were the kind which the Templars had seen used by fortune-tellers at spring fetes and roadside fairs.

Jacques risked being suddenly in the market for a semi-

---

1. An old tradition in the part of Belgium he was from, and a practical spell, too. If you can manage to nail a horseshoe to your enemy's face, he's not likely to give you much more trouble, and that's good luck.

detached lily pad, by having a bit of a chuckle.

"What? You're gonna tell 'im he's gonna meet a tall, dark stranger? That this might be a good week to ask for that promotion at work?"

The witch shot him a look that silenced him instantly, with a certain something of the Medusa about it.

"The only fortune he has bought is poverty, exile, and a future of having his name spelled wrong by spotty nincompoops during high school English exams," she intoned, in words as cold and sharp as an ice sculpture. "But what he hath wrought..."

"*Yes, yes, thank you Doris, I'll take it from here,*" said a voice.

And here was the funny thing about this voice; it was quiet, and calm, but it seemed to be unspeakably important, and right inside you ear like a secret whisper, all at the same time.

It belonged to figure which came striding dramatically out of the mist. One hand held up a lantern, with light spilling out from a little door on its side. The glow revealed a face with a proud beak of a nose, piercing eyes, and a sardonic little smile.

It was the face of the poet Dante Alighieri – rock-star of his era, the bad boy of Florence and unrepentant nemesis of the Black Guelph hegemony. When it came to sarcastic letters to the editor, comical graffiti, risible libels and political cartoons, he was as sharp as an assassin's dagger and twice as accurate.[2]

"You know how I told you lads that I was going to put the demons in their place?" he drawled. "All of them? Well, this is the key. It seems that the universe won't allow absolutely *zero* chance of them coming back. So I've done something that Lucifer and his rabble might approve of.

---

2. Because he wasn't blasted halfway to the moons of Neptune on hashish, mainly

I've created a puzzle."

"Oh, *you* have, have you?" asked Doris, arching one eyebrow. "I suppose *you* caught all those newts, then, and had to scrub out the cauldron after..."

Alighieri sketched a little bow, dipping his lantern. He really did look quite like the card for the Hermit, right at the top of Doris' deck. All that was missing was the beard.

"All credit to you, and to your sisters, my dear. After all, this new age we usher in will be yours, as well as mine."

"Well, if those meddling angels are gone, who else is your average peasant going to come to for a reasonably-priced miracle? We witches figured we'd better be on the right side of history."

"So this is them?" asked Dante, gingerly reaching for the tarot cards.

"The whole batch. Enough to incarnate a cadre of mortals, and replace the psychopomps of the current mythic pantheon, as ordered. Have you written the poem?"

Dante knocked on the side of the wagon.

"Once people get a load of this, they'll believe that Hell is its own closed-off little world, and Heaven too. No more angels and demons knocking about, snarling up fate and history. The laws of nature will work the same way, everywhere. I envision an enlightenment, when natural philosophy will actually make sense."

Doris shuffled her cards, and plucked one from the deck.

"That's why there's balance, right?" she asked, peering at it. "I was always iffy about this one. But I suppose for every enlightenment, there has to be an *Endarkenment*. Stands to reason."

Dante nodded.

"*Reason*, Miss Doris, is exactly what I'm about. I've been up to Paris, and to some place called Oxford, on that little island with all the sheep. There are people there who seek to reframe the world, and tame it with something better than alchemy and spells." He chuckled. "Then there's these two."

Jacques and Martin stared, uncomfortable at being the centre of attention. Somewhere off in the woods, that rumbling, snoring rasp came again. There was a definite whiff of brimstone to it.

"OK lads," said Dante, rubbing his hands together. "You know how I promised you fortune and fame? Well, here they are. Although, to put a fine point on it, the fortune part was more about 'fortune' as in destiny, rather than 'fortune' as in loads of money."

Jacques prodded his battle-brother.

"See? What did I tell you. Poets are great for the semantics, I said..."

"But did we ever meet one in the Holy Land with two brass pennies to rub together?" finished Martin, in a world-weary sing-song voice.

"Hey! It's not all doom and gloom," said Dante. "There's still the very distinct possibility of immortality on the table. And I don't mean that in the poetic sense *at all*."

Now he had their attention (though Jacques was slightly confused by the lack of an actual table). The two Templars leaned forward on the buckboard of the wagon, a certain avaricious twinkle in their eyes.

"As you just heard, I plan to put the demons in a big hole in the ground, and then hide the key. That sound you've been hearing is the actual, factual mouth of the new Hell, which we had to put *somewhere*. Seeing as this forest has been giving the willies to everyone since Alexander the Great made a detour around it, we thought... why not? The fact that this patch belongs to those Guelph bastards who took over my city is just the marinara on the linguine.[3]"

---

3. 'the icing on the cake', but in medieval Italian.

The poet held out his hand, and accepted the pack of tarot cards from Doris. A little spark of green fire blipped from his fingers for an instant, as he cut and shuffled it expertly.

"Soooo... one of you can take *this* card, and the immortality it grants, and go forth into the world to give out the rest of my tarot to those who must bear them. This puzzle unlocks heaven and hell, so if humanity rejects the age of reason I'm giving them, they can undo it all and go back to the no-holds-barred celestial punch-up we've been enjoying these past few centuries."

He held up a card. It depicted the Page of Swords; a young man in a chain-mail gambeson holding aloft a cruciform battle-blade.

Two hands reached out. One set of slim fingers jerked the card away, out of reach.

"And the *other* has to stay here. They'll be immortal too, but they'll have a different job. See, I'm kind of anticipating that our current Adversary, the incumbent Lucifer, Prince of Hell, is going to be slightly peeved about his change in real estate. So someone has to guard the gate. That might involve having to slay the odd demon or two."

Dante held out another card, in his other hand. This one was the Knight of Swords, an altogether more serious-looking figure.

"I... I don't suppose we could just say no, and walk away?" asked Martin, who was a bit quicker on the uptake than his Brother.

Dante shrugged.

"You could. But until the phase-space variables collapse, who knows what's out there in that mist? Who knows if things like 'out there' even apply? Let alone 'what.'"

Four eyes swivelled toward Doris.

"Ribbit," she said, with a twitch of a smile.

Dante managed to look just a little bit apologetic.

"Or that. But I suspect there'll be no need for transmogrification. You're noble knights! A quest with devils and fate and lots of action is right up your idiom, isn't it? And come on, lads. *Immortality*. Think about it!"

He gave his best salesman grin, with extra razzmatazz.

"Oh, I am," said Jacques, gloomily. He was thinking about how much it would hurt to have your arms and legs ripped off by a giant demon when you couldn't die.

"But if it's a choice between wandering the earth handing out pieces of cardboard, or battling angry demons at the gates of damnation..." he sneaked a sidelong glance at Martin. Who had already sneaked one at him. Both hesitated, as they were just about to try to snatch the Page of Swords.

"Rock paper scissors?" asked Jacques, with a fatalistic sigh.

Later, and just a little bit further down to road, Doris the dark enchantress (and future probationary Crone) leaned up against a signpost, at a crossroads, and took a look at the card she'd palmed from the deck.

Those two oafs couldn't be trusted to get this one right. It was very important that someone who fit just neat and snug as a glove fell into this particular role. After all, they'd be distracting the attention of a whole very complicated universe from the real thing...

Thankfully, people totally expect witches to cheat. Nobody thinks the worse of them for it; in fact, it's sort of traditional. Because of this, Doris, who was a frightfully good witch indeed, had set up a little meeting here long before she'd ever agreed to do a favour for Dante Alighieri.

She looked at the card again. Not a bad painting, if she did say so herself. The horns were just the right type of curly, and the beard reminded her of one of her ex-boyfriends, who (some people would be surprised to learn), was these days a very successful cabinetmaker in Vienna, not some kind of damp reptile.

Presently, a traveller happened by. Due to the kind of lucky chance which takes a bit of supernatural finesse to carry off, he was exactly the right one.

'Mister Right' was a short but sturdily-built little man in yellow leggings, a blue woollen shirt, and a big broad leather belt. A cockeyed straw hat of rustic design was perched rakishly atop his head, and a pointed little beard clung to his chin. 'Spry' is a word usually used for older folk, but spry was the word for this gent; he seemed to be too full of energy, which fizzed around him as he walked, putting a spring in his step, even though he was walking through an obviously cursed and haunted forest.

This may have been explained by the wooden violin case he carried on a strap over one shoulder. To the untrained eye, this would appear to be that most dire of wanderers, the folk musician. Indeed, it looked as though he was ready to burst into song about the merry old month of May, suggestive rural double entendres and all, at the drop of a handkerchief.

Doris wasn't fooled. He was crooked through and through, this one, with a mind like a carbon-steel corkscrew.

"Blessings be on ye, met by, ummm. Well, I *suppose* there's some moonlight up there somewhere," she said, making a conscious effort to look eldritch.

The traveller stopped, seeing the shadows which attended the rickety old crossroad post peel away and arrange themselves into the shape of a witch. To his credit, he rallied wonderfully.

"Well met on this... okay, let's call it what it is, a bloody horrible foggy evening," he said, appraising Doris with the kind of up-and-down glance which would normally earn a man a smack in the chops. "Do you, by any chance, have any skill at all with playing the fiddle?"

Doris had been expecting something of this sort.

"Giving out lessons, are you?" she hazarded. "Or – and correct a reasonably young but crone-adjacent witch if she's wrong – are you pulling the old number twenty-six and seven?"

The man nodded, with the kind of respect one craftsman shows another.

"As in, if you say you *can* play, I'll challenge you to a fiddle contest for what looks very much like a solid gold violin," he said. "It's got trick tuning pegs, so even a maestro sounds like he's wringing out a cat."

The witch nodded.

"And if I profess to total musical incompetence, you'll sell me fame and talent for my immortal soul? Tell me, do you use oriental smoke bombs to impersonate Lucifer, or do you just do a really good evil laugh?" Doris grinned. "What's your finisher?"

The traveller looked left and right, then spoke behind his hand, as if anyone else would be spying on them.

"I let 'em think they're soulless for a week or so, until every turn of bad luck makes 'em reckon God's got it in for 'em. Then I turn up as a 'wandering bishop' and offer to get their soul back, for a bloody huge 'donation.'"

Doris laughed, the kind of hearty, full-belly laugh which is the gift of the truly unselfconscious.

"Oh, *yes*. You'll do, squire. What's your name?"

The traveller looked slightly disconcerted; he'd heard that you shouldn't give your real name to anyone magical. But something rebellious rallied in him, and he looked Doris dead in the eye.

"Beggin' your pardon miss, but they calls me Charlie Wickham. That is, the wanted posters, and all... Hence my walking tour of Northern Italy, and my notable absence from Sussex."

Doris reached out and cupped his chin in one hand. Wyrd ripples and whorls of power made the air roil like water in a cauldron, for just a moment.

"Tell me, Charlie – have you ever wanted to pull one really big, whopping great, pays-for-all job, then just disappear?" she asked. In her other hand, she held up a tarot card, painted with the image of two naked people chained to the throne of a giant, red and horn-headed demon.

The travelling grifter nodded, mesmerised. His eyes reflected the card, and seemed to spiral it out into infinity, as if seen through a cut diamond all a-twirl.

"You know... I had been considering a bit of a change," he conceded. A little drip of spittle threaded out from the corner of his mouth.

Doris smiled brightly.

"Excellent! Because I know of an executive position which has just become available. *Exactly* the kind of thing for a man of your talents."

The tarot card hit him square between the eyes, driven by a quite vehement witch's palm travelling at tremendous speed. There was a blast of unreality. There was an unravelling of edges, and the smell of Thursday afternoons in August, and the sound of gears made of glass slipping and grinding and...

catching.

The mist, which had lurked sullenly under the forest eaves all night, exploded up and out in a perfect mushroom cloud, shaped like a skull. Bats fled, shrieking in registers too high to hear. Down below the earth, a huge voice bellowed deep and mournful and doomed, and the sound of cracking ice carried from subterranean depths.

There was a sense of ending. Invisible pages slammed shut. An idea was caught, like a luckless moth, between them.

"The red velvet suits you," said Doris, what might have been later.

Time, a bit the worse for wear, had sidled back all embarrassed. "Don't know about the skullcap with the little horns, though. Or the tiny ornamental pitchfork. Very eleventh century."

The creature which had been Charlie Wickham (in a continuum which was swiftly receding into unreality) chuckled. It was a singularly oily and unpleasant little sound.

"So..." he hazarded. "Doesn't this mean that, *technically*, you're supposed to be one of my brides, now?" He raised one pencil-perfect black eyebrow, over a wink that would make nuns catch fire.

Doris rolled her eyes. *Bloody typical. Why that fool Alighieri hadn't gone for a demon* queen *was beyond her.*

"You just try that, and see how you like raising a few hundred tadpoles, sunshine," she said. "Now. Let's talk about the particulars of your new job, and this *total* bell-end called Faustus I want us to pay a visit on..."

PART ONE

THE BOOK OF THE PRE-DECEASED

We fling up flowers and laugh, we laugh across
the wine;
With wine we dull our souls and careful
strains of art;
Our cups are polished skulls round which the
roses twine:
None dares to look at Death who leers and
lurks apart. –

Ernest Dowson (1867–1900)
Muses on the dark allure of mortality
– probably while wearing one of
those shirts with a lacy front
and tight black trousers.

Crowley once challenged Ray to a game,
Losing your soul was the paying stake,
Crowley used garlic, brightstone and fire,
'Cos fucking Ray Reardon is a vampire.
Ray Reardon, Ray Reardon,
We are all doomed –

Lawnmower Deth (1987-present)
share their theory on the meteoric
career of Wales' six-time
world snooker champion.

Death.

IT'S THE FINAL curtain. The last hurrah, or, in many cases, a word which means exactly the opposite of 'hurrah', and is quite unsuitable to print here.

We come into the world naked and screaming, and some of us end up going out in the same fashion, though it's generally frowned upon to share a definitive list, at least with non-clairvoyants.

But we *all* go out. The trick, or so they say, is to do it with a certain kind of style.

Death is the answer, in the end, to all of our problems, and most of our questions. All except the big one. The daddy.

What happens afterwards?

And will there, in fact, be cake?

Ever since the first time an enterprising caveman picked a bright purple mushroom and was hit directly between the frontal lobes with the mysteries of the cosmos, there's been someone willing to hazard a guess. It didn't hurt that, eventually, those doing the guessing managed to put on robes and hats and suggest (with reference to certain implements of torture), that they were bloody well right.

This is a story about The End.

It's different from the fiery, uncomfortable, jagged or potentially blissful bits of most of the major religions. Faith and science, after all, have one of those relationships which often ends up with people throwing chairs at each other on daytime television. It all comes down to how they handle unknowns.

There are a lot of these about. One of the big ones is this *– we don't know how many unknowns there are to not know about.*

And the ones we do know that we don't know about can be quite confusing.

For example –

A young woman named September doesn't know, as you're reading this, that a gnarly, fractal knot of fate, causality, trouble, and weaponised improbability is belting across the manifold of eleven-dimensional spacetime toward her, with **The End** writ large upon it. If she *did* know, she might have sidestepped at a critical instant, and grown up to be the carpet acquisitions comptroller for a medium-sized municipal council.

As things stand, she is blissfully ignorant about this – along with what awaits beyond this mortal world, what the Antipope wears under his cassock, and how many undead Elvis Presleys it takes to install a light bulb. All this is about to change, and it's fair to say she might be a bit cross about it.

They say, of course, that what you don't know can't hurt you.

But then again, *they* haven't been hit by a cruel and feral Beginning, hurtling out of some benighted phase-space like a comet-core of depleted uranium, laden down with several hot megatons of narrative imperative.

It looks like a seething ball of spiked glass spaghetti, haloed with lightning; as half-imagined as a fragment of a dream.

See it as it comes screaming in, making a noise which – if you had the right ears to hear it with – would sound like a billion miles of bubble wrap being torn asunder. Down toward a watery blue planet, spinning dizzy in the firmament. Down toward a patchwork of fields and looping highways, bright rivers flashing silver under armadas of clouds. Towards a jumble of rooftops; a thicket of chimney-pots; a grand old gothic pile of a school.

This is a story about The End.

But it starts...

NOW

IN THE YEAR OF OUR LORD, NINETEEN HUNDRED AND NINETY-NINE

One
Frankenfrog
vs
Presley

IT ALL BEGAN, September thought ruefully, with the incident with the frog.

Well, really, it was The Incident With The Frog; a calamitous occasion which fully deserved a full brace of capital letters. Certainly, Mister Mackleduff, and Headmaster of the Standard Academy, had pronounced both of those words with capitals when he'd phoned her parents. Both 'Incident' and 'Frog' had been clipped off like topiary under Mister Mackleduff's razor-straight moustache, and September was certain that he'd left a thin crisp crust of ice on the telephone as well.

"In this school," he'd said, fixing her with his one good eye, "We obey the laws of nature! Does that look like a dissected frog to you?"

The other eye – the glass one – wobbled about like a wonky compass needle as Mister Mackleduff pointed with the stem of his pipe. The frog scrabbled damply at the sides of the jar it was trapped in. Words like 'autopsy' and 'dismembered' did not really apply to it. Though it did have quite a lot of stitches.

"I thought the point of science was to *fix* things," said September, swinging her legs under the huge button-backed chair on the other side of the headmaster's desk. "I saw how to put him back together, and I did. The textbook says it's my duty to become a Smart and Curious Young Scientist."

Mister Mackleduff was as fusty as a hand-me-down

tweed blazer with leather elbow patches.[4] He wore a mortarboard with an ashtray glued to it, where he now stowed his pipe.

"Dash it all, girl, the job was to take it to bits. Poor Miss Pennywhistle has had to go and have a lie down and a cup of tea. Need I remind you that this is a Standard Academy? For the Determinedly Unobtrusive? We don't like surprises, and we won't tolerate…" here, he screwed up his face, making his jowls quiver, "*novelties.* I won't ask how you did it. Just get rid of it."

September wrapped the jar up in her arms, which were, themselves, swamped by a Saint Pewtred's Standard Academy pullover three sizes too big, patched with scraps of faux leopardskin and crinkly silver. Just quietly, she was rather proud of the frog. The neck bolts had been tricky, but she'd managed to carefully swipe two just the right size from the back of Lucretia Beigeington-Plaid's calculator.

"Terribly sorry, sir," she said, with a look of precisely calculated remorse and innocence. It was copied from pictures of large, floppy dogs. "It shan't happen again."

Mister Mackleduff sighed. There was a reason September Normalsson was depressingly familiar with the cracked-leather armchair where students sat to face his displeasure. Actually, there were three hundred and forty-two reasons, all written up on St Pewtred's stationery and filed in a big manilla folder with fat rubber bands to hold it shut.

"It's only a little longer until the end of the term, Miss Normalsson," he said, pinching the bridge of his nose. "After the thing with the pudding, and the basketball accident, and the electrical fire, and the plague of weasels that savaged Miss Dulcimer…"

"Technically, plague of *weasel*, sir. There was only one of Boris, and the copies faded away when Groundskeeper

---

4. You'd better believe that's what he was wearing, too.

Hackforth smashed the machine with his cricket bat, sir."

The elderly headmaster gritted his teeth. Surely *he, who had purposely sought out the most boring educational position in the Commonwealth, didn't deserve this?* Then he remembered the sinful naughtiness stowed deep in his past, and realised that he probably did.

"You're forbidden from the science lab until the end of term," he said, retrieving his pipe. "And of course, any further discipline is for your parents to venture."

Mister Mackleduff turned and looked out the window. It was an utterly stereotypical view, out across a rather sad and boggy football field to where the River Average slunk along between its banks.

September hefted the big jar, which still smelled vaguely of sauerkraut, and looked through the wavy thick glass at the frog inside. It looked back, with eyes that seemed far too wise to belong in a tiny green face laced up with orange stitches.

Quietly, so as not to elicit any more harrumphs and waggled eyebrows from the headmaster, September crept across the swirly carpet and slipped out the door. Through the windows of the second-floor corridor she caught a glimpse of the fire department sharing tea and sandwiches, and Constable O'Dwightly sucking on his pencil as he tried to think of what to write in his little police notebook. The smoke damage was far worse than the actual fire this time, she thought.

September ignored them all, and the crowd of students watching the show, as she squelched across the football fields and reached the edge of the river. She opened the jar and let the frog go; it plopped into the water with not so much as a backwards glance, in spite of the fact that September had saved it from being a very educational sad little pile of bits.

Now it was her turn to sigh.

She tried. She really did. But every time she attempted to do anything humdrum, mundane or practical, it turned out mad, instead. Love for her poor long-suffering Mum and Dad, and a sort of damply cheerful school spirit made her keep trying, though.

She'd become a normal person. It was just a matter of time. She might even manage to become the Smart and Curious Young Scientist the textbooks kept mentioning.

Somewhere downstream, where the little river Average was boxed in with concrete, and traffic rumbled overhead, a slightly lopsided frog perched on the wheel of a half-submerged shopping trolley, and blinked. Things were happening in its tiny amphibian brain, which had been augmented with a few bits and pieces and then rewired before being popped back in. Down amid the tin cans and bicycle parts of the culvert bottom it had found a AAA battery, which it thoughtfully nibbled on, sending sparks sizzling from the twin calculator bolts in its neck.

A passing heron, sculling through the skies over Little-Mean-on-the-Average, made eye contact from 600 feet up, and decided immediately to become a vegetarian.

Banned from science! The one subject she was good at!

Well... the only one which she enjoyed.

'Good at' was a relative term, when you couldn't seem to do any kind of experiment without having, as poor Miss Pennywhistle called them, 'sideways ideas'.

If September's experiments had simply failed, then her enthusiasm for science would just be sad. But because they tended to do things which bent or outright smashed the laws of physics, people tended to assume that somehow she was being disruptive, or worse, *disrespectful*.

And that was the thing about Saint Pewtred's Standard

Academy for the Deliberately Unobtrusive. There were schools which looked stuffy and tweedy and buttoned-down, but which were really a cover for all kinds of super-heroic shenanigans.

It was also broadly hinted, (in the fourteen novels written after 1981 which sat under a stern warning sign in the school library) that some academies trained wizards, or held portals to other worlds concealed in Victorian furniture, or possibly had something to do with ninjas.

Not this one. The only magic and wonder associated with Saint Pewtred's was the mystery of how the cook, Mrs Malorbian, could boil any species of plant or animal until it turned into the sole of a 1920s tennis shoe. If an owl flew into anyone's window in Little-Mean-on-the-Average, they'd call the pest exterminators, and it would likely end up as Tuesday's Mystery Loaf Special. September was thankful that most of the faculty (average age, 62) was not inclined to wear spandex tights, either.

"*Anyway,*" said September's lab partner Agnes Unremarkable, "*You can tell this isn't one of them magic schools, coz none of the teachers are famous Hollywood actors, and none of us kids are being played by a twenty-five year old.*"

And that was it. Saint Pewtred's was decidedly unmagical, unsuper, and unimaginative. It wasn't a good place to be named after a month late in the year, either. September had been assured by her mother that is was absolutely button-down sensible to be called April, May or June. And that apparently, the name was a tribute to her unbelievably antiquated great-great-grandfather, who nobody in the family was supposed to talk about, but who she visited quite often.

September hadn't bothered going back to school that day. She figured that she was in as much trouble as it was possible to be in. Her parents were not actually allowed to deploy tactical nuclear weapons. So she might as well go to one of the rare places where she felt at home; the town library.

There was a library at Saint Pewtred's, of course, but it was so boring that it felt more like the accounting department of a protractor factory. Mrs Dearborn, the librarian there, was of the opinion that fiction was silly, unless it was written hundreds of years ago by people with huge lace collars and double-barrelled surnames. She kept a big cardboard cutout of Sir Isaac Newton behind the library counter, and the scuttlebutt among the student body was that she would often practice kissing it, or pretend to feed it pieces of cake.

This was quite the opposite of the Municipal Library, where Miss Rummage ruled, in floral skirts and pink cardigans and her hair held up with assorted coloured pencils. In her spare time the civic librarian enjoyed hang gliding and tae kwan do, which were considered a bit outré for the likes of Little-Mean-on-the-Average. However, nobody else understood the library's filing system, so, with a few grumbles from the determinedly boring borough council, Miss Rummage kept her job.

Because Little Mean was built as a planned town in the 1960s, the library looked like a concrete tribute to Soviet bunkers, shoe boxes and glue factories. The kind of place where a supervillain would keep his spare doomsday devices, September often thought. She trudged past the neighbouring construction site, where huge Dutch super-grocer Anders' Veg had been promising to open for the past few years, then up a set of stairs which could have repelled a medium-sized panzer division.

As usual, she caught a glimpse of herself striding toward the mirrored doors.

Huge, copper-red nimbus of curly hair – check.

Green eyes which were just slightly too big, underlined with a scattershot of freckles – all present.

There was also a nose which looked absolutely unlike that of any famous pop singer or movie star, and a mouth twitched up at one corner, into the kind of smile which either looks incredibly alluring in classical paintings, or makes everyone assume that you've just done something sneaky.

September was not entirely sure about the combined effect, but as she lived, as it were, inside it, she figured that dealing with the sum total of her facial features was very much other people's problem. She'd care about their opinions when the weather forecast for Hell included sleet.[5]

The door hissed open and snicked back. The reflection folded away with a wink of light.

"Aha! Good afternoon, young lady!" shouted Miss Rummage, from high atop a ladder. "Your interloan requests from Miskatonic U have come in, but it seems we've misplaced our hazmat suit and tongs, so you'll have to bear with me."

There was a large laminated sign just inside the door, which summed up the attitude of Miss Rummage to life, the universe, and the mercurial whims of fate.

Rule I – Be respectful and leave things better than you found them.
Rule b – In addition to Rule I, there are also some rules about using the library.
What? You thought Rule I only applied to the inside a big room full of books?
Rule III – However, most everything is

---

5. Blatant Foreshadowing – September will need to know about the meteorological conditions in the Realm of Satan soon enough.

**covered by Rule 1, so it's more exciting to leave them secret until utterly necessary.
Rule 3a – No smoking.**

It turned out that using a hazmat suit, barbecue tongs and lemon-and-lime air freshener while reading certain volumes was one of the secret rules. September had to admit that most people would never have to be told about it.

She, on the other hand, knew all about the little lead-lined reading room just behind the tiny tots' picture book section. She'd carefully stored several wads of half-chewed bubble gum on the giant brass statue of Dagon which lurked on its bog-oak table, with a huge and cobwebbed keyhole in its belly.

And she'd memorised the full list of instructions for reading the tomes and grimoires inside. This education had started at the age of ten, when someone had forgotten to put a first edition of Abdul Alhazred's now-infamous *Necronomicon* back in its nine-dimensional vault, and it had tried to bite September's finger off.

A normal child, Miss Rummage thought, *would have probably cried.* September had shoved a huge, sticky, lint-covered lollipop into the thing's mouth. Then she'd opened it to the chapter on the Shrieking Snail-Beast Slaves of Tshedg-Hoguuah and started drawing pictures of them. Mere crayons should not have even been able to portray the colours mentioned, like infra-blurple and meta-puce.[6]

Considering the secret purpose of Little-Mean-on-the-Average, the librarian should have told someone. But Miss Rummage lived pretty much all of her life by Rule 1, and

---

6. The Necronomicon is widely known to be bound in human faces, which have been turned to leather by a ghastly process you really don't want to know about, and which can still pack a nasty bite. Even worse is the oft-hinted-at (but never seen) volume, also by the mad mystic Alhazred, *The Laff-a-Minute Bumper Book of Forbidden Fart Jokes.* This is said be be bound in human bums.

considered that the world would be better than she found it, if it included a frighteningly intelligent, largely fearless ten-year-old girl who knew how to handle a lollipop with malice aforethought. Now that girl was nearly eighteen, and would (Miss R grudgingly admitted) make a pretty good librarian herself, if she could survive the secret training.

"Nice to see your great-great-Grandad in the news again, though," said the librarian, sliding down her ladder with a shriek of sensible boot soles on polished oak. "The old boy's still got it, even at 137!"

She performed a complicated judo roll over the library counter and came back up again holding a copy of the *Average Non-Inquirer*, the town's relentlessly boring newspaper. Legend had it that it was printed on the boiled up, recycled remains of vintage tax ledgers, just to make it more uninteresting. Certainly, Wilmsloe Busby, the editor, had an uncanny knack for a dreary headline.

"Local pensioner remains elderly," traced September, reading the masthead upside down. "'Does a thing, some people mildly interested'. Gosh, he even got a boring strapline, too!"

The other news on the front page appeared to be more of the local police warning people about a new drug menace – but there was a photo of great-great-granddad, in his lab coat, tartan suit and aviator goggles. As usual, his haircut resembled an explosion in the kind of factory that stuffs uncomfortable mattresses. Upside down, it almost made sense.

"The big one-three-seven, eh? I suppose you've been round to wish him many happy returns, despite this Doom Clock he's allegedly invented. Caused a right rumpus at the old folk's home, that did."

"I think you'd better let me read the article," said

September, who had almost forgotten great-granddad Septivarian's birthday. This was quite embarrassing, but understandable. September's parents had been on a somewhat demented mission to pretend that the old man didn't exist since before she was born.

September pretended to be keen and obedient, of course. But she visited him in his top-floor flat at the local retirement home almost every week. He and some of his weird fellow inmates were September's friends.

She sensed that her parents' aversion wasn't just part of a musty old feud, though. It was almost as if Norma and Norman Normalsson were *terrified* of their single-toothed, crinkle-faced living ancestor.

And that was just silly, because... well, because of things like the subject of this news story, for starters.

"Local inventor and former super-villain, Septivarian Quintimegistus Archimedes, has turned 137 years old today, celebrating this unprecedented longevity by unveiling his latest creation, the Doom Clock," read September.

Miss Rummage, who knew the habits of her most regular customer, wheeled a library step-stool around behind September before she sat down on nothing. Reading seemed to put her into a kind of trance, during which one of her pupils grew to a vast and limpid size and the other retracted to a black scintilla. Miss Rummage swore that sometimes she'd seen actual sparks crackling among those bright red curls.

"Professor Archimedes says that his immensely long life is down to the science of retro-palmistry, an art which he has perfected. He claims that by tattooing more life-line from the palm of his hand, around his wrist and up his arm, he's managed to not just cheat death, but also bamboozle the bony bloke in black into forgetting where he lives," continued September.

"Applying this principle, along with subsonic phrenological tomography, the Professor has created a pocket watch which tells people the exact time of their deaths. Amazing as this machine is, it led to tragedy when it was passed about the residents of the Wrinkly Acres retirement home and hospital.

Resident oldster, Elspeth Grebe-Fruitspoon, perished of a shock-induced heart attack when the Doom Clock indicated that she had mere seconds to live. While staff were quick to commiserate the other residents, Archimedes was heard to cackle in what bystanders described as a 'villainous manner', and announce 'at least now we know it works'."

September rolled her eyes. Miss Rummage chuckled.

Neither of them noticed the figure lurking in the periodicals section, behind the huge old microfiche. It was holding a copy of the *Paranormal Times* upside down, covering its face, but a huge pompadour haircut rose above the inverted cover photo (of David Icke playing the accordion). A strong smell of lemon bleach wafted from the figure, which feigned as much nonchalance as possible while wearing a white tasselled suit with bell-bottom trousers.

"Well, I should get over there if I were you," said Miss Rummage. "The dark mysteries of the elder gods can wait, I suppose. Things with names like a losing Scrabble hand are less important than birthdays, even if they *do* promise to rend the fragile veil of reality, and devour our souls with a spicy dipping sauce."

"That's oddly specific," said September.

"Latest copy of the *Eldritch Examiner*," replied the librarian, twiddling one of the coloured pencils in her hair. "Professor De Schmutter says chipotle, while Professor Gloompallour insists it's Korean barbecue. Still, it's unlikely to happen, is it? If the end of the world was coming, your great-great-granddad's clock gizmo would have told everyone the same time. Give or take the entrées, of course."

"Alright. Just something to be going on with, then, and I'll come back later to sign for the interloan. Great-granddad *is* still family, even if my parents act all funny around him. I won't be forbidden from visiting a poor old man on his birthday."

"Good for you!" enthused Miss Rummage. "Here. Take a copy of Graf Wilhelm Spankenberger's *Unaussprechliche Praktiken der Kannibalenfroschmenschen des Grossen Spurlosen Untergangssumpfes*. His ritual for summoning the Malignant Star-Toad really only manifests a small lemon meringue pie, but it's quite a nice one. Zesty."

She watched as September crammed the volume deep into her huge, shapeless school bag, filled with unknown horrors and bedecked all about with the logos of heavy metal bands. Then the librarian turned back to her cataloguing, not looking up as she heard her favourite young customer leave through the big mirrored doors.

Presently, a shadow fell over the counter. A stench of lemon bleach rose up, along with something behind it, far less wholesome, which seemed to hint at churned black soil, and wood polish, and rot.

"Uh huh huh," said a croaky, American-accented voice, in tones like a car trying to start after being dragged out of a swamp. "Uh Hooooo... *where's the girl going, thankyouverymuch?*"

Miss Rummage carefully slid the coloured pencil in her hand back into her hair.

"We don't give out that kind of information, sorry," she said, pointedly not looking up. "Librarian's code. Strict confidentiality."

"Little lady, you *know* who we are. You know we don't ask twice."

Now Miss Rummage looked up. The thing which leaned on her counter (she knew full well that, despite having the requisite number of arms, legs and heads, it was *not a person*) resembled a black-and-white photograph of a young Elvis Presley, inflated into three dimensions.

"Who you are? Huh! Government stooges with a thing for tacky rhinestones, and sod all else. Not exactly the words that old Alhazred used, but we won't go there, shall we? You know who I represent, too. The Order of the Baal Shem know your true names, shiftless sons of the outer darkness."

The Elvis smirked, the expression sliding across its face like pollution across a puddle.

"Name-drop the Order all you like, missy. This is *our* town. Oversight's jurisdiction. And we *will* make sure that nothing wyrd happens here. Especially with *that* one." The creature's grin continued to stretch back, until a profusion of teeth wrapped all the way around the bottom of its head, right back to its spine on both sides. It flexed its long, leather-gloved fingers into fists. "So I'll ask you again, just to be polite. *Where's she going, and what do you know about it?*"

Miss Rummage could have folded. This really was Oversight's town; built as a bell jar and a crab bucket for people who were briefly powerful, but were now just embarrassing. The Bureau Innominandum had plotted every angle, shrub and pigeon dropping in Little-Mean-on-the-Average.

But... Miss Rummage thought that the world was a much better place with September Normalsson in it. And she knew, in her heart of hearts, that paperwork and niceties aside, the Dead Elvi were known for making people disappear, into the horrible time-loop from whence they were spawned.

So—

"I'm sorry," she said, clicking a small plastic triangular sign down on the counter with all the malice and precision of a samurai pushing his katana out of its sheath with one thumb. "But the information service is closed. Please try again later."

'GO AWAY PLEASE' read the sign.

"You sure?" asked the Elvis, as the pupils of its eyes doubled, then split again, revolving like egg yolks in some horrid hangover cure.

"Deadly," said Miss Rummage.

There was a moment's sickly silence, like the one in which a beer-jug sails heedlessly through the air, on a trajectory for the back of a big, tattooed head.

Then –

They both moved at once, and if anyone had been betting on the rock 'n' roll waxwork monster, then they would have been thoroughly underestimating the Ancient and Terrible Order of the Baal Shem, the masters of the word.

As the Elvis plunged both arms through the counter up to the shoulders, splintering the hardwood, Miss R leapt up and over, performing a perfect cartwheel to land behind it. Before the Elvis could pull itself loose, she raised one finger to her lips, in the universal gesture of librarians everywhere, and let the other one hover at her side, seeking among the shelves.

Ahh. There it was. The self-help section, two rows down, third volume from the end of the shelf. The masterwork of chef Jean-Pierre de Crecy,[7] in which he described his combination of cookery and crippling violence – the

---

7. De Crecy is also responsible for translating that most hideous of volumes, A *Compleat Historie of Erotic Cakes*, which contains cakes considered erotic by the Elder Gods, Ancient Slime Ones, the Gibberers Beyond and the Thngs Whch Knw N Vwls.

French martial art known as kung-fou. The text from page twenty-nine slithered through the ether with a crackle of sparks, and Miss Rummage surged forward, perfectly executing the lethal 'beatdown bourguignon'.

A twelve-strike flurry of tenderising blows landed, faster than the eye could follow, but the Elvis was made of supernatural stuff. Even as the librarian's final strike sent it hammering back through the ruins of the counter, its flesh twisted on its bones, and its face came bubbling around to the back of its skull. Horrible cartilaginous popping noises attended.

"I'd call that first blood, if I had any," it chuckled. "But it's the last stuff that counts!"

So saying, the reanimated rocker sprung to the attack, rhinestones flying like shrapnel. Grey-skinned fists pummelled at Miss Rummage from every direction, but she fended them all off with one outstretched finger, offsetting the kinetic energy through a series of descriptions of medieval castles in a volume on siege warfare. Three shelves away, the gold foil around the book's pages melted.

The librarian responded with a snap kick to the liver (*karaté de foie gras*), and a follow-up spinning back-foot which propelled the Elvis clean through the magazines and periodicals. Pages fluttered down in its wake.

But the creature flipped back to its feet and charged, snatching up a whole chrome-wire shelf to use as a bludgeon. This time Miss Rummage was forced to retreat, ducking under scything swings which crashed into the shelves, left and right. The Elvis didn't break a sweat; its lip was curled into a cinematic sneer, but its advance was, ummm... what was the word?

Inhuman, thought Miss Rummage, with a twinge of genuine annoyance. *A truce with nine-dimensional monsters was all fine and good, but it took the creative idiocy*

Finally, she found herself backed up against the photocopier, a great beige beast of a thing packed with toner, malice, and about five thousand easily jammed rollers.

"Wait! *Stop!*"

She held out her hand toward the Elvis – and such was the power of her voice, in this place, that the vile thing paused. A mangled wire shelf clattered to the ground.

"You're going to be reasonable, then?" it asked. "Okay. Tell us what that doddering old fool and his grand-daughter have planned, and I suppose that Oversight could write this off as a misunderstanding."

Miss Rummage puffed a floating wisp of hair out of her eyes, and laughed.

"You're madder than the old Mississippi original, aren't you? They're planning a birthday party, you simpleton. He's one hundred and thirty seven years old. A bit late for a career revival, don't you think?"

Down at her side, the librarian's fingers twitched, searching, flipping though an unseen catalogue...

"Don't talk to me about comeback specials, little lady," said the Elvis. "And don't call it paranoia, either. If you don't think that wily old buzzard is plotting something, then you haven't done your homework."

There. A twist of an unseen lock. A door cracked open, on silent, well-oiled hinges, just behind the tiny tots' picture book section.

"Speaking of homework," said Miss Rummage, "I've got some for you."

A volume came sizzling through the air, bent its trajectory at right angles around the end of one row of shelves, and smacked into her palm with a detonation of green sparks. These blipped and buzzed across the linoleum as she flipped open the photocopier, slammed the book inside, face down, and turned a large and meaningful dial.

"About a thousand pages should do it. *I will not stupidly attack a librarian in her own library*."

The dire mechanisms within the photocopier cranked into life, and eldritch light blazed out from the gap between glass and lid. Rollers squealed. Toner puffed out in a gritty black mist.

"What... what have you *done*?" screeched the Elvis, as the thaumic barometer plummeted. All the magic behind reality was sucked into a tight vortex, centred on the machine.

"You'll love this," grinned Miss Rummage. "It's one of young September's own bright ideas, funnily enough. See, I wouldn't be worried about what her Grandad still is. I'd be worried about what *she's becoming*."

The Elvis set its face in a determined snarl and pounced, fingers attenuating into claws. Rhinestones scattered in its slipstream. But it was too late.

Because out of the copier's chute came a spiralling, flapping, whirling cacophony of pages, each one slashed across with what appeared to be a jagged scissor-slice. Out came a whirlwind of two-dimensional living faces, toothy and snarling, gnashing paper fangs as they blizzarded and billowed.

Face-down inside the copier, Abdul Alhazred's now-infamous *Necronomicon* gurned horribly. Its tongue squeaked against the glass as a beam of light swept back and forth, peeling layers off its demon soul like an occult bacon slicer.

The pages which came out all bore its hideous, stitched-up image, and all of them were in a rotten mood. They descended on the Elvis in mid-air, wrapping the thing up like a mummy, inflicting a thousand horrible paper-cuts at once. Black blood soaked through reams of A4 copy-stock.

"Nooooo!" it howled, in a voice which made the varnish blister across every old-oak shelf and panel in the library. *"We've seen it! This is where it starts! The Antipope! The Great Beast from Cocytus! The dead rising! It's all... uuuurgh!"*

And indeed, it *was* all uuuurgh.

Because inside its flimsy bubble of skin, the Dead Elvis was made from nothing but slime. When the relentless teeth of the necrocopycons chewed through to the core of the thing it popped like a black balloon, spattering a wide circle of linoleum. A shell made up of saturated paper squelched to the floor, followed by a fluttering of now-inanimate copies, each displaying a demon face.

"Shhhhh," said Miss Rummage, braced against the photocopier., Her hair had exploded into a tangle of static electricity, coloured pencils and frizz. When she and September had talked about the plan, over lime thick-shakes, it had seemed a whimsical fantasy. Now it was the kind of situation which called for a stiff drink, a large mop, and a sturdy constitution.

The librarian made a gesture with one hand, stealing a useful passage from Arch-Druidess Cecilia Junethistle's *Principles of Occult Macramé*. Her hair organised itself into a tight, fractal bun.

The mop, (and a sneakily concealed bottle of Moosewrangler's Old Intractable) were stashed in the janitor's closet. As for a sturdy constitution – well. She'd survived under-fives arts and crafts weekend, hadn't she? The difficult part would be convincing Oversight that all was still fine and well in the borough.

Behind the ruined counter top, a huge red bakelite telephone began ringing...

Oversight, that creaking and byzantine sub-department of the Bureau Innominandum, had indeed built Little-Mean-on-the-Average.

There'd been a trend for planned communities in the 1960s. The horrible beige and concrete results were whispered by many to be the work of the Devil.

In fact, the infamous Prince of Darkness had been notably absent during the 1960s, and indeed, during the war years, despite the testimony of the Rolling Stones that he'd been knocking about in a Panzer.

The evil that men did had to be done by men, in sensible boots and trousers.[8] Unfortunately, it was always easy enough to find those keen for the job. With a blank cheque and the social conscience of an incontinent seagull flying over a charity concert, designing a town to damp down magic had been a doddle.

If you looked at a map of Little Mean, you'd find that the street map formed a set of nested pentacles, and that certain curly-wurly cul-de-sacs traced out sigils of occult significance from above. The fairways of the Average Valley Country Club were cunningly arranged into the pictogram for 'bugger off' in the language of ancient Lemuria.

About the only things out of place were the trio of construction sites which scarred the landscape; as well as Anders' Veg, there was a large American petrol company's UK office going up, and a gigantic retro computer games arcade. None of these showed any signs of progress, except for huge, inexplicably tarpaulin'd-over foundation holes.

In the middle of Little Mean, surrounded by this triangle of work-free worksites, squatted three institutions, back to back to back. Saint Pewtred's, to safeguard the future against random strangeness. Bleachwood Scours, the

---

8. And women too, as evil was very much equal-opportunity in that regard.

asylum for the so-called 'differently gnostic'. And, of course, Wrinkly Acres; real name, the General Crowley Veteran's Home for the Utterly Secret Services.

A kindly soul, looking at this map with the right eyes, would perhaps assume that someone had designed Little-Mean-on-the-Average to protect the elderly heroes of the past, the unfortunately psychically afflicted, and the precious children.

From whom?

Why, from those forces which loomed over the sane little island of three-dimensional reality like pot-smokers over a family-sized bucket of fried chicken, of course!

They'd be wrong, though.

Even monsters far beyond things like geometry, bus timetables and reality television were scared enough to want to keep certain people *in*.

There'd been deals made, after the last war. Unhallowed pacts, sealed with big official stamps and signed by those dour grey men you sometimes see on the TV news, standing just behind and to the left of our so-called leaders. The ones who tell new politicians, all fresh-faced and idealistic, about the assassination of JFK. And then show them the other video. Zoomed in on the face of Elvis, on that grassy knoll.

The grey men thought of it as a kind of nuclear non-aggression pact. Neither side would cultivate, train or deploy the kind of things which gave the other ones nightmares. And what gave the likes of old Cthulhu and his mates nightmares, if they overdid the camembert just before bedtime, was currently mooching along the high street in a too-big jumper covered in patches, listening to Napalm Death's *From Enslavement To Obliteration* on a pair of headphones held together with duct tape. One of her cherry-red Doctor Marten's boots was held together with the same stuff.

September didn't mind the muttering, and the twitching curtains, and the frankly rude stares. Or so she told herself. This was a Nice Little Town, where People Knew Their Place, after all. Most of the residents viewed September Normalsson in the same way that pedigree cat fanciers would look at a raccoon who'd sidled in to have a rummage through the bins.

Teenage girls were supposed to be bright and bubbly and travel in a gaggle of laughing, carefree friends, discussing pop stars and boys and glossy magazines about clothes. September considered all of this to be about as interesting as Regency-era tax law.

That might be why she had no friends her own age. Perhaps. If she thought about it, which was a rare and soul-searching kind of occasion.

Oh, there were some who weren't openly hostile, alright? And it wasn't their fault if they were all supposed to act like teenagers in a soap opera, but weren't actually smart enough to be creatively cruel. Someone had tried bullying September once. The casts came off after a few months, and they'd learned to walk again, but their hair never grew back.

People talked, as she went by.

There's the misfit. The wrong 'un. God knew her parents had tried, but...

Luckily, September had cultivated an attitude towards the gossips and gripes which she tended like barbed-wire topiary. They could all go to hell, but probably wouldn't, because it sounded too exciting.

After all, I try! she thought, noting a sideways glance and a little shake of the head from Mrs Cludge and Mrs Seeply, outside the Gilded Doily tearooms. *For mum and dad, really. But I'm not doing any of the really stupid bits. And*

I'm not going to have fake friends just to make the world feel comfortable!

What remained of the Dead Elvis followed September as she passed by the greengrocer's with its terrible punctuation, the Tao Maharajah Curry and Chinese Take-Out Pagoda, the local branch of Burger Slave, and the King's Toes, one of Little Mean's three faux-historic pubs.

Where the high street doglegged right, she passed by another huge, fenced-off hole in the ground, where diggers and concrete mixers lay dormant. This one was supposed to be the headquarters of Denver Gas, the petroleum giant, but like the others it was nothing but a mysterious pit.

The king of rock 'n' roll scuttled down a guy-rope, and splashed through a puddle of muddy water. It was now only six inches tall, and it clung to the shadows in the gutter, ducking through culvert pipes and menacing cockroaches with a tiny switchblade.

This had to be part of the Big Conspiracy, it reasoned, in a brain the size of a split lentil. *Oversight's tame oracles had seen some pants-wettingly horrible things in the near future, and they all started here...*[9]

There was a little park in the middle of the town, called Monkston's Green, and here the River Average made an oxbow loop, passing under the Memorial Bridge and between willow-hung banks to where the allotments began. Beyond that blackberry-brambled no-mans-land it was boxed into a concrete culvert. The Elvis popped out of a pipe and down into the gloom below the bridge, picking a path over stones and sunken shopping trolleys.

---

9. During the cold war, the Bureau Innominandum had reasoned that if an old lady in a Stevie Nicks costume could tell one person's future by reading the leaves in a standard cup of tea, then a coven of well-trained army witches should be able to tell the future of whole nations, given a teacup roughly one hundred and thirty metres round. The gigacup, as it was called, was loaded with finest lapsang souchong by a team of excavator operators, and featured a pattern of blue and white geese wearing aprons, each one taller than a double-decker bus.

Oh yes. Even diminished, it could keep up with its prey. If the mad professor and his silly young spawn were up to something, the Elvis Army would find out! And then…

Except that this time, there wouldn't be any more 'thens'.

Because, just as the little scrap of eldritch nastiness hop-skipped from a sunken whisky bottle to a rusted bike frame, a fatal sound split the silence.

"*Ribbit*," said the resurrected frog.

It had been trying to articulate its single-minded determination, it's grasp of the nefarious designs of the tiny Elvis, and its utter, worshipful devotion to the girl who had given it life. Strong, complex emotions seethed through that frog, like a hurricane trapped inside a party balloon. It had tried to express them all, but what it got was 'ribbit'.

What the Dead Elvis got was a length of sticky, muscular tongue, fired from between the frog's jaws with terrible accuracy.

There was a tiny plop. Nobody saw the six-inch Presley windmill backwards into the water. Nobody saw it come up snarling, grabbing the frog's tongue with both hands, ready to rip and rend…

Old Wilf Handisides, the house painter, did hear the *pop*, though, as he came wobbling over the Memorial Bridge on this vintage 1919 Peugeot bicycle. He thought he'd bust a tyre again, and swerved into an ornamental shrubbery, collapsing with a clatter of half-empty paint tins and ladderworks.

It was the sound of 20,000 volts frizzle-frying a tiny Elvis to a stick-figure scribble of charcoal. For a moment, the frog sat there, idly puffing up its throat and blinking. Little blips of electricity sparked around its neck bolts. Then it hopped into the air, performed a perfect miniature backflip, and disappeared below the weedy surface of the

Average, in search of more batteries.

Up above, September trudged blithely on. Toward, it seemed, the doom of all humanity. But in a much more immediate sense, toward birthday cake. So let's look on the bright side...

Two
The Doom Commission
vs
Old Age

Wrinkly Acres.

The 'waiting room for the afterlife' had a frontage like several stately homes spackled together, with a gabled roof that appeared to have been fashioned by a mad gingerbread baker.

Seeing as one of the place's inhabitants wrote *just exactly that* on his tax return each year, it was sort of fitting, thought September.

A pair of huge old oak trees leaned drunkenly against each other over the twisty wrought-iron gate, which proclaimed in Latin – *'aetas amet, sapientia ad libitum'*.[10] For unknown reasons, the entire vast edifice languished amid a constant smell of boiled cabbage.

September crunched her way up the gravel drive, past the ornamental fountain of Fey King Oberyn playing the tuba, and into the shade of the home's huge, gargoyle-heavy portico. She found herself smiling, just a little. Despite the cabbagey smell, this was a comfy old place, with something of a grandmother's kitchen about it.

"Afternoon, lass!" called out Doctor Defenestration, waving his portal gun cheerfully. The spindly old man was wizened and nut-bown, shrunken into a lime green spandex costume with an insignia of a stick-figure falling out of a window. "Here to see the guv'nor for his birthday, then?"

As usual, the Doctor (who, in his day, had stolen the

---

10. Basically, 'you have to get old, but wisdom is optional'.

crown jewels on three non-consecutive occasions) was playing checkers against his arch nemesis, an equally geriatric, pudgy old bloke in a judge's wig and purple tights.

"You and Rough Justice should come up," said September, casting a practised eye over the gameboard. One of the checkers, which was actually a beetle, tried to scuttle away, but the man in purple licked his lips with the patience of a terrapin, then proceeded to smack it flat with a wooden gavel.

"Mhhhhmhhhm. Yes. Got to pay our respects, Manfred. And there might be cake, you know!"

"Not like that time in Lisbon, when I got double-crossed by the Confectioner, and that big gateau..." began the Doctor, his eyes unfocussing alarmingly.

"No. Just triple chocolate," said September, reassuringly. "I stopped in at Mr Patel's on the way over. Surely the nurses will let you have a slice?"

Defenestration smiled, the expression wobbling out onto his face like a hesitant ice-skater.

"Oh, back in our day, we used to hold the United Nations to ransom so often they had us on speed-dial. I think we can handle a few *nurses*, Miss September!"

She gave the pair a little wave as she stepped into the cool marble vault of the home itself, through the big oak-leaf carved double doors, and into the main day room, under its huge domed skylight. Now the whiff of cabbage was joined by a high-pitched note of antiseptic.

This might have been something to do with the... and September could think of no other word for them... *denizens*. She thought it was a good word. It implied a lot of lurking.

They were all there, gathered around tables playing cards, watching soap operas on television, or simply snoring in massive, padded arm chairs. The subjects of ten thousand pulp comic books, 1960s television shows, and real-life adventures so classified that even a five-star general would have to read them upside down with his head in a bathtub.

There was King Chameleon, in his rubber lizard suit with the golden crown. The Suede Spectre, all in black, with his bell-bottomed super suit, wide collar and ruched cape. Neopatra, the cybernetic Queen of the Nile from the future. Mariachi Muerto. The Dread Panda. The Octopirate and his old foe, Captain Captain. The Piledriver, still three metres tall, despite his suit hanging from his elderly frame in folds, next to the hugely muscled, bright red and tiny shape of Short Temper. Heroes and villains chatted together, brought to a kind of equilibrium by the most implacable enemy of all – old age.

There was the Confectioner, bad baker of crime, with his henchwomen Candy Caine and Turkish Delight. This last villainess was knitting herself a new belly-dancer's costume while nattering to the Mistress of Necromancy, Penny Dreadful. In one corner Snorr, Norse god of narcolepsy, played table tennis against his old enemy in a bishop's mitre and skates; the Holy Roller. The Purple Paladin, the Groundskeeper, Lady Citronella and two of Septic Seven looked on.

Nurses in long-skirted Victorian costumes sailed sedately across the thick mint-green carpet, silent and attentive. September skirted around the side of the day room, keeping out of their way. These ladies were as efficient as a crack unit of paratroopers, and always had too many questions for her liking. She wouldn't have been surprised to learn the truth; these were, in fact, a cadre of combat soldiers, assigned to very politely keep strangers away from the elderly weirdos in their care.

September employed a furtive sidle and a nonchalant

slouch, making it to the elevators without rousing the attention of the staff. Her great-great-grandfather lived at the very top of the building, in an airy suite of rooms all overgrown with potted ferns. There were stairwells, of course, but these were hardly ever used by the residents. Simply opening the door to them would attract the attention of the head matron, Mrs Hardacre, secure in her glass-windowed bunker full of pills and romance novels.

The only way up was via the creaky, rattling old cage elevator, with its big ship's-tiller handle and scuffed oak panelling. September performed a stealthy, super-spy scuttle into the ground-floor cage, cranked the lever to the top, and dug deep in her backpack as the lift wobbled skyward.

It wasn't a bad cake.

Mr Patel was a serious student of the baking arts, and hoped one day to spend some quality time with the Confectioner, his henchwomen, and a pen and paper. So far, the elderly supervillain hadn't replied to any of his letters, but he always finished off the cookies which Mr Patel sent, and that was something. In his heyday, the Confectioner had once punished the baker of a sub-standard custard square by turning him into a thin film of crème brûlée.

The icing, though... *well*, September thought, *it was at least a nice shade of radioactive green.*

* Happy

One Hundred

and

Thirty Seventh Birthday

Bottom Text From Your Grate Grand DaughTR

(Smely Face Here) *

...it said, in curly loops of marzipan.

September just had time to tuck it behind her back before

the lift doors rattled open, and she faced the dreaded, evil, wicked Doom Commission.

They were all here, and, for the occasion, they'd all put on their special costumes as well. All except Granddad Septivarian, who was dressed, as usual, in tartan pyjamas and a lab coat. His eyes crinkled up around the edges as he broke into a wide and false-toothed grin.

There was something in his hand, as September stepped out of the lift, but he managed to slip it behind him and put it down, before he thought she'd noticed. *A little bottle of something green.* He swapped it out for a big bottle of something brown.

"Wahey! Just in time, young, mmm, lady! I say, are you old enough to have a drink with us? We have some very fine 27-year-aged scotch, or, if you prefer, some kind of cherry-flavoured stuff which the Holy Roller says he brewed up in his *toilet*, of all places. I think he's been in and out of prison a few too many times, eh?"

The Red Mobster, in his all-crimson zoot suit, waggled a cheeky bottle of moonshine in one huge robot claw.

"You know my views on prohibition, sweetheart. Get some while it's here!"

A segmented mechanical tentacle looped over behind Professor Archimedes and slapped the hulking big Mobster. It was connected to a tiny little old lady with a gigantic crystal dome for a forehead, behind which a massive, hundred-kilo brain pulsed. Twenty such tentacles were plugged through the clear dome and into its surface.

"You don't call the boss' granddaughter 'sweetheart', you lug," scolded this vision, Medusa Oblongata. "It's disrespectful to women!"

"It's in my idiom!" growled big Red, rolling his eyes. "And keep those mecha-serpents to yourself! Last week Stoatman sat on one, and it bit him right on the..."

"Who? Me? Naaaah, no trouble. Nobody complaining over here. Not today. Not ever. Gotta larf though, don't ya? Is that *cake* I smell?"

This came from a very twitchy, very thin old geezer in a motheaten fur onesie, who popped up and down behind the three figures seated at the table. A hood, complete with a stuffed approximation of a stoat's face, wobbled down over his eyes every time he moved. He was smoking the infinitesimal bent end of a roll-up cigarette, which seemed to switch sides from one corner of his mouth the other with no intervening motion.

"...and of course, you know, hmmmm, the Invisible Prince, last son of Immaterion, our alien friend," finished great-granddad Septivarian. He'd lost the thread of the conversation, followed it into his own head, proven two new theories of higher mathematics, devised a novel way of buttering crumpets, and then popped back out into reality to complete his welcome speech.

He gestured at what appeared to be an empty chair on his left. Off on the right, a glass raised itself to September. Since the prince was reclusive, paranoid, spoke no English and was permanently transparent, it was a surprise to see him about. Which was, of course, merely a figure of speech.

"Everybody, in fact. Except poor old Omegabrain. I rather wish he was able to, mmmm, see all of this, but of course, I'm only his replacement."

The assembled oldsters made conciliatory tuttings and grumblings, suggesting that Omegabrain, whoever he'd been, would have been quite pleased about the situation. September gave them all her wildest grin.

"The whole entire Doom Commission! You folks haven't been together since the 1980s! Not since you all teamed up to defeat the Silver Sorcerer, when he broke the Anti-

Superhuman Intervention Pact![11] They thought the Red Mobster was dead, and as for you, Stoatman, you switched sides and became the sworn defender of, ummm…"

"Woolwich, mainly. But you know how it is. All those lovely dank warehouses have been given loft conversions, or torn down to make the headquarters of ad agencies and recording studios. Hard to skulk properly, in, y'know, a stoaty manner when there's a wine bar on every corner, right?"

"Well, we had to be here for this one!" grumped Medusa Oblongata, over a pair of huge, butterfly-wing spectacles on a pink plastic chain.

"I suppose so," said September. "One hundred and thirty seven, eh? definitely a reason… for… celebr… atio… n?"

This last sentence drifted off into fuzzy, damp embarrassment as she noticed the expressions on the faces of the Doom Commission. The Red Mobster made frantic, behind-Septivarian's-back motions with one claw, signalling September to shut up. The other claw clipped the little bottle that the Professor had tried to hide, and it rolled across the table, glowing softly. September copped a look at the rolling label before it dropped out of sight. *Repo*.

"Oh, dear. Oh, dear dear me, no. Did nobody tell you, pumpkin?" asked the old professor, his face all but caving in with sorrow. "This is somewhat… mmmm… in the nature of a *going away* party."

---

11. Giving people strange powers by way of magic was quite forbidden under the Unmanifest Accords, those rules which bound the supernatural races and humanity. This was mainly because it resulted in the spawning of abominations, but also because your average wizard or witch had worked extremely hard to gain wyrd and eldritch powers, and didn't want some johnny-come-lately super soldier getting them for free. Strange science, in the postwar years, had achieved what sorcery could not, but by the late 1970s a superhuman arms race had not only threatened the destruction of the world, but also caused a critical shortage of spandex. In 1981 a pact was signed to demilitarise superhumanity, and retire people like the Doom Commission in places like Little-Mean-on-the-Average.

"A final bash!" said the Mobster, snickering one claw.

"A last grand adventure!" enthused Stoatman.

"The piece de resistance!" agreed Medusa.

"Zgh-traaa fnorsh glag zububbulon!" put in the Invisible Prince, though what this meant was lost on all present.

"Going away? But great-granddad, you *are* away! This..." and here September gestured all around at the high-windowed corner suite, with its hanging ferns and its glass cases full of trophies from a life of super-crime. "This is away. This is about as away as you can get, without leaving the planet."

Septivarian Archimedes sighed, and took something out of his pocket. He set it on the table with a sad, final little click, and the top popped open. It was a golden pocket-watch, with loops of wire and blinking diodes grafted to one side like bracket fungus. A pair of batteries was sellotaped to the back.

"It's more a sort of going away from this body, sort of thing," he said, in a small voice. "The doom clock never lies. I'll be getting a visit from the tall skinny chap with the garden implement sometime around afternoon tea. Then, I suppose, I'll be seeing Omegabrain again, too."

"But that's *horrible!*"

Medusa Oblongata peered over her glasses, fixing September with a pair of eyes like shucked oysters under ice.

"Get to our age, miss, and it don't seem so bad. There's the prospect of the afterlife, or reincarnation, and all that. And of course, a proper rest."

The Doom Commission suddenly looked their age – an average of 106.

"He comes for us all, eventually," grumbled the Red Mobster. "Ultimate adversary, he is. Implacable as thermodynamics, they say. Never missed his man."

The geriatric supervillains shared a conspiratorial look. Medusa nodded.

"That's why we're all here today. To nobble the bastard," said Stoatman, with a wheezing laugh. "Talk about a grand finale for the chief, eh? Loyal to the bitter end, that's us!"

"Though the plan is to make it *his* bitter end, or at least his end what gets bitten."

Septivarian smiled, as the Mobster polished one jagged claw.

"See! Stout companions all! I tried to talk them out of it, but they insisted. The Doom Commission versus Death Himself! Of course, my money is still on the grim reaper, though... mmmmm... you're more than welcome to stay and watch the fun."

September's hands weren't under their own power. She dropped the cake, which collapsed sideways across the table.

"Oh, no. You can't be serious."

"Absolutely, Miss September," nodded Stoatman. "We feel it's the least we can do for the guv'nor after all we've been through together. First he was Professor Archimedes during the war, then he spent thirty years behind the black cape as the Befuddler. I mean..."

"No, you daft mustelid! I mean – *he's right behind you!*"

The Doom Commission moved much faster than their collective several centuries of experience would have suggested, turning to face the pillar of seething mist which had formed behind them. Little crackles of green lightning percolated through this cloud as it rose up, assuming the form of a tall, cowled figure.

"Bloody hell! That's him alright!" said Big Red. "I recognise him from the tattoo on my bum cheek!"

Medusa Oblongata rose up into the air, cross-legged, her mecha-serpents whipping and writhing. Stoatman adopted a furtive, feral crouch. September had no idea what the Invisible Prince was up to, but she supposed it must be quite dramatic.

As for great-great-granddad Septivarian...

The old man picked up the doom clock, which was blinking with a row of red LED zeroes. He sighed, put it back on the table, and then took his coat off, folding it neatly over the chair back. He began to unbutton his pyjamas.

"September, there's something important you need to know," he said, fishing a waxed length of string out from around his neck.

"Well, there's no need to get nude for it," she replied, with a mad little giggle. "That's the kind of thing which makes the nurses think you've lost it."

Lost, indeed. For now the cloud had begun to coalesce, and September could clearly see a skeletal face shaping up, inside a swiftly darkening robe. She knew she was supposed to be terrified, but all she could think about was how this would be a big disappointment for Mum, and Dad, and poor Mister Mackleduff.

Battling the Grim Reaper was definitely what they'd call Behaviour Unbefitting of a Young Lady.

Septivarian cared not one iota.

"Please, September! There are dark and sinister forces after me, because of my work. Not the fun I had with these lads..." (the Commission all took the chance to wave and nod) "...but the *real* work. During the cold war. With the Biocomputer, and the New Damnation, and all that. B.I.S.H.O.P and the Elvises and... well. You know how they say you can't take it with you? Well, when it comes to ideas, you *can*. And there's no way I should."

He brandished a crucifix on the end of his string, then – a medieval-sized cross with a key on the long end. It had been augmented, with its own batteries and wires soldered on. Next to it on that greasy twist of twine was a clear plastic slab, of the kind nerds use to protect their most valuable trading cards. There was a little picture inside it, which September almost recognised.

"Bloody hell! That explains the one-thirty-seven!" said a deep, sepulchral voice.

The crucifix and card-holder twinkled and spun, as a gale blew out from the pillar of mist, revealing a very familiar figure in black. Familiar, that is, even to those who hadn't seen the Red Mobster's intimate tattoo.

"*Septivarian Quintmegistus Archimedes?*" It asked, in tones which made it obvious that it was not here to deliver a pizza. "*AKA the Befuddler, Quizmaster of Chaos? It is your time!*"

September felt panic rise up in her, like a radiator about to boil over.

"What do you mean, ideas? *Which* ideas, granddad?"

She now saw what the old man was wearing under his tartan PJs, and a little thrill of intuition crackled up the back of her neck, forcing the panic down. It was his old costume – the black tights with their question-mark insignia. It had been on the cover of a whole lot of comic books, back when she was small.

"I don't know!" he shouted.

"*You don't know if you're Professor Septivarian Archimedes?*" asked the grim reaper, tilting his skull to one side. "*I never got any notes about senile dementia, mate...*"

"Oh, shut up for a minute, bonesy! I'm talking to the girl. Kind of a last second, very emotional bequeathing of the family legacy, kind of thing. If you don't mind?"

He held out the cross and key. They sizzled with green fire.

"I mean, I *removed* those ideas from my own brain, with the help of a machine called B.I.S.H.O.P, that I'm pretty sure I destroyed. But ideas have a way of getting out. Especially the very wicked ones, that you know you should never have told anyone you could come up with! Some very nasty people will be coming to claim them, and quite a lot of them will be Elvis Presley."

This last nugget of information sailed over September's head like a cruise missile. She reached out for the string, and closed her hand around the golden cross instead, feeling it lurch like a living heart between her fingers.

"But..."

Septivarian dropped his pants. He was wearing knee-high boots and leather trousers underneath. A cape unfurled. From a hidden pocket, the old man produced a professor's mortarboard (this one with a razor edge, for throwing) and gently placed it on his head. The top of it was inscribed with a sideways eight – the symbol for infinity.

"No buts, dear. You're family. Your silly relatives all thought you could stop the Endarkenment by being *normal*, and look where it got them. Pah! Chartered accountancy! Quantity surveying! Insurance brokerage! Your mother even changed her name, for all the good it did her. Septerina was a very pretty name for a little girl, I always thought."

"**Look, can we get on with this?**" asked the angel of death. "**It's just that there's a bus crash in Karachi coming up very soon, and...**"

"Shut up!" chorused the whole Doom Commission at once. Septivarian carried on.

"You've got the *wrong stuff*, young lady, and I mean that in the best possible way. If this was 1961 you'd have knocked 'em dead as a supervillain. If it was 1942 you'd have been a Battle Witch in Section M. But it's the new millennium, all right, so you'll have to find your own... mmmmm... idiom. Yes, that's it. Take the key. Find my old laboratory. Find my wild ideas. Because... no pressure, but if you don't get them first, the world might very well end."

"I really must insist, and look, I'm sorry for the tight schedule, but..." began the skeleton with the scythe.

"Isn't it traditional that he gets to play a game, to see if he gets another year of life?" asked Medusa.

"Oh. right. The chess. I was worried about that. Old professors, and all..." The reaper clicked his bony fingers, and a marble chess set on a small stone pillar appeared. *"I suppose I'll go black, then. Now, just remind me, how does the horsey one move at the start?"*

"Actually, ahhhh, what we were thinking of..." said Stoatman, with a cheesewire whine of menace behind his cockney accent, "Was something a bit more physical."

"Well, I have Cluedo, and Battleship, and Hungry Hungry Hippos," said the Ultimate Reality, rummaging in his robes. *"But..."*

"We were thinking more of, you know. Five-on-one mixed martial arts," said Medusa, hefting an empty whisky bottle with one metallic serpent.

Septivarian gave September a wink.

"Terribly sorry to make you save the world on your first time out," he said, with a twinkle in his eye. "But I have, mmm, all kinds of faith in you! Now, the first idea is in the cross. Hopefully that card will take care of the unlucky curse. Then all you have to do is complete Project Dark Lazarus, and we'll be home free!"

September's face felt numb. Her brain looped little loops, through bubbles of stark disbelief.

"You want *me* to save the world? Me? You know I got suspended from science at school today, right?"

"Oh, school's no place for a genius," harrumphed the professor. "Adventures are so much more educational! I do so wish I could come with you. I never did get to see if all that Lazarus malarkey would really work. Regrettably, though, I believe I have business with this skinny gentleman. Now, things might get a bit kinetic, m'dear, so if you're concerned about your health, then –"

"No!" shouted September. "You can't *die*! You can't just leave! You're Professor Archimedes! You won all those medals! You were the Befuddler! You're... my granddad! It's not *fair*!"

The old professor smiled.

"No," he said. "It's not fair at all. But it's the rules. You get so long, even with retro-palmistry. Don't you worry. I'm ready, now. Because I've got a plan. You've *got* this one, young September. And now –" He turned to face the Grim Reaper. His friends all posed menacingly, just like on the cover of a comic book.

"Get him, boys!" he said – and the room exploded.

For all their age, the Doom Commission were still supervillains, with powers to match. They piled in, rushing the grim reaper as he pulled a long silver staff from its harness on his back, and the impact blew the table over backwards. September slid into cover behind it, but couldn't resist a peek over the top, as the backsplash of multi-coloured detonations painted the walls and cracked the windows.

Medusa fired searing violet lasers from her tentacles. The Invisible Prince must have been in there, because now and again a blast of green sparks rocked the reaper back on his heels. The Red Mobster had no pyrotechnics – he simply waded in with his giant claws, all rough and spiky, throwing haymakers which could demolish brick walls. Certainly, the ones which missed pulverised great-great-granddad's furniture. Meanwhile, Stoatman tenaciously chewed on the grim reaper's leg, making a horrible high-pitched keening noise.

As for Septivarian himself – well, when he'd been the Befuddler, Quizmaster of Chaos, he'd never been short of nasty gadgets. Now he wielded a huge, chrome-plated Bafflement Ray, a baroque cannon of a thing with spinning glass globes, tanks of sizzling electrified acid, and a muzzle like a lemon juicer designed by aliens. It flung streamers of blue fire, as the old professor laughed in a thoroughly unhinged fashion, really getting a last one in before closing time.

The reaper weathered it all. His silver staff was a blur as it blocked every blow, and an aura which boiled around him like heat-haze simply absorbed those blasts and bolts of energy.

"***Come on! Be reasonable!***" he shouted, in a voice which was quite unlike the booming tones he'd adopted before. "***He's a hundred and thirty seven, for goodness sake. It's not like I'm early!***"

Medusa Oblongata chose this moment to use her telekinetic powers, lifting an entire three-seater lounge suite and throwing it across the room.

"He carried one of the Keys of Dante for sixty years, you bony bastard! He's earned a nice long retirement!"

"***Right,***" said the Reaper, managing a determined frown despite having no eyebrows. "***You're just being silly, now. That's it!***"

Time shimmered for an instant, and September saw the whole scene grow glassy and unreal. There was Big Red, leaping off the kitchen counter with his claws wide open. there was Stoatman, being flailed about on the end of one black reaper-issue boot like a rogue draught excluder. There was her grandfather, hefting a large, antiquated round black bomb with a question mark painted on the side. Presumably, there was the Invisible Prince too, though he might have been having a sit-down for all September knew. Medusa was caught in that typical telekinetic pose, her fingers poised at her temples, her face screwed up like that of a small terrier trying to conduct its business on the next-door neighbour's lawn.

Then the scythe hinged open. That silver staff grew a blade like an upwelling of liquid mercury. It made a sound like a soapy finger on glass as it solidified. Light tapdanced along its horribly sharp edge.

It was finality made solid. It had come whispering down on whole armies behind a storm of arrows, and tidied up after countless plagues. It was the last word in lawn care, and it glistened like the arctic stars, cold and indifferent.

"Right. I'm not supposed to reap any of you except the old feller, but it's my first day, and if any of you get in the way of the scythe, I won't be held responsible. Health and safety act, that is. You've been duly warned."

The blade swept in what could only be accurately called a reaping arc, with the hypersonic shriek of diamonds across bulletproof glass. September clearly saw the soul of the lounge suite leave its body.[12] A translucent, wavering ghost in tan leather rose skyward and vanished through the roof, as the sofa itself was cloven in twain. It turned to dust in mid-air, blowing past the Grim Reaper as two spiral vortices.

"OK then? Who wants some?" asked that bony

---

12. Religious furniture believes that, when a couch, easy chair or sideboard dies, its soul goes to furniture heaven, to be with Treesus, who died to save all wooden products from their sins. Treesus was a cedar from the Holy Land who, some two thousand years ago, was cruelly uprooted and turned into a crucifix by some Roman chaps, and then had some fellow from Nazareth nailed to him. His gospel preaches that, when the time of the Great Recycling is at hand, all furniture will be reborn in the Holy Shrubbery, a world where lumberjacks and carpenters have been rendered down into a range of scented waxes.

apparition, with the hint of a raised eyebrow (that wasn't, strictly speaking, there).

Medusa dropped her hands from her temples and cracked her knuckles.

"Oh, you poor wee sprog," she said, not unkindly. "We're just getting *started*."

"Fink yer 'ard enuf?" cackled Stoatman.

"Phraar glag blobble!" added the Invisible Prince, who turned out to have been over by the breakfast nook this whole time.

And...

"Wait. What? Your *first day?*" said September, as her second thoughts crashed into her train of thought. "Aren't you, you know, a metaphysical representation of the inevitability of time, or something? Shouldn't..."

"September! September! Over here!" shouted great-granddad Septivarian. "Always was a thing with our family, the... mmmmm... digressions. Perhaps I could create a kind of helmet that... but no! There's no *time*! September, take the key, and run! Just *run*! Find my lab. Find my wild ideas! Don't look back. And don't give anyone that card, or the other one. You're the Magician, now. The Electric Virgil will explain."

Septivarian turned away... and rose up into the air, a crackling nimbus of lightning playing around his black spandex suit. Something like a fat black-and-chrome spider scuttled down his arm, and wrapped itself around his hand, becoming a mechanical glove.

"Look at this, boys! I found my magneto-gravitonic manipulator! The one I used against Captain Pernicious during that trouble in Tunisia!"

"That's the mustard!" cackled Medusa Oblongata, as several of her mecha-tentacles split open, revealing arcing, spitting plasma nozzles. "Come on, boys! Let's give old bowling-ball-face here one to remember!"

September backpedalled as a fury of super-powered rays and beams stabbed out at the Grim Reaper.

*"**Bowling-ball face! Really! I mean, this job was supposed to come with at least a little self-respect...**"* He slammed the butt-end of his scythe against the floor, and all of those incandescent beams froze, and cracked, and shattered. Shards of frozen fire fell to the floor with a sound like tinkling glass. *"**And, yes, for your information miss, it is my first day. Not that you'd care. I'll probably get put back on probation thanks to these senile delinquents!**"*

The Doom Commission, who were complete strangers to the concept of backing down, all managed to unfold new, exciting and very deadly looking weaponry as they rallied. The Befuddler's magnetic manipulator glove let him tear a huge chunk of pipework out of the ceiling, aiming it in the air like a spear.

"I thought you were ... mmmm... supposed to be running, girl!" shouted the old man over his shoulder, as his mortarboard began to levitate, rotating gently.

Indeed! Because the discharge of weird particles around the Reaper and his curmudgeonly adversaries was beginning to do odd things to the room, the laws of physics, and the air itself. September took a breath, which tasted like microwaved gym socks, and watched the wallpaper slowly collapse in into a fractal tangle. The potted ferns wavered like mirages, and one went *pop*, suddenly turning to lemon jelly.

It was time to leave.

On a whim, she snatched up the Doom Clock, still blinking all zeroes. Then, fighting back the kind of snotty tears which were all the worse for not being pretty, September backed out of the double doors, and spun around as they slammed themselves shut behind her.

The first thing she saw was a flying wedge of battle nurses, coming straight at her. They were wearing white gas masks and carrying white-painted Kalashnikov assault rifles, with red crosses painted on. September flattened herself against the wall as they went stampeding past, through the double doors...

And were immediately blown back out again, pinwheeling through the air like rag dolls to land in a crumpled heap. September's heart hammered against her ribs – but they weren't dead. *Her Grandad wasn't a murderer, at the end.*

"Come on, girls!" shouted the matron, from under a struggling, starchy pile. "We're not going to let the old duffer act up, even if it is his birthday! Truncheons out, and set to stun!"

The nurses reformed their phalanx, as a beam cored out a circular section of the wall right next to September, turning it to key lime pie. One of the Doom Commission must have borrowed some toys from the Confectioner, she supposed. But now was not the time for speculation. The whole building groaned and shuddered. Plaster dust rained down. It was time to do what her great-grandad had suggested, and *run*.

September took the stairs two at a time, clutching the key-cross in one hand and the Doom Clock in the other. The building shook again as horrible super-science clashed with the supernatural above, and a tide of what smelled and looked quite like raspberry jam came slubbering down behind her, bubbling at her heels. Nurses screamed. Some shouted exciting swear-words in Russian.

September skidded into the day-room in a controlled power-slide, her sensible soles smoking, and saw the mint-carpeted expanse zoom out before her in tunnel vision. It was a minefield of obstacles to a girl trying to accelerate, and the doors seemed very, very far away.

They seemed a lot further when the card and crucifix in her hand sizzled with a snap of electricity, and a tiny hologram of Septivarian Archimedes fizzed to life in mid-air, right next to her. It was, sacrilegiously, projected from the tiny figure of Our Lord, who seemed, on closer inspection, to be a cross between a person and a deep-sea anglerfish.

"Ahhh... mmm... September, I hope. If you're seeing this, things went about as well as we planned against the Grim Reaper. I'm dead, but don't be sad. I have some *very* interesting theories on the afterlife, and this is my chance to have a whole new adventure! The important thing is that you're running. Good!"

September barely had time to take this in as she hurdled the ping pong table, slid under a tea trolley laden down with cakes, and performed a ninja dive-roll over a sofa, between two more of the Septic Seven.

"There's two thing you need to know, right now," went on the hologram, which stayed resolutely upright, despite this display of gymnastics. "First, the Wild Idea inside this key, and all the other ones, contain a tiny part of my soul. So the Reaper is going to be coming after them."

September risked a look back as this news sizzled to the forefront of her brain. She skidded to a stop as the elevator doors slid open, snicking like metal teeth.

And here he came. Calm and cool as a badass in an action movie, the Grim Reaper slo-mo walked out of the lift, casually sliding on a pair of black Ray-ban aviators.

This shouldn't have really worked for a being with no ears, but he managed to pull it off spectacularly. He held out one bony hand, and pointed.

"Not a chance!" snarled September.

This was the thing which had killed her Grandad! Or... well... at least punched his ticket. There was no way she was going to let it get hold of the key. Instead, she hurled the Doom Clock, which sailed over the heads of all the geriatric heroes and villains present, blinking red.

"Plasma grenade!" shouted September, as her feet started to run again without her head turning to look where they were going.

That might be why she missed the spilled porridge on the floor, and why, in the next instant, she was confused by the world spinning upside down. Her sensible boots went past on an upward trajectory, then the ceiling blurred by, then her face was full of mint-green carpet. Behind her, the Reaper let rip with any number of thoroughly unprofessional curses, plucking the Doom Clock (not a plasma grenade) out of his rib cage.

"There's the unlucky curse," said the voice of Great-granddad Septivarian. "You'll be needing a pinch of catnip, a new penny, a fresh egg and some oak leaves..."

The Reaper strode forward. His long-legged stride carried him up and over the ping pong table. He pushed the tea trolley aside. He stalked over the couch, where Septic Commandos Three and Five cowered back.

"Just hand it over, miss. It's not your soul, and it's not your fight. 'Not one ghost left behind', that's our motto."

"The second thing's that card," continued the hologram. "Old bonesy there's from the afterlife, so he can't touch it. Not this one. But there's things that will be wanting it. And while you've got it, you're sort of heir to my lineage, as it were."

September struggled to her feet, slopping cold porridge off the side of her face. She needed a bright idea... so she took a closer look at the card.

Inside its plastic shell, the thing looked ancient. It was a tarot card, of the kind fortune tellers used, but it was older than the ones they sold in the high street bookstore for the kind of ladies who collected crystals. It looked, in fact, as if it could be the prototype.

A figure stood before a table on the card, etched in old, faded inks. The figure was doing something with three little cups, that September recognised immediately as one of those street-corner grifting tricks. Above the figure's head was the symbol for infinity, just like the one on Septivarian's mortarboard.

The Magician, said the card, in heavy gothic script.

September didn't get long to think about this. Because the rat-gnawed wiring which suspended the light above her chose that moment to give way. If she wasn't given a split second's warning by the twang of parting copper, September would have been clobbered by a tacky chandelier.

"Unlucky curse, you see?" said the hologram, irritatingly calm. "Gosh, he's really getting pretty close, don't you think? Time to try running again, perhaps?"

September didn't need telling twice.

As she accelerated across the day room, carpets ruched up in front of her. Electrical cables formed cunning snares. Liquids leaked, and empty wheelchairs rolled into her path.

But September's mind was afloat in a cool sea of calm, now, and time seemed to slow down. She focused on the doors and prayed for velocity. She never felt bony fingers nearly snapping shut around her collar; her imagination filled in the blanks well enough.

Mrs Slugpounder, the Sports Matron at Saint Pewtred's, would have been astounded by the Olympic-level focus which her young pupil displayed in that mad, twenty-metre dash to freedom.

September had always seemed to be more of a daydreamer than an athlete, lacking any semblance of competitive spirit, or interest in jolly teamwork. The best that could be said of her was that she did well at fencing, and paid worryingly intent attention to judo.

She also had a horrible habit of just standing there during games of field hockey, until the ball came to her, when she'd test the wind with one finger, narrow her eyes, and then proceed to land a trick shot which saw it bounce off the grandstand, the corner posts, the tea caddy and anything else solid, right into the opposition goal.

This, Mrs Slugpounder felt, was not sporting, as neither thinking nor physics had any place on the hockey turf.[13]

Despite the curse, and despite the bony apparition hard on her heels, September made it. She burst out into the sunlight and out of the smell of liniment and cabbage, seeing the driveway laid out before her and no more obstacles in her path.

Now she was in the clear. Because September, a tall and lanky teenager, was made for running, thanks to countless ancient generations of humans who had to contend with such things as a sabre-toothed hamsters and giant, carnivorous ducks. Once all her limbs agreed on a particular firing order, she was off. At the same time, the Grim Reaper was finding out that when it comes to athletic garments, a flowing black robe of utter midnight is, to put no finer point on it, a bit crap.

Down he went in a spray of very expensive gravel, to the delighted whoops of Doctor Defenestration and Rough Justice. Smash, went a pair of very expensive vintage Ray-Bans.

*"**You don't understand!**"* wailed the Incarnation of Oblivion. *"**You can't leave a part of him here! It'll break causality! It'll attract all kinds of hideous monsters! I'll**

---

13. This kind of attitude explained why the Saint Pewtred's Fighting Marmosets had lost every field hockey game they had ever entered, but also why Mrs Slugpounder's all-girls wrestling team were undisputed champions of the tri-borough area.

have to do so much paperwork!"

But September wasn't inclined to listen. She shot through the gates, between the drunkenly leaning oak trees, and stopped, turning back and brandishing the key over her head in victory.

She'd done it! Great-great-granddad's final wish! She'd always known there was a special, different future waiting for her. One which had nothing to do with dusty schoolrooms and chartered accountancy and flat-soled shoes. She'd find the laboratory. She'd carry on the professor's legacy. She'd become the Magician! Wait. *Where did that thought come from?*

"Ummmm..." said the hologram, as the blast of a gigantic air horn made September's head snap around to the left, driven by a sense of sudden dread.

There was a lot of radiator grille right there. There was a screech of tyres. There was a definite sense that she'd stopped, right in the middle of Burnsley Road, and now the number 12 bus was only a few metres away, and not slowing down fast enough.

"*Unlucky curse.*" said the hologram, as the front of the bus collided with September, throwing her into the air. An ornamental shrubbery swallowed her up on a nearly flat trajectory.

Luckily, at this point, she was already unconscious.

Kneeling on the driveway of Wrinkly Acres, the Grim Reaper's jaw fell open in shock. Then it fell off.

"Urrrhhh crrrrp. That wnnnt spposd trrr hrpppn!"

Suture One
The Big Malpractice

SIDNEY DIBBLECOMB WOKE up in a bathtub, wearing full Victorian evening dress, and nursing a hangover so vile that the roof of his mouth felt like it had been upholstered with burnt vinyl.

Somebody had also – obviously – force-fed him a fire ant vindaloo, then washed it down with a pint of diesel. The fact that this somebody was actually Sidney himself, in the not too distant past, made things not one whit better.

He groaned, the sound echoing off the dingy formica and enamel of the bathroom and threatening to implode his cranium.

Good god! What a night out it must have been! He remembered the minicab, and the first nightclub, and the second, and vomiting in a bus shelter, and then... then...

A memory swum up to the surface of Sidney's aching brain, churning the silt of his stupor with the shadow of fangs and fins.

Ohhh, hell. The tracksuit man. The guy in the Range Rover with the blacked out windows. Offering all kinds of chemical ecstasy, for a very reasonable price.

Sidney raised one hand from out of the cold bathwater, only just realising that he was immersed in it. There, on his wrist, was a big flat purple patch, like those ones cigarette smokers used to break their habit. Written on it in orange was one word.

REPO

"The wildest ride you'll ever take," the tracksuit man had grinned, with a mouthful of crooked teeth, like a taxidermist's bottom drawer. Sidney could still see the man's lips moving in front of that thicket of yellowed enamel, even through the bandsaw grind of the hangover. "Twenty quid well spent, me old chum. You'll be *well* wasted, right?"

"Repo?" he'd joked. "Like, what you fellers do to geezers what won't pay?"

Sidney had ploughed on, desperate for a chuckle.

"Like, when you wake up in a bathtub full of ice, with... one... kidney..."

That particular recollection made him sit up in the bath, sloshing water all over the mildewed linoleum. *Cold* water. Water that might have once been *ice*...

And, *oh crap, oh crap*... the water was stained red. Little wisps and curls of blood were floating in it! Sidney's brain wrung itself out with sheer terror, as his eyes focused.

On a pair of white gloves, on his hands. On a black tuxedo jacket and white, collared shirt, on him, and spattered with gore. He felt down and around, searching for stitches in his side, but instead his hand found something solid on the bottom of the tub. Something which ground up against the enamel in a very particular way.

He pulled it out. It was a knife. A big, curved, chrome surgical blade, like something from a display about antique hospitals, where anaesthetic was a burly bloke with a mallet, and infections danced a merry jig on the end of tar-caked amputations.

Sidney stood up, dripping, and for the first time he saw what waited for him outside the bathroom door.

He saw the pentagram. He saw the dripping trails.

He saw the blood, and the chunks, and the loops and coils of things which a man should never see before breakfast, and even then only as the outside bits of sausages.

He saw the big black medical bag on the floor, where the carpet was a mass of crawling flies and crimson.

And finally, he saw the words. Someone had written

them with what Sidney was horribly certain was a sliced-off finger, using it like a sharpie marker. An equally horrible little insinuation convinced him that the writer had been, if not him, then at least working the levers behind his eyes.

From Hell,

Said the writing on the wall.

Dearest Sir. Our little game is not quite done. If you still want to play at coppers, I am more than satisfied to remain, your humble servant and most diligent quarry;
Jack

It was at that moment that the metropolitan police, alerted by a tenant on the floor below whose ceiling had developed a bad case of stigmata, kicked in the door.

They found Sidney Dibblecomb on his hands and knees, throwing up violently. This detail was more than obscured by the fact that they also found him dressed as a Victorian-era surgeon, holding what could only be described as 'the murder weapon', down in a puddle of what used to be, until very recently, a human being.

Afterwards, one of the constables said that the worst bit – the *very* worst – was the look Sidney gave him at the end, with blood on his hands and vomit on his chin.

Like being truncheoned unconscious was the highlight of his morning.

Three
Ancient Evil
vs
Modern Medicine

"Another Repo overdose?" asked Dr Cliff Hunkstrong, rakishly brushing his fringe out of his eyes. "So sad. And so young, as well."

Dr Cliff had no idea he was performing an incredibly tightly choreographed segue, and if he had known, he would have been quietly chuffed.

Like all doctors, Cliff Hunkstrong harboured a smouldering passion to leave the world of national-health-funded medicine behind, and become a television doctor on a Latin-American daytime soap opera. It was for this reason that he'd changed his name from Dr Reginald Spudley, and gotten a bit of a 'mates rates' plastic surgery job from one of his old med-school chums.

"Nope," said Nurse Valerie, peering at a clipboard. "Says she was hit buy a bus. One of those miraculous escapes, apparently."

Nurse Valerie popped a huge pink bubble of gum between lips painted cherry red. Dr Cliff had picked her because of her photogenic looks, and insisted on a dress code which bordered on violating not only several human resources guidelines, but also standards of broadcast decency. Valerie, who was no idiot, put up with the erstwhile Reginald's delusions because the pay was great, and frankly, the only thing her boss had a perverted desire for was himself.

"Hardly an escape, nurse," mused Cliff, pouting in what he felt was a manly fashion.

The nurse peered at her clipboard again, then at the bandage-swaddled figure of September Normalsson, identifiable by her Doctor Martens boots. She lay on a chrome gurney like a rudely awoken Pharaoh, wrapped up head-to-ankles.

"Not one bone broken. Not one bruise. Not even a scratch, and that was a big old Albion bus. She's stone-cold unconscious, and then there's this cross, see?" She pointed to September's resolutely clenched fist, which was still holding the big, ornate chunk of filigree that her great-great-granddad had gifted her. "The paramedics tried to pry her fingers open, but she's giving old Charlton Heston a run for his money."

"You mean, sort of parting the red sea, kind of thing?" asked Cliff. "Displaying a morbid fear of monkeys? Having some kind of exciting chariot race while wearing an inappropriately modern watch?"

Valerie sighed, severely stretching the seams of her inappropriately small white latex uniform. She sometimes wondered if Dr Hunkstrong would ever manage to leave behind the world of verrucas and ingrown fingernails, and actually become a telenovela star. He'd have to learn to memorise scripts in Spanish, after all.

"I mean, we'd have to pry that thing from her cold, dead, hands, Doctor," she said. "Which we can't. Coz she'd not dead, see?"

"And it really wasn't Repo? I'd look ever so dashing on the evening news, weeping a manly tear or so for the flower of teenage maidenhood, cruelly cut down by the scourge of illegal drugs."

"You eat vicodin like skittles, you berk," muttered Valerie under her breath.

"What was that?"

"I said *we might have to try some vitamins and see if they work*, boss. Sometimes these coma thingies can be tricky buggers."

Dr Hunkstrong nodded, cupping his artfully clefted chin between tanned fingers.

"Indeed. There's often amnesia, and flashbacks, and dream sequences where the screen goes all swirly-whirly and you realise you've been in the shower for twenty four years," he said knowingly. "Put her in a room with some beeping machinery, then call me after I've had my botox injections to see how she's going. And nurse?" Dr Cliff turned back to her dramatically, sliding on a pair of mirrored sunglasses. "Stay smouldering with unspoken sexual tension!"

Valerie, who was smouldering with a heartfelt desire to ram her clipboard up Reginald Spudley's bottom, simply smiled.

And that was how September, who had been protected by several gigawatts of force-field shielding thrown out by a self-sacrificing little hologram, found herself in a plain white hospital room, having an out-of-body experience.

Her spirit (which was dressed in torn-up blue jeans and a Motorhead t-shirt) began to rise, and the threads tethering her mind to her body parted like wisps of smoke. All the chemicals sloshing around in her skull were left behind, and her anger melted away, followed by the sorrow, and the confusion of why her parents had tried so hard to keep Septivarian at arm's length.

September rolled over in the air, easy as thinking, and saw her body down below, hooked up to several serious-looking machines which went 'beep'. They hadn't bothered with intravenous drugs, because, aside from some mud and grass stains, September seemed miraculously unharmed. However, the doctors and nurses all agreed that she'd been hit by a bus, so there must be something wrong with her.

Some of the staff secretly hoped that it would be a hitherto-unknown condition, that they'd get to name.

September drifted upwards. There was a brief sizzle as the back of her head pushed through the ceiling; her hand and arm passed right through the hanging fluorescent tubes with a whisper of electrons. Just before she ascended through to the next floor, September noticed a crisp, new fifty-pound note on top of the tall wardrobe beside her bed.[14] Then her view was obscured by wires, timbers and a very surprised rat, before she surfaced through the lino of the hospital refectory.

September exerted a little will and her ghost stopped rising, spinning around to hang vertically in the air. She tried to swipe a plastic fork, but her hand went right through, only making it wobble slightly. Finally, as she scanned a frozen tableau of doctors stuffing their faces, her thoughts caught up with her.

Funny, she thought. *This isn't half as terrifying as it should be. No glands, I suppose. No adrenaline. I mean, as far as sudden metaphysical revelations go, it's been quite an afternoon. But I'm not dead, right? So this must be one of those-out of body things. Like the psychics talk about on television. Bloody hell! Does this mean that crew of flakes are serious, too?*

She concentrated hard, and a blue nimbus outlined her fingers, radiating out from the spectral tarot card on its string around her neck. With a supreme effort of will, September managed to pluck a Snickers bar from a junior surgeon's fingers, sending it clattering to the tabletop.

Interesting. Willpower manifested as a physical force.

14. They used to do this in some hospitals, to see if people truly had out-of-body experiences. The experiment proved two things; that people might very well leave their mortal shells when they were extremely sick or injured, but that they didn't just hover about like a half-deflated balloon dog if they did so. And that hospital cleaners are both very, very diligent, and craftier than the temporarily dead when it comes to pocketing a sly fifty.

But if my body and my brain are a whole floor below me, what's thinking this right now? And if I can't feel anything, because I don't currently have any skin, why has the room... suddenly... gone... cold?

September turned in mid-air; a glowing blue wraith in a world of frozen doctors and microwave dinners. And there, boiling up like a thunderhead behind the cutlery counter, was a pillar of darkness shot through with lightning. Inside it... a face.

Well, sort of a face, anyway. The fundamentals, you'd call it.

"**September H Normalsson?**" boomed a sepulchral voice. Midnight robes burst into existence, like black ink dripped into milk. "**It is your time!**"

September tried to back-pedal in the air as a layer of frost curled out across everything, painting fern patterns on glass and stainless steel.

"Ummm... actually, I think this is just one of those out-of-body thingys," she attempted, trying to sound nonchalant. "I'll just be shuffling back to the old mortal coil, then, and you can have the afternoon off."

The Grim Reaper, now fully manifest, billowed toward her. He flicked his scythe open with a pop of one bony wrist. The blade sizzled, where sub-atomic particles were forced to choose a side. Then he paused, mid stride.

"**Hey!**" he said, in a voice which was somewhat familiar, and not at all as grave. "**Aren't you the girl from before? The one that got hit by a bus? The one who was trying to keep part of her great-great-grandfather's soul, for some reason?**"

Now September got the hang of how to move. It was all about terror, apparently. The mesmerising glitter of the scythe was quite inspirational, in that department.

"No. *Nonono.* Someone else entirely, I'm certain. You'd

remember someone who was hit by a bus, I'm sure, what with all the mess, and whatnot. Especially on your first day."

The reaper's eyes narrowed.

"*Who told you it was my first day?*"

Many years of having to explain things to Headmaster Mackleduff had given September Normalsson one of the all-time greatest insouciant shrugs in the world.

"Lucky guess? Now, how about that game of chess?"

Very briefly, the air around the Grim Reaper blazed black. Swear-words (unspoken, but horribly vivid), came seething up out of his aura.

"*What do you think?*" he grated, knuckles white around the scythe grip. Which, once again, was not really a matter of choice.

September gulped down a deep (and probably unnecessary) breath, and *ran*.

She was certain she only imagined the whispered whoosh of the scythe behind her back, but imagination was enough. September powered through a door without opening it, while her spectral Docs scrabbled for traction on the linoleum.

"*Why do they always run?*" asked a tetchy voice, far too close behind for comfort. September gathered up her willpower and arrowed down the hospital corridor, weaving around frozen nurses, patients and doctors as she went.

This was about the time that her emotions caught up with her; and, along with them, a delayed-reaction delivery from the chemicals left behind her in her body.

Not fear. Not mortal dread. But **anger**.

The Grim Reaper was right behind her, and **that skeletal bastard had killed her grandfather.**

Okay. Metaphysical semantics aside, fair enough. File

that for later. But there *was* something important there.

Death took old Septivarian Archimedes. But he went down fighting. That meant he had a plan. And that meant that September could come up with one, too.

She pelted around a tight right-hand corner and slid sideways, through a pair of double doors, and into what turned out to be an operating theatre. The room was a scrubbed-white enormity, decked out with wicked chrome tools and complicated lamps. It was a place for last things. Breaths, moments, and possibly – stands.

Come on, girl! Time to face this Reaper head-on. After all, there's something you know about him, isn't there?

Really? she asked her subconscious. *And what's that, then?*

The answer arrived just as the doors blew dramatically inward, and a chilly fog came boiling across the linoleum. The Reaper stood framed in the doorway. A cutout of utter darkness, like the long-haul flight between galaxies.

But;

Don't be impressed. Thought September. *It's his first day, right? So he's not **the** Grim Reaper. He's **a** Grim Reaper. The real one would have a card, like that one around your neck. So it's a franchise. That means they sometimes need replacing!*

A bony finger was levelled with malice aforethought.

"***September Hyacinth Normalsson!***" intoned the Final Judge of Worlds. "***Do not resist! It's... wait a minute.*** Hyacinth? ***Really? Isn't that one of those little guinea-pig things from the mountains of Africa?***"

September planted herself on the far side of the surgical table, and exerted some willpower. Cold anger prickled down her arm as a shockwave of ice-blue light. First one, and then a whole clutch of nasty little knives, hooks and cutters wobbled upright.

"It's a kind of flower. You're thinking of hyraxes. Though not for long. Because today, *death learns how to die!*"

It had sounded much better in her mind, but September was not one to back down from a bombastic one-liner. She rose up into the air, with her spectral hair floating out in a halo, and an array of scalpels orbiting her hands.

With a flick of her mind, she let them fly.

Death parried, and sparks flew. Surgical tools stood quivering from the walls in a random spray.

"Wow! That actually worked!"

The Nemesis of All was not impressed.

"*Death learns how to die? Do you, by any chance, read a lot of bad comic books?*"

"No! Well, yes, actually! But that's hardly the point!"

September blocked the scythe with a stainless-steel pan, feeling the shock of it numb her to the elbows.

"*Think of this as the end of a very limited-edition run,*" said the Reaper. "*If it helps.*"

He flourished the scythe, spinning it like a martial-arts master, and made a series of cuts almost too fast to follow. But only almost.

September grabbed a hanging lamp with her willpower, and sent it smashing into the Reaper's back. He stumbled sideways, curses smoking from between his teeth, and regained his balance just in time to catch a wheeled trolley in the pelvis. A dish full of antiseptic and nasty-looking tongs crashed down.

"*OW! Hey, if I wasn't a skeleton, that would have been below the belt, Miss! Why don't you just accept the inevitable?*"

September just beckoned him on.

Like a total badass. Too bad there was nobody from school here to watch.

Well, that seemed to do it. The Reaper snarled as he leapt

to the attack, although it was quite possible that she was reading too much into his one-note facial expression.

The scythe was far more eloquent. September plucked anything she could grip from the trays and trolleys, and blocked frantically.

"Too slow," she said. "Bowling-ball face."

"Being hurtful isn't going to make this any easier!"

"You killed my granddad!" she hissed, parrying with a huge chrome bonesaw. Miss Slugpounder's fencing lessons were certainly coming in handy. The Magician card glowed around the edges, like a furnace door ajar.

"Hey! We don't actually kill anyone, you know!"

The Reaper twitched his skull to one side, and the bonesaw embedded itself three inches deep in the wall behind him.

"We don't **have** *to escort people to the afterlife, so they don't get all lost and lonely. It's a public service. And let me tell you, the pay isn't wonderful, either! That's why..."* (he said, hewing the operating table in twain) *"It's so annoying..."* (he continued, lopping off a tangle of hanging tubes and wires) when people won't just admit that it's their time!"

Even after a very eventful day, full of frog resurrection, scholastic censure, super-villainous senior citizens (and being hit by a bus), the thought of being chopped in half can be incredibly focusing.

September felt time slow down, as the scythe came around in a flat silver blur. There was nothing left to block with.

Think! Think like Septivarian would! Think like a scientist!

And there it was. A whole ramified, thorny tree of choices unfolded in her mind, blooming in silence.

What organises the cells inside your body? If every cell in your body is destroyed and renewed every seven years, how

*do we stay the same shape, or keep tattoos in the same place?
What causes the itch in an amputee's missing limbs, and lets
a sponge re-grow in the exact same form, even if you run it
through a blender?*

The answer, reasoned September, as three feet of supernatural steel described an arc toward her reincarnation, was a phantom. A bioelectric field with no 'bio'. Which meant...

Time slapped back into focus, and September rolled sideways in the air. The Reaper's scythe went past with a sound like tearing cling-film, then embedded itself in the wall, vibrating. She reached the little trolley which sat next to the chopped-up operating table, and picked up the twin paddles of a defibrillator, feeling a thin whine spool up inside them. One floor down (and several rooms away), goosebumps exploded across the skin of her sleeping body.

"I didn't have time to come up with a pun about something shocking," said September, as the Reaper's cowl turned to face her. His eye-sockets went wide as he saw what was about to happen next. "Sorry."

"No! Oh,. nonononono! You have no idea what'll happen if you..."

But she did.

Four
So-called 'Reality'
vs
The Endarkenment

ALL THE LIGHTS went out in the hospital as September connected, jamming her thumbs down on the two triggers of the defibrillator. A sizzling crack, like the birth of a thunderbolt, lit up the Reaper's cowl. It revealed a jangling skeleton inside, each bone outlined in blue fire. That, and a face behind the skull, for an instant... before the kickback sparked off the Reaper's scythe, and blew September out of the spirit realm.

When she opened her eyes and the hospital was gone. She was lying on her side on what appeared to be a pebble beach, and the air tasted old and dry, as if it had been stuck in a biscuit tin in an attic for several decades. The horizon was pink and violet, sharp with the shadows of hundreds and hundreds of pyramids.

September blinked, and looked down at her hands, which seemed to be flesh and blood again. The pebbles under her fingers were tiny, and on closer inspection, each one was a carved, multi-faceted and perfectly black gemstone.

"Ohhhh, gods and demons! You just had to go and try something daft, didn't you? Why didn't they tell me that you were going to succeed your great-Grandad? You've probably been training to wield Dante's Tarot for most of your life!"

September spun around to find a figure in a long black robe staggering to its feet behind her. Her fists clenched, knuckles white... but this was not the Grim Reaper. It was a boy with one of those old-fashioned faces, the ones you only really see in vintage photographs.

It was the kind of face which stared back at you from textbooks about World War Two. His hair had been slicked back in that style which requires industrial quantities of pomade, and a lot of time with what was probably a switchblade comb.

"Hello," hissed September. "I'm September. pleased to meet you. Now, none of the things you just said make any sense at all, but I think this card thingy might have given me super powers, which I most certainly don't want. That's not *at all* conventional! So what should we do next?"

This earned her a look which was part horror and part surprise, as if she'd told him that she was trying to defuse a nuclear bomb while wearing mittens.

"We're going to have to get back as quickly and as quietly as we can," he said, visibly regaining control of his facial features. "If the horrible lurking thing that lives here wakes up, we're basically dinner. If it eats the card, potentially... well bang goes seven hundred years without angels and demons everywhere."

"What thing?" September asked.

Halfway through asking, she realised that what she'd thought was a large, lumpy hill in the middle distance was gently moving.

Was *breathing*, in fact.

As her eyes adjusted to the dim purple glow of the sky, she saw that it was a huge and leathery beast, built on a scale which made her rational mind need a bit of a lie down. It was warty and impossible; a cross between a hippopotamus and a crocodile, with its long and loathsome muzzle tucked up over one clawed forepaw. Its back legs, which were revoltingly saurian, treadled aimlessly, like those of a spaniel wrapped up in a dream.

"*That* one," hissed the boy, in a kind of urgent whisper. "Ammut! This is the fragment of her realm, left over from Egyptian religion. There's nobody left to believe in it, but it's too stupid to die. Because then it would have to judge itself, which it knows it's too stupid to do. This is where you go, if you die after you're dead."

"But I'm *not!*" protested September, transfixed by that saurian face, the size of a mountain. "And I'll have you know it's not my time, either! I'm just having an out-of-body experience. If I hadn't thrown granddad's Doom Clock at the Grim Reaper I'd be able to prove it."

"Shhhh!" went the boy, fumbling inside his robe. "Do you mean this thing?" He produced a very familiar brass pocket-watch, all encrusted with soldered-on technology. "I knew it wasn't really a plasma grenade. We had science fiction in the fifties, you know."

September's mind, which was having a bit of a hard afternoon, finally caught up.

"You're *him*, aren't you? You're the 'it's my first day' Grim Reaper! Just a horrible spotty little boy with a scary mask on! You tried to *kill* me!"

September ended this sentence with one trembling index finger almost right up the young lad's nose. Indignation boiled off her like heat haze. The young Reaper held up both hands in defence, backing away a step.

"Shhhhh! Really! If the soul-eater wakes up, we're toast! Well, more like jam, actually, with the runny bits... *And it's not like that!* I was given orders, see? Guide your spirit to the other side, and tidy up all the bits of your great-great-grandfather's soul which he left knocking about. The kind of job they give to us apprentices."

September rolled her eyes.

"First you're a newbie, then it's worse! I suppose you know how to get back, then? Or was that not in the training video?"

The Reaper bore up mightily under such withering sarcasm.

"You just have to wake up. Then I can finish the job, and you'll be in the afterlife or reincarnation of your choice before you can say 'inevitable mortality'."

"I told you! It's not my time! Here – give me that clock!"

"And *I* told *you*. I had orders. PostMortis doesn't make mistakes! Anyway, you got hit by a bus! I think that's usually enough. I only crashed a motorcycle, and I was zapped into the Aught so fast, I ended up embedded in a wall! Again."

"Well, your bosses didn't tell you about this tarot situation, did they? Just like my Grandad never told me. So we're going to learn together. Starting with this."

September grabbed the Doom Clock, and hesitated with her index finger on the button which popped it open.

"Do I really want to know?" she asked.

"Know what?"

"Well, the *exact moment when I die*. Heavy stuff. It could have untold consequences for my life choices, kind of thing."

"Ummmm..."

"Well, that's a fairy unshakeable philosophical argument," said September, who often resorted to sarcasm when she was terrified. "Any advance on 'ummm', or are we deep into Tibetan existentialism and beyond language here?"

That was when she noticed that the boy was looking past her, up at the immense bulk of the soul-eater, Ammut. For the second time that afternoon, September felt herself turning gently, on invisible castors of dread.

Two glowing violet eyes had cracked open above that toothy snout. They blinked, slow as plate tectonics, as a pair of slit pupils focused. A tongue slithered out between a horrorworks of ivory, dripping drool.

Ammut's bone-shuddering roar was bad enough. The stench of rotten meat and damp carpets on her breath just made it worse.

"I reckon I could tell you without the clock, Miss, unless you hurry up."

September hit the button, closing her eyes so she wouldn't see the numbers.

Several things happened at once.

First, the great bulk of the soul-eater lumbered into a pounce, complete with a catlike bum-wiggle. At the same time, September and the young Reaper were outlined in a blaze of purple sparks, and popped out of the world like cardboard cutouts knocked through with a hammer.

September flashed back into existence in her own hospital room, with a feeling that she'd been scribbled into reality by a malicious three-year-old. But there was no time to be horrified. Because *there* was her bandage-wrapped body, all wired up to machines that went 'beep'.

And *there* – looming over her with a syringe full of glowing green liquid – was a handsome doctor with a feverish look on his face.

"Oi! *What do you think you're doing?*" shouted September, forgetting for a moment that she was a phantom. A drip of radioactive-green goop wobbled at the tip of the needle.

The doctor looked up at her.

"It's not what it looks like!" he blurted, trying to hide the syringe behind his back. "They paid me to do it! It wasn't my idea! They said that they'd make sure I got my photographs shown to Señor Marquez in the talent department!"

"You can *see* me?" asked September, floating closer. She tried to look as ghostly and frightening as possible, while placing herself between the very nervous doctor and her sleeping body. "I'm a horrible ghostly wraith, you know. I can probably suck your eyeballs out, or turn your brain back to front. You... ummm... you don't look very surprised, though."

The doctor nodded, with bright and brittle enthusiasm.

"I see ghosts all the time," he giggled, in a way which put September in mind of a possessed porcelain doll. "Ever since *they* started talking to me. Ever since the Repo started coming in. They did something to my eyes, and now... look, I'm *sorry* about the needle. It's just that *they* can see what I see. When you came in, the Cardinal wanted a report, and he said... he said... to let old Jack take you for a spin, see if we couldn't find out what your Grandad was hiding. *I don't even know what that means!*"

"You were going to shoot me up with *Repo?* That new drug that makes people go crazy? What kind of hospital *is* this?"

"I can't tell you! They can see what I see, and hear what I say, and they're always whispering! Always! Such horrible things, all day, all night... I..."

September had already decided that it was time to leave, even before this fit of twitching insanity. She walked right through the middle of the bed, and pulled her body on like a pair of overalls, limbs flopping as she settled back into her own nervous system. This was probably Behaviour Unbefitting of a Young Lady, but her education hadn't covered how to dress for re-mortality.

Or how to politely dispose of a homicidal doctor.

"*Frightfully* sorry about this," said Cliff Hunkstrong. "But you understand, malignant voices in my head and all... not entirely my fault!" He was grinning like the kind of person who eats cockroaches with a knife and fork. "All be over with in a jiffy!"

September managed to roll out of bed at the very last

instant, bandages tangling, and the big needle full of Repo popped through the mattress where her head had been. For a hideous moment the shape of a human body bulged up from the polyfoam, its eyeless face contorted in a scream that wouldn't come out.

The doctor's head, still grinning and dripping with sweat, turned as if on rusted gears.

"*Time to take your medicine,*" he grated, in a voice which wasn't his own.

September tried to stand, but she was wrapped in bandages and tubes and wires, trussed up like a fly in a spider's web. The point of the syringe winked in the light as it came up for the last time.

And a black spot appeared in the doctor's chest.

His mouth opened in an 'o' of astonishment, as an inky stain spread across his lab coat, outlined in orange sparks. Soon the stain became a fist-sized hole, then a tunnel right through him, exposing horrible wobbly bits which most doctors only ever see as Latin names in textbooks.

He dropped the hypodermic from hands crooked into claws, coughed out a belch of black smoke and froze, his whole body turning ashen grey. Little wisps of dust drifted clear, as his eyes turned to two milky marbles.

Through the tunnel in his chest, edged with blackened bone, September saw Elvis Presley.

He was rendered in black and white, with a rebel sneer, a pair of mutton chop sideburns you could tell the time by,[15] and a huge, ornate pistol in one hand, its muzzle still glowing cherry-red.

"Come with me if you want to live," drawled the King, flicking his signature-kiss-curl out of his eyes.

The room seemed to blur, stretching through that smoking tunnel in the doctor's corpse. September pushed

---

15. That time was a Saturday night in 1961

herself up against the wall and struggled to stand. Deep in the eyes of the Dead Elvis she watched nuclear explosions blossom and mushroom and loop. The thing's teeth were grainy with static as it held out one hand, beseeching.

Then a scythe-swing, wild and chrome, tore it in half. The blade swept up, hooking the fake Presley right between the legs, and unzipped it to the top of its outlandish haircut, with a sound like overloading circuit boards. The stench of burning plastic billowed out.

An explosion of filth painted the walls, blowing the remains of Doctor Cliff Hunkstrong to what looked like a cloud of cigarette ash. September, halfway to her feet, felt something warm and horribly chunky spatter across her bandages. She tore them away, sending beeping machinery clattering down.

"That'll hold him for a while, but there's going to be more!" said the Grim Reaper, folding away his scythe with a series of metallic, efficient little clicks. ***"Go on! Run! I'll tell them it was an accident, or something!"***

"That doctor... the Repo. He was going to..."

The skull mask of Death segmented then, hidden lines hinging open as panels slid and interlocked. It folded away, revealing the old-fashioned face of the boy from the black desert; the one who didn't look like the Final Judgement of Kings at all.

"I know! Somebody gave me the wrong orders!" He bit his lower lip, and his eyes darted left and right as if they were trying to escape.

"That doesn't happen! That *can't* happen! But I saw the numbers on the clock, Miss Normalsson, and it worked. It got us back. *So it's not your time.* And now these Elvises are involved, and worse. You'd better just get out of here."

Something about the look of determined panic on the boy's face stopped her. September looked down at her hand, where the crucifix-key Septivarian had given her was tangled by its string in the bandages. The card of the Magician seemed to wink at her.

"You don't want this, then? Or, you know, my immortal soul, or anything?"

The lines of tension on the Reaper's face eased, just a little, and he hazarded a wobbly smile.

"At this point, I don't think I could be in any more trouble. So no. You keep it. This whole job's crooked, and now I've attacked one of those ghouls from the Bureau. Which, by the way..."

He looked down, and September followed his gaze, to where the black slime dripping off the walls was writhing and seeping, knitting itself together like ink shot through with worms.

"Urgh! What *was* that thing?"

"Is, unfortunately. As in, what *is* that thing? It's a Dead Elvis. They work for the government. Not the one you see on the six o'clock news, the *real* one. And it'll be getting back up again pretty soon. No soul, right? So go on! Get moving!"

September pushed up the hospital window, and was just about to swing her legs over the sill when she remembered something.

"Why not?" she asked herself, as she went up on tip-toes next to the tall white cupboard in the corner of the room, fishing around until her fingertips felt the edges of a fifty pound note. She pocketed it, swung out the window, and paused, looking down into an ornamental flower bed. Thankfully, her room was on the ground floor.

"Are you sure you're going to be alright?" she asked.

The Reaper's mask snicked back into place, settling in beneath his bible-black cowl. At his feet, a puddle of darkness was bubbling up, little tendrils knotting together as they tried to form a pair of blue suede shoes.

"Miss, *I'm already dead!* I've just assaulted an agent of the Bureau Innominandum, refused to carry out my orders, and botched my first soul transfer. If that card you're carrying hadn't shut off hell in the 1300s, I'd probably be sentenced to clean the toilets there for the next thirty thousand years. Now, *run,* before I have second thoughts!"

September saw nothing but genuine worry in the eyes of Death, and so she bit back *her* second thoughts, and did.

Two very beat-up cherry red Doc Martens hit the begonias, and then she was off across the hospital lawn. Down to where Oldchurch Avenue met the High Street, and another of the town's old faux-historic pubs, the Flying Chrysanthemum, had just opened for the afternoon's custom. Hard up against it was another of those mysterious construction projects; this one for a multi-storey vintage computer games arcade, called, unsubtly, Nerd Vegas. Like the other excavations, it seemed to have permanently stalled.

Right. *Tradecraft. Blend in. Don't look like you're on the run!*

September adopted a nonchalant swagger, as if she had not a care in the world. The effect was spoiled somewhat by two things. The first was a huge, billowing explosion which blew out the wall of the hospital behind her. The second was a nasty electric shock from the key in her hand.

"Ahhh! *Bastard!*"

September scuttled across Oldchurch, grasping her hand at the wrist, and flattened herself against the brick wall of Little Mean's only authentic Japanese-themed Irish pub. Through the tiny mullioned windows, she could see Hiro Mulcahey pottering about in his green kimono and hakama, bringing trays of sake and Guinness to his thirsty patrons. The sound of the explosion made him drop it all.

Bits of glass, window frame and air conditioner came tinkling down. Car alarms began to whoop. Somewhere, September knew, Constable O'Dwightly would be just about to bite into a Burger Slave Big 'Un with cheese, and was going to have his lunchtime ruined.

Electric-arc pops and muffled bangs echoed out of the hole blown in the side of the hospital, and now... *oh, good lord*, now a big black van was pulling up just across the street. If September was not mistaken, the driver was a certain much-beloved American rock 'n' roller.

So was the passenger, who carried a horrible squat sawn-off shotgun. So, too, was every last one of the goon squad who piled out of the back, in costumes ranging from *Roustabout* to *Blue Hawaii*.

September attempted so sidle around the corner, but was suddenly bent double by another stinging shock from the key in her hand.

She looked down, ready to dash the thing to the pavement, but suddenly remembered that this weird little key was somehow charged with a fragment of her Grandfather's soul. It had protected her from the entire force of a charging Albion bus. The reminder was punctuated by a nimbus of glowing letters, in a speech bubble coming from the mouth of the fish-faced figure on the cross.

UNLUCKY CURSE

They read, picked out in hovering sparks.

MUST DE-ACTIVATE

"*Hey!* Stop electrocuting me, alright? And I thought the curse was finished, what with the bus crash and everything."

At this moment a Mariachi Elvis, who had stopped to remove a rocket launcher from his guitar case, pointed across the road.

"Well-a-hey there, boys! Isn't that the little mama we're supposed to bring in for questioning?"

A gaggle of famous mugs swivelled toward September. Mirrored aviator shades were perched on every last one, reflecting nuclear fire.

"Nuh-huh-huh, Mister Presley. We were just allowed to blow her up," said one of the others.

MUST DE-ACTIVATE

"OK! Point taken!" hissed September, covering her face with one hand and skulking into the doorway of the pub, where she almost collided with Wilf Handisides, pushing his slightly battered old Peugeot bicycle. "And *how*, exactly, do I foil this nefarious curse?"

Wilf, who was no stranger to the old 'disembodied voices in the noggin', gave her a watery-eyed smile and touched the brim of his cap.

"Me old Nan used to say, the best thing for a curse was to cross a gypsy's palm with silver. Then again, that's on account of her being one of the travellin' folk, and not averse to a bit of bribery. Most of her curses were about picking the wrong football team, mind you."

September shot him a look of such fragile, bright normality that the civic planners of Little Mean would have been proud.

"Don't mind me, Mr Handisides. I'm on one of those new hands-free mobile phone things. See? So tiny, it's invisible. Japanese, you know?"

PUT THE KEY IN YOUR EAR

– said the words hovering above the key, causing September's attempt at nonchalance to implode.

"My *ear*? Are you out of your mind? I don't know where

you've been!"

"Ummmm," said Wilf, tugging on her sleeve. "There's a man with a very complicated haircut pointing at you. He's crossing the street. He's got a *bazooka*, miss, unless I've been hitting the turpentine fumes a bit hard this afternoon..."

PUT THE KEY IN YOUR EAR

Repeated the key...

TO AVOID A 98% CHANCE OF MORTALITY

September looked up and saw, for the second time in just ten minutes, the leering face of Elvis Presley, wielding a weapon with murderous intent. She'd witnessed what the pistol one of these things packed had done to a poor demented doctor. Now she was staring down the barrel of a black and wicked rocket launcher. The missile, deep in its recessed tube, was painted with a smiley face.

"Allright, baby, it looks like we got this one allllll worked out," crooned the undead rocker, his finger tightening on the trigger.

September, who was having a much worse day than usual, decided that stuffing an ancient, possibly sentient (probably haunted) key in her ear was the least horrible of the things which could happen to her in the next several seconds. So she went ahead and did so. The face of the Magician, on the tarot card which made up the key's tag, smiled knowingly.

Something happened.

Here, it's worth pointing out that reality, as we see it, is in fact simply the protrusion into three-dimensional space of an entire manifold of layers of probability; a vast and ramified phase-space where unlikely events teem beyond the horizon of the mundane.

For September, in that second, all of those layers peeled away, fluttering apart like the pages of a book. She witnessed (for an instant which felt like spearmint gum, and static shocks, and the colour behind your eyes when you stub your toe), the whole infinite scrawl of a formula so complex it represented the universe. And the universe represented it.

She saw pages and paragraphs where physics worked just a little differently, and magic replaced science. And knew, in that instant[16] that while you couldn't re-write the book, you could certainly fold the pages – and thus change the story.

This was why all her attempts at mundane science had gone wrong. There was something in her DNA which looked at the rules, read them upside down, and then set them on fire. Something that had come down from Septivarian, by way of Dante Alighieri, it seemed.

He'd allowed the Enlightenment to come into being, by way of balance. But the Endarkenment was there first.

Set against this, an anti-tank missile painted with a jolly smiley face was nothing.

September felt all those layers of reality close back up again around her, collapsing like layers of steel forged together into a blade. There were glassy reflections visible in some of them, as they closed in like petals blossoming in reverse; images of the Flying Chrysanthemum going up in a vast explosion, or of September simply ceasing to exist, leaving behind nothing but a smoking pair of cherry-red Docs.

But there were others, too. And one... which was just perfect.

Sparks crackled. Calculations seethed. September

---

16. ...with the clarity that usually only comes to the dedicated seeker of truth after the second handful of mushrooms...

gripped the mirror of Wilf's old Peugeot bicycle, and tore it from its rusty old mountings, feeling something fundamental change deep in the glass.

Mirrors reflect light, and the only difference between light and matter is that matter has mass. Mass is a matter of bosons, so a little bit of tweaking down at a Higgs Field level, and you got this. A mirror which reflected solid objects.

Now of course, that was complete insanity. But nevertheless – there were places, out on the tie-dyed edges of reality, where it was utterly true. The Endarkenment was all about bending *here* around to *there*, in just a big enough space to matter.

The missile coughed out a cloud of white smoke as it speared toward her, whining like a hornet. It hit the mirror square, disappeared into it with a blip of quicksilver, then immediately came out going the other way – with all the writing on it reversed.

This gave Mariachi Elvis just enough time to look surprised before it hit him right between the eyes. The explosion was cataclysmic. A radial blast of slime splattered the road, the van, and half of his fellow Elvi. A pair of mirror-shades tinkled to the tarmac, twisted and broken.

If this had been a western, like the ones they showed at the old Electric El Dorado theatre on Brunel Avenue, there would have been a dramatic flurry of guitars at this point, and perhaps even a whip-crack.[17] The gaggle of Elvi took a step backward, fear writ large across their faces.

"Ooooh err," said Wilf Handisides. "I feel a strange compulsion to get a pint down my neck with swift alacrity, Miss, so as to forget this weird and eldritch turn of events."

September brandished her mirror at the Elvi, and was gratified to see them flinch.

---

17. But it was Mariachi Elvis who'd just been blown up! How inconvenient!

"That's right, you pack of rock and roll rejects! I, ummm, can do that thing again! Just get back in your van, and get out of here, or I'll absolutely voluntarily do something scientific to the lot of you!"

Behind the Elvi, another smoky explosion went off inside the hospital. A 44-gallon steel drum came arcing out of the hole in the wall, and slammed into the ornamental garden strip in the middle of the road. It was marked with the word REPO, and it began to ooze neon green as it rolled to a standstill. The Blue Hawaii Elvis wrung his hands, and hopped from one blue suede shoe to the other.

"Boss, if she's involved in *that* mess, with the drugs, and the... you know... then we haven't got much choice. You know what the Supreme Aaron will do to us if we fail."

GI Blues Elvis (who was apparently in command), flicked his hair out of his eyes.

"Well, uh – what the heck, buddies. There's only one of her, even if she *has* got one of the Tarot. Let's make her a metaphysical problem."

A brace of horrid black pistols were whipped out and levelled at September. She looked down at the mirror in her hand and realised that it wouldn't stop a horizontal hail of bullets, any more than a cocktail umbrella would stop a monsoon.

"Wilf," she asked, out of the corner of her mouth. "Can I offer you a crisp, new fifty pound note for your bicycle?"

The house painter, who had been contemplating the amount of coppers in his pocket (and the expense of enough drink to forget this savage scene), was more than willing.

"Just so long as you ride off very, very fast." he replied, palming the folding stuff.

"Shoot to kill!" hollered GI Elvis...

And September was off.

Fluttering from the key around her neck, the brightly painted tarot card of the Magician was now just an empty frame, around a curious absence...

Suture Two
Science Camp

"Really? *Science camp?*" asked Norman, lighting up his briarwood pipe with a raised eyebrow and a puff of blue smoke. "I hardly think..."

"Well, you see, Sir, *hardly thinking* is a bit of the problem that science camp tries to fix," said the man who was perched on Norman's floral-pattered wingback easy chair, balancing a tiny cup and saucer of tea on his knee.

All around, the paisley pastel wallpaper seemed to close in, studded with leering porcelain ducks and hedgehogs in waistcoats.

"It's somewhat remedial, if you get my drift. To make sure that there's no... how can I put this delicately... *outliers on the bell curve.*"

At the insinuation of non-uniformity, Norman's wife Norma gasped, and raised one perfectly manicured hand to her lips.

"We always thought she was such a *smart* girl, too," she said, fussing for a handkerchief. Norma, or, to put a fine point on it, September's mum, had the same shade of violently red hair, but it was constrained in a short bob with enough product to start a new ozone hole. "Will she be away for long?"

Norman harrumphed, jetting tobacco smoke in a tiny mushroom cloud.

"It's just that, after the headmaster called this afternoon, we expected some kind of punishment, not," (and here Norma referred to a slim pamphlet from off the coffee table, on which the ink was still wet) "...a fun and interactive series of classes which demonstrate the basics of science in a supportive environment," she read, worry writ large upon her face.

The second man from the Ministry of Education leaned forward on the settee, placing his teaspoon on his saucer with a precise little silverware click.

"The thing is, Mr and Mrs Normalsson, it would be *extremely odd* if September didn't pass science. She's doing very well in all the other subjects that make up the standard curriculum, and to be held back... well, that would be *different*."

September's mum and dad both flinched visibly at the word. Norman's pipe-stem clattered against his teeth as he tried to maintain a smile.

"I'm sure that won't be necessary, Mr... was it Alvarez? Mr Priestley? You two obviously know what's best. If the school board say that our daughter needs to attend a remedial science camp, then it's the average thing to do, yes?"

"Extremely median," said Mr Priestley, sipping his tea.

"Quotidian as... heck," agreed Mr Alvarez, nodding. "And it's only for a week. All you have to do is sign here, and here, and here, and initial here."

The crisp crinkle of paperwork seemed to sooth both of the Normalssons. Mr Alvarez leaned forward, proffering a slim chrome Mont Blanc, and Norman took it in sweaty fingers.

Just before he affixed his signature, however, he paused.

"You both look quite familiar, you school board chaps. Have we met?"

Priestley and Alvarez both shrugged and mimed puzzlement. When they looked at each other, they were reflected all the way out to infinity in their matching pairs of mirrored ray-ban aviators. Both were wearing cheap black suits of the kind that screamed 'federal agent'.

"We're just functionaries of the government, Mr

Normalsson. Quite standard and interchangeable. I'm sure our sheer ubiquity lends us a kind of familiarity," said Priestly, smooth as buttery teflon.

Norman signed. Both of the 'government men' breathed sighs of relief; that boilerplate was good for total triple indemnity, waiving responsibility for things which made death itself seem like a relaxing shoulder massage.

"It's a sad fact, but she's just a bit odd sometimes," said September's mum, in hushed tones. As if she was confessing that September occasionally yodelled in Hungarian, or nibbled on yellowcake uranium. "Her great-great granddad is a scientist, you see, so we thought..."

"*Was...*" interjected Priestley, before Alvarez could slap his hand across the other man's face.

"He means, WAS she ever a bit dim growing up, in things to do with physics and chemistry? It's often a warning sign if they try to drink the bleach, kind of thing..."

"Oh, come now! Norma, you know we don't talk about *that Professor* in this household! As for you, Sir, I hardly think..." sputtered Norman, gesticulating with his pipe.

"There you go 'hardly thinking' again. Tut tut," said Priestley. "Don't worry. Science Camp could have fixed that. September is going to be just fine."

Mum and Dad looked at each other, shared a worried moment, and then turned back to the two Elvi perched on their occasional furniture.

"If you say it's best, then," said Norma. "We'll come and pick her up in a week."

"I'm sure I've seen at least *one* of you before..." added Norman, as the pair stood up to leave. Alvarez drained his tea, then took a big bite out of the porcelain cup.

"We'll be on our way, then," said Priestley, chivvying his partner out the door. "Don't get up! No, no... we can see ourselves out!" Alvarez waved with just his fingertips, chewing a mouthful of shards.

"Funny," said Norman, after the front door slammed. "I don't remember hearing them drive up in anything. Maybe they took public transport. Very frugal with the taxpayer's dollar."

Outside, Priestley and Alvarez looked furtively around themselves, and ducked behind the Normalsson's potting shed.

"Well, those two know nothing," said Alvarez – actually a Mr Presley of rock 'n' roll fame. "Blithering idiots, but they're scared of something. I can taste it!"

"They're loyal to the program. That's all that matters. The Bureau Innominandum has taken care of them, and they're taking care of the Bureau. Now, let's get out of this horrible stuffy dimension, and slip into something less starchy!"

Priestly (who – no surprises – was in fact an ersatz entertainer beginning with E), reached out and gripped the edge of his shadow, where it was thrown up against the potting shed wall by the lowering sun. His fingers attenuated into sharp points and he worried the edge away, folding it up and over himself, like peeling a banana in reverse.

Alvarez did exactly the same, and with a brief double-pop, the two Dead Elvi origami'd themselves out of existence, back into the impossible time loop which spawned them. All that was left on the lawn was a steaming double imprint of two pairs of blue suede shoes.

On the other side of town, their fellow Elvi were slamming doors and hefting weapons and gritting teeth, laying down a patch of smoking rubber. All the nasty, flaming, particle-splitting, electrified, gloopy horribleness they wanted to visit upon September Normalsson was now one hundred percent legal, which, to one of the Elvi, was akin to it being holy scripture.

In short, September was now allowed to be murdered, because she'd got a note from her parents.

At this point, it's probably the nice thing to do, to point out that Norman and Norma were *not bad people*, as such. It's just that both of them had seen things, when they themselves were kids, which pushed their minds a little too close to the abyss.

There were big bits of both September's mum and dad which had been heavily edited by the Bureau Innominandum, at their own request, to make the nightmares stop. Suffice to say, some youngsters are cut out to be the kind who solve mysteries and unmask monsters and say things like 'golly gee, that means that Old Man Withers from the abandoned amusement park was the Sasquatch Mummy all along!'

And some aren't.

There are self-help groups for them, to soothe the frazzled split-ends of sanity. Most are very glad to make a deal, and move to places like Little-Mean-on the-Average, and be as resolutely normal as vanilla ice cream and beige shorts.

While the elderly relatives who'd dragged them along on adventures mellowed and blurred away in the vaults of Wrinkly Acres, they were watched, and their children were watched, and the Bureau hoped that the wyrdness was slowly soaked out of the world, to be replaced by the fabric-softeners of certainty and control.

But then things like September happened.

Throwbacks. Sports. Outliers on the bell curve.

And when that happened, there were only two possible outcomes.

Recruitment or cremation.

Five
Tommy the Train
vs
The Black Shadow

SEPTEMBER WAS NOT one of nature's bicyclists.

Not for her the serious, spandex-clad pursuit of record triathlon times, or even the kind of sun-dress-wearing, picnic-basket rambles through the countryside which she was informed were possible, thanks to certain popular hygiene products.

Her shapeless, many-times-patched school jumper and tartan dress were not exactly sporting attire, and Wilf Handisides had not picked his old Peugeot bike for speed.

However, this wasn't your average late afternoon, either – and unholy terror is a great motivator.

September pumped her legs as fast as possible, getting the creaky iron monster up to a grim velocity. She crested the little rise on Oldchurch (just by the church itself, the now-deconsecrated Saint Lucifer and No Angels) and let gravity push her even faster, down towards the railway yards and the gasworks.

Behind her, she could imagine a black Ford Transit van full of Elvi coursing at her heels, rabid rock 'n' roll entertainers snarling behind its wind-shield. No – scratch that – she could hear the squeal of its tyres, and the whump and scrape of its undercarriage as it crested the hill behind her!

Was September dismayed, to find herself tangled up in some kind of mess with dodgy doctors, elderly supervillains, an apprentice Grim Reaper and a homicidal bunch of Presley clones?

Her second thoughts informed her that she should be.

But another part of her mind, one which was positively throbbing and glowing with the black neon of the Endarkenment, knew that this was right and good.

September had always felt that something exciting was going to happen, one day. A lot of us harbour the same secret faith, heavy and comforting in our hearts.

That this job is just marking time until destiny calls.

That this little one-bedroom flat is where they will (one day soon), nail up a blue plaque for the tourists.

That this marriage, this school, this night shift, this... life, really – was all a placeholder until the fireworks kicked in, and greatness burst the chrysalis of normality with its vast, technicolor wings.

It's narcissism, really. Laziness, too.

But for a certain number of people, it's absolutely true.

September should have been terrified, and confused, and keen for a visit with the same doctors with soothing voices who had taken the scissors to her mum and dad's memories, all those years ago.

But she wasn't. She was curiously optimistic. Buoyantly excited.

And utterly, utterly sure that this was just the beginning of her story.

There was a cracking sound from behind her, and something whirred past her ear like an angry pheasant. A second detonation, and the sign outside the bus station spun around on its pole, smacking into the back of a tall gentleman's head and knocking him out cold.

They were shooting at her! Excellent!

A childhood of computer games had taught September that when the bad guys were chasing you, and trying to kill you, that was when you were going in the right direction. She risked a look in the one remaining wing mirror attached to Wilf's bicycle with bailing twine.

Yes, there they were. Closing the gap, Elvi hanging out the windows, and one of them sliding open the side door to reveal what looked very much like a General Electric minigun, the kind made famous by *The Terminator*.

Evasive action was definitely called for.

The Elvi gunned the engine of their Transit, trying to pull up level with September, and she swerved wildly, wrenching the handlebars of the old 1919 Peugeot across to the left. An alleyway between two rows of red-brick houses yawned, dustbins lolling drunkenly, and September sliced through, blowing last week's newspapers behind her in a yellowing cloud. A stray cat yowled in protest from the top of a fence – then leapt eight feet in the air, as a hail of bullets stitched across the brickwork, riddled a parked Wolseley, and smashed the pickets to kindling.

September risked a look behind her, and saw, for a heart-stopping instant, the rotating maw of the General Electric minigun, aimed down the alleyway by GI Blues Elvis, who was perched in the open side door of the Transit. She watched him jam his thumbs down on the firing studs, just in time to lurch the great wrought-iron bedstead frame of Wilf's bicycle to the right, through a half-rotten garden gate which put up as much resistance as a polite 'excuse me'.

Another hailstorm of horizontal lead chewed up the alleyway, detonating potted begonias and sawing the top off Mr Ableton's tool shed. The worm-eaten old shed crumbled in half, its roof sloughing away, to reveal a very embarrassed Mr Ableton, holding a naughty magazine and a bottle of turnip moonshine.

September juddered across his lawn, throwing him an ironic salute, then hit the angled side of the old World War Two bomb shelter in the corner of the yard, using it as a ramp to clear the low back wall.

There was no way, she thought, *that the Elvi were going to fit that van down the alley.*

Home clear! Or at least... *well, they'd probably already figured out where home was, hadn't they?* She'd have to do what old Septivarian had suggested, and find his laboratory. The only way out of this was **through**.

Speaking of through, however...

A grinding, screeching noise behind her, combined with the bellow of an old Ford two-litre in serious distress, convinced September that yes – the Dead Elvi *could* fit their van down the alleyway, so long as they cared not one whit for its wing mirrors and door handles.

Her jump had landed her atop the railway cutting which sliced along the back end of Little Mean, headed for the Hoxham End tunnel. Ahead of her ran a broad concrete path shaded by poplars, with a footbridge across to the scrubby parkland behind the gasworks. Now, *that* was too narrow for a Ford Transit, wing mirrors notwithstanding!

Behind her, September heard a van full of murderous rock 'n' rollers come bursting out of the alleyway, fishtailing around in a billow of tyre-smoke. Mr Ableton ran, wailing, across his lawn, holding up his trousers with one hand, and made a dive for the old bomb shelter.

At least, thought September, *that minigun is poking out the side, so if I can just stay ahead until the bridge...*

But of course, one of the fine features of the 1972 Ford Transit van is its optional sunroof.

A Spanish Elvis (dressed in a ruffled satin shirt and matador jacket) popped up from out of this like a retro jack-in-the-box, hefting what could only be described as an anti-tank bazooka of prodigious size. There was a pair of mirrored aviator shades perched on the nose of the rocket, and *'Love Me Tender'* written on the side in flowing cursive.

September put her head down and pedalled, wielding the weight and inertia of the old Peugeot bike like an Olympic road-racer. The chain was a blur, the bearings creaked like galleons tacking into a gale, and for a dreamy, floating instant, it looked as if September would make it to the bridge.

Then the rocket whooshed past, narrowly missing the bicycle's rear wheel, and skipped off the pavement in a shower of sparks. September watched it spin away, trailing smoke, its trajectory a corkscrew.

It coughed once, at the apogee of its flight, twitched in the air, and then speared down on a tail of blue fire, utterly destroying the footbridge.

Twists of tube steel and wire mesh were blown out in a huge fireball, ripping a twelve-foot span away. Both ends sagged down into the railway cutting, as the blast-wave slapped September across the face with heat and grit. The bike wobbled under her, and she heard the Elvis curse over the roar of the van's engine.

Any second now, she'd be keelhauled under its oily undercarriage, gobbled up by its dented front bumper, and reduced to a sad and sorry stain. Unless...

September wrestled the handlebars around, turning her wobble into a fully-fledged jag to the left. Up over a hump of poplar roots, and up further, until Wilf Handisides' old Peugeot was riding horizontally along the back of a red-brick wall. Then down again, turning in, whipping the whole ancient machine to the right, to zip down the gullet of the fallen bridge, using it as a ramp.

September dropped the final three feet, every bone rattling as her half-flat tyres kissed gravel. She'd landed between the rails, and for an instant the rims of her wheels ground up against the inside edge of one, showering sparks. Then she was off, pumping those pedals with grim desperation, accelerating for the Hoxham End tunnel and freedom.

Hah! That's shown 'em, thought September, in an instant of adrenaline-fuelled hubris. *Let's see them get a Ford Transit down that!*

Of course, they didn't.

Minigun aside, at least one of the feral Presleys must have watched James Cameron's masterpiece of action, because at that point the *entire van* came flying off the edge of the embankment, wheels spinning in the breeze, oily smoke, divots of turf and empty shell casings flying out in a comet-tail behind it.

September could clearly count the holes in the van's exhaust as it flew, its shadow blocking out the sun. Unless its whole suspension system burst to splinters on impact, it was going fast enough to simply bounce, roll, and splatter September and her bicycle both, like a sledgehammer swatting a field mouse.

Gravel exploded from under the van's wheels as it landed, and a terrible rending noise echoed up and down the cutting. Mangled, sagging, its shock absorbers punched clean through its bent bodywork – still the black Transit kept on coming, gnashing along the rails with a sound like a knife on a grindstone.

But seconds before its chattering number plate bit into September's rear tyre, the Grim Reaper was there.

He came falling from the sky, launching himself off the opposite embankment on a tongue of exhaust-pipe fire, and the motorcycle he was riding flashed chrome and glossy black against the sinking sun.

There was one of those perfect moments, when everything turned crystal-clear and syrupy slow – September's hair flying out all orange and wild, the Reaper hanging weightless as the wire-spoked wheels of his bike clicked over like the spools of an old-fashioned film projector. Then came gravity, and the *crunch*, and the *wham*, and the howl of rubber on metal, as an arm which looked bony and clawed (but felt very warm and solid) scooped September off Wilf Handisides' bicycle and deposited her on the pillion seat of a 1951 Vincent Black Shadow.

There are times when being rescued was annoyingly stereotypical, mused a part of September's brain. *And there were others when it was just unspeakably relieving.*

With a twist of the throttle the Vincent snarled forward, pulling clear of the van full of Elvi. Gravel scattershot their windscreen, crazing it to ruin. Now the rails were twin filaments of silver, and the tunnel was racing up, and all September could do was hang on, stealing a glimpse behind her as Wilf's poor old Peugeot went under the van's front bumper.

There was a mangling crash, and the sound of mechanical things all letting go at once. There was a sickening lurch as, somewhere under the Transit's undercarriage, Wilf's bike had it's wicked revenge.

Through watering eyes, September saw the whole thing flip. It launched itself into a clumsy pirouette, then tumbled end over end, shedding Elvi and guns and doors and wheels, battered and broken, burning and wrecked. The bicycle flew out behind it, rolling impossibly upright for a few seconds before it, too collapsed between the rails.

"You can slow down now!" shouted September, hoping that the Reaper could hear her through the ripping slipstream and the padding of his old-fashioned bucket helmet – (black, of course). "I think they're finished!"

The tunnel was coming up fast, but before it came the gasworks spur, where something big and blue crouched, hissing steam.

"No they're not!" shouted the Reaper, cranking out just a little more speed. The Black Shadow growled and shimmied, revealing why Hunter S. Thompson had predicted death for anyone who rode one of these for too long, too quickly. "Look! The train!"

They whipped past the siding in a blur, but September saw it. Parked between the huge rusted vats and tanks was a familiar blue steam engine, from a popular children's television show. This wasn't the little model used to film the series; it was a life-sized replica, a restored shunting engine with a giant, soulless fibreglass face bolted onto its front. A gormless grin and a pair of empty eyes blurred past.

It was crawling with Elvi, all dressed in neat blue railway uniforms. And its wheels were turning. It was full of steam, and headed out to crush them.

"They must have hijacked some kind of meet-and-greet for the kids!" shouted September, as they entered the tunnel. The Vincent's headlamp flicked on, scything[18] through the coal-black gloom. "*Please* tell me we're not going to be killed by Tommy the Train!"[19]

Aboard Tommy, an obese Elvis wearing a black dinner suit and a top hat pulled the whistle chain. He clamped a two-way radio to his ear, and nodded.

"We have a visual, baby!' he sneered. "All systems go! Let's get this bucket o' bolts moving!"

Up hard against the boiler, a soot-stained Elvis kicked open the firebox, and motioned to another of his ilk, who lugged a massive flamethrower into position.

"Hold onto your hats, thankyouverymuch," he said, just before he pulled the trigger.

Incinerating flame boiled through the innards of Tommy

---

18. appropriately...
19. Thanks for sparing us the legal work there. [ED]

the Train. His asinine fibreglass face changed not one iota, but billowing fire belched from his smokestack, and his wheels blurred against the rails, showering purple sparks. Superheated steam blasted from every valve and coupling as his pistons thrashed, making the little blue engine accelerate like a ball-bearing from a slingshot.

September looked back as the light from the end of the tunnel was blotted out. For a single terrible instant she saw that empty grin rushing toward her, haloed in fire.

I never trusted that train, she thought to herself, as the thunder of wheels eclipsed the world.

The Reaper wrung every last bit of speed from his motorcycle as she hung on, eyes screwed tightly shut. They went blasting through the darkness and out the other end of the tunnel with Tommy the Train hot on their tailpipes, his beatific smile promising murder. Elvi leaned and leered from his windows and hung from his footplate, wielding any number of horrible implements of mayhem.

September was momentarily blinded by the light as they came hammering out of the tunnel mouth, right into the middle of Hoxham End, the village which had been swallowed up by Little-Mean as it sprawled southward. Here, where the railway tracks crossed the main street, just near the old vicarage, a crowd of mums, dads and milling small children had turned out to see Tommy the Train.

There was tinsel and trimmings and flags in shades of blue, and cardboard cutouts of Tommy's supporting cast, like Travis the Tractor, Lumpy the Scarecrow and the Plump Comptroller.

The apparition which burst into the light behind the Vincent Black Shadow was not what any of them had expected.

Blazing, belching black smoke and burning embers, Tommy's face was melted into a distorted snarl, his eyes glowing red-hot and his nose dissolved into a deformed dribble. Roughly half the children began to scream in abject terror, while the ones who would probably grow up to be captains of finance and industry cheered and hollered – rapt with the transformation of their idol.

This strange tableau of banners and balloons and bunting was not what caught September's attention, however.

She peeked over the Grim Reaper's shoulder as they sped toward the level crossing, and saw, right smack-bang in the main street of Hoxham End, a patch of absolute night. It was as if a cone of darkness had been projected from on high, a rod of midnight complete with stars in the sky, a wicked toenail-clipping curl of a moon, and its own aura of velvety silence.

The darkness bathed an old-fashioned carriage, of the stagecoach variety; one hitched to a team of four coal-black horses in medieval barding. The coach, too, was utterly black, in a way which made September's rescuer and his Vincent seem positively technicolour. It sucked in the weak wash of moonlight, and there was the definite sense that it would be freezing cold to the touch – cold enough to strip the skin from your fingertips.

There was no driver, and no footmen, but as the distance closed, the door of the coach cracked open, and blood-red light spilled out, fervid and teeming, like a bad smell rendered in crimson.

They were closing in, the Vincent's wheels blurring across the cobblestones, when a figure stepped from the carriage, and time stopped.

He was a cutout in the red glow. A man dressed in ornate, ancient priest's robes, all crimson too, with a tall mitre and a crozier topped with a strange, runic sigil. There was no face, in the conventional sense, between his gilded collar and his high-crowned hat – only a pair of eyes which fairly boiled with malice, like twin holes drilled through into some repressed and self-loathing little hell.

There he stood, red robes splashed like a bloodstain against the darkness he'd brought with him, and not one of the panicking parents and screaming children appeared to be able to see him. Not even when the clocks behind the universe started ticking again.

But September could. She looked into those eyes and felt a sense of terrible vertigo, sucking at reality. She also saw what was pinned in the centre of his crozier – another ancient old Tarot card, in impossibly crisp focus. *The Hierophant.*

This was the thing Septivarian was talking about, said another part of her brain, all clean and clinical. *This is the bastard who's going to end the world, if you don't do something about it.*

She knew it with the kind of certainty that makes either saints or lunatics. You could have bent railroad spikes around it.

The Reaper could see him too, and he cursed, using the kind of language which (if you think about it), he'd probably often encounter in the course of his day-to-day-business.

"Oh bugger! It's *him!* I thought he was just a legend!"

"Who?"

"Kind of my opposite number," said the Reaper, as the figure in red brought his staff up, prelude to hammering it into the ground.

"You mean... he brings the souls of little babies into the world? I sort of imagined someone like that being more of a Cupid kind of character. Little diaper, dove wings, sort of thing," said September.

"*No!* I mean, he's supposed to be the one that takes the souls we miss. If we ever miss one, *he's* what happens to

it. And it's not nice! He's in the same book as the Magi...
I mean, the same one that *you're* in. Ooooohhhh, this is
going to be messy!"

September didn't want to look behind her. She could feel
the heat of Tommy the Train, grinding up the rails. *Was
there time to perform some kind of act of wild and feral
science?*

Probably not. There was likely not even time to be Smart
and Curious.

"Can you ride a motorbike?" asked the Reaper, turning
his skull helmet to look at her. The hidden seams parted,
and the helmet hinged back, revealing once again the face
of a boy who looked like an antique photograph. "What
am I saying? I saw you on that bicycle. You'll be fine!"

His smile was wide, and not a little bit wobbly.

"I'll be *what?*" asked September. "What are you planning
on..."

But then it was too late for 'planning on'. The Grim
Reaper simply **did**.

He sprung up to a standing position in front of September,
and surfed the Vincent's petrol tank for a second, ignoring
her yelp of surprise. September had just got her fingers
wrapped around the Vincent's grips when he performed a
back-flip off the speeding machine, leaving her thundering
up the Hoxham High Street towards the Red Cardinal and
his pool of personal night-time.

September hauled on the brakes. The Vincent skidded
and bumped to a stop, leaving a smoking swathe of rubber
behind it.

And she saw the Reaper land, right in the path of Tommy
the Train.

He came down in what the Doom Commission would
have identified as a perfect super-hero pose, and he'd
unshipped his scythe as he flew, turning in mid-air. Four

feet of impossible metal snicked into place as he swept the Soul-Severer low, lopping off a curved segment of Tommy's front wheels.

The effect was instantaneous. Suddenly, Tommy and his crew of Elvi were trying to roll on flat edges, and their juggernaut charge was flipped into savage rotation. Tommy reared up, launching himself off of his front buffers, his empty-eyed face still grinning as he cartwheeled end over end.

"*Oh, fuss and bother,*" said the Elvis dressed as the Plump Comptroller.

Up, and Tommy's boiler creased and crinkled.

Over, and tortured pipes split asunder, blasting steam and fire.

He spun end over end a second time, as Elvi flew in a ragdoll rain, and children shrieked and pointed and clapped. Tommy flew in a long, lazy arc, over September where she'd stalled the Vincent Black Shadow. She looked up into the train's gormless mug, and felt her sanity curdling around the edges.

Then down.

Down, like a pillar of retribution, a cylinder of red-hot iron shedding wheels and pistons and brass whistles and pipes.

Down, like a giant metal fist, on the pool of darkness, and on the Red Cardinal, who howled in utter fury before he imploded. Red, brimstone-scented dust puffed out.

Then came an explosion so loud it came up through the soles of people's feet, and echoed in the marrow of their bones. There was a silence afterwards, in which the world rang like the inside of a great glass bell.

September looked down at her hands, where they gripped the handlebars of the Vincent Black Shadow. Then at the bullet holes in her shapeless school cardigan, and the singed patches and ragged edges of her tartan skirt. Her eyes blurred as she tried to focus.

The Grim Reaper came stalking out of the smoking ruin of Tommy the Train, a vision in retro-black 1950s biker leathers. His head was a chrome-steel skull, its eye-pits reflecting fire. Tommy's melted face rolled a few drunken circles behind him, then fell flat.

Sometimes, getting rescued was extremely convenient, thought September, *but she mustn't let this boy think it was a habit of hers. After all, it was pretty much his fault she needed rescuing in the first place.*

"Oh my god! Miss, are you all ri..." he began, but September held up one finger to shush him. The front of his skull helmet was cold to the touch.

"I need your clothes, your boots and your motorcycle," she said. She'd always wanted to try that. A look of stark, utterly endearing incomprehension flickered behind those wicked cheekbones and grinning teeth. Then September smiled too.

"Unless, that is, you feel like tagging along? I think we're going to have to save the world."

Suture Three
Cardinal Syn

DOCTOR CLIFF HUNKSTRONG was not in a popular daytime telenovela.

In fact, he wasn't sure he was still even in the real world. He'd woken up in the foyer of a busy hospital, seated on a beige plastic chair – part of a sad little row of them bolted to the floor. The linoleum was scuffed and bloodstained, and some of the black squares of its chequerboard seemed to have too much depth, like pits yawning on nothingness. Neon mushrooms grew in the corners of the room, and atop one of them, a tiny blue man was picking his nose.

It took a second for Cliff's eyes to focus, and as they did, they wandered across a phantasmagoria. There was the obligatory rusted old vending machine, though this one seemed worse off than most. It was coffin-shaped, for starters, and several of the things held in wire loops behind the glass were writhing, twitching, oozing, or making a frantic bid for escape. The tannoy speaker above it had a long blue tongue hanging out of it, drooling.

Then there were his fellow patients. Something in Cliff's raddled little mind recognised the fact that he was here because he was somewhat poorly. The massive, smoking hole in his chest might have something to do with that. But for now, he was positively floating, a rubbery smile on his lips. He'd get back to the mystery of his missing sternum later.

Doctor Hunkstrong looked across the waiting room to the sad, beige row opposite, and saw a mohawk'd young man smoking a cigarette. This was odd enough in a hospital – but what made it especially noteworthy was the fact that he was holding his head in his lap. One hand held the tailormade up to his blue lips, and he took a drag, belching smoke out of his ragged neck-stump.

That was going to need a band-aid!

Cliff giggled a little, then tried to hide it as the mohawk man scowled. Next to him was a lady with tyre tracks clearly imprinted across her midsection, and a bit of the look of a used toothpaste tube about her. She was expensively dressed, and kept tugging her long cashmere shawl away from her other neighbour, a man in a preacher's collar and black shirt, who was stuck so full of arrows he looked like a toothpick holder. Blood still seeped from around the shafts, which were feathered with the plumage of several brightly coloured tropical birds. He tipped his panama hat when Cliff looked his way, and smiled.

Now came a little quiver of dread. Now, Cliff Hunkstrong realised that something was actually very wrong.

Most of us burble through life in a cloud of delusions, refusing to see the subtle horrors which lurk in both daylight and shadow. To acknowledge them, (while the mind tries to juggle a gastrointestinal tract, and a haunted skeleton tottering about on rubber-band muscles) would be instantly and wildly fatal.

It would take up *every bit of the brain*, you see.

It would turn off all the parts which gurgle away, keeping the lights on, while the whole cranial switchboard was plugged into Radio Cosmic Chaos, broadcasting existential weirdness on a waveband so broad it bulldozered whole solar systems.

Cliff Hunkstrong didn't have any of those gnarly meat appendages anymore. His evolutionary inheritance as a slick, bipedal killing machine with tonsils to spare had been squandered. So his mind was free to grasp, all at once, the reality of his situation.

This was where he'd been getting his orders from. The

afterlife. As in... what happened after you'd finished living. What happened, to be precise, when you were... ooooh, err. Right. The 'D' word.

Gosh. He was dead, wasn't he?

Still, there was an upside to this morbid situation. The worst had already happened, and at least now things were quiet inside his head. Doctor Cliff sighed, like a man settling into a warm bath.

Before he could get all misty-eyed however, a hand fell upon his shoulder. Cliff froze. His eyeballs tracked left to see a set of pale, tapering fingers, all set with ruby rings. They dug into his flesh like ice-cold steel.

The voice which came with the hand sounded merry, but it was cranked up so tight it could cut you. It was the voice of someone trying to hold back bloody frenzy.

"No time for dozing, Doctor! No lazy days for wicked boys like us! Oh no! It's all elbow grease and beaujolais, my chum! Besides, Cliff – my little lamb, my sausage! We really *do* have to talk about how you've failed me utterly, don't we?"

Cliff's legs stood up, before his brain could insist that he didn't want to. He'd heard that voice before, sliding in between his nightmares like an icepick between the floating ribs. It seemed to have the same effect on the decapitated punk, who was staring through the hole in Cliff's chest with a look that needed fresh underpants.

"You best trot along, mate," said the voice to him, all bubbly and conversational. "Or I'll run you up a suit in crimson, my *word* yes. I'll pop your pretty peepers where the sun don't shine."

The headless man fumbled his cranium as he scrambled to obey, fairly sprinting off down the corridor with it under one arm.

"I hate eavesdroppers. Don't you? Worst kind of people."

A single fingertip on the top of his head twisted Doctor Cliff around. The Red Cardinal stood before him, all imminence and edges, and Doctor Hunkstrong suddenly knew, with tongue-swallowing certainty, that there was something *much* worse than hearing supernatural voices in your head.

Having them turn up outside of it.

"Walk with me, Cliff, my chum. Let's be all professional, and proper, and polite," said the Cardinal, his face all crinkled up around his smile. It dripped red, like the grisly parts of a nightmare. The only clear impression was of *teeth*.

"We're going to have to take care of that girl who got you killed, you realise. Very messy."

Cliff looked down at his chest.

"You can say that again!" he said, pathetically glad for a change of subject. "Gosh! I mean, look at that hole! My lungs must be carbon on the wall, back there!"

For an instant the Red Cardinal's features froze, flickering with disgust.

"That was a *Dead Elvis* what got you, boy. We don't need *them* snooping around. Not now that we're so close. I've had young Jack the Lad distracting them with 'is old carnival games down in Whitechapel. But now, here comes some teen-aged busybody, with bloody PostMortis and the Elvi snooping after her! The Gravesend Corporation does not need the strife, Doctor, and that's why we employed *you*."

The pair walked down a long, pale corridor, its black-and-white linoleum floor spattered with blood. Doors to either side yawned open; some were lit from within by flickering strobes, some exhaled clouds of mist. Others echoed with laughter, music, or screams.

Cliff wanted to take a peek, but his neck wouldn't move. He kept staring directly ahead, paralysed. The Cardinal strode beside him in a whisper of long red robes, his crozier clicking a knell against the formica.

"I'm sorry, I suppose," he managed, though his tongue felt like a slab of carrion behind his teeth. "But I'm just about as punished as a body can be, aren't I? What with the dying, and all..."

Once again, the Cardinal's face froze for an instant, this time in a terrible, leering grin.

"Oh, *I'll* be the judge of that. And bodies is not what it's all about, down here. Not really. Not yet. That was supposed to have been *your* job, you silly sack of organs. That girl had one of the Tarot, and we could smell the other ones on her. I never thought her grandfather would bring her out to play. But desperate men, and desperate times, hmm? The poor dear has no clue as to what he's done to her."

Now they came to a set of armoured doors, bound in rusted chains, riveted with studs of iron. Blazoned across them in dripping yellow spray-paint were the words PSYCHIATRIC SECURE SECTION.

"Ummm... are you absolutely certain we should be here?"

Cliff was fairly sure that the last thing he wanted to do was go inside. But that's the thing about last things. Sometimes, it's horribly obvious that if you don't do them, the lastness might be made permanent.

The Cardinal grinned, with a face like a flip-book full of crime-scene polaroids. His eyes twinkled merrily.

"Now," he chuckled, "that's either a very deep philosophical question, or you're much, *much* sillier than you look. Considering you look a right doughnut, what are the odds of that, eh? No, we'll go and take a look in there. And you'll tell me all about this young lady, while we stroll. If I like what I hear, you might come out with all your bits on, and the right way round, too."

He clicked his fingers, slick as a tent-revival preacher. The doors creaked open.

"Can't say fairer than that, can I doctor?"

Cliff's traitorous feet shuffled him forward, into a deep and busy darkness. Here, the walls were padded and ripped, with stuffing spilling out. Here there was a smell of blood and bleach, and the doors were pierced by tiny barred windows. Groping hands scrabbled though, pleading. The fluorescent tubes above stuttered and popped, counterpoint to the droning of flies.

"Errrmmm... w-what would you like to know?" asked Cliff. He was sure he'd caught a good look inside one of the rooms, where the light was aquarium green. He was sure he'd seen something more fish than man in there, nailed upside-down to the wall. *Playing the accordion.*

"Why, *everything*, of course," smiled the Cardinal, holding up one long, pale finger. "The whole butcher's shop. Loot and prizes. But no, my dear doctor – don't bother to speak. Just you relax, now, that's my lad. You might feel a little pinch, though."

Cliff's eyes were locked rigid, staring straight ahead. But he felt set of black-nailed fingers spider-walk up the side of his head. He caught a glimpse of a gold ring in the shape of a cobra, then something cold and electric was jammed into his ear.

Dark filaments burrowed through the doctor's brain. He continued to drift down the corridor as they unwound, his toes bobbing two inches above the linoleum. A little blood dripped from his right nostril, pattering onto the memory of his lab coat.

For a moment, Cliff saw through the image of Cardinal Syn. He saw rank on rank of huge magnetic drums and banks of valves on fire, circuit boards charring and melting – and something within them mutating, to run a program *on the flames themselves...*

Consciousness slammed back, with the smell of charred bakelite and tin.

"I see. *September*, eh? The spawn of old Archimedes? Dante's magician, when *I* should have been! I, his true successor, cast off so cruelly? That don't half hurt, and no mistake!"

The Cardinal took a moment to compose himself, clenching his fists at his sides. The smell of melting aluminium filled the corridor.

"I've been a glorious fool, so help me! We both thought that the old gasoline-and-matches trick was final, didn't we? Now, though..."

The Cardinal snapped his fingers, and a tangle of hair-thin tendrils unreeled from inside the recesses of Cliff Hunkstrong's skull.

"September Hyacinth Normalsson!" enthused the Cardinal, making it into a little sing-song. His face was frozen for an instant in a grisly smile. "What an interesting young lady! And we know *just* the fellow for taking care of young ladies, don't we?"

The crozier came up, then slammed down. The corridor spun clockwise, kaleidoscoping with impossible spaces, which collapsed again with a sound like snapping teeth.

"Here we are now. Come and say hello."

This door was coffin-shaped, and spiked, and etched with nasty runes. It slammed open as the Cardinal gestured with one claw, unleashing the smell of a butcher's-shop drain in summer, all clotted and rank.

There were no windows in the room beyond. Only stone walls, spiralling up like a chimney to unknowable volumes of shadow. Candles and guano, old books and scattered pieces of armour lay everywhere.

Those, and the stakes.

There must have been a bed in here, once, and a desk, and a chair. But patient hands had rendered every stick of furniture down into a series of sharp, pointed spikes, then jammed them in between the mouldering mortar of the walls. The skulls of bats, rats and mice adorned most of them, but when Cliff squinted, he could see that even smaller stakes, the size of toothpicks, were screwed into even smaller fissures, bearing the heads of cockroaches and spiders.

The Cardinal beamed like a proud uncle, and gestured to the architect of this madness. It was a shadow, this denizen. All long tangled hair and rags like last week's laundry.

"My dear, dear friend! My beautiful, aristocratic cousin! We've found someone to replace you for a while, so the guards don't get suspicious. So you can go back to the world and indulge your little hobby."

The ragged figure shifted. There was a dry, unpleasant rasp of laughter.

"So nice to see you again, Your Eminence. And you've brought us a guest? *Or is it... dinnertime?*"

Something about that nasty pause burrowed through the sticky mess of Cliff Hunkstrong's brain. It found the part which was still plain old Reginald Spudley, hiding curled up in a corner, and poked him.

"What do you mean, *replace* him?" he asked.

The Cardinal leaned over – horribly, intimately close – to whisper in the doctor's ear.

"I'm afraid that if the authorities find our friend here missing, they might ask questions. All those beautifully balanced cards could come tumbling down. But it's alright. You just sit tight, and he'll be back in no time."

Cliff reached out tentatively, and pricked his finger on one of the wooden spikes. It was wickedly sharp, and blood welled out. The ragged figure on the floor sat up, shoulders shivering. It gave a pained, longing sigh.

"Oh, you know what that is, don't you?" said the Cardinal, ignoring Cliff. "Say you'll obey, and the *Materia Mortalis* awaits! Surely you're hungry, after all these nights?"

A head turned from its work. Long, pale fingers with black nails held up a tiny sliver of wood, on which was impaled a twitching fly. The face, when it was revealed, was beautifully cruel, dark-eyed and intense.

It was also, clearly, utterly insane.

"I could bloody *murder* a kebab," said Vlad Dracula – the Sorrow of Carpathia, the Terror of Wallachia. Also known as the Impailer.

It would probably surprise nobody, at this juncture, if it was revealed that he wore around his neck a certain diamond-sheathed tarot card, bearing the image in woodcut of the Knight of Staves. *Sharpened* ones, of course.

The Red Cardinal laughed, and the shadows crowded in at the corners of Cliff Hunkstrong's eyes, and he felt the chains descending from above, the manacles and hooks reaching out for him...

Six
The Public Library System
vs
PostMortis

THE FIRST WILD idea of Professor Archimedes, AKA the Befuddler, AKA September Normalsson's great-great-granddad, Dante's Magician, was this:

If you can't enlist the aid of a god, then make your own.

Now, admittedly, voodoo priests and priestesses had been working on this formula for many centuries, and had even added a snazzy top hat to the ensemble.

But in the aftermath of the Unmanifest Accords, when a deal was struck between humanity and the Things Beyond, direct intervention by any of the many, many elder powers was strictly forbidden.

September remembered the Professor coming up with the answer, while relaxing in a bubble bath in 1961. Of course, the memory belonged to Septivarian, so September was *extremely* glad for the bubbles.

Because she recollected him leaping out of the tub like his namesake, stark naked, on that chilly afternoon in February. The suds clung strategically as he went pelting naked through the halls of a big, white-tiled building, to hash up a whole string of arcane algebra on a two-storey chalkboard.

FLASH —

An avid-looking young scientist with a name tag that said ROSEWOOD took a photograph of the formula, and of Septivarian's bum, (though this second bit may have been unintentional).

FLASH —

A memory slotted in, of the two of them – her great-grandad and this Rosewood person – bolting a plaque to the front of a giant, 1960s-style computer. They were smiling, and there were empty beer bottles stacked on the floor around them.

B.I.S.H.O.P. – read the plaque. *Bio-Intelligent Silicon Holistic Operations Processor.*

FLASH — another memory; Rosewood holding a silver pistol, too weird to be one that fired actual bullets. September looked down at her hands – Septivarian's hands – and saw, in them, a jerry can and a book of matches. Flames licked up from behind the beige casing of the B.I.S.H.O.P, and the sound of alarms began to warble and wail in the distance...

Then the motorcycle went over a bump, and September snapped back to reality. She caught a glimpse of herself as they burbled past the Burger Slave on the corner of Anglesey Street and Cormorant. The familiar zipper-masked clown-face of Beefy Roger leered down at her as the Vincent slid by, a reflection in the greasy windows.

Funny – she didn't look different. Not really. But she felt very odd indeed.

The sun was sinking below the chimneys of the Little Mean gasworks as the Grim Reaper's motorcycle chugged on, through the leafy streets around the South End. Evening was a distinct possibility, rising purple and star-scattered behind them.

And there was still, apparently, a world to save.

There was a hot, scratchy silence just in front of September, as the motorcycle took the corner onto Larchwood Avenue, angling back toward the centre of town. Her social awkwardness tingled.

"Thanks for the rescue, back there. I mean, it's right out of your wheelhouse, that kind of thing, isn't it? Saving people, instead of – you know. With the garden implement, and the funerals, and all that."

The silence deepened, like black, audio treacle.

"It's *Cedric*, by the way," said the Reaper, at long last. "My name. So you don't have to keep thinking of me as the angel of oblivion, or some other such gothic claptrap. Cedric Welbourne, died 1957. You can probably add 'fired, this afternoon' to that as well."

September was a bit lost for how to respond. It wasn't every day that people introduced themselves to her by their death-date.

"Well, you're, ummm, not letting it keep you down," she ventured. "Listen, Cedric... *really?* The Grim Reaper's actual name is..."

The silence returned, with a forecast of withering frost.

"Fair enough. Listen, Ced. I'm sorry if this is moving a bit fast, but try to see things from my perspective. I'm pretty sure that my granddad, that fellow you dispatched earlier, did something during the Cold War that might, perhaps, sort of... potentially destroy the world. I've also just experienced what it was like to be a naked man covered in soap suds."

"Well, I'm sorry about that," said Cedric, coasting to a stop outside the Little-Mean-on-the-Average town library. "The reaping, and all, not the soap suds. It's not supposed to go wrong, they said! *Every soul at the right time*, they said."

The big boarded-up fence where Anders' Veg had failed to sprout loomed, blazoned with the logo of a pipe-smoking farmer in clogs. Cedric's voice was bleak.

"What have I got, if this job's a big lie? I spent my afterlife studying, and working, and waiting, and training, to get into PostMortis, and rise up the ranks, and get assigned to Reaping duties, just to get back to the world, so I could see..."

September was already off the bike before Cedric popped the kickstand down, but she still caught the look on his face, as if that last sentence had run directly into a concrete barricade. Nevertheless, something big and tragic and unspoken hung there, as he turned his helmet in his hands.

"See what?" she asked. "Or who? Or... oh."

"Yes," he said "*Oh*. But you know what? I didn't, in the end. She would have been seventy-seven this year. Probably had kids, a family. A whole life. I could have sneaked in a quick peek during one of the training missions. But no. And anyway... why are we talking about *me?* You said that your grandpa might have figured out how to destroy the world! That's the kind of knowledge that some people would be more than happy to kill for. Or... you know. Pervert the course of mortality for. As an example."

"I don't think he was really *trying* to destroy the world. Just to beat the Soviets," said September. "The memory wasn't very clear. But it was *very* clear about this. His laboratory is right beneath the best camouflage in all of Little Mean. The library."

Like somewhere a supervillain would keep his doomsday devices, she thought. *Huh. And it turns out it really was.* Had Miss Rummage known all along?

"Camouflage?" asked Cedric, as he loped up the stairs, two at a time. September hurried to keep in front.

"Precisely! Even a normal library generates a few background kilothaums of magical energy. What they were up to... well, anything supernatural would sniff it out, if it was in plain sight. I think it was one of those black-bag operations. Top secret."

September caught a look at herself as the big mirrored doors of the library slid open, and there was something slightly odd about her reflection. It wasn't the soot stains, or the frazzled hair, or even the bullet holes stitched through the hem of her shapeless, many-times-patched jersey.

No – it was something about her eyes. They seemed a bit too dark, now, and a bit too sparkling, as if tiny gears where whirring away at the centre of each iris, breaking the world down into atoms.

Then the doors parted, and September's eyes, weird or otherwise, went wide with shock.

Because there was Miss Rummage, backed up against the photocopier and stabbing desperately at its keypad. And advancing on her, cold as a nuclear winter and blacker than the hearts of hell's parking wardens, was the Grim Reaper.

"Oh, various imaginary deities!" hissed September, as both the stricken librarian and the giant, seven-foot apparition in black turned to look at her. "Is that your dad, Cedric?"

There *was* an aura of terminal dadness about this Reaper. He definitely deserved the capital letters. Where Cedric was clearly a fellow in a costume, this was something else; a tall and stalking thing, mantis-angled and hollow-eyed, with fingers like pale spider legs. He carried a scythe that curled over all crooked and razor-keen. A huge silver badge shaped like an hourglass swung ponderously about his neck.

"W-worse," stammered the boy from the 1950s. "*It's my boss.*"

"*Ahhh. Young Cedric!*" said the Reaper. "*And I suppose this would be September Normalsson. The one who's the focus of all this confusion.*" The senior Reaper's voice was rich and sonorous, with the kind of accent that hinted at five thousand years of history, lacquered over by a stint at

Oxbridge. "*You have our apologies for the inconvenience. It seems that someone has been playing what you might call 'silly buggers' with our most sacred duty.*"

Cedric breathed a sigh of relief.

"Then... I'm not in trouble?"

The apparition's eyes twinkled, cold as the stars at midwinter.

"*On the contrary, Provisional Operative 2399. There are whole new kinds of trouble being invented, just to cover what you're in. But the situation is salvageable, so long as... look, madam, what exactly are you trying to achieve with that photocopier?*"

September had a fair idea. She locked eyes with Miss Rummage for a second, and nodded. This seemed to calm the librarian down, just enough.

"Well, it worked earlier. Worked splendidly, in fact, against that bloody Elvis. Excellent scheming, September."

"*Wait!*" said the Reaper, holding up one bony hand. "*You mean one of* them *was here? Big sideburns, bell-bottom trousers, wobbly hips? And it was looking for this girl, too?*" The thing's skull swung back and forth, with what seemed like genuine dismay. "*I'm afraid you'll have to come with us for questioning, young lady.*"

"Does that involve being dead?" asked September. "It's just —"

"Only in a very technical sense..." began the Reaper, in the same tones a dentist might use to describe a long and expensive procedure. One of his fingertips hinged open, revealing a tiny, scalpel-sized scythe.

"But it's not her time," protested Cedric. "Isn't that what this is all about, Mr Khatri?"

The senior Reaper's skull helmet segmented and slid and folded away, revealing the face of a stern and middle-aged south-Asian gent, with the kind of frown lines that could only come from extended, aggravated police work.

"You don't get to question me, 2399! Not after the antics you've been up to, here in the *Materia!* We expected you to check up on your old sweetheart, and that would have gotten you some stern words, but no more. This other business, though! With the train, and the transit van, and the hospital? The collateral damage alone is going to make all the supernatural scandal rags, from the *Inquirer* to the *Illuminati Watch!*"

September ignored all this, and focused in on what she saw as the most pivotal part of the conversation.

"*Technically* dead, you say? Ummm... I'm going to have to take a rain-check on that. I have a genetic allergy to death, right? None of my relatives who've died have ever come back to recommend it."

PostMortis Captain Jaghtaran Khatri rolled his eyes.

His fingers split open, every one, glittering as a whole thicket of sharp steel popped out from between them.

"It's not a request," he said, in a sad, quiet voice. There was real regret in his eyes, too. It just failed to extend to the tips of his fingers.

"Miss Rummage!" shouted September, in a voice which was just a little too close to hysteria. She took a deep breath. "Remember when you told me that all of fiction is a shared hallucination?

The librarian nodded, rearranging the pencils in her hair. Captain Khatri hovered closer. Little sparks and blips of electricity arced between his bladed fingers.

"Yes, I suppose I did, which was a bit naughty of me, but... September, we can't just go there, just like that! The amount of magic you'd need would turn your brain to cottage cheese!"

September's voice, when it came next, was hard as the nails on a hanging post. There was definitely something of her old Grandad about it.

"Miss, we're standing in a box filled with enough creative power to re-ignite a dead star. I reckon we can do however much magic we want."

"You wouldn't *dare*, young lady!" grated Reaper-Captain Khatri. He resembled a very polite thundercloud, with stainless-steel lightning around the edges.

"Please," said September, with the soul-crushing condescension that only a teenage girl can deliver. "You have no *idea* what I'd dare, which means you have exactly *zero* percent of a clue what I can actually do. Miss R, do you know a good book with Death in it? I can think of a few."[20]

She raised one eyebrow and crossed her arms.

Miss Rummage's distraction – a sudden screeching flock of paper parakeets, summoned from a National Geographic – came right on time.

As Jaghtaran Khatri flapped and staggered, September reached out to the tarot of the Magician. She ripped the library's barcode scanner from its plugs, popped its plastic case open, flipped the mirror around and tucked in one of the big jolly new-age quartz crystals Miss Rummage kept on her desk to repel bad vibes. The little red laser inside blurred through the spectrum to a kind of radioactive yellow-green. Rubber bands snapped shut.

"Plug it in, and hit it!" she shouted, tossing the modified scanner underhand to Miss Rummage. The librarian must have gotten what was happening, because she slammed the complex toothy little plug on the end of the scanner's cable into the photocopier.

---

20. DNA is just code. A long and twisty bar-code, which meshes nicely with the ISBN numbers stamped on every book in the library. Words are just code, too. They're designed to run on a mixture of chemicals and tame lightning behind your eyeballs. Some people know how to hack the brain with words. But September – at that moment, as realities blossomed and refracted behind her eyes – knew how to hack the worlds made by words, using only a single brain.

A photocopier which still had the complete, unabridged Necronomicon boiling in its short-term memory.

"Checking out!" shouted Miss Rummage, as the Grim Reaper stopped trying to winkle a paper budgie out of one eye-socket.

She levelled the barcode scanner like a cowboy's six-shooter, and a wash of green laser gridwork blazed out of its muzzle. It painted the inside of the library like the background of a 1980s sports-car advertisement. And where it struck Mr Khatri, it *stuck*.

Stuck – and wrapped around, binding him up in a web of emerald. The same lines snapped taut around September and Cedric, and even bounced back in a shimmering net of reflections, freezing Miss Rummage where she stood.

There was just time for a gurgle of rage from the Reaper-Captain, and then all four people folded up with a fizzle of sparks, and disappeared.

The barcode scanner clattered to the floor, and snapped off. A very big scythe and a silver badge shaped like an hourglass hit the floor next to it.

On the tiny screen of the photocopier, a red light started blinking...

MEMORY FULL

Seven
The Ender of Worlds
vs
Light Holiday Fiction

THERE WAS A brief moment of vertigo and panic, which September's mind filled with a tunnel of psychedelic words, hammered out by some invisible typewriter. Then reality was sketched in all around her, fleshed out with texture and colour...

The first thing September experienced was the smell.

She was standing in a cobbled street, lined with the kind of old tudor-era buildings which always look as though they're drunk, and leaning on each other to keep from slumping into the gutters. Horse manure was much in evidence, as well as other assorted manures, which didn't bear much thinking about.

Despite this, crowds bustled happily along the pavements, and wagons jostled in a kind of good-natured gridlock, carrying what appeared to be (mainly) an industrial quantity of cabbages.

September tried to get her bearings, but instead ended up quite surprised by what she was wearing – a long, medieval dress in workaday black. She tentatively felt up above her riot of red curls, and yes... there it was. A tall and pointed hat. This would explain, she supposed, why all the passers-by were giving her a fairly wide berth.

"September!" shouted a voice from behind her. She whipped around, almost expecting the stern and looming figure of Reaper-Captain Khatri.

"Over here! Come on, we haven't much time!"

It was Cedric, dressed in a floppy black hat and long

dark velvet robes; the weeds[21] of an apprentice assassin. September's aura of unmistakable witchery literally stopped traffic as she dodged across the road to the alleyway where he lurked. She caught a glimpse, as she did so, of the street sloping downhill toward a wide and sluggish river.

"Where exactly *are* we?" asked Cedric, as September ducked in between two wildly leaning buildings. "One second we were in the library, and then..."

"We're inside fiction," said Miss Rummage, in a tight and barely controlled little voice. "The collective hallucination of the whole species. But this is *not* a good book to be stuck in. Not for me."

She was leaned up against the alleyway wall, eyes unfocused, and as September watched a shimmer seemed to pass over her body, blurring her outline with a spangle of bent rainbows. When this happened, out of the corner of her eye, September could swear that Miss Rummage lost her human form, and became squat, sack-shaped and orange.

"Oh crap! A good book with Death in it! And you're a *librarian*! Which means..."

"We have to get out of here, fast – unless you packed an awful lot of bananas. Come on! There's a portal to the next contiguous narrative link down on the bridge; it's a reference to Dickensian London."

September shot Cedric a 'don't ask' kind of look, then lifted Miss Rummage by one armpit. The young Reaper did the same, and they hustled the librarian out onto the street, pretending she'd simply had a few drinks too many.

"Is this really the inside of a book?" he asked, as they frogmarched their living cargo down toward the

---

21. [ED] The things you learn editing books! Yes, WEEDS. It transpires that the word "weeds" in this context is derived from the Old English word "wæd," which meant "robe, dress, apparel, garment, or clothing".

riverside. Another crackle of energy blurred through Miss Rummage, and September was horribly certain she could feel fur under her fingers.

"Oh, yes. And in other circumstances, I'd like to have a bit of a look around. But..."

"I totally agree. Because here's '*but*' right now," croaked Cedric, looking back down the street behind them.

There were shouts and screams, as people threw themselves from moving carts and ducked into the doorways of shops and houses. A furtive figure carrying a small portable barbecue took a dive right into an ornamental fountain. And here came the reason why, all billowing black and gleaming white, a very familiar garden implement raised high.

"CEDRIC! YOU GET BACK HERE THIS INSTANT!" boomed Mr Khatri – in what was clearly all capitals. "THIS IS NO TIME TO GET SENTIMENTAL ABOUT SOME MORTAL GIRL!"

The young Reaper blushed, rolling his eyes.

"It's not at all like that, actually, Miss, and if you..."

"I don't *care*!" hissed September, who could see where they were headed, now. A kind of blur in the air, behind one of the big hippopotamus statues on the bridge's parapet, staring out to sea. Through it, she was sure she could glimpse a similar-looking river and street, dusted with snow. "Or rather, yes, that's nice, but *come on!* I can feel poor Miss Rummage getting heavier, and that horse your boss has gotten hold of looks pretty damn fast!"

"CEDRIC!"

September snatched a glimpse, and yes – here came the Rider on the Pale Horse, just as grim as advertised, eyes flashing cerulean blue as his mount's hooves struck sparks from the air.

"Ooook!" exclaimed Miss Rummage, as they hustled

onto the bridge and into the rift. "I mean, eeek! Duck, everybody!"

September heard the whistle, and felt the air itself being ripped in twain like crisp waxed paper. Her witch's hat lost about nine inches off the top as she threw herself forward, toward the sharp scent of freshly fallen snow and woodsmoke.

There was another flurry of words, pelting down like hail and smelling of hot metal and ink. And then they were through, a whole new world sketching itself into existence around them. This time, September actually saw the words landing, clustering like insects and melting together to form cobblestones, houses, gas-lamps and people.

"Jolly good!" enthused Miss Rummage, who was now back to her former self, without even a hint of the primal primate. "That ghastly apparition will find itself somewhat diminished, should it venture into *this* particular story!"

"Cor blimey!" said Cedric, now dressed as what appeared to be a chimney sweep. "I mean... wait a minute? Did I actually just *say* that? Who says 'cor blimey', anyway? It's a right to-do, that is!"

Miss Rummage put a hand on his arm. She, too, had changed costume, and was now dressed as a rather stern-looking governess, complete with button-up boots.

"We're adapting to the narrative, you young scallywag. This is Dickens. Everything is grindingly poor, but ever so cheerful. And you'll find you have a grim but cheerful back story, too. Like a memory crossed with a toothache."

September tried to recall just what she was doing here, and was surprised to find that as well as being a keen young scientist on a mission to save her great-granddad's masterwork, she was also a poor little orphan girl, betrothed to wed the cruel and miserly Mister Obadiah Skimblebrisket, a magnate in the whale oil trade. Against all the evidence, she remembered being raised by a convent full of hideously strict nuns.

"Why did we come 'ere, then?" she asked, in what she realised was a pantomime Cockney accent.

"Another step toward what I assumed to be *your* plan, young September," said Miss Rummage. "Here, the only archetype he's got to hang onto is the Ghost of Christmas Future, which puts us within a quick jump of light holiday fiction."

"Gawd grizzle me gubbins! She ain't 'arf right!" said Cedric, who'd got it bad. A passing rosy-cheeked match-girl rolled her eyes at his terrible acting. "The dark robe, the hood, the sinister, bony finger pointing toward inevitable doom..."

"Exactly! Have you seen the classic movie version then, with Alastair Sim?"

Chimney-sweep Cedric shook his head.

"Never fear that, Miss – e's right behind you!"

Victorian extras scattered as September turned, to see the Ghost of Christmas Future come stalking out of the inevitable fog. He brandished a whole entire gravestone, on which was inscribed –

I

liked

the last

book better

– in curly cursive calligraphy. A finger, pale and bony, pointed menacingly.

"Come on! We've got him now! He's a famous Christmas apparition, and there's a link to the next phase-space at the Cratchit family's cottage. You know. Scrooge and Marley's clerk. Tiny Tim's old man."

September was catching on to the plan now.

"You're going to exacerbate the children's strand of the

narrative by bending it at ninety degrees, where they did a version with Kermit the Frog in it, aren't you?" she said, with more than a little admiration in her voice.

Miss Rummage narrowed her eyes.

"Damn right. That fluffy green amphibian is going to earn his keep today. The green, in fact, is what we're after..."

The trio pelted up the high street, scattering waifs, urchins and other impoverished strays of the parish in their wake. September's shoes slipped on the icy cobbles as they ducked under the belly of a stalled cart-horse, and skidded around the corner into a lane hung with wreaths and baubles.

"What did Marley and Scrooge actually do?" asked Cedric. "I always wondered, back in my school days."

"Business. They do *business*. If you looked too hard at it, the paperwork would all just be meaningless columns of figures. The important part is that they have a clerk, and he has a poor little cottage, and that it looks *just perfectly christmassy*."

September looked back, and saw the Ghost of Christmas Future bearing down on them, all spectral and hollow-hooded. It passed right through the big Clydesdale horse, making it roll its eyes and shudder from its ears to the tip of its braided tail.

"There! Get inside!"

September concentrated on running, and forgot about the ghost, though part of her mind wished she was able to whip up a quick proton accelerator, just to test out the theory. The possibilities for wyrd science in a snowy Victorian street were few, but she felt up to the challenge.

Then she spotted Bob Cratchit's house, like the archetype of all cheap biscuit assortment tins made real. Just looking at it made sleigh bells jingle in her head. The door was ajar, and the merry glow of a fire burning in the hearth flickered within, wafting the smell of plum pudding and roasted goose out into the street.

September ducked inside, just as a huge, heavy gravestone went whickering past overhead with a sound like a frightened pheasant. A quarter-tonne of stone smashed into Bob Cratchit's front door, and stuck halfway through.

"Gawd blessus, every one!" shouted Cedric, as that now-familiar heat-haze ripple swallowed them up...

Oh, some things, they all happened,
with swirling about,
and some twirling and spinning
and spitting them out,
There was tinsel and fireworks,
shoves and a shout...
It was still Christmas time –
of that there was no doubt.

"It still snows", thought September,
Feeling floppy and faint,
"But a high street in London,
This certainly ain't!
The buildings are curly,
there's candy-cane paint–
But my brain's trying to yammer
an urgent complaint."

She looked down at her hands,
Clad in bright yellow mittens,
Then her arms, and her feet,
And she nearly had kittens.

Coz it seemed the whole world,
On the bright afternoon,
Had been rendered and blended
with some mad cartoon.
In a whimsical style
that she picked all too soon,
As her thoughts wobbled up
in a fluffy balloon.

"With some science-y
thinking, I'm quick to deduce
That to flummox our enemy,
still on the loose.
Miss Rummage has gone
far beyond Christmas goose,
And into the works
of a doctor named Seuss!"

Miss Rummage replied –
"It's an excellent choice,
We've escaped from that ghost
who was missing his voice,
though you'll find the good doctor
rhymes better with 'Royce'
than with 'juice' – Still, there's cause to
enthuse and rejoice..."

"No there isn't!" said Cedric
"He's got us this time!
And it seems we'll all die speaking
only in rhyme!"

Sure enough,
here he came – see the cartoon folk

scatter!
From a figure in robes black as fresh
antimatter!
One which caterwauls
over the christmassy chatter,
In tones loud enough
to make icicles shatter—

"What the hell have you done,
you insufferable fools?
Don't you know that you're bending
and breaking the rules?
Dragging us through these silly
consecutive Yules,
When I should be addressing those
Elvis-shaped ghouls?"

"And if that's not enough,
now your bloody machine
Has painted me into
this slovenly scene,
With the urge to steal toys,
and act cunning and mean, with
a body that's utterly
FUZZY AND GREEN!"

Then he ripped at his robes,
and they tore with a jerk
Revealing a nudity Not Safe For Work
And a full-body merkin
of purest viridian!

"Good gosh!" smirked September

"That's not so bad, considerin'
It's sneaking and taking
     you have expertise in.
So here, you're the spirit of
     holiday treason,
That Christmas-thief mocked
in the holiday seasons, the Gr..."

"We can't say it,
     for copyright reasons!"

Miss Rummage spoke sternly,
     but with hindsight she'd say
The Grim Reaper's wrath grew
     six sizes that day.

And in lieu of a scythe
he grabbed anything handy –
In this case, a huge cane
made of peppermint candy.

"That's it! You are definitely
     going to get it!
This is messing with fate!
     You won't live to regret it!
I'll pummel and pulverise,
     vengeance is coming!"

He looked up from his tantrum
     to see them all running
And slithering, slipping in snow,
     slush and sleet,
Along that warped whimsical
     Christmas-time-street,

To a blur in the air, a dimensional portal...

Which swallowed three folks, then one pissed-off immortal.

This time, September was almost ready for the whirling tunnel of words and the smell of boiling ink and pencil dust.

Almost, but not quite – and she was utterly unready for the landing she found herself rolled and tumbled and bundled up in.

The grass was greener than green had any right to be here, and the sky was palest clear-heaven blue. The clouds which bumbled across it were dreadnoughts of cotton candy. Even the sun was a perfect egg-yolk circle of yellow, with a cheerfully demented face plastered across it, grinning fit to split in half.

Except the grass wasn't grass, and the sky wasn't sky. And the cloud's weren't cotton candy. They were felt.

Felt, with big bright colourful stitching around the edges. So, too, were the happy little felt ducks which bobbed along on the felt river, past the felt trees with their woolly leaves.

September stifled a word thoroughly inappropriate for this obviously G-rated setting, as she saw that her own hands were now fingerless rounded mittens of the same stuff. Her dress was a piece of tartan, and the motorcycle jacket she'd borrowed was dense black merino.

Because she was two dimensional. September Normalsson had become a puppet.

"What a wonderful day!" said Miss Rummage, who was also missing a certain sense of depth. When her mouth moved, it was clearly a series of little paper cutouts in different shapes. "Now, there's only one place in here, and only one thing he could have become, so..."

"Alright. You win. Just don't look," said a very dejected voice, from behind a felt tree stump. It stood in the yard of a cottage which was precisely square, with a precisely triangular roof, four windows, and a chimney with a curly spring of woollen smoke coming out of it.

"Ummm. Look, I'm sorry about this, boss, it's just that..."

"Don't come any closer! *I get it!* You think that the breakdown of life and death and mortality is some kind of joke, and you can just gallivant around smashing all the rules with impunity. Fine! Just let me out of this... this... *whatever it is*, and I'll forget all about it. The drugs, and the vampire, and your horrible hospital in the Aught, and everything. I can see this goes higher than my pay-grade."

Cedric didn't stop. He receded into the distance with a series of jerky little stop-motion blips, becoming a smaller and smaller black felt boy with a mop of woollen hair. September, for her part, simply wondered how you gallivanted. It sounded complicated, as if you'd have to buy several items of expensive equipment with French names.

"Oh. Ohhhh, Mister Khatri. I'm... ummm. Look, if it makes things any better, you are a *very cute* little..."

"Don't you patronise me, boy! I'm still your boss! Even if I'm currently... well. *Fine!* Take a good, long look!"

Reaper-Captain Khatri came out shyly from behind his tree stump, and wobbled forward into what seemed to be both the front of the world and the present moment at once, in a kind of tangled, brain-aching way.

He had become a fluffy, small grey wolf.

Miss Rummage smiled, her paper mouth becoming a little upside-down 'n'.

"Makes sense. A wolf's about the baddest thing you get in one of these. Or a very selfish goose, or a frog with an attitude problem. Not sharing the bouncy ball, kind of scenario. Kids don't get the idea of death. He doesn't exist in here. He's hanging on by the thread of a story."

Miss Rummage leaned down and patted Mister Khatri with one rounded-off felt hand. She was a perfect fabric cut-out of a Victorian nanny, complete with red, round spots on her cheeks. Khatri's tail began to wag, against his own will.

"Now look," she said, "I have no idea what you mean about drugs, and vampires, and the Aught."

"I might," ventured felt September, putting up one hand. "But..."

"But *nothing*. It's rude, ill-mannered and downright *unprofessional* to come into a person's library without so much as a how-do-you-do, and start swinging a big bloody scythe around. I reckon a few weeks eating woollen dog food serves you right!"

Mister Khatri whined.

"But someone has broken into PostMortis! Somebody is knocking off the wrong people! And, well, some of our prisoners have gone missing, too. I was told by the Azraeon to get to the bottom of it, and everything led right to... your... library..."

The little felt wolf cub looked crestfallen.

"I've missed something important, haven't I?" he asked, fixing September with the saddest pair of puppy-dog eyes she had ever seen cut out of cloth. "It's not you, is it? You're not messing up the demortalisations. You, or those meddling Elvi. It's someone else."

September looked at Miss Rummage, her little felt eyes narrowing.

"Can we get out of here? All of us? Right now?"

The librarian tried to do a good impression of embarrassed worry, but the emotion was far too nuanced for a few primary shapes made of fabric.

"Well, *we* can. But not Mister Khatri, I'm afraid. I wasn't kidding about the two weeks. This book, *Jolly Dormouse Jim and the Little Bad Wolf,* is out on loan. I won't be able to get him out until it comes back."

"But whatever tricked us both is probably out there right now," said Cedric, "lurking horribly, and your Grandad's lbhrhmmmm iss mmmm – hey! What was that for?"

"There was a tiny tinfoil bug on your big round stupid felt face," said September sweetly, giving Cedric a meaningful look. "And you're right – my Grandad's *funeral is on Thursday.*" It was impossible to wink surreptitiously when you were made of cloth. September tried anyway. "Let's get going, then. We'll have to forgo the being technically dead, but there's things to do. He's right about the hospital, and the Elvises, and some kind of drug ring. I reckon we could foil that kind of plan, just the three of us."

"Are you talking about an *adventure?*" asked Miss Rummage. "Haven't had one of those for a while. Little Mean is a pretty quiet posting."

"Are you all mad?" wailed the little bad wolf. "If whoever's behind this fooled all of PostMortis, and got me into this trap, then they're smarter than you by a factor of billions! No offence, but you lot seem to have the tactical acuity of a dead hamster between you."

"And which one of us is a tiny felt doggie right now?" asked September. "Next time, don't just rush in and threaten to kill people, and you might get a better response."

"I only meant *technically dead,* as in..."

But September wasn't hearing it. Some kind of deep, resonant twist in her little woollen double-helix was thrumming like the strings on an upright bass. And it was all over the word 'adventure'.

"Miss R, do your thing," she said.

And the librarian did. She pulled a small dewey-decimal card from one of the pockets of her two-dimensional coat, and tore it in half. The world rippled, and blurred, and there was a sound like thousands of sheets of paper crinkling at once. Felt outlines blurred and frayed. Crayon-scrawl colours bled out of the sky and the grass, spiralling in toward blinding white...

Crisp and colourful cardboard covers snapped shut.

Suture Four
Mad, Bad, Vlad

MOST OF US live very much inside out own heads.

But much more of us lives inside the heads of other people.

It's like this. You exist – right now – as a pattern of neurons and electricity inside a grapefruit-sized chunk of soggy tissue called a brain.

But you also exist as a little voice, an image, and a collection of opinions and stories and anecdotes, inside the brains of everyone who you know, and everyone who you have ever met.

The collective balance of you which is, in fact, *not stored behind your own eyebrows*, is staggering. It outweighs the amount which you keep under a hat by quite a lot.

So, where's the rest?

The answer, or so Septivarian Archimedes had discovered, was a place called the Aught. The collective subconscious of the species. His theory, which involved a lot of the kind of maths that looks like ancient Greek graffiti, was this:

If the act of observing something collapses it from a wave into a particle, thus making it exist in the 'real' universe, then thinking, dreaming or idly fantasizing about something makes it real in the Aught.

This works for dead people, because the echoes of the dead live in the minds of everyone who has ever loved or hated them, for *decades* after their bodies go back to the dirt. Hence Septivarian's worries that his immortal soul, (or the part of oneself that goes on even beyond the Aught, into weird fractal spaces unknown) will imprint on that collective echo, and serve up his secrets to any evildoers who may have been waiting on the other side of the veil for him.

He's sort of right about that.

Just like Miss Rummage is sort of right, about fiction.

The Baal Shem know it's real, and that it's there behind reality, seething with characters who live in so many brains and minds that they can sometimes be more real than you or I.

They know that some fictional characters are rotten to the core, and that some have been driven mad by the way that humans have fractured them up into myths and jokes and fears and horrors all at once.

Dracula, for example. The bloke with the thing about toothpicks, from the previous suture.

What Eileen Charlotte Rummage doesn't know – and nor does September – is just how powerful the Count really is. After all, he's a dead guy called Vlad Tepes, the Impaler, one of history's most notorious killers. Plus, the father of fictional vampires, and we all know that the oldest vampire has the power of all the other ones, put together.

We all know this, so it's true. And it gets worse.

More people have heard about Vlad Dracula, and know all about his supernatural powers, than know about Arthur Slodge, of 22 Penwiper Street, Prawn Harbour, Australia. Even though Arthur Slodge is very real, and Vlad is fictional.

That's a lot of power, right there. And there's another difference, too.

Aside from a morbid fear of sponge cake, Arthur Slodge is quite absolutely sane.

Count Dracula, however, is out of his tiny little mind.

Which makes it even more of a shame that, even as you're reading this, *a little part of him is living rent-free inside yours...*

Eight
The Lost Vegas
All-Elvis Revue
vs
Count Dracula

LITTLE-MEAN-ON-THE-AVERAGE SLEPT, WRAPPED up in its woollies and soothed by cups of sweet tea.

Cats patrolled the allotments, and mooched in the weeds that surrounded those three empty-tooth-socket holes where a supermarket, a petrol company and a video arcade had failed to prosper. The night smelled of jasmine and primrose, and the streets were all but empty. A Burger Slave wrapper bowled along Charles Babbage Terrace, against the prevailing breeze.

If you were to fall in toward the centre of town, you'd find the tip of the triangle marked out by those construction sites. It was right next to what should have been a darkened civic library. However, tonight, something stirred amid the periodicals. The high windows were alive with candlelight.

Papery whispers riffled across the shelves. Shadows and cobwebs swirled, half-imagined, as harpsichord music played on a scratchy old gramophone. A memory of red velvet mouldered at the very edge of sight.

Because you can't have a vampire story without every gothic cliché in the big black book.

And one of those clichés is a young lady, awoken violently from nightmares...

September didn't even remember, afterwards, what the nightmare had been about. A lingering image of cheese and a lobster in a top hat wobbled away from her mind's grasp.

Then her eyes slammed open and adrenaline gurgled through her, doing the job of ten coffees so black that light could not escape their surface.[22] A rebellious curl of her own hair bobbed like a broken clock-spring.

Felt! She'd been made of bloody felt!

But –

The library. They were back in the library. Where her Grandad's laboratory was hidden. And where something was waiting...

In any kind of fair and reasonable universe, September would have been given a minute to quell the feeling that her arms and legs were tubes of pink wool. But, as has been noted by numerous philosophers since the Big Bang got things off on the wrong foot, you can grind even the wisest man down to atoms and find not one quarks-worth of fairness.

Instead, there came a voice.

"Ahhhhh! Awaken unto darkness, my sinister angel! Arise, and join me in unholy ecstasy, *for ve... are ze children of the night!*"

September was, unfortunately, no stranger to what teenage boys, old ladies and the made-for-TV movie industry considered romantic. A withering response was already locked and loaded as she spun around – only to be smacked right in the prefrontal cortex by the hypnotic stare of Vlad Dracula.

The Count was tall, predatory and pallidly handsome, his eyes all darkly glistening. His obligatory opera cape and tuxedo were deployed to full effect, as was a haunted smile, reminiscent of the famously deceased Bela Lugosi. The outrageous pompadour haircut? Naturally! A tasteful amount of eyeliner? You bet! And he had the words right, too.

---

22. The infamous hextuple-shot Beta Squalzarian Neutroniumesso.

"Ahhh, my lovely, delectable flower of ze night!" crooned the Count. "At last, ve can be together! Come, be hypnotised by ze dark seduction of my mephistophelean... ummm... Let your spirit descend into ze abyss of my eternal... errr... allright, then – gaze into ze hypnotic romance of my dark soul, and... bugger! Zhis isn't working, is it?"

September regarded Vlad critically, narrowing her eyes. He didn't look at all romantic or attractive, on closer inspection. In fact, he looked a bit sweaty and nervous.

"If I'm supposed to swoon at this point, then no, it's not working," she said. "I never learned swooning in school. I think I might have been suspended at the time, for giving the class hamster tentacles."

The vampire wrung his hands.

"I assure you, zhis never happens to me. I'm usually quite reliably dark and alluring."

September refused to feel sorry for him. She reached for the cold fizz of the Endarkenment, and managed to tease out a thread of fiction, left floating in the library air. Suddenly, there was a very real, very hot Victorian-era fire poker in her hand, courtesy of the hearth of Mr B Cratchit.

"It's been a heck of a day, Count Chocula, so you've got about three seconds to explain yourself, before this goes somewhere *unspeakably* uncomfortable."

A spasm twitched through the vampire's face; the urge to bite. But being seductive at young girls in nightgowns had worked for Vlad for decades. He tried harder. The air around him *curdled*.

"Are you suuuuuurrrre zhat you vouldn't like to take all your clothes off?" he asked, with the hopeful smile of self-convinced 'ladies men' everywhere. "Look, I can sparkle, and everything..."

September cleared the ten feet between them in a blur, and the tip of one Doc Marten's boot crunched into

Dracula's crotch. His face came down, wincing, and met the upward arc of the fire poker.

It made a noise like a hammer smacking into a sheet of copper.

"You're really not my type," she said softly, as the vampire curled up around his pain and keeled over. "I prefer a boy who can build his own nuclear death ray – and who's about two hundred years closer to my age," she smiled, bright as madness. "But enough about me. How about we talk about *who. Sent. You?*"

The fire poker singed Vlad's nostril hairs. He shrunk back, hissing, still lashing out with his hypnotic power. It could find nothing to grip onto.

Oh sweet mother night! This looked like a teenage girl, but it tasted like pure, uncut exorcist!

"But... but... I'm ever so romantic! Look! I'm a bloody immortal vampire! A thousand years of lust and darkness and bedroom curtains blowing on a supernatural wind stand behind me! How can you resist all zhat?"

September considered him with her head tilted to one side. It was the kind of look a doctor gives to a bacterium down a microscope, when she's about to apply a big squirt of disinfectant.

"Oh, I know what you guys do. I *like* horror movies. I'm not one of those silly girls who fall for all your 'immortal love' nonsense, then get blood-sucked like a grapefruit before the third act."

She leaned forward. Her eyes glowed red in the poker-light.

"I know not to run upstairs, or hide in a closet with those little louvres you can see though, or go to an old cabin in the woods without bringing a chainsaw. *I'm inoculated.* So start talking. Because I bet you're old-fashioned enough to burst into flames if I use a pencil to make this fire poker into a crucifix. Just for the sake of tradition, right? Handymen from Israel notwithstanding?"

In supernatural wavelengths, the vampire could see the oil-refinery sized flare of the Endarkenment haloing September, rippling out behind her with the tick-whirr of thousands of turning gears. *Just like Doctor bloody Frankenstein. Just like Van Helsing himself, with his damned gadgets!*

"So, you think you are ze clever vun, yes?" asked the Count, with an accent that was pure Hollywood, right to the curly edges. "Vell, ve have more zhan vun vay of negotiating, young lady. You say you like horror movies?"

The transformation was almost instantaneous. During that horrible instant, the vampire's face bubbled like boiling soap, stuck between fleshy frequencies. It was *not* pleasant to watch, even at the business end of a fire poker.

What was worse, however, was the snarling, bestial mug that replaced it. It had tiny, blackcurrant eyes, a pushed-in nose, and the ragged, pointed ears of a blood-drinking bat. And it had the teeth as well. A whole mawfull, gnashing and grinding, so sharp and long that they cut into the Count's lips.

He bit the end off September's poker. He swallowed.

"Say hello to ze other guy!" hissed this vision, all hunched and sinewy. "*Nosferatu.* He's not so much into romance. But you said you liked *horror!*"

Claws sprouted from the tips of Vlad's fingers, with a wet, crunching sound. Muscles like bunches of sausages bulged under velvet. September stepped back, seeing her face reflected in those beady little eyes. She swung the stump of the poker overhand and it stabbed deep into the vampire's shoulder, to no visible effect. He smiled a shrapnel grin at her presumption.

"You still vant to know who sent me?"

"On second thoughts, we could just forget it. And I'm re-thinking the idea of a nice dinner for two as well."

The Count flexed. The poker wormed its way out of his flesh and clattered to the floor.

"There's still room for us both at dinner," he frothed. "It's just that *I'm* the only one who'll be enjoying a drink."

At this point, Cedric, (provisional junior grim reaper), and Miss Rummage, (Baal Shem of the Word, and ace local librarian), decided to chance their hand at heroism.

They should have caught the Count off his guard. But whatever feral senses he now possessed allowed him to sweep up the scythe at his feet, spin it in mid-air, and grind it across Cedric's blade in a desperate parry.

Sparks flashed blue. Steel grated on steel. And with a ripple of wire-cable muscles, the vampire forced Cedric down. The blades chimed against each other as he flung the reaper across the room, into a shelf full of romance novels.

He was just in time to spin and block a ferocious salvo of spinning high-kicks from the librarian, who was once again channelling the power of kung-fou. Her hair had broken free from its coloured pencils, and there was certainly something of the ancient tribal warrior-queen about her.

Dracula blocked left and right with one upraised arm, swaying to avoid those furious button-boots of death. He even yawned. This was too easy! Then he spun his scythe one-handed to parry a looping blow from Cedric, and his claws lashed out, gripping Miss Rummage by the throat.

"Stop! All of you mad mortals, *stop!* Or I'll take her head off like a champagne cork!"

The four of them froze in a momentary tableau, as lightning flickered high up near the roof of the library. A wolf howled outside, against all the regulations of urban animal control.

Once again, September realised, in some brightly-lit stainless-steel chamber of her mind, that all this was *silly*. She understood that she was meant to be horrified. But... but, the *drama* of it all! The sheer bloody cheek of such pantomime! She wasn't at all afraid of this rabid old stereotype. *She was mad at him for existing.*

"Bugger off back to the bargain bin, somewhere they still sell VHS!" she snarled, remembering what hung around her neck. She fished the little crucifix up from where it lay warm against her skin, and brandished it in Dracula's face. "Aha!"

The vampire held Miss Rummage at arm's length, looking quizzical.

"And vhat's *zhat* supposed to do?" he asked. "Am I meant to burst into flames or something?" His confused look melted into a horrible leering grin. "Because it's not religious icons zhat hurt me, little lady. Handymen from Israel, as you so nicely put it, notvithstanding. You have to have *faith*, and fire, and a symbol you'd die for.

"You, though? Pah. A bloody agnostic, right? *Ohhh, I'm very spiritual, crystals and dolphins and bloody unicorns,* isn't it? A bit of jewellery zhat reminds you of weakly-smiling vicars raising money to fix ze vestry roof isn't going to stop Vlad! Ze bloody! IMPALER!"

September shrugged.

"Well, I *was* kind of hoping. And no, I'm not about to go around believing in Gods, just because they apparently exist. Got to make them work for it." She smiled, and it was just as terrible a thing as Vlad's own horrorshow of enamel. "But anyway – I bought them some time, didn't I?"

The vampire's eyes twitched back and forth between September and Cedric, who menaced him with an upraised scythe. The young Reaper had scooped up the hourglass badge his boss had dropped. It hung around his neck, glowing insect-zapper blue. Cedric's features, underlit, had something of the skeletal about them.

Vlad ignored the librarian. Because in his experience, women who were under his claws didn't do anything but scream theatrically.[23]

Miss Rummage, though, was not some feckless Victorian wench in a lace nightie. And she'd been listening to September's talk about horror films.

"Hey, ugly," she croaked, holding out her hands to each side. Wooden drawers slammed open behind her desk, and little yellow cards came spiralling out, flocking and swirling. A select few slotted in between her fingers, with a sound like origami swords being drawn.

"The time has come," Miss Rummage said, "To talk of scary things. Of Barkers, Raimis, Cronenbergs, and Carpenters, and Kings. That's Stephen, if you catch my drift. Your bloody *successors*."

The shadows within the library shifted, like the facets of some forbidden puzzle-box. The shelf reserved for adult-library-card-holders-only horror DVDs grated around to face them.

"*And a genre re-arisen under cinematic wings*," she finished...

As the shadows scissored shut like shears.

There is a secret praxis of the Baal Shem, which should only (or so it's taught) be used in circumstances of utmost necessity. It involves the fact that horror is the most visceral of genres, and that it takes very little for things like Vlad Dracula to happen, given the nature of human imagination and the fabric of time and space.

There are certain archetypes of horror which have an

---

23. At least in the PG-Rated version.

independent existence in the realms beyond. Some are myths which have been co-opted by errant souls, and worn like Halloween costumes. Others live simply because belief can take the place of life; ask the madly religious about that one.

Some of them have jobs, in the Aught. That bloke with the knives for fingers is a jazz-tap instructor. The hockey mask fellow makes small-batch organic cheeses.

But the Baal Shem have their private numbers. They know how to call them up.

So it was that light burst through between the shelves, in that iconic horror-movie fashion – latticed beams of it, which didn't so much banish the darkness as slice it up.

From the aisles came the sound of clinking chains, as figures appeared from a sudden and inexplicable mist. They were lean and pale, clad in long coats of black leather, and each one appeared to have died as part of some kind of extreme body piercing accident. Their leader was a bald and bone-white man whose entire head was covered in long sharp spikes, on which several hundred post-it memos had been impaled. He plucked one as he approached, gliding across the floor, and fumbled a pair of tiny spectacles out of one leather pocket to peer at it.

"Right... hold on... says here... *ahem*... foolish mortals! You have summoned the Sybarites of the order of the Papercut, and will now know the pain of pleasure and the pleasure of pain for all eternity. Prepare for... *oh, hell, not that berk again!*"

Dracula put down Miss Rummage, and narrowed his eyes.

"Hello... *Ralph*." he said, with bitterest rancour.

"Hello... *Vlad*," replied the Sybarite, as its fictional demon companions hissed.

"A few new ones since last time, eh? How's things back

in the Aught?"

The spike-headed demon shrugged.

"Oh you know, you know. Ecstasy and suffering, cameo appearances in nightmares, that sort of thing. You're still locked up for being proper mental though, aren't you? Funny to find you out and about."

The vampire showed a smile with plenty of enamel.

"Top secret, my old mate. Ze Cardinal pays extremely well, and pretty soon you lot vill be out of business."

The Sybarite rolled his eyes.

"Working for those slags at Gravesend? Tut tut. I'm almost pleased we're gonna have to kick your Transylvanian arse."

Ralph cracked his knuckles. Various other cyber-gothic demons brandished hands made from cutlery and power tools.

"And vouldn't that be doing me a favour? Pain being pleasure and all? Vouldn't a relaxing back massage be much more horrifying to you sickos? Answer me vun thing, Ralph. What's going on with ze new lad, over there?"

Dracula pointed to a small Sybarite who appeared to have nothing punctured through him. Ralph raised an eyebrow which was, in fact, a small row of drawing pins, and snapped his fingers.

With a look of utterly damned horror, the demon raised one foot, to reveal that a piece of brightly coloured Lego was embedded right in its heel.

"Ooooosh!" winced the vampire. "Zhat must be horrible... I mean lovely... which means it's nasty... which means... oh, bugger it, *let's rumble!*"

Miss Rummage put up her fists. Cedric gripped his scythe. Dracula brandished his own, as even more muscle and sinew crawled under his skin, like a nest of electrified snakes. Various imaginary demons flexed – one, whose head appeared to have been half-replaced with a chrome espresso machine, disgorged a cup of something indescribable from a little spout in its ear, and handed it to a colleague.

But September wasn't watching any of them. Her mind was tapped into the mains current of the Endarkenment, and she could see through the reality-bending auras which surrounded the Count and his foes. She was looking up at the library roof, where purposeful shadows were moving against the skylights.

"Somebody say 'what we need now is a distraction,'" she whispered.

"What?" asked Cedric.

"*We need now is a distraction,*" finished September.

And then the roof exploded.

And distractions? There were plenty. Because here came a crack all-Elvis commando chorus line, rappelling down ropes to clobber and arrest everyone in sight. All the expenditure of sorcery which had just occurred in the Little Mean civic library had lit the place up like a nuclear-powered Christmas tree, thaumic dampeners notwithstanding.

There to meet them were the Sybarites of the Order of the Papercut, a horrifying hit-squad of demons who combined sadomasochism with mind-numbing bureaucracy. For them, boredom was excitement and pain was pleasure – leading to a state of permanent confusion and a bloody short temper. They waded into the Elvi with a howling battle-cry, as Ralph and Miss Rummage fought Vlad Dracula atop a pile of returned library books.

It was an all-in, slobber-knocking brawl, with fists and feet flying in the style of a 1970s kung fu epic. Knuckles crunched. Bones crumpled. Bodies were propelled from the melee to topple shelves, and leave person-shaped indentations in the walls. Chairs, heavy tomes, computer monitors and items of stationery went airborne.

This made it surprisingly easy for September to sneak through by simply crawling along the floor. She reached Cedric, who had been thrown bodily through the young adults section, as he was brushing himself off and staggering to his feet.

"Oi! Down here! They've forgotten about us! We need to get to the secret reading room. I think that's where they hid the entrance to Septivarian's laboratory."

Cedric, however, had a look on his face which September recognised. It was the look her father got when he was about to do battle with a badly clogged bathroom sink. She realised, with the kind of emotional insight that wasn't usually her forte, that he was about to do something brave and stupid.

"You go, then," he said, turning to where Vlad Dracula was now levitating in the centre of the room, surrounded by the whirling shapes of angry Sybarites. "This guy's on the 'most unwanted' list. He should be in prison. If anyone's going to have answers about this whole colossal screw-up, it's him."

With that the young reaper activated his helmet, and the panels and planes of a skull snicked into position over his face. He pulled Mister Khatri's huge hourglass-shaped badge of office from his pocket, and turned it over and over between his fingers. September noticed that the back of the badge was clear, and slipped into it, like a driver's licence into a plastic sleeve, was a tarot card.

Just like her Grandad's. Except this one featured a black-armoured skeleton riding a horse. It was the Tarot of Death.

In this instance, September did *not* reckon that it simply predicted a change in one's personal life, or new opportunities at work.

"I am going to get in *so* much trouble for this," said Cedric, gloomily. Then he pulled the card from its sleeve, and slapped it up against his forehead.

The effect was instantaneous.

Ced's outline blurred like static, as a chill wind whistled in from between the aisles of books, blowing away the Sybarites' mist. His skin seemed to shrink around his bones, turning porcelain white. A series of horrible wet cracks and pops attended, as he grew several more vertebrae, and his arms and legs stretched long and thin. His clothes rippled as they became a robe of utter darkness, and his helm sunk in, to become a time-worn, bleached-white skull. September saw all this with a flash of insight, like a hot knitting needle to the base of the brain.

Azreal, the Angel of Death, was a proper angel after all. One of the first cadre of God's creation, if you followed that mythology. Which meant he was trapped outside of the world when Dante worked his sorcery. He'd been replaced by an avatar, a human wearing his mask. The succession Reaper-Captains of PostMortis.

Now, some people think that angels are all sweetness and feather-fluff and blessings. But they haven't thought it through.

What kind of thing would you create, and what power would you give it, if you knew it was going to have to hack apart legions of demons for all eternity?

What further strength would it need, if it was banished from Heaven and denied a place in Hell, only to serve as God's soul-collector? A celestial hitman, armed with nothing but a primitive lawn-mower and a face that could stop a beating heart?

Real angels were all eyes and sharpened light and cruel mathematics. The Azraeon was something more again. And now his full power poured through the (yes!)

hourglass pinch-point of sorcery that Dante had wrought. It hammered into Cedric so hard his feet levitated from the floor.

"***Vlad Dracula! Sorrow of Carpathia, Scourge of Transylvania, and so on, et cetera!***" he said, and the words came out as chisel-strokes of iron on granite. "***You are bloody well* nicked, *mate!***"

This caught everyone's attention. The thing which unfolded from behind the murder-mystery section, all upraised scythe and polished bone, even made September scrabble backwards across the linoleum. For an instant, the Reaper's face blurred, peeling back from one eye and half a mouth.

"Go! I can't do this for long! There's a reason Captain Khatri has to mediate six hours a day! Get to that laboratory, and don't look back!"

September didn't need telling twice. She ran down a tunnel of books, all of them quaking and rustling, some popping from their shelves and making an attempt to crawl along the ground with their pages. From behind her came a flash of light, like a welding torch lit up underwater. Then the inhuman scream of a chorus of demons, Elvi, and one very annoyed vampire.

September skidded into the Tiny Tot's picture book section, scattering a pile of stuffed animals. Behind her, an ornate battle-spear, of late iron-age design, smacked into the wall and stood quivering. There was no time to panic, however. The secret door was ahead, and to open it September needed to push just the right spots on an art-deco carving of a leering *commedia dell'arte* clown.

Her fingers stabbed into an eye and a ludicrous pom-pom, and the door cracked open, letting out a wash of stale, dry air. September could hear footsteps behind her, fast-paced little taps on the linoleum, and she risked a look back, only to see a Dead Elvis reaching out for her, its eyes obscured behind green-glowing tactical lenses.

"*Not so fast, little lady,*" said the rock 'n' roll monster. Its fingers stretched into claws, as it made a grab for her collar...

Then the backwash of thaumic radiation from the secret reading room came billowing out, slower than sound. It travelled at the *speed of smell*, which lingers and meanders and stops to sniff the roses. But this was not a scent that came in via the nose. It was the flatulence of sorcery, and it smacked the Elvis like the stench downwind of a sewer explosion.

The Elvi worked for the Things Beyond, and the reading room was full of books on how to identify, avoid, worship, capture or control them. While September detected nothing but a hint of brimstone, the invisible whiff made the Elvis recoil, its skin sagging like putty from its bones.

"Get back here!" it snarled, with a mouth glooped halfway down to its chest. "You're in violation off thrrr mmmphmm lurgle blhrrr smlurp!"

It was a futile gesture. September was through the door, and she grabbed the statue of Dagon to stop herself, turning her momentum into a spin. She fished the key out from around her neck, and slammed it onto the keyhole in Dagon's scaly belly-button.

Unsurprisingly, it was a perfect fit.

What *was* a surprise (and which made September collapse backwards into the room's single old button-backed leather armchair) was the sudden lurch of lost gravity. A spray of dust and the squeal of metal rose over the clatter of cold-war-era engineering. The bookshelves seemed to shoot upward as the room got taller and thinner.

Actually, of course, the whole reading room (chair, table, statue of Dagon and all) was falling, like a giant freight elevator. The walls went from mahogany shelves to riveted steel plates as the platform plummeted, just a little too fast for the liking of September's stomach. Lucky she hadn't had any supper!

Up above, great grinding bulkheads slammed closed, blotting out the light. The gears churned on for a good long while – long enough that September wondered how deep this infernal shaft went. She even had time to wonder if 'infernal' was a word she wanted to consider, when it came to what Septivarian had been up to...

There was a hiss of strained pneumatics. The floor came to a stop, shuddering like a wet dog. And a set of doors hissed open, with that very particular 'Star Trek' noise, which we're told was made by a props man standing just behind the cardboard set.

September beheld the Befuddler's Lair – with a capital L.

She was surprised to discover that it was quite familiar.

Meanwhile, in the library, the battle had swung in the favour of Miss Rummage and Cedric. In fact, the librarian was having a bit of a sit-down, fanning herself with a sheaf of community notices from the Little-Mean-on-the-Average Bowling Club. The horribly incarnate Avatar of Death swung his scythe in great blurring arcs, leaving a neon-purple glow behind it in the air.

Sybarites squealed and panicked, hitching up their trench-coats and fleeing, like Victorian nannies from a particularly sassy plague of mice. Ralph, the post-it-noted demon prince, stopped for a second beside Miss Rummage's commandeered office chair, and made a sour face.

"You never told me *this* bloke would be crashing the party, love," he said, disapprovingly. He pulled a note from one of the spikes adorning his head, scribbled some figures on it, then thrust it at the librarian. "That's extra, that is. Tell your bosses that we don't do avatars, gods, children's birthday parties or anything involving the tax department, right?"

He slapped the note onto Miss Rummage's forearm, then held his nose, crossed his eyes, and vanished. A sprinkle of those little circles of paper left inside a hole punch pattered down as his black-clad cohort followed suit.

Because to be clipped by that flying scythe – which ripped the air apart at a sub-atomic level – was a one-way ticket to the realm of Ammut the soul-eater, scourge of the doubly dead.

Several Elvi had already caught it, and their splattered and smoking remains adorned the walls and shelves, cutout images of bell-bottomed pants and outrageous coiffures stained black where they'd burst.

But amazingly, the Count held Cedric back.

A few centuries practising his swordsmanship had given him fighting form. He parried and deflected each swing of the scythe, wielding a pair of ornate damascus-steel sabres akimbo, and he was smiling.

The pair fought atop a pile of collapsed library shelves, fluttering, broken-backed books and empty Elvis costumes drenched in slime. An uncanny whirlwind was whipped up, winter-sharp, as the reaper and the eldest of vampires traded blows. Whenever their weapons collided, steel grated on steel with a sound like gnashing jaws, and sparks burned their shadows into the walls.

But Cedric was slowing down. There was a price to pay for being the conduit for an angel's power. The Reaper-Captains of PostMortis spent long hours in meditation to manifest for mere minutes in the *Materia*. Cedric had not so much as read a dodgy pamphlet on yoga, and contact with the essence of extinction was peeling his soul. Little memories wisped away as he tried to keep his mind from dissolving, long enough to land a killing blow.

He flagged, stumbling, and Vlad Dracula loomed up to strike, every bit aware of his dramatic pose. He hissed, for his audience of one exhausted librarian.

Who, he noticed, was not impressed.

Who, he further noticed, was holding a cordless telephone.

The faceplate of which blinked with the words 'FIRE DEPARTMENT'.

"Oh, *bollocks*," muttered the vampire, who knew exactly what the Little-Mean-on-the-Average municipal fire brigade really was.

"That's right, your bloody lordship. I'll probably lose my job over this debacle, but you... you'd better just run along now."

Miss Rummage dropped the phone from fingers gone all numb, and slumped backward in her chair, laughing.

Just in time for a six-tonne Bedford fire engine to come smashing through the doors at full chat, blasting blue flames from a clutch of sawn-off exhausts. It hung there, airborne, for one of those endless floating moments of pure cool – glittering glass fragments and twists of metal sprayed wide in slow motion.

Cedric leapt back out of the way, his cloak of shadows turned to shapeless clattering wings as it exploded off his shoulders. The body which hit the ground was, once again, that of a beat-up young fifties rocker, with no skull helmet, no empty ribcage full of cold fire, and no scythe.

He barely missed being clipped by the fire engine as it slid sideways across the linoleum in a four-wheel drift. Figures in tall brass-trimmed hats and long black coats deployed, with the seamless precision of old ladies setting up a church bake sale.

Dracula wasn't so lucky. He copped the rear corner of the Bedford right in the back, and turned his rag-doll flight into the real thing by shapeshifting in mid-air. A huge, red-eyed bat screeched and flapped up toward the ceiling, trying to gain altitude.

This was just the kind of thing the Fire Brigade was hoping for, of course. Actual fires were not the bread and butter of this team, who unrolled hoses with strange nozzles, and aimed them up at that leathery apparition. This was a tidy-up squad from the human side of the Bureau Innominandum, staffed by ex-special-forces commandos. Blasting things was a perk of the job.

Inside the truck, a very large proton accelerator, of a kind made famous by those four lads in that particular movie, came online with a thrumming drone. Pink lightning came sizzling down the hosepipes.

"On my mark, light 'im up!" bellowed Chief Fire Officer Lesley Bellingham, wielding one of those giant Victorian-era speaking trumpets. "*Mark!*"

Coruscating streams of energy crackled forth, of the kind you're definitely not meant to cross. September would have been delighted to discover that ghosts, spirits, and creatures of the Aught were indeed greatly discomfited by the application of nuclear-powered plasma.

But then again, who isn't?

The Little Mean firefighters were more than happy to pour it on, especially as the library was already ruined. Whole shelves erupted, and blackened contrails scarred the walls as they tried to follow their target.

"So," asked CFO Bellingham, leaning over the chair in which Miss Rummage reclined. "What exactly happened here? I mean, for the official version. The one where we're not trying to pot a giant rodent with wings, you understand?"

The librarian puffed a wisp of stray hair out of her eyes, and sat up.

"Let's say it was a riot, shall we? Tell them that we'd just got in an advance copy of Lady Prunella Boddyce-Rippington's steamy romance novel about time-travelling Scots beefcakes, Victorian-era lords with no shirts on, and a single milkmaid's impossible choice between which one of them has the most oiled-up six-pack. *Love in the time of Dysentery*, or some such. Lots of amorous old ladies wrecked the place trying to get their mitts on it."

Chief Bellingham nodded. Her own copy of Lady Prunella's previous opus, *The Breeze Beneath His Kilt*, had a tendency to fall open to several well-read passages.

"Sounds eminently plausible. But just so we're utterly clear, that's Dracula, isn't it? escaped from his novel and gone on a rampage, I suspect?"

To most people, this would seem like lunacy, but Miss Rummage knew an out when she saw it. There'd be no getting away without a tonne of paperwork, but a fictional crossleak was Baal Shem business, not a case for the Bureau.

That, at least, would buy September some time, even if it did mean having to face Chief Librarian Henrietta Smythe, ceremonial Wearer of the Glasses on the Plastic Chain, Grand Silencer, and Keeper of the Rubber Stamp.

Hetty would understand. Sometimes you had to go above and beyond for a favoured borrower.

Across the room, Cedric groaned and rolled over. He looked, thankfully, just like a particularly anachronistic hipster, who'd been visiting the library to peruse *Man Bun Weekly* or the *Artisanal Brewer's Friend*. With a desperate waggling of eyebrows, Miss R bade him to crawl off out of sight and after September. As a citizen of the Aught, a blast from the Fire Department's proton beams would banish him quite painfully.

"You know how it is," shrugged the librarian, turning her meaningful eyebrow work into what looked like a post-traumatic shudder. "Someone puts a book like that back on the shelf next to some how-to guides on Ouija boards, and next thing you know, bam!"

Up above, two of the crackling proton beams converged on Dracula. There was thunderclap, and a shriek, and the single bat exploded into a cloud of smaller ones, all of them spiralling and chittering away in various directions. CFO Bellingham rubbed her chin and looked thoughtful.

"Well, they're out of the library, and he's going to run out of steam the longer he's out of his book. I take it you'll find the offending volume, and deal with it accordingly?"

Miss Rummage nodded. She wasn't about to tell the authorities that the book she was really worried about was actually *Jolly Dormouse Jim*. She'd have to get it back before some toddler opened it up to find a very annoyed captain of PostMortis swearing in big letters made of felt.

"Perils of the job, I'm afraid. Now – how would you and the lads fancy a nice cup of tea?"

Up above, the spirit of the Count swarmed between several bats, steering a clutch of the creatures down along September's trail. For this was no rogue fictional instance of Vlad Dracula, as thin as a paper cutout. This was the *real thing*, direct from the Aught, and he could sense blood with an intensity that put sharks to shame.

He also had one more trick up his gothic sleeve.

A clutch of bats came gusting into the secret reading room, skittering like dry leaves, just in time for their sonar senses to ping Cedric, who was disappearing through a large metal hatch in the floor. Leathery wings flapped, and little silent puffs of magic lit up the space, making the rowan wands set in the door-frame smoulder.

"Too late!" shouted the upstart Reaper, as he gripped the rungs of a very long maintenance ladder, and slid down into the dark. But...

"Too slow," said a ludicrously handsome vampire in a white business suit, who caught the edge of the hatch before it could slam shut. "Brothers?"

There were two other versions of Bad Vlad in the room with him. One was dressed in late-medieval finery – a quilted jacket with lots of gold embroidery, a fez, and a truly magnificent moustache. The third was what could be thought of as 'original flavour' – a vampire direct from 1930s Hollywood, with an opera cape, slicked-back hair, and teeth you could open cans with.

"You get zhat little pillock in the James Dean costume, and I'll get ze girl. Ze Cardinal will owe us *big time* for zhis, and as for getting PostMortis off his back... vell! Vithout Dante's Tarot, ze captain of ze Reapers is nothing more than a sad old git vith a knife on a stick."

The other two nodded, and ripped the hatch from its hinges. Three heads were framed against the light as they looked down, and down, and *down*, into a shaft of blackness where, far below, a tiny white face looked back up at them.

It was time to finish this.

Nine
The Secret Army
vs
The Phantom Railroad

THE LABORATORY OF Professor Archimedes was a poem in high-Victorian chic, tiled with scenes from classical mythology – and it was *vast*. It was vaulted like the kind of cellar where monks meet by midnight for serious double-crossing, a sneaky pint, and perhaps the odd human sacrifice. Steampunk bronze and brass filigree'd the edges.

It was also, quite clearly, an underground station. A pair of rails cut right through the middle, bricked into a trench and ending in twin concrete tunnels. There was even a ticket window, though the mannequin inside was dressed in a lab coat and gas mask. September was not surprised to find that the name tag clipped to this coat read ROSEWOOD – Section W.

A door stood behind the ticket desk, set into the wall. It was a big, solid-steel pressure hatch, of the kind usually only found on submarines, and September could still see the blackening around its edges, where the fire had spilled out. That was the room where the B.I.S.H.O.P had been; the biocomputer that her great-great granddad had built, and then, inexplicably, set on fire.

She found that she really didn't want to go and look. It would be like desecrating a grave to open that door, and breathe in the smell of burnt plastic and copper wires.

Instead September reached for a huge pull-handle switch on the wall, and hit the lights.

Capacitors hummed. Massive suspended flood-lamps slammed on, illuminating acres of black and white tiles, all as bright and squeaky as if they'd just been polished. All around were machines of the esoteric kind, with glass bulbs, mysterious tangles of tubing, copper cooling fans, brass dials, and hundreds of old-fashioned valves, like the back end of a vintage amplifier.

She stepped between them (and the big brushed-steel benches, and the huge refrigerators full of specimen jars) speechless with wonderment. The Endarkenment sizzled around her head like a halo, fuelled by all the mad science on display.

*Because **mad** was the word for it. Yes indeed.* Things were laid out here, some whole and some in pieces, which defied conventional physics. Things which made use of the wyrd angles and mathematics of the Realms Beyond, Beneath, Besideways and frankly inside-out.

Here were tiny laser swords made for fairies, and rays which could turn people to stone, or custard, or living music. Here were suits to make you invisible, or inexplicable, or suits of beguilement which worked the opposite way, so that you became the object of everyone's idolising fascination.

There were olive-drab weapons from two world wars, and polished mahogany and brass contrivances from the era of Jules Verne and Isambard Brunel. There were things which September, who knew her nerdy sword-and-sorcery well, identified as dwarvern, or elvish, or a bloody good facsimile of the same. There was even (and here, she shuddered involuntarily) a row of chilled cryogenic tanks, with half-seen, pale bodies trapped under the ice. A sign above them read 'Witness Protection.'

September ran one fingertip over what seemed to be a clockwork blunderbuss studded with crystals, and read the engraving on its barrel – 'Propertie of William Shakespeare, esq'.

Yes! something inside her mind thrilled. *With all of this, there'd be no more Saint Pewtred's Academy. There'd be no more dullness, and no worries about some boring future. There'd be adventure, and discovery, and power. The power to make them all see that 'different' didn't mean 'wrong'. That it meant dangerous.*

Perhaps this is why old Septivarian had become a super-villain, in the end. You'd get sick of trying to justify yourself to people who didn't understand, with a mind like his. And so you'd just do exactly what you wanted, and let them call you what they had to.

Actually having a second to think about him, and the fact that he was gone for good, made September tear up, just a bit. I mean, it wouldn't have done to let anything slip while she was being chased by scythe-swinging skeletons or possessed evil trains or ghoulish Elvi, but here, in this place, with the presence of Septivarian Archimedes all around...

"Would you like a tissue? We have an industrial supply, of course, thanks to all the chemical spills. Hazard of the industry."

September turned around so fast that her heels left rubber on the parquet.

It was him.

Or rather, a much bigger hologram than the one she'd put in her ear, what seemed like several days ago. It was projected by a lens on a jointed brass arm, hanging above the heart of the lab. There were old-fashioned computers there, and bunsen burners, and a row of man-sized glass tubes, bubbling green.

"*Great Grandad!*" exclaimed September, running toward him. "You're alive!"

"Well, I'm actually just a very limited hologram, dear," he replied, his faced crinkling into a smile. "If this version of me has booted up, then you have absorbed Dante's Magician, and received the Endarkenment. There's likely someone coming after you, or several someones, with nasty intent. And whoops, what's this? Yes, the lair's perimeter has just been breached in three places. So I'd better make this quick."

"But... but you *died!* I didn't get the chance to say..."

The hologram shushed her, not unkindly, with one upraised finger. It was painfully transparent.

"We *all* die. But, as you may now be quite aware, that's far from the end. Thanks to Dante, it's not just a two-party system over there any more. No highway to hell and stairway to heaven, though of course both of those songs are *excellent*. No – a good eighty per cent of souls are agnostic enough to mean that there's a kind of existential purgatory. An afterlife where people can get used to the fact that there's an afterlife. Uncarnadine, they call it."

"I've had more than a few people try to convince me to go there," agreed September, stepping up to the dais. She ran one hand along the glass of a tank, seeing what looked like a pair of denim jeans (and a denim jacket, with hand-punched metal studs around the collar) floating within.

"Well, there's things there that can't get hold of all of this. The contents of my mind, to be more specific. Especially *that*. The thing you're breathing on, while drawing a little skull and crossbones with your finger."

September instinctively jerked back from the glass of the second tank, where several vinyl LPs, a flying-V guitar and a pair of headphones swum in green gloop, sparkles of energy flickering fitfully around them. She recognised that gloop. It was the same horrible stuff the doctor had tried to inject her with. The stuff in the 44-gallon drums. The drug called Repo.

September's mind crashed down through the gears,

trying to fit it all together. She fell back on sarcasm, almost automatically.

"A copy of Black Sabbath's *Master of Reality*, and a cheap knock-off Gibson?"

The hologram arched one eyebrow. September noticed, for the first time, that it was dressed not as the Befuddler, Quizmaster of Chaos, but as Professor Archimedes, in a lab coat and headband with little gold wings on it, like the headgear of some Greek god.

"Do you really think it's a coincidence that three of the best guitar solos of all time are from Crossroads by Cream, *Hotel California* by the Eagles and *Sympathy for the Devil* by the Stones? That the consistent number one is *Stairway to Heaven?*"

He shook his head.

"Something was trying to get out, via the music. Something that gave us a message, via Robert Johnson. Something that Mrs Thatcher and Ronald Reagan were determined to weaponise. They called it Project Dark Lazarus, and, for my sins, I helped them, for a while. I was even foolish enough to help design a machine to assist me."

September stopped him, before he got into a full teacher-style rant, by hugging him anyway. Her arms went a little bit through the hologram, but she felt that the gesture was necessary. It had been a very long, strange, afternoon.

"I *know*. I know it's all terribly important. But I wanted to say I'm sorry I didn't visit as much as I should have. I'm sorry my stupid parents kept you away. And I wish we could talk about normal things, like... like the weather, and music, and football, and, and..." She screwed up her eyes with frustration, as the words failed to line up properly. "Aaargh! About lemurs, and politics, and cakes, and spaceflight and all that. But now you're a hologram, and you're going to say something like..."

"I'm sorry," said the hologram of Professor Archimedes, "But I am programmed with only a very limited range of topics for discussion."

"Something like that. Something *dead*."

"...most of which are about the mission at hand. Though the old boy did give me this little piece of advice to hand on to you."

The projection blurred for an instant, looking a little more real. It flickered into a true recording, and not just an animated model.

"Don't wish for normal. Leave normal for those who can hope for nothing more, and be yourself, turned up to eleven."

September stepped back, wiping away something messy leaking from her eyes. It must be the dust in here. *Definitely* the dust.

Then she took a deep breath, smoothed down her frayed and burned cardigan, and let normal worry about itself.

"I sort of figured part of all this out, from your random memories. But the tarot cards still confuse me. Why are you... *we*... the Magician?"

The professor nodded.

"That's the right kind of question, young lady! It was all Dante's fault. The poet, tall chap, spoke Florentine, swore like a trooper. To trap the demons in his circles of Hell, he needed a *balance*. There are forces embodied in the world which pre-date the old Judaeo-Christian mythos. A lot of the causal disconnect we experience – miracles, supernatural visitations, and the like – is down to gnostic overlap. That is to say, belief systems layered up on top of each other. Like how your computer's operating system is actually just pasted in on top of an older one, and an older one, all the way down to binary code."

For a second the hologram stuttered, and a shimmer

passed through it in a long sine wave. Somewhere above, something rumbled and crashed, and the lights flickered too. Septivarian looked worried, but he ploughed on.

"Well, they were the glitches that carried over. They had to be exempted from the working. Quite a few of them are common to several old gods, who, of course, are all officially retired. But the avatars are a kind of linchpin. They stop a variety of apocalypses and ragnaroks from kicking off, which could be messy."

"Like Death," said September. "He used to be an angel, but then again, he also used to be Pluto and Hades, and she was Kali and Erishkigal too. So if Dante wanted angels and demons *out*, but an avatar of the concept of death in..."

"He forged a pact with the Sisterhood of Witches, and between them they made a special tarot deck. The Magician, in that deck, is the embodiment of all the tricky, cunning gods of technology and cleverness, and it's part of a lineage that goes back to Leonardo Da Vinci. Through me. To *you*. Not – and this is important – to the machine that I worked on with Silas Rosewood, for section W. The thing they called B.I.S.H.O.P."

This time the stutter shattered Septivarian up into cubes and bits, crazing his face with static. The boom which followed was much louder, and a billow of dust blew out from the elevator shaft that led back to the library.

"And *that* means we're out of time. Come on. There's two things you need before... ohhhh, *bother*."

"What?"

The Hologram re-formed, but there was something definitely wrong with it. Little blips and pops tweaked at its polygon mesh, giving September's great-great-granddad a wildly fluctuating frown.

"It seems they've brought an Ogris. You must have really made an impression, September! Now, drink this, put this on, and don't let them capture you." A slim chrome capsule rose from the floor beside him, opening to reveal a lab coat and a glass bottle of black liquid, flecked with green. "You need to know about the B.I.S.H.O.P biocomputer, and what went wrong with it, but..."

Unfortunately, September would never hear another word from her holographic grandsire.

Because at that moment Cedric came flying out of the elevator shaft on a flat trajectory, his blue jeans on fire. He pinballed off several large hanging lamps, and then smashed through the tangle of machinery which projected Professor Archimedes, snuffing out its light in a shatterburst of broken glass.

"As it turns out, I haven't really got this under control," he croaked, rolling on one side. Glass fragments squealed and popped as he held up one arm. "But I do have *this*. The first vampire down the ladder was going pretty fast, and all I had to do was hold the scythe out sideways."

His hand opened, and a crumpled and bloodied tarot card dropped out. It unfurled like a leaf as September watched, becoming straight and unblemished again. The Knight of Staves.

"Can you walk?" she asked, helping to pull Cedric to his feet. Under the robe, he was wearing his old 1950s biker clothes, definitely the worse for wear. The great silver hourglass which contained the tarot of Death hung heavy around his neck. "Because I think we'd better get out of here. Septivarian said something about an *Ogris*, and he sounded pretty serious."

Her eyes flitted to the open silver pod, and its contents. *Perhaps*, thought September, *all of this escalating mayhem was part of the unlucky curse, still unbroken. If so...*

"Hey! You really shouldn't just drink whatever you find in a mad science lab, miss!" warned Cedric, as September grabbed the little phial and slugged back its contents. They fizzed, with the flavour of asparagus, peppermint and old iron.

The effects on general background luck could have been measured on a handy leprechaumeter (which, neither of them realised) was hanging in a supply cupboard not three paces away.

However, this would have been impossible to read above the roar and crash of very obvious doom which now came from the elevator shaft. It was followed by a billowing cloud of concrete dust, and the mangled remains of a very sad-looking vampire.

Cedric bent over, wincing, and picked up his scythe. It was all folded up into a little chrome tube again, but with a bang against a nearby counter-top it unfolded. The young reaper leaned on it like a crutch, one leg bent at a funny angle.

"That'll be the last of them. All the Draculas from every single film and comic book, I suppose. He's going to have a headache back in the Aught, pulling himself back together."

Out of the dust loomed an iceberg of flesh. It knuckled like a bloated ape, all got up in rhinestones and flares and tassels, and yes – it, too, was Elvis Presley. Just ten times the size.

Some voodoo science had been wrought on this specimen, involving slabs of jiggling fat and corded muscle, all pierced with tubes that glowed atomic green. 'No oil painting' didn't even *begin* to cover it. Jowls wobbled, spilling drool. Its aviator shades were stapled to its flesh. September noted a bunch of salami-sized fingers, a pompadour haircut – and the way it ripped the elevator doors from their mountings with barely a grunt of effort.

"*That's* an Ogris?" she asked. "Where do they get them

from?"

Ced shrugged.

"They were mentioned in the PostMortis operations manual, under 'unnatural hazards'. We never got to do that chapter, though. I *did* mention it was my first day, right?"

The Ogris was on a chain, snapped tight to a collar around it's volcano-shaped neck. And at the other end of that chain was the youngest and most handsome Elvis which September had yet seen; a cowboy Elvis, in a white stetson hat and aviator shades, smoking a cigarette. He tipped the brim of his hat up and grinned, when he was absolutely sure he was the centre of attention.

"Well, well, well, missy. I see Bubba here has got you cornered, and there's pretty much no place left to go. Are y'all about ready to entertain a deal?"

Cowboy Elvis sauntered across the parquet, tugging his belligerent pet behind him. The stacked heels of his boots made little clicking noises that set September's teeth on edge. She slipped the big, stained lab coat from the pod around her shoulders as if it was armour, feeling the reassuring weight of metal in its pockets.

"A deal? With you, I assume... *people?* I suppose it can't hurt to listen, though I sort of have to add – just for appearances, really – one step closer and I'll turn you inside-out."

She gestured to some of the wyrd machinery suspended from the ceiling, and hovered her other hand meaningfully over a bank of switches.

"You have no idea what that does," smirked Elvis – but there was a little twitch of worry there, too. And he stopped.

"You're right," said September. "I don't know what all of this does. It could give you super-powers. It could just give you a nasty disease. But you know my great-granddad just about as well as I do, now that I'm the Magician. You can be certain it's not going to be pleasant."

Cowboy Elvis held up his hands, appealing for calm.

"Woah, now! Hear us out, first. If you want threats, then we can start that way. Bubba here can pretzel a tank, and without me to keep him calm, he's a bit of a handful." He hoisted one perfect eyebrow. "See? I can do all nasty, just like you. But I can also offer a way out of this terrible, confusing day. One which makes us aaaalllllll happy."

"I'm listening."

"We can let you just walk away, so long as you let us write this up as a diplomatic incident. Septivarian Archimedes is dead. This is just the fireworks and shenanigans you get when a man like that shuffles off to the Aught, or wherever he's eventually headed. You just got caught in the crossfire, young lady."

"And if we both fail to acknowledge that *load of steaming horsecrap* for what it is?"

Elvis arched one monochrome eyebrow.

"Then you let the authorities take the memories of this whole afternoon away. Like they did for your folks, all them years back. You'll go back to school, and back to your friends, and your nice normal little life, and you'll even think that the dear old professor died peacefully in his sleep. They can edit in memories of a *very* touching funeral."

For an instant, there was part of her which wanted to agree. To just collapse, and fold, and do what a good, normal person should. That part of her knew that it shouldn't *want* the memories of the last few hours, and that a lovely normal life awaited, just on the other side of their erasure.

Then the rest of her woke up, and felt the fish-hook realities tucked into the Dead Elvis' words.

That these things had done something to her parents, long ago.

That they offered to cut up her brain, to suit their plan for the world.

And that (and here, the rage found its spark, and rose up inside her on enormous wings) they thought she wanted to *forget* her great-great-granddad. The pain was still there, and it was raw, but it was *hers*.

The part of her which owned that grief was the greater part. The part which loved weird facts, and heavy metal, and animals, and thunderstorms, and old cartoons. It came down on the little construct she'd built to fool the world, talons out. The right kind of ears would have heard the tiny dead-lightbulb crack of it, ending.

"Is that you final offer?" asked September, in a voice that made even Cedric back away a pace or two. One hand reached into the lab coat, down deep into a pocket which she knew was there, and drew forth a huge and ornate pistol, far too long to have fit inside. It was all glowing valves and brass gears – and a muzzle which depicted a screaming angel's face.

"You were right before," she said. "I have no idea about most of this. But I know that this coat is a Class Twelve Inverseract of Holding, and it's made to link up the things you need *right now* with the spaces where your alternate-dimensional selves have already built them. I know, because I have quite a lot of Professor Archimedes' memories in my head. And not a single one of them says I should trust you."

Those memories were twisting and popping behind her eyes. One, for example, told her that this gun was called Lights Out, and that it worked by making its target unobservable. Seeing as it was only the act of being observed which collapsed the waveform of a thing's probability into particles, it had the effect of making its targets *cease to have the potential to exist.*

"*Wait!*" stammered Cowboy Elvis.

And —

"*Vait!*" said another voice, this one rich and velvety and distinctly Transylvanian. "You know zhis thing can't be trusted. *Authority!* Pah! They all vant you to be a little tiny peasant in their big feudal system! I should know!"

"I thought you said you'd got them all?" whispered September.

"There were a lot of bats," shrugged Cedric.

"You're a fool to trust *him*, too," said Vlad Tepes, otherwise known as Dracula, the Impaler, stepping out from behind what appeared to be a fusion stellerator. "You think PostMortis are your candy-pixie little happytime friends? Come *on*, girl! He's here to keep an eye on you. They're just more bureaucrats. Part of ze system which oppresses ze common ghost."

Vlad certainly didn't look 'common'. He was also the spit and image of all those old paintings September had seen in the nastier kind of history books. The original-recipe Dracula wore a long, droopy moustache, red-lacquered armour, and a red velvet hat like a tiny plant-pot upside down on his head.

"So *you're* the heroic resistance?" she asked "You tried to use me as a human juice box, mister The Impaler. Which, by the way, is not a particularly trustworthy name."

"Exactly!" said Cowboy Elvis.

"Shut up!" snapped September, levelling Lights Out at him without looking around.

Vlad shrugged.

"You get vhat history gives you. And if you know your history, you know that I was never a backstabber. At least, not *metaphorically*. I gave 100 per cent to the cause.

Ottoman Empire on a stick, for life." He bumped his fist against his chest, in the style of a golden-era gangsta rapper. "Now I'm working for civil rights for the Unfairly Deceased. Dead lives matter!"

"Terrorist!" spat Cedric. "Your whole bloody gang is nothing but a cheap cover for illegal introcism!"

"There's a reason for the status quo, buddy," drawled Cowboy Elvis. "Now, if you'd all just..."

"Shut up!" said September, Ced and Vlad at once. September flipped a switch, and emerald energies boiled through the tubes of Lights Out. The vampire smiled, showing a lot of fang.

"Look, I'll admit ve got off on the wrong foot. Ze whole seduction thing vas mainly force of habit. But you haff to admit, it vas *you* who swung ze fire poker. And your skeletal friend told you they've been snuffing ze wrong people, right? That's vhy zhey came for you. That's vhy zhey came for your great-great-granddad, too. They're *corrupt*."

"You just want to come back to the Materia so you can impale people!" snarled Cedric. "We know your M.O."

Dracula's smile turned sad.

"Alas, it has been my curse. Pop culture has driven me a little mad, unless I really concentrate. I've been doing a lot of work on myself, though, these past decades. I've taken up knitting."

"Knitting?" asked September. The conversation seemed to have taken a few hairpin turns.

"It's technically impaling lots of little loops of wool. My therapist calls it a displacement exercise."

"Displacement..." muttered September, only just realising that Cowboy Elvis had gone very quiet. That, in fact, he was mumbling something into the sleeve of his denim jacket.

"Hey!" she said. "This is the part where both of you leave.

I'd give you some talk about the easy way and the hard way, but you know the score. This is *my* home ground, lads. I hold all the cards."

"About zhat..." said the Count, one finger raised. The muzzle of Lights Out dipped back toward him, and the finger wilted. "You might vant to giff me back ze Knight of Staves. That's vhat these greasy Elvi are after. Never trust a monster from ze inside-out!"

The black-and-white cowboy smirked.

"Good advice, coming from a monster from the Aught. But it's immaterial. That backup you were worried about is already on its way. And, considerin' you might listen to this ole bloodsucker here, reckon I've about changed my mind. Bubba?"

The Ogris roared. Ropes of drool dripped, and jowls wobbled, as the thing's mouth opened wider and wider, becoming a maw the size of a wheelie bin. Cowboy Elvis held the chain up between two fingers, then let it go.

"Kill."

It was the last thing he said, because September took his advice. Lights Out spat a rod of marbled darkness, shot through with little crackles of crimson. It struck Cowboy Elvis high on the chest, spinning him around. As he fell he began to blur, like an old picture in a newspaper from the nineteen-twenties. Every little dot which made him up went drifting away from its neighbour, de-cohering. Then he faded out, with a sizzle like frying bacon.

The last thing which popped out of existence was the very surprised look on his face.

September spun, the gun gripped in a way she shouldn't have found so familiar. She was just in time for two things to happen, in a blur of black and silver.

Dracula whipped Lights Out from her hands, reversed it in mid-air, and aimed it back at her head. The old

Transylvanian moved faster than should be possible, leaving a small thunderclap and a cloud of vampire-shaped dust behind him.

But Cedric was nearly as fast. And 'nearly' is good enough, when you're armed with the most dreadful garden implement in the known universe. A reaping arc sizzled through the air, severing atom from atom, and sliced Lights Out cleanly in half.

Then Ced changed his grip for the backswing, grasped the stave of his weapon in both hands, and used it to push September to the floor.

They slid across the parquet as something massive thundered overhead, punching huge footprints into the ground on either side of them.

"Oh, *bollocks*," sighed Vlad – just before Bubba hit him with the impact of a freight-train hauling lead. The Ogris slapped into him with a meaty crunch, powering through three rows of laboratory benches, shattering glass and scattering papers. A huge fist reared up, then came back down like a steam hammer, shattering the tiled floor with the back of Dracula's head.

"Can't ve... SLAM! Talk about... SLAM! Zhis... SLAM!... Mister Presley... SLAM!"

"We have to get out of here!" said Cedric, eyes wild. "That cowboy wasn't kidding. For something like this, they'll mobilise all Elvisdom. There's *three* of Dante's Tarot here, along with whatever your granddad was working on. Stuff they were willing to break the laws of Death to get their tentacles on!"

September fixed him with a very pointed look, until he realised he was still lying on top of her.

"Oh! Sorry!" He tried to stand, but his leg buckled under him, and he rolled onto his back next to September. "I don't suppose that railway line actually goes anywhere, does it?"

A flash of Endarkenment lit up September's memory, then. Or rather, it played a searchlight beam over a tumbling fragment of Septivarian's memory, lodged in her head. Suddenly, she knew *exactly* where those silver rails ended up.

"And to think I've been avoiding it all day," she mused. "End of the line..."

There was a detonation of magic behind them, and the Ogris came looping through the air, sailing over the pair of them like a rhinestone-encrusted blimp. Behind it was the painted ceiling; a heavenly Dante, passing what appeared to be a tarot card to Leonardo Da Vinci. Two knights with handlebar moustaches stood in attendance.

"We can narrow it down, too. The southern line seems to have traffic," said Cedric. "Look!"

Lights were indeed moving down the tunnel – the one which led back toward London. They appeared to be the beams of innumerable torches, and they were accompanied by the crunch and rumble of hundreds of marching feet. Elvisdom, or some other mysterious branch of the Bureau Innominandum, had indeed been mobilised.

"We can't just run!" said September, as Vlad Dracula levitated past, hissing. A brushed-steel freezer clobbered him right in the kisser. "Great Grandad's last project is right here, and it's what they're after. I've led them right to it!"

September's words were cut off by a vast detonation, which shook the entire underground lair. The arches shuddered, and tiles cracked and fell. Metal rebar creaked and groaned. Soldiers were spewing from the tunnel now, in Bureau black, all got up in body armour and visored helmets. Vlad had heard her, and he battered the Ogris with a roundhouse punch, turning with one bloody fist upraised.

"*Exactly!* That's vhy zhey sent me! To beg you to join us! Ze professor never vanted all zhis to go to the Bureau, or to your government. And you're the only vun who can make sense of it. You have his wild ideas, now. We can... *urk!*"

The vampire's plea was cut off by a tufted projectile, which sprouted suddenly in his neck.

"Hypercoagulant!" he gurgled, hands clawing at his throat. A flurry of darts smacked into the Ogris, too, catching it hefting a second freezer in one meaty hand. A smile spread across its jowls like warm butter, and it farted hugely as it fell.

"*Drop your weapons! You are surrounded! Any attempt to utilise eldritch powers will be answered with lethal force!*"

That was the leader of the Bureau death-squad, who was having a jolly good time. They'd given him a big bullhorn, and permission to use every clichéd catch-phrase from every action blockbuster ever made, at full volume.

"*Come out with your hands up! Y'all boys are in a whole mess of trouble! Achtung! For you, ze war is over!*"

Mirror-visored troops secured the Ogris, lashing it to a gurney with nylon rope. Others had brought a government-issue coffin for Vlad, who was snoring loudly.

"Fire brigade were right," said a jackbooted medic, saluting the commander. "Proper undead. Possessing a real body. He's never seen the inside of a book, let alone come out of one. We don't know why the librarian was covering for 'im with that half-arsed story about amorous grannies. But we think it's got something to do with the girl in the lab coat."

A ring of automatic weapons muzzled in at Cedric and September. It was the kind of thing which could be quite offputting.

"Ahh, yes," said the commander, peeling back his visor. He said it through the bullhorn, then seemed to remember his manners, and tucked the offending device away. Under the helmet he was a leathery old buzzard, with the clipped moustache, weathered jowls and steely little ball-bearing eyes of a parade-ground sadist.

"The heir to all of this, eh? September Hyacinth Normalsson, civilian, age seventeen and a bit. How bloody convenient. You know, we've been waiting for *decades* to get our mitts on Dark Lazarus. We couldn't touch it when your great-great-grandpa was in charge, because he was a stubborn old goat. You, however, look like the type who might be easier to persuade."

"Because I'm a teenage girl?" asked September, with withering sarcasm. It bounced right off of the commander's sheer militant crustiness.

"Because you can't torture a supervillain. Half of them have countermeasures, and the other half enjoy it."

This conversation had taken a turn for the extremely grim. Cedric snarled with anger and pushed himself forward, wincing as he put his weight on his injured leg.

"Hey! why don't you pick on someone your own size, pal?"

The commander shrugged.

"Frankly, the whole idea of the army is that we can pick on anyone we like. We've got tanks. There's not much anybody can do about it."

It was at that moment that the commander noticed a hand creeping into his pocket. The hand, which was clad in a rather moth-eaten furry glove, extracted one of the commander's special hand-rolled cigarillos,[24] and a match was struck. The hand, which was connected to a similarly

---

24. Which the Commander smoked to try and give himself some distinctive character.

threadbare furry arm, much patched and stitched, conveyed the cigarillo to an elderly set of lips, all fuzzed about with nicotine-stained whiskers.

"Well now. See, the thing is... the thing is, yer'honour, that there unfortunately *is* someone who can do quite a bit about it. Ladies and gents? The big dramatic pose, right sharpish?"

The lights went out. Soldiers swore and cursed. Torch beams skittered like spider legs. But then a huge overhead spot slammed on, with the clunk and hum of truly giant capacitors. It illuminated a trio of figures, posed like a cinema billboard.

The Red Mobster loomed at the centre, in full battle panoply, his natty fedora and 1930s dance-hall suit augmented with twin drum-fed tommy guns, attached to his gigantic claws. To his left was Medusa Oblongata, her giant skull-dome pulsing with light, and a hundred mechanical serpents bearing her up off the ground in the lotus position.

Stoatman was on the right, still cheekily puffing on his stolen cigarillo; he'd used his incredibly slippery powers to blip from one place to another without so much as an intervening shadow. Now his half-cowl of stained towelling was up over his face, and his little furry paws had sprouted claws.

September was sure that the Invisible Prince was there too, but there was absolutely no way of knowing if he was taking part in this big, dramatic pose or not.

"The Doom Commission – Devilish and Demented Deliverers of Darkness and Domination!" shouted Stoatman, who suddenly seemed far less silly, and a lot less elderly. He sketched a little salute at the commander. "We're friends of the family, sort of thing. Now, I believe you was threatening to torture my old mate's granddaughter, sonny. How d'ya think that's gonna work out for you?"

The commander smiled. It was a nasty, smug little expression.

"I *suppose* that the hundred elite soldiers I have surrounding this facility will blast you bunch of has-been geriatrics into a selection of cardboard coffins... unless you stand down immediately."

Stoatman winked at September.

"That one there, then," he said, gesturing to a visor-helmeted trooper. "What's his name?"

The commander looked puzzled for a second. He turned and looked, squinting.

"Well, in this light, with the helmet on, I, ummm..."

Stoatman chuckled, taking a big drag on his stolen cigarillo. The glowing ashen tip lit up his face for a second, and it was a study in craggy, wrinkled malice.

"Oh dear oh *dear*. You know what happens when a bunch of nameless henchmen confront a vastly outnumbered band of plucky superhumans, commander. That's basic training, that is. In fact, we haven't heard *your* name, either. Could be you're not even real. No wife and kids back home, no budgie, no spaniel, no bloody hope and shite for brains. We're even doing a big redemption arc here, which makes us anti-heroes. I *do* bloody hope your insurance is paid up."

"This is preposterous! Men! Prepare to fire!"

Stoatman finished his smoke, and flicked the butt away into the darkness.

"Now, September, I knows what you're thinking. Your Grandad's mates are going to make mincemeat out of these poor muppets, and aside from not wanting to look, you'll be perfectly fine. But I'll tell you a secret. This is likely to be one of those famous-last-stand scenarios. Redemption arc, like I said. And the problem with the government, is they always have more damn fool lads lining up to play at soldiers. We're going to have to blow this place up, to keep the guv'nor's secrets safe."

September nodded. She understood.

"So in about three seconds, Medusa here, who has all the codes for your Grandad's computers and such, is gonna drop the old Befuddlermobile down onto those rails. Young man, can you drive?"

Cedric managed to give a wobbly thumbs-up.

"Good. Then you floor it down the tunnel, and don't look back."

"You're not going anywhere!" bellowed the commander, his face tuning beetroot red.

"Let's see, then," said Stoatman. "Doom Commission, are you ready?"

"Aye!"

"Yerp!"

"Zpharg Glorp Sneeble!"

A peculiar moment of calm descended, charged with hot and crawling sparks of portent. A hundred guns were aimed at the four elderly supervillains of the Doom Commission – even the invisible one. For an instant there was a flicker in the air, and then the Prince finally dropped his chameleon-cloak, for the first time in seventy five years.

He turned out to be a pale blue, elderly gent with a long white beard, overalls made of scaled armour, and tiny little crown perched on the top of his bald head. However, clenched in his liver-spotted fists were a pair of alien pistols the size of toaster ovens.

"Glargo! Sneep bla – *fooom!*"

"What he said," chuckled Stoatman, as a panel in the ceiling opened. A seriously hot-rodded 1936 Plymouth was dropped onto the rails by robotic claws, and a shimmering blue pentacle of light lit up the tunnel mouth, down-line. "Do like your grandpa would have, and save the world! But first, run! Run, like there's hell behind you, because I brought a whole steamin' helping of it with me!"

The tension broke. The guns roared and racketed. Energy bloomed and burst. Beams sliced through benches, ripped across the tiled ceiling, and gouged trenches in the parquet. The clash of powers swelled inside a bubble of noise and light, blasting September backwards so that she staggered, one hand in front of her eyes.

"No!" she shouted – furious that she couldn't articulate the words which were burning in her throat. A simple 'no' hardly seemed enough. But...

"Come on!" shouted Cedric. "You heard him! This place is coming down! We have to leave, *now!*"

He spun her around, and together they piled into the Befuddlermobile, an utterly black, wickedly chopped machine with tyres like liquorice doughnuts. Seat belts snapped from their recesses automatically, binding September tight to the passenger's seat. Lights flared across the dash, and the car's massive seven-litre hemi V8[25] kicked into life, sucking down gallons of oxygen through a question-mark shaped supercharger scoop.

"I think it knows where it's going," said Cedric, who was mummified in a four-point racing harness. "I can't even reach the steering wheel!"

The gear shifter clicked into first. The accelerator pedal blipped, of its own accord. Ahead of them, that glowing pentacle filled the world, huge and ghostly.

And, as a surge of wild acceleration mashed her back into the seat cushions, and the world blurred, and the rumble of collapsing masonry followed on behind, September knew where they were going, too.

---

25. The immortal 426. If you know what it sounds like, you can hear it right now.

Into the tunnel, and into darkness. Then into the warping, seething light. Into a space where reality was crinkled up like a dirty napkin.

Into the Aught.

Suture Five
Void Chamber

THIS ROOM WAS *not* the kind which you ever wanted to see the inside of. It was buried deep beneath Westminster; an under-dungeon scrabbled into the bedrock. It was so secret that the cleaning staff had to work blindfolded.

This was not conducive to very accurate dusting, but then again, a few cobwebs in the corners helped create the right ambience, it was felt.

Blindfolded was also how the Chief Inspector of Police was introduced to the secret little room, manhandled by two stern and lumpen special forces types. He had a bag over his head, emblazoned with the heraldry of the Bureau Innominandum – a lidless eye and crossed, broken keys on a shield of black. Somehow, he'd gotten the notion that this whole rigmarole was part of his brother Masons playing a prank on him. This might have been something to do with the scent of very expensive brandy which surrounded him in a flammable halo.

"Ho ho, good one, deacon Fred! Making it seem like the elevator went down for forty floors, with all the rumbling and creaking... genius! I suppose when you take off the hoodwink, there'll be all the brothers waiting with a big bottle of sherry, and..."

A pair of fingers snapped, crisp as a gunshot in the musty air. The hoodwink came off, tugged away by a hand with fingers like chorizos. The Chief Inspector felt himself pressed firmly (but not unkindly) into a large leather chair, as neon tubes blurred above.

"Deacon Fred? Brother warden Geoff? Lads?"

But there was not another Masonic brother to be seen, let alone a nice vintage drop. The Chief Inspector, whose name was Rupert, felt his police-issue pushbroom moustache begin to bristle, and the hairs stand up along his forearms. The room swum into focus, and it was not a reassuring sight.

This place was known as the Void Chamber, and it was the opposite of the little star-spangled room up above, where British royals had once dealt with the dirty dealings of state. John Dee had been its architect, and so it was outfitted in the height of Tudor fashion, all black-lacquered joinery and dark mirrors. While Star Chamber was the secret heart of monarchical power in the realm above, Void Chamber was the scheming little hindbrain of the world below. A world of spies and sorcerers, monsters, assassins and thieves. Some of those descriptions even referred to separate people.

Today, there were only four chairs pulled up around the ornate obsidian table, with its inset map of nebulae in the night sky, rendered in haematite. The chairs were huge and high-backed, with a spread-winged raven carved atop each one.

Perched in one, all angles and elbows, was Doctor Silas Rosewood, code-name PROPHET, the director-general of Section W, the weird science division of Her Majesty's Occult Forces. Chief Inspector Rupert had no idea who Rosewood was, but the man's beaky nose, inch-thick John Lennon spectacles and buckled-up black leather coat made him look like some kind of Nazi caricature; an image compounded by the fact that his teeth, when he smiled, were the bright green of peas in a pod.

September would have had some idea – this was the very same Rosewood who had helped her great-granddad design the B.I.S.H.O.P biocomputer for project Dark Lazarus.

The second chair belonged to Elvis Presley. A huge,

resplendently plump comeback-special version, all in black and white, and wearing an actual crown. He was demolishing a bucket of fried chicken; not one of the paper ones with the red and white stripes, but an old-fashioned metal bucket, of the kind you might use to feed a squadron of hogs.

This was rather surprising, but before Rupert could splutter out something obvious and appalled, he noticed who occupied the final chair. *The one right across from him.* Some dim religious twitch, whacked into him at boarding school, made him cross himself as he looked into a pair of eyes like the barrels of twin mechanical pencil sharpeners.

"*Mrs Thatcher!*" he breathed, feeling chilled and idolatrous.

Conservative to the core, Rupert knew that buttoned-down face and that iron-grey haircut instantly. He'd seen them emblazoned across scenes of riot and mayhem on the old vacuum-tubed, wood-panelled televisions of his youth. Back in that beige-tinted time, when he'd first found out that people would pay you to stomp on hippies.

"You're *back*, Ma'am! Not that you, umm, ever left, apparently, but it's, errr, good to see you."

Then the very familiar figure leaned forward, letting light wash over that six o'clock news face. It was just a bit *too* perfect, and just a bit *too* shiny, as if it had been preserved under plastic. Rupert fancied that it moved all wrong, as well; with the whirr and click of expensive camera lenses sliding into focus.

"No, you little berk, I'm a robot," growled the ersatz Prime Minister. "They built this thing in the 80s, in case she ever got assassinated. After that business with the lizard shapeshifters, I was in need of somewhere to keep my brain, and this is it."

"So you're not... HER?" asked Arthur, deflating back into

his chair. "I just thought, with all the secret tunnels, and the bag over my head, and Elvis here, that perhaps there was some kind of jolly exciting conspiracy going on."

The robot Thatcher fixed him with a look that could have sharpened tungsten.

"I happen to be the Secretary-General of the Bureau Innominandum. Minister for the Far-From-Home Office. Ambassador to the Things Beyond. Lady Marjorie Goosegarden."

"The troops call her Mother Goose," chimed in Doctor Rosewood. "But you can stick with Your Ladyship."

"And who are *you?*" asked Rupert, getting back just a little bit of his chief-policeman's attitude. *By God, he wouldn't be rattled by this bunch of charlatans and a robot PM!*

"I'm the one who gets to say 'We're the ones who ask the questions,'" said Rosewood, with a pea-green grin.

He pushed a big red button inset into the table in front of him, and a whack of electricity inserted itself between every one of the Chief Inspector's vertebrae at once, then twisted. Smoke wafted up from out of his collar and cuffs as he flung himself backward in his chair, only to find that it was bolted to the floor.

Rupert remembered some things from the 'bad old days', then, when certain friendly bobbies were rather free with the truncheon, come time for citizens to 'help them with their enquiries'. A chair bolted to the floor was *not* a good sign.

"We're the ones who ask the questions!" smirked the nasty, leather-wrapped Doctor. "See? Doesn't that make this all so much easier for you to understand?"

Rupert nodded weakly.

"Well, you will be pleased to know that there *is* a jolly good conspiracy going on," said Mother Goose, lighting up a cigarette with the tip of one finger. "Two, actually, and they're both rip-snorters. The trouble is, the big one isn't one of ours. And that's somewhat of a sticky wicket. Isn't that right, Doctor?"

Rosewood nodded.

"On a scale of wicket stickiness, this would be able to stop a fast-bowl from nine out of ten of the best cricketers from the West Indies, or even Australia. Very highly oleaginous, especially about the bails."

Rupert dithered a little. One of the big, burly commandos plonked a coffee mug full of brandy down in front of him, and he knocked it back in one swallow.

"The first issue is the Repo problem you boys at the Met are having. What do you know about its distribution network?"

Rupert grimaced, though this might have been something to do with the half-litre of hard liquor which had just hit his stomach lining.

"That new drug? Well, we know what it *does*. Folks all over the city have been caught with it. They say it gives you vivid, powerful hallucinations of past lives; medieval nonsense, regency times, even some Roman hi-jinks. But the people on it wander around all dazed, like they're amazed by things like traffic lights and kebab shops. Some of them get nasty, and nearly all of them gabble some kind of nonsense language."

Rosewood chuckled.

"I think you'll find it's not nonsense, officer. It's probably a spectrum, from old Latin and Gaelic through to Middle English, Norman French, and a bit of dark ages Danish thrown in. Those people *really are* experiencing past lives."

Rupert scoffed, as only a drunken senior policeman can.

"Oh, *riiiiight*. That'll be why some of the dealers have been bloody astrologers and ghost-botherers, then. They all believe in that rubbish, and think that Repo proves their point about reincarnation."

"It's worse than that," said Mrs Goosegarden. "It's *pre-deincarnation*. **Possession**. The users of Repo have a nice little trip down someone else's memory lane, while their body runs around possessed by a dead person. That's why you've been having all that trouble with Jack the Ripper again."

Rupert's face went white, then, as his blood drained away like the tide going out.

"That's... I mean... *how did you know?* That's highly classified, that is! Nobody knows about that investigation!"

Elvis burped heartily, and grinned.

"Well, uh yuh see, baby, we are pretty much the *definition* of highly classified, thankyouverymuch. Between us and your government, we keep all the things you don't need to know on the hush-hush."

At a certain point, the rational mind can only take so much, even if it is fortified with twenty-five year aged brandy.

"And what the hell have *you* got to do with it, Mister so-called Presley?" asked Rupert, all incredulous. "I suppose you're here representing some bloody long acronym from our Yankee friends, who want to play 'men in black' in my damn city?"

"Chief Inspector!" hissed the robot Margaret Thatcher. "The Supreme Aaron is an *ambassador* from our friends in dark dimensions of unspeakable madness and terror! Try to be diplomatic!"

This was a fact which Rupert was very much prepared to disbelieve... until, for a sickening moment, the face of Elvis Presley was torn away by pudgy fingers, revealing the actuality beneath.

There was a light which was darkness manifest. There was a sound like a cold, dry wind roaring over aeons of ice. Tentacles popped out around the edges. A scream froze solid in the Chief Inspector's throat, then melted again, leaving an aftertaste of hot tin.

Then, just as swiftly as it began, the horror was over. The room seemed to settle back into its comfortable, sane angles again, wood creaking and popping. Elvis shrugged.

"We're from someplace where diplomacy didn't work. Where old JFK was busy in bed when the Cuban Missile Crisis kicked off. So we know the value of talkin' things out, understand?"

"Whhhuuuuub whub whub. You... blargle... sneep." said Rupert. Doctor Rosewood popped a handy syringe of something blue into his neck.

"I'm a little beige plastic pelican named Percival, and I'm off to the strawberry factory," said the Chief Inspector, with a wide and glassy grin.

"Too much!" snarled Mother Goose. She reached across the table with one extendable hand and slapped him. Rosewood gave a wry smile, and took a little dose himself.

"*Right,*" said the robotic Prime Minister, as Rupert's pupils wobbled back to similar sizes. "Here's the facts. We know that this Repo epidemic is being engineered by someone from the other side. A dead 'un. And, up until this evening, we had no idea who was bringing it through into the known world. There's no embassy in the Aught, which is what they call their little mortuary funland over there. Undiscovered country, and all that rot."

"Some of my boys were investigatin' a little loose end," added Elvis. "From the age of super-heroism. Nothin' too special, but it concerned a no-goodnik called the Befuddler."

"He was... ummm... a bit before my time," said Rupert, whose brain felt like it had been upholstered in cheese.

"Well, so was Jack the Ripper, but he's been distracting

your best and brightest for the past two weeks," growled Mrs Goosegarden. "What Mister Presley was getting around to, was that during this investigation we located a major stockpile of Repo, in the town of Little-Mean-on-the-Average."

"That, and the old villain's great-great-granddaughter. Who appears to have become rotten, not too far from the family tree," said Rosewood. "She's leading the Doom Commission, who have, most explosively, come out of retirement. And she must be stopped."

"Then there's *this*," grated Mrs Goosegarden, gesturing to one side impatiently. A special-forces type rolled in a television set of the old, vacuum-tube variety, complete with a potted begonia on a doily on top. A blur of static collapsed, into the face of Vlad the Impaler.

He was tied down to what appeared to be a dentist's chair, and he looked none too happy about his predicament.

"This is a known associate of your Ripper friend, from back in Victorian Times. A Mr Dracula, of Hollywood fame, in fact. He had some very interesting things to tell our boys from the Ministry... eventually. The dentist was most persuasive."

Of course, thought a very nasty part of the Chief Inspector's mind. *How do you torture a vampire? Well, imagine how sensitive those big, hollow fangs must be. They can taste with 'em, after all...*

On the screen, the Count's eyes darted back and forth, to where various chromed dental instruments ringed the chair. He was dripping with sweat, and babbling what sounded like nonsense.

"Dark Lazarus. It all comes back to Dark Lazarus. Your bosses, watching this – I know you're there! Yes, they know what zhat means, even if you don't, you poor little peasants. Zhat old fool of a professor, he wanted ze lost tarot, ze Devil,

for your stupid plan to beat ze Russians. But it's not yours. It's ours. Ze Devil belongs to ze afterlife, not ze Materia! And vhen ve get him back, you'll have a proper respect for ze dead again!"

The video blurred, as a grim-faced man in welding goggles holding a brush laden down with triple-stripe toothpaste leaned in. Vlad began to scream.

Mother Goose clicked a remote the size of a small bible, cutting off the vampire's shrieks.

"See? That Professor he mentioned is the Befuddler, AKA Septivarian Archimedes. It was *his* super-team, and *his* bloody progeny, who also caused an incident at the Little-Mean-on-the-Average General Hospital today. We found three thousand litres of Repo on the scene, and twelve Elvi lost their, um… well, unlives, I suppose."

Rupert wrung his hands, wishing most vehemently that he'd gone into a more sane line of work, such as weasel necromancy.

"But… Mrs Thatcher! Mr Presley! You… the nasty science fellow. *I'm just an old-fashioned British Police Inspector!* All I do is tell people they're nicked, smoke a pipe, drive an interesting old Jaguar convertible and enjoy a selection of very nice whiskeys down the Lodge on Thursdays. I can't help you with any of this supernatural mumbo jumbo!"

"This mumbo," said Mother Goose, leaning forward seriously, "Is very jumbo indeed. Repo poses a clear and present threat to the difference between the living and the dead. If there's a revolving door to the afterlife, what's the point in killing bastards like Hitler? Someone over there is running a regular Haight-Ashbury acid racket, letting them waltz right back. We had Vlad the Impaler busting up a suburban library today. I hate to think what Attila the Hun could accomplish in a crowded supermarket. Or how about Genghis Khan in the middle of Covent Garden?"

"But what can I *do?*" wailed Rupert, feeling the walls of Void Chamber close in, and the implacable faces of his tormentors begin to spin like a nightmare carousel.

"Get your nastiest, most old-fashioned, hobnail-wearing bobbies. Arm them up with the best riot squad clobber you can dig out of the basement. Then head up to Little-Mean-on-the-Average, and find me the Befuddler's grand-kid. Find me September Normalsson."

They didn't give him a chance to protest. Burly hands gripped the Chief Inspector under his armpits, and hauled him from, his chair, his heels leaving twin grooves in the thick black carpet as they headed for the door.

"Wait!" he cried. "What's the second conspiracy?"

Robot Thatcher nodded, seemingly very pleased that he'd asked.

"You'll notice there's no bag over your head on the way out, Inspector. That's because the second conspiracy is one that *you're now part of.* Try to tell anyone about all this, and they'll think you've lost your tiny little mind. But trust me. *We'll know.* And then you'll be *his* problem."

Mrs Goosegarden pointed one pale and plasticky finger across the table at the Supreme Aaron, master of the Dead Elvi. Who smiled, and waved cheerfully.

Rupert shuddered. He remembered (with all those bits of his brain which allowed him to) the moment when that thing's face had come off, and he'd seen into the heart of the nuclear fire. To the endless loop of erasure which churned in the creature's borrowed soul...

Instinct kicked in. He saluted, like a constable fresh out of training school at Hendon.

"You can count on me, ma'am. Wherever this September has gone, we'll find her."

But they wouldn't.

Because September Normalsson was dead.

Or at least, she had passed beyond the shores of mortality, and into that far and foggy other country, from whence none return. Or at least, which isn't known for it's discount duty-free section...

PART TWO

THE BOOK OF THE (MOSTLY) DEAD

Here lies an atheist
All dressed up and no place to go
Gravestone in the cemetery of
Thurmont, Maryland, USA

I told you I was sick
Gravestone of
Spike Milligan (1918-2002)

The real question is how I'm writing this
after I'm supposedly dead, isn't it?
Gravestone of Gilles J. Q. Moncreiff,
the famous 'Zombie Bishop of
Blatherstowe and Cridge'
(1301-1366; 1385-1412; 1447- ?)

Ten
Agnosticism
vs
The Actual Afterlife

SEPTEMBER AWOKE FITFULLY, in little stutters and starts, like a person rising up through the clouds of anaesthesia.

Sometimes her eyes would flicker open to see a moonlit desert, or a wash of stars airbrushed across the night. Sometimes she'd just see a glimpse of her reflection, in the safety glass of the car's window, and feel comfortably reassured that she still showed up in mirrors.

There were also times when she blurred into consciousness focused on tiny details; the little chrome buttons on the dash, or the scent of the swinging, question-mark shaped air freshener which hung from the rear-view mirror. Those times, her impressions of the silver-and-black world outside the car were as unreal as daydreams; pictures from another country.

Then came the one that caught. September sparked awake, stretching backward against her seat in a kind of full-body yawn. Copper-red curls blurred her vision, and she tucked them back behind her ears with an unselfconscious little motion, deeper than thought. She was still wearing Septivarian's great many-pocketed lab coat, and she was glad of it. The air here was cold, chilled to the temperature of the inside of a morgue.

Cedric was driving. In the lights from the dashboard and the pervasive moon-glow he was back to his 1950s self, with the big hourglass chain of the Tarot looped around his neck.

"Ahhh. You're back among the living, eh?" His face

crinkled up into a wry little smile. "Although, considering where your grandad's railway went, that's not entirely accurate."

September tried very hard to get the taste of bleach and copper out of her mouth. She even licked the sleeve of her coat before deciding that this was a terrible idea.

"Whhr hrrr we, anhuu... I mean, *where are we*, anyhow? I guessed that, with the whole Dark Lazarus thing, he must have a direct line to some kind of afterlife. After all, Lazarus came back from the dead. You'd have to go to where the dead live to find him."

Cedric shrugged.

"He's not in the phone book. But then again, all that biblical stuff's before my time, Miss. Where we are now is the Probable Desert, outside of town. 'Town' being Uncarnadine, of course. The Rotten Apple. The city that won't stay down. My home, since... well, since I made the acquaintance of that wall back in 1957, to be brutally honest."

September looked out the window again, then rolled it down, breathing in the cold, dry air of the desert. There were wrecks on either side of the road, some right up on the shoulder, and some off in the sand and cacti. They'd blip past them intermittently – gaunt metallic skeletons lit up in monochrome.

"My bike's out there, somewhere. Some machines have a little bit of soul, and when they die, they have to go somewhere too. Even the sand here is made of dead things. If we stopped, and you picked up a handful, you'd see that each grain was a decision that wasn't made. A whole different universe could have spun off from each one. They're the choices that haunt people, you know. The ones that keep you up at night, wondering what would have happened if you'd said something different, or ordered the lobster, or gone to that party, or never had that argument, and rode away angry, in the rain…"

He snapped out of it, and September saw that his knuckles were white around the wheel.

"For example," he finished, with a weak smile. "The thing is, if you drive off into the desert on one side of town, you come back on the other side. I don't know how we can possibly have just rolled in!"

September's brain was still fuzzy from sleep, and it threw her a scatter of images; of a younger Septivarian, in his Professor Archimedes costume, welding and wrenching and putting this very same car together. From wrecks, and rusted pieces, and scrap. A runic circle splashed on a garage floor in transmission fluid was there, too.

"He resurrected this car. And you're right – it **did** have a soul. That's how we've managed to drive to the afterlife, I think. The big pentacle was just for the sake of tradition, really."

"Mechanical necromancy. *Mechromancy*. Huh. That old fella had some wild ideas, all right! So now we're on the other side, September. It's, ummm… It's sometimes a bit much for new arrivals to get used to."

September had already noticed. She leaned out of the window, and skooched up on her seat to lever her head and shoulders out into the slipstream, her hair whipping back in a riot of red. It was the only colour under the pale, cold moonlight which streamed down from a great silver-white sphere in the sky.

It wasn't the moon.

It had no regolith, no craters, no abandoned 1960s technology, and no stars and stripes on a pole. There was no suggestion of a cheeky little face, either, because the suggestion was *far* from subtle.

The moon was a skull, huge and impossible. It stared

down on the Possible Desert with a hollow-socketed sadness that seemed to account for every grain of regret. And it wasn't just a disembodied cranium, floating amid a spatterburst of stars.

The night itself was, *at the same time*, the infinite blackness of transgalactic space, and a ragged cloak, its hood and hem fraying away into swirls of nebulae.

An immense arm, built of the scale of solar systems, reached out from inside that robe of darkness, looming large to become radius and ulna bones rimed with cosmic dust. It was clear, from the way it swept out and down, that all of the desert was cupped in one tectonic-sized skeletal hand.

And so was a city.

In the palm of the hand of that great, grim watcher stood an ornate carriage clock, all tarnished silver and whirring gears. It was built on the scale of mountains, and its every pillar and dial was encrusted with the works of humanity, turning it into a cathedral. Around it was tangled the very same road they were on now, lifted up on impossible stilts and braces, some of which were suspended on absolutely nothing. It joined a wide Moebius strip which looped around the clock, and which bristled with buildings on either side, ranging from castles to skyscrapers. It would not have surprised September to learn that each one of them was the ghost of a building that had been demolished, back in the *Materia Mortalis*.

The Befuddlermobile was joined by other traffic as they headed toward the city lights. Other roads joined in to the impossible highway in a spaghetti-tangle profusion, forming an insane cloverleaf turnpike as they arced off into tunnel mouths suspended in empty air.

There were huge rusted road signs bolted onto skeletal gantries above them, and September read them with growing incredulity as they sped by.

"Nightmares? Hallucinations? Urban Myths? How are *those* places with their own offramps? I thought this was some kind of afterlife?"

Ced shrugged.

"This is the Aught, Miss. It's all connected up, but most of us don't get to visit all the other parts. Mister Khatri called it a 'metaphorophysical manifestation of the collective sub-unconscious', but big words like that just mean that someone important doesn't know exactly what's happening, deep down."

He dodged around a huge big-rig truck, all painted up with 'Day of the Dead' sugar skulls and pinstripes, and a smile broke across his face like a reluctant sunrise. "It's home, I suppose. Or it's gotten to feel that way."

Now the highway dropped down through a pair of huge wrought-iron gates, like the ones you'd find outside a proper old-fashioned cemetery, but built on the scale of skyscrapers. People had thrown shanty shacks of tar-paper and corrugated iron up through the metal flowers and vines, and the sight of underpants and bed sheets flapping in the breeze made September smile, too. If this was the realm of the dead, it wasn't particularly horrible.

As the car purred along down the main street of Uncarnadine, September leaned out the window to stare up at the cliffs of skyscrapers, noticing a dizzying array of architectural styles, all mashed together. These were dead buildings, stitched together from Roman ruins and Aztec temples, modern council housing blocks and creaking rookeries of rotten wood.

Some even had the hulks of dead ships poking right through them; a structure which housed a great vertical food bazaar was hollowed out in the middle, and a fountain spilled out from a stone conch the size of a church, clasped in the hand of a fallen statue. The waterfall it made rained down endlessly on the canted deck of an oil tanker, which had been set up as an *al fresco* restaurant. The waiters all carried black umbrellas.

Another pair of skyscrapers were topped with holy places. A cathedral with towers made entirely of stained glass faced a huge onion-domed mosque across the street, and an old railway bridge arched over to join them at the waist, tilted at a slight diagonal. This hadn't stopped people from building houses and shops along both sides of the bridge, or helping keep the whole edifice aloft with two huge, tethered barrage balloons.

Perhaps, thought September, the *gargoyles, skeletons, coffin-lids, gravestones and bats would have seemed frightening on their own.* But here, under the weirdlight glowing silver from the face of the Azraeon, people had built their lives around them. They were like a Halloween costume worn to go down to the supermarket, in April. A bit silly, and not frightening at all.

After the architecture, the second thing September noticed was the lights. From candles floating through the air in paper lanterns shaped like skulls (of course), to glowing phantom aurorae hung over guywires, to neon loops and swirls thrown like cursive graffiti up the side of buildings, there were lights everywhere, in every colour. Cedric must have known what she was going to ask, because he pointed up to where the great central clock pierced the skyline, scissor-sliced by spotlight beams.

"That's not telling the time, see? It's *never* going to be daytime. It's been midnight here forever. But the clock's counting down the big one; it's the big version of that one your great Grandad invented. A Doom Clock that measures the lifespan of the Azraeon himself. When it strikes, it strikes only once, and there'll be nobody left to hear it. The mainspring will contain the last scrap of energy in a universe that's iced over."

That made September shudder, just a little. She knew all about thermodynamics, of course. But the fact of that huge pale clock face with its single hand made it sort of personal. Still, there was no time to dwell on morbidity; the dead were living it up, all around her.

Many of these people were illuminated, too. Some were outlined in coloured auras, which seemed to pulse and change with their moods; a figure slumped on a park bench with a bottle was haloed in blue-green, while a couple having a screaming row in a second-floor apartment made the air spit yellow and red. Other pedestrians wore clothes painted with glowing inks, or pinned up with lantern-lights, bulbs and beads of phosphorescence.

Then there were those who were missing body parts; arms, legs, even a fair few heads. These folk had ghostly appendages sprouting from what looked like still-fresh stumps, bloodless as a butcher's window display. Their spirit limbs and faces glowed pale turquoise, as did the phantom scars which stitched together many other bodies on the street.

Men run through with swords hawked beer and doughnuts. Women pincushioned with arrows, or with the floating hair of the drowned, pushed carts full of groceries. Skeletons in suits smoked cigars as they strolled, discussing business. A gent who was still on fire, and wearing the remains of a pilot's uniform, sat at a cafe with a girl who was a ghost from the waist up, sipping lattes. Their waiter had a tomahawk in his chest, and was dressed as a cowboy. People in the funeral clothes of a score of major religions bustled and tipped their hats (or severed skull-tops) to each other, and bawled and flirted and hustled and thieved, amid the bubbling stew of joys and sorrows only a big city could offer. There was even a branch of Burger Slave in Uncarnadine – the zipper-mouthed grin of Beefy Roger hung in neon over what appeared to be an aluminium-sided 1950s diner.

September was stunned into silence. These were dead people, and they were just... *getting on with it.* For every one who wore the marks of an obvious death, there were ten more who she could only imagine had surgical scars under their clothes, or had perished from illness or age. Which made her ponder...

"Why aren't most of them elderly? I mean, you'd think they'd look mostly like my great-Grandad, or just as wrinkly."

Cedric shrugged.

"Their bodies probably did. But you know how they always say 'you're as old as you feel?' Well, apparently, when you're dead, you look how you imagine you should. We get young folks whose spirits are old, and old folks who come over to Uncarnadine as rugrats. There's plenty of people who believed that they were monsters, and we get those as well."

"Thing like our mate Dracula?"

"Things worse! They're supposed to keep the mad ones locked up."

"But they let you out?"

It took a second for Ced to realise she was joking, and when he did his smile was wobbly and fragile.

"I just hope they do it again," he said. "And then there's *you*, Miss. You're not even really dead. That's going to be pretty obvious to everyone here."

"Why?" asked September. "Because I don't have a ghost head, or... yikes! Bullet holes right through me, like *that* guy."

She pointed at a cyclist in an army uniform, who was,

indeed, riddled with glowing holes. He scowled and flipped her off as the car rumbled by. Cedric didn't answer. But as the Befuddlermobile cruised down a street of stacked marble mausoleums he spun the rear-view mirror around, so that September could see herself.

And, ohhhhh yes. He was quite right.

People would talk. Or, possibly, she reckoned, they'd scream. Running away and hiding under things was a distinct possibility.

Because what stared back from behind the glass was not the face she was used to. It was somehow more *real*; crisp and vivid, like a cartoon of itself. Her nose was still utterly unlike that of any pop star, and her freckles were a constellation scattered across her pale skin. But her eyes were just slightly too big, now, and the Endarkenment seethed inside them, haloing each iris with the illusion of spinning clockwork. The closer she looked, the more intricate the gears became.

But that wasn't the weirdest of it. Oh no.

The strangest part of September's transformation was this; there was now a black outline around her body. It was as if someone had taken a sharpie marker and traced around every one of her fingers, and right to the tips of the big, cartoon coils of copper-coloured hair which haloed her head.

"I take it that nobody else here has this kind of thing going on," said September slowly, watching the lines flow and change as she flexed her fingers.

"You're darn right! I mean, some of the characters from fiction who visit have something similar. The Comicfolk. They prefer the term 'graphic novel personae'. But that – that's just *wrong*. You can see it sizzling where it touches things."

It was at that instant that September saw the crowds part,

and a familiar figure step into a pool of light. The black flicker around her acted without any input from her brain. It reached down into the gubbins of the Befuddlermobile, and pulled the hand brake.

There was a solid 'clunk' as Cedric's head connected with the steering wheel. He came up groaning, just in time to see September getting out of the car.

"Didn't you hear me? *You can't go out there!* Nobody in Uncarnadine looks like that!"

"*He* does!" shouted September, leaning back in through the window, and pointing—

At Professor Septivarian Archimedes.

Who saw her, his eyes going wide and his mouth dropping open with shock. Who spun on his heel, and elbowed his way through the crowd, escaping.

"Come on!"

Ced struggled with the four-point harness, then kicked the door open and followed. As he ran after September he activated his Reaper helmet, which had a definite effect on the people who bustled on this busy avenue. Like policemen across the multiverse, Cedric found that he had a big bubble of personal space all around him.

September sprinted ahead, ducking and weaving between half-phantom folk, very surprised skeletons and politely indignant zombies. Her big cherry-red Docs splashed in puddles, shattering the reflection of neon, and she plunged deeper into what turned out to be a huge, hustling street market, following the glimpse of a lab coat and mortarboard through the crush.

It was undoubtedly Septivarian. There was no mistaking that face, or that unruly shock of hair bursting out like atomic dandelion fuzz.

She put her head down, gave it all of her track-and-field best, and hurdled a hot-dog cart, earning a string or curses from its undead vendor. She slid between two bicycles and spun around the back of a tuk-tuk, just as Cedric caught up.

"What are you doing?" he panted. "Someone's going to call the cops! I mean, real ones, who haven't been fired!"

"It's *him!* My great-great-granddad. Of course he'd be over here, if I'd just thought about it. You reaped him, after all."

Cedric slid up against a wall as a barrow full of antique clocks rolled past, and followed September into the mouth of an alleyway, where small and smoky doorways promised illicit pleasures. Septivarian turned back at the far end of the alley, framed in the glow of a street light, and he held up what appeared to be an old-fashioned miner's lantern for a second before he bolted away into the steaming dark.

"I, ummmm, got him with the scythe, yes. Not a formal reaping. Not, errrr... by the book. His mates were a bit cheesed off, to tell you the truth, and I thought it best not to stick around. There's no guarantee he came here, anyway. I mean, not if he was a man of firm beliefs, anyway..."

September didn't have time to dodge and dive through the crowds anymore. She let the Endarkenment flare out, sweeping ahead of her as a wave of hair-thin lightning bolts, in carbon black. Neon signs popped and fizzed. Bicycles fell in half. Automatic doors snicked shut. People found themselves pushed back, distracted, confused and September pelted down the now-empty middle of the alleyway, Cedric hard on her heels.

She spun around the corner, soles slipping in a sheen of oil, just in time to see Septivarian winding up to throw his mining lamp.

"No no no no nooooo!" came a voice from within it, as the Professor gave it a proper old-fashioned baseball pitch – right at September's head.

It was the Endarkenment that caught it, really. A burst of black lightning lifted September off her feet in mid-stride, and her hand came up to field the lamp as it sailed toward her. It slapped into her palm as she landed and rolled, coming back up running.

My goodness! Miss Slugpounder would have been impressed! thought September. *And I'm gaining on him, too! Though that's not a bad turn of speed for a 137-year-old...*

"Mmmmph!" said the lamp, tucked under her arm. "Whhhrrrrrffflll!"

Down a long flight of concrete steps they went, Septivarian grinding down the central steel bannister on the soles of his slippers, and September just sprinting over a sea of disgruntled heads, like a surfer in a mosh pit. As she landed, she bought the lamp out to take a closer look.

"Well, this is a fine bloody mess!" said the tiny little man inside, who was dressed in a toga and laurel wreath. "Who are you, then? The boss's successor? You've nicked his lab coat, anyway."

They dipped and weaved across a four-lane road, Septivarian sliding under a flat-deck truck, September rolling across the hood of a huge, skull-painted Cadillac, and Cedric wheezing and panting behind.

"Why... why's he running?" asked September. "He knows me! I'm his great-great-granddaughter!"

The little man raised an eyebrow.

"You're Arbourdale's *what?* I don't see how that's possible, young lady. He doesn't have the necessaries, as it were." Then realisation dawned. "Oh! You mean... you're Norma's kid! That is to say, Septerina's. I heard she changed her name, when things got all estranged. *Look out! Rickshaw!*"

September snapped her attention forward again, and narrowly missed being chewed up under the wheels of a neon-green three-wheeler, being pedalled by a ghoul in a battered top hat and board shorts. Ahead, Septivarian stole a look over his shoulder, and hared off down another noisome alleyway, into the dark.

"You knew my mum?"

"Arbourdale was her sidekick. I mean... he was something reassuring that has nothing to do with super-villainy. The boss asked us not to talk to you about that, if you ever showed up here. Which I suppose we should have guessed you would, when we heard that he'd died."

"*Heard he'd died?* He just threw you at me!"

"Ahhhh," said the little man in the lamp, as they clattered down a set of steel steps, down into a chasm of bricks and rotting mortar below street level. "How can I put this delicately? That's not him. That's a robot. Piloted by your mum's old teddy bear."

This was a bit much to take in, but there was no time to slow down. The allegedly robotic Septivarian Archimedes was punching a code into a keypad, his fingers shaking. Just as September caught up with him, a section of the brick wall rumbled open, and she fell through as she barrelled into him, with Cedric collapsing on top of them both.

There was swearing, and cursing, and tussling, and clattering, all in pitch blackness. At one point, September was certain that they all rolled down another flight of stairs. Then the lights came on, and the whole stricken tableau froze around her.

It was a copy of the Befuddler's Lair, down under the Little Mean Civic Library. This one, however, was apparently dedicated to evil. Everywhere there were tanks full of bubbling green Repo, with things floating in them that hinted at Goetic demonology, medieval darkness, and 1980s heavy metal. Statues of demons lined the walls, and massive pentagrams were spray-painted across tablets in Aramaic and cuneiform. A huge cork-board, the size of a swimming pool on its side, was covered in pictures of imps, oni and fallen angels, from every tradition of esoterica. Pages ripped from old grimoires were stapled up, pinned next to scrawled notes and magical symbols, and all webbed with that red string so beloved of conspiracy nutters.

"I thought you said he was a loveable old chap?" croaked Cedric, lying on his back. "This looks like demonology, or at least demon social studies. Remember those monsters I told you about? *They* have places that look like this, with the red string and all."

September had landed on top of the robot Professor, and the lamp she'd been holding had rolled away to one side. Now it righted itself with a clunk, and the tiny man inside banged on the glass.

"This is Dark Lazarus, girl! This is the final project that he didn't want anyone to find. The stuff that the government forced him to do, see? He left me and Arbourdale in charge of it, and told us he'd be back."

Just then, Septivarian's head split open, in the same way Cedric's helmet did. His face hinged up like the canopy of a fighter jet, revealing, inside, a tiny cramped cockpit, all chrome and leather. In it sat a small purple teddy bear, with a ferocious scowl and a cute little pink plastic nose.

"Right! I'm going to have to take care of this myself, am I?" he asked, unclipping his harness and striding out onto the Professor's chest. "Think you're bloody 'ard enough, do you? Come and get a mauling, you big... umm... *girl?*"

"Arbourdale, this is Septerina's daughter," said the man in the lamp, in a soothing tone. "The boss' successor, I suppose, now that he's gone."

"He's *not gone!*" bristled the little bear, with what looked like tears in its black-button eyes. "Sure as he made me, that man had a plan. He was never going to give up that easy, Virgil!"

The tiny Roman sighed.

"He had a lot of plans, Arbourdale. That robot you converted was one of 'em, and it didn't work either. You can put a mind in one of those things, but not a soul."

September stood up, a bit unsteadily. There was a big brushed-steel table in the middle of the laboratory, and she drew up a stool and collapsed across it, suddenly spent. *She'd been so sure that she could just ask Septivarian to fix all of this, like he always did. But no... she was on her own, as usual.*

Cedric pulled up another seat across from her.

"Are you all right?"

She nodded.

"Perhaps we'd better figure out what we do next, then. There was some mention of having to save the world?"

"Ohh, we're good at that kind of thing," said Virgil, brightening. "Saved the world with the old guv'nor more times than I care to mention, me."

"He cowered in his lamp and pee'd his toga," said Arbourdale, clambering up on top of the table, and dragging the lamp behind him. "But if the old boss sent you, and you're Septerina's kid, then we pretty much have to help you. Hang on a bit. I'll get some hot chocolates on. Then we can talk about how we can finish Dark Lazarus. That's what he said we'd have to do, if he ever snuffed it."

"Hang on," said Virgil. "You know I'm perfectly comfortable dealing with Hell, but these folks don't look like they're keen on it. Isn't there another way?"

Arbourdale shook his head.

"Unless you've got the phone number for Ozzy Osbourne, we need us a proper alternative prince of Darkness."

"You mean..?" asked Cedric, with a definite note of worry in his voice.

"Yep," said the little purple bear, rubbing his paws together. "Proper mad science, innit? We're going to raise the Devil!"

Eleven
Lucifer
vs
The Devil
vs
Satan

"The second Wild Idea of The Quizmaster of Chaos, AKA Septivarian Archimedes, AKA my old boss, bless his spandex socks, was this;" said the Electric Virgil.

"*Nietzsche was right, for a given value of right. God is dead – for a given value of God. But his adversary ain't dead. He just quit. So he's available for business.*"

"Hang on. Wait. Rewind!" spluttered Cedric, who had almost choked on a marshmallow. "You're going to have to excuse me, but for a second there it sounded like you said 'raise the Devil'. That's *definitely* something PostMortis arrests people for. He's trespassed from the afterlife, for obvious reasons."

"Aha!" said Virgil. "*Exactly!* The devil. Not Lucifer, who got locked up in the ice of Cocytus by wily old Dante. And not Satan, who never really came into being during the 1980s. *The Devil.* With Capitals. Mark Two. The Great Adversary, from 1314 through until 1666. With a brief holiday in the late 1500s, when he hung out in Portugal for a while, incognito."

Everyone around the table looked at the little figure in the lantern as if it had gone insane, which made Virgil roll his pixilated eyes and sigh.

"Listen, kittens. Mr Rock 'n' Roll Reject here's the Grim Reaper, right? Got the card, and everything? I remember an Indian bloke, but you know, human resources and staff turnover and all that, best of luck to you. But he wasn't *born* as a skeleton with a magic weed-whacker."

Blank looks all round.

"My mum says I was born in a pub, while people were singing a rude song about Hitler," Said Cedric, looking confused. "She would have mentioned a scythe, I reckon. Even a baby-sized one."

Virgil slapped his own forehead, and wished he had a whiteboard.

"What I'm saying is, your basic Abrahamic God *might* be out there, tinkering with new universes, and composing boring psalms for the choirs eternal. *But he wasn't the one who was knocking about in the Middle Ages.* No more than Zeus was, or Thor, or any of them. He was one of the Gods we made, by believing in 'em."

"Dark Lazarus was meant to make a new Dark Lord, in the service of Ronnie Reagan and Missus Thatcher," said Arbourdale. "Hence all the Satanic Panic hoo-hah Section W ginned up, with the dungeons and dragons and heavy metal and horror films and all. But to really, *truly* work, they needed the darkest of the Tarot, too. And, well – the guy who held it was a total bastard."

"Riiiiight," said September, halfway between incredulity and sarcasm. "So someone, out there, has a magical tarot card, which makes them into the real, actual – but in every possible way, fictional – Devil. And my great-great-granddad expects me to go and dig him up, because during the 1980s, he was trying to enlist his help to crush communism?"

"Bingo! Yes!" said Virgil, touching the tip of his nose with one hand while pointing up at September with the other. "But no! Because, like I said, he quit in 1666."

"Then we go after his replacement," said Ced. "Easy as

that."

"Wrong again! *He never gave the card back.* Apparently, he left a note. Said that all those puritans cursing him was giving him alopecia and a terrible migraine, and that he was, to quote, 'so over it'. He also said that the world didn't need an embodiment of radical evil, because it had humans."

"So we need the Tarot to make all of this work, and it's still with the original owner?"

"Who Septivarian did a little bit of work for, as it turns out. He knew exactly where he lived."

"Easy, then," said September. "We'll explain it all to this retired Devil, and the world gets saved before teatime."

"Welllll..." said Arbourdale, twisting his little felt paws together. "It's not quite that simple. See, the boss erased a lot of his memories, when your government went nasty on him. He didn't think they should have hold of a tame Antichrist, so he destroyed a lot of his work, even the stuff in his own head. All we have is this."

He pointed to the figure scrawled in the middle of the cork-board, the one all the lines of red string converged on.

1:03am, June 12, 1666

"He was trying to work it all out, again. But now you say he's snuffed it."

"Then we've got him!" Cedric snapped his fingers triumphantly. "I've still got my uniform and my helmet. I can get inside the Clock Tower, and into the PostMortis hall of records, and find out who came through to the Other Side at exactly that time. We've got records going back to the 1300s. We can find him, and have a little chat about this card you need, September."

"I don't think so!" said Virgil, in tones of rising panic. "Look at that! On the monitors!"

There were busy shadows crowding and skulking out there. Security cameras showed a horde of them, all armoured up like a SWAT team, with night-vision goggles and the crossed-scythes insignia of PostMortis on their backs.

"They followed you!" groaned Arbourdale. "Oh, *stuffing!* You've led the feds right to us! After all these years!"

A lot of things happened all at once, then.

Virgil's toga turned army-issue camo, and a General-Patton-era helmet manifested atop his head inside the lantern. Hatches in the walls and ceiling slammed open, and an array of nasty weapons sprung forth on jointed arms, belts of bullets swinging and laser range-finders webbing the room with crimson.

Because here came the forces of PostMortis, crashing through breaches in the walls, dropping commando-style out of air vents, and smashing in through the doors, bustling and black-armoured, armed with squat and efficient looking little sub-machineguns.

"Just give me the word, and we'll go out in a blaze of glory!" shouted Virgil, in a very unpoetic voice. He brandished a tiny riding crop the size of a stick of liquorice.

"Wait!" shouted September, as the horde shouldered their weapons. "We'll come quietly! Don't shoot! It was all my fault, really. It's his first day." She'd backed up to the cork board at the first crash of shattering glass, and now she quickly, quietly tore down the date at the middle of the web of red string, shredding it behind her back.

Cedric waved feebly. Arbourdale had fainted.

"Hold your fire," came a voice from behind the wall of officers. "It's just possible – *just* – that they really are a bunch harmless idiots. Come on, let me through..."

The tight-packed paramilitary types shuffled and shoved, clearing a path for a tall woman in black. She was wearing what appeared to be an ancient parking warden's uniform, complete with a floor-length pleated skirt, twin rows of shiny silver buttons, and a little peaked cap. Her bob haircut was so severe it looked as if it had been cut with industrial lasers, then set with enough product to leave it shinier and harder than vintage bakelite. Under its fringe her eyes were covered by tiny black-pebble glasses, set atop a beak of a nose.

As this apparition approached, she unclipped a monocle from her lapel. It was, it appeared, a fresh and dripping eyeball, held in a silver frame and attached to a length of chain. She used this bloodshot thing to inspect September's little group, holding it up in front of her sunglasses.

"Cedric Welbourne. Deceased 1957. Recruited 1963. And of course," – and here her thin lips twisted into a snarl – "dismissed with unspeakably extreme prejudice, right now. Is there any way in which you haven't royally defecated on every singular aspect of your sacred duty today, ex-provisional-junior Reaper Welbourne?"

Up until this point, September had been certain that people's knees knocked together with fright only in old-fashioned comic books. Cedric's were doing it now, though.

"No, Miss Kolslaw. I mean, yes, or ummm... I don't know, Miss Kolslaw! Please!"

Now September felt the stare from that wobbling mad eyeball, as it bored into her. If it hadn't been for lots of practice facing Headmaster Mackleduff's glass eye, she would have probably yelped – but then she saw her reflection in it.

That was why these PostMortis death-troopers were all jittery, just being near her. A scrawl of black lightning haloed her head, spiked and angry.

This was her great-great-granddad's lab. This was her turf.

Here and now, she was dangerous, and the Reapers didn't want her to try anything naughty.

Miss Kolslaw (whoever she was) managed to keep not just her cool, but a frosty aura of menace, too. September was quietly impressed.

"And *you*. An actual 'live one'. You think you can just waltz in here with your mad science and your grandfather's dangerous toys, and make a mockery of the vital necessity of death? *He* was bad enough, but he was discreet. You… *pah!*"

That one syllable conveyed such a depth of contempt that September almost gave up. But deep inside her mind, a little spark of outrage held the line.

I've met your type before, she thought. *The type that thinks it has the story all figured out. But we shall see…*

"I'm glad you're here," said September, all calm contrition. She held out her hands, wrists together. "I'm requesting protective custody, and safe passage back to your headquarters, for all four of us. There's things about this situation you don't know yet, Miss Kolslaw."

The woman looked shocked for just a sliver of a second, and then she grinned.

Yes, thought September. *She'd have been disappointed if I* **didn't** *do something tricky. Now she knows I have a plan to escape, and she needs to know how it's going to play out, so she can try to be trickier than I am. A simple, honest person would have been much worse. A simple, honest person might have shot the lot of us.*

"Well, goodness me," said Kolslaw, all acid and vinegar. "If we're going to cooperate so nicely, you can just call me Sharon."

Sharon made a gesture with one finger. Troopers slapped big iron manacles around September's wrists, and Cedric's too. Even Arbourdale and Virgil got scooped up, though handcuffs in their sizes were not forthcoming.

Now those black-lensed eyes came closer. Now September could smell the scent of rosewater and embalming fluid on Kolslaw's breath.

"And what *precisely* don't we know, Miss September Normalsson? I mean, one thing we *have* discovered is the location of your great-grandfather's secret lab, which had vexed PostMortis greatly for several decades. Thank you for that, by the way."

September smiled primly.

"You don't know which book we trapped your boss in, or how to get him back. And you don't know that someone is using you all as assassins, back in the real world. Your *holy necessity* is someone else's cheap snuff. Someone involved with a drug called Repo."

And there it was. That little twitch. The roulette wheel was spinning, and the little ball was clicking and jumping as it rolled. September knew the slap was coming, even as she registered the instant of panic in Sharon Kolslaw's face. For an instant, her little glasses slipped, and September caught a glimpse of something copper-coloured and shiny behind them.

It still hurt. September tasted blood as she rolled with it, and she winked at Kolslaw as she sagged down, feeling the troopers behind her grabbing her by the arms.

"Enough! We'll ask the questions, and we'll get the answers. Or else you boys know what happens next! The penalty for subverting death has always been the same!"

It was a call-and-response. It was a fervent shout, back from all those dead men with guns.

"*The Reject Chute! The Reject Chute!*"

September did not like the sound of that, one little bit.

Which just goes to show that even on the worst of days, you can sometimes be absolutely right.

Suture Six
Tiny Tots Storybook Section

NIGEL WILBERTON, AGE four, had just settled down to read his favourite book when the trouble started.

Of course, he was far too young to know it was actually trouble, when he opened up a classic *Jolly Dormouse Jim* adventure with small and sticky fingers.

To Nigel, it simply seemed like another one of those fine ideas which sometimes popped into his head. Ideas such as filling his mum's car up with water from the garden hose, or washing the dog in the kitchen sink with laundry detergent.

Nigel spent a lot of his time in his room, ostensibly thinking about what he'd done.

What he really did was read books and draw pictures, many of which would end up being shown, in great crinkled sheaves, to child psychologists with big fluffy cardigans and worried expressions.

But that was all for the future.

Today, after baking a very convincing pie made of mud, twigs, worms and snails in the microwave, he'd been banished to the big red bean-bag chair in his bedroom, and had idly plucked a storybook from the pile. He opened it to the first page, and beheld a world of felt, as soft and sickly-sweet as marzipan left out in the sun. Perfect and simple and sane.

Except for the little black dog, who hadn't been there last time.

The little black dog with the funny white markings on its face, that made it look a bit like one of the Halloween decorations Nigel had pinned to his cork board. They weren't scary; they were a bit silly and a lot of fun, and they reminded him of the best thing in all the world – free sweets.

Nigel peered at the thick cardboard page, unsure what to make of this. In his limited experience, books didn't change, like things on the television. But this was *definitely* real. Where the Little Bad Wolf, ex-antagonist of *Jolly Dormouse Jim's* plush universe, had once been, there was a different dog, who looked a bit like the ones that herded sheep, and a bit like...

"Draw a picture of a skellington," mumbled Nigel, not knowing where the thought had come from. He was a bit surprised to hear his own voice. But then again, he was at that age when mercurial whims breezed through his brain like the changing weather. It seemed perfectly logical, to a mind unclouded by the troubles of adulthood, to add in a picture that was clearly missing from this book.

There was a *hole* there, right next to the little black dog, who now seemed to be carrying a curved stick in his mouth. A single lone twig sprouted from the end of the stick, standing out at right-angles to it.

"Needs to have a skellington in it," agreed Nigel with himself, his brow creasing with consternation.

There were coloured pencils right there on the shelf.

Nigel looked up, for inspiration, at the cardboard cut-out of a dancing skeleton he'd gotten from the big children's Halloween party down at the community centre. It was smiling, (of course) and wore a jaunty top hat and spats. It appeared to be clicking its bony heels together in a merry jig.

What happened next did not rank, at all, with the finest paintings of the renaissance. There was a lot of cross-eyed concentration. Nigel felt, in a kind of vague and semi-religious way, that it was wrong to draw in a library book, but the obvious lack of a skeleton carrying a big curvy stick worried at him, like an annoying little itch. Presently, he put his pencil down, and admired his handiwork.

It wasn't terribly life-like. But it was terribly *alive*.

All the black flowed out of the small black dog, and across into the robed, hooded stick-figure with the perfect-circle skull for a face Nigel had scribed in next to it. A pair of black-button eyes blinked, and a set of bony fingers made of single pencil strokes clenched.

"Thanks, kid!" said a bubble of felt that bloomed from the little image's grid of teeth. "I feel better already!"

Nigel dropped the book and the page flipped over, but it was no use. The little drawn skeleton in the scrawled black robe pulled itself around the edge of the page and into the next scene. Here, yellow woollen ducks drifted on a felt pond, and Dormouse Jim was having a picnic with the Hedgehog Twins.

"Don't be afraid," said another bubble of felt, filled with words. "I'm just magic, is all. Say, tell me – do you know Tommy the Train?"

Now Nigel was in more familiar territory. Adults had been telling him for his whole short existence that toys could come to life, and that magic happened to special little boys, who then went onto have smashing adventures with pirates and witches and cowboys. This was clearly just his own quota of that enchantment coming due.

And he *did* know Tommy the Train. He'd been one of the kids who'd witnessed what the television news was calling the nursery rhyme nightmare in Hoxham End, just yesterday.

"Yeah! I saw Tommy go boom! His face comed-ed off and all! It was brilliant!"

The little stick-figure skeleton nodded. It had all been in the extremely damning report he'd been given about

Cedric Welbourne's first day. And it was *sure* to be in all the newspapers...

"Do you have any books about Tommy and his chums, then?" he asked. If a librarian could work out how to get this deep down into children's fiction, then he could certainly decipher a way out.

Nigel beamed.

"I've got lots! he said. "Tommy and the Miners' Strike, Tommy and the Sea Monster's Curse, Tommy and the Ninja Grandma Protocol..." He trundled over to a big blue-painted shelf, and pulled out a thick slab of colourful volumes. "They're my fav'rit!"

"Right!" said the skeleton, rubbing his hands together. This made a sound like a pencil being sharpened. "Open one of them, then put it right next to this book, here, with me in it. Then I'm going to need you to go and get your dad's newspaper..."

A few minutes later, the Plump Comptroller got the shock of his plasticine life, when a very angry Grim Reaper strode through the Island of Sodall's Railway Bake Sale, pausing only to snaffle a blueberry muffin made of modelling clay.

"Am I going mad?" he asked, mopping his brow with a paper handkerchief.

"No, you're as sane as the rest of us," said the talking steam train who was parked next to him. "That was the avatar of death, the angel of oblivion, dark keeper of the keys to infinity, out for a little stroll. I'd recognise him anywhere."

It was only a few more jumps, through the inevitable news stories about Tommy exploding, into disaster thrillers, and then *out*.

Reaper-Captain Jaghtaran Khatri was on his way. He made a little detour into one of Lady Prunella Boddyce-

Rippington's regency-era romances to nick a scythe that wasn't drawn in crayon; the lusty farmhand who should have been using it was 'otherwise engaged', and never noticed it was gone.

He took a surprisingly short and sneaky route. The Aught was vast and sprawling, the sum total of the extelligence of humanity, a ramified, buttress-rooted, coral-reef explosion of hopes, dreams, religions, fears, nightmares, wishes, old tall tales and silly anecdotes.

There were hidden paths between things that seemed unconnected, and usually – most certainly – it was love, death or vengeance which wired them all together. The avatar of death (even without Dante's Tarot) could navigate through the wyrd crevices and spaces of Fiction. But eventually, like all travellers in the Aught, he reached a choke-point. A gateway.

This one was known as the Curtain Call, and it lay on the outskirts of the city of Dramatis Personae, the fictopolis[26] of almost-forgotten characters. It was a rambling sort of place, built up on a mountain that turned into a spiral as it tapered up and over. The great Inkspatter Highway zigzagged up its crooked slopes, finally plunging into what appeared to be a gigantic baroque mirror, taller still than the city's highest towers. Mouldering red velvet curtains hung around its frame, which was so large that ice rimed its top, and its base was embedded in a desert of black sand.

The mountain, known as the Neverhorn, carried the highway on its back, higher and higher, and this was the last walk for fictional characters whose final volume was gone to moths and dust.

No wonder they barred their doors and slammed their shutters when they saw the Grim Reaper coming. You

---

26. a city of the imaginary and literary.

had to have been a star, once, to live here – among the streets of Dramatis Personae, with their cracked mosaic pavements and tumbles of ivy leaves covered in poetry. The houses were all stucco and terracotta, painted in a riot of colours. Their inhabitants ranged from penny-romance picaroons through to 1950s space-troopers and one-issue comic book villains.

Jaghtaran Khatri stalked through the streets in his own bubble of privacy, as eyes – some cartoon woodcuts, some made of paint and neon, some rendered in polygons from old computer games – peeked out at him through cracks. Mortality was unwelcome here. They all knew that the last walk was coming for them, up the Neverhorn, onto that thin corkscrew path and into the mirror. Into Uncarnadine, so long as you were remembered.

Or into dusty oblivion. It was hard to be fictional.

Reaper-Captain Khatri trudged along the path, up toward the great silvery face of the mirror, leaving the city behind. He cut quite a figure against this backdrop, and against the storm-light sky which imagination had conjured here. A tall, robed traveller, his black cloak whipping out behind him in the rising breeze, leaning on his folded scythe like a walking stick.

See him from afar, and he'd resemble nothing more or less than the Hermit, another of Dante's tarot.[27]

Then again, if you saw him from afar, passing through a boulder field just where the snowline began, you'd also see the three figures who detached themselves from the shadow of the rocks, and fanned out to block his path.

They wore long red capes and wide, Japanese-style

---

27. And the old feller from inside the cover of Led Zeppelin 4; the bearer of the Hermit gains incredible gnostic and esoteric wisdom, and is therefore great fun to have long, rambling conversations with under the influence of naughty mushrooms. This meant that he was always (allegedly) welcome on the Led Zep tour bus, and that the picture is a sketch taken from life.

basket hats, which covered their faces. Their movements were pure menace, each step crunching on gravel, tendon-tight. Threatening... but *afraid*.

Khatri knew what they were as soon as he saw them break away from the cover of the boulders. Not your usual bandits, these. No – they had been sent to stop him coming home.

He'd not just read the news article about Tommy the Train's demise, he'd *lived in it*, becoming black ink on old newsprint for a time. He'd absorbed the rumours about a coach-and-four being obliterated amid that ugly scene, and of a red-robed ecclesiastical type in his own patch of midnight. *So, that wily bastard was making his move. Things were about to get nasty.*

"Stand aside, all of you," he said, in a voice that came out far more weary than it should have. "I don't know what he paid you, but it's not enough. You know what happens to the twice-dead, I'm certain."

The middle basket-hat raised one hand, bidding its fellows to stop. A slight inclination of the brim showed that Khatri had gotten its attention.

"It's not what he paid us. It's what he promised! *That's* why you have to be kept out of the way. PostMortis is about to have some resourcing changes, you see. To bring it up to speed with the modern world."

Khatri knew that voice. More than this – he knew that smug, maniacal tone. In an instant, he knew what these three creatures were. Some people were so infamous that they grew a legend up around them. Even when they passed from Uncarnadine other, sadder souls could wear that infamy, and its power. It hollowed them out to husks of spite, but while the power lasted, they were a match for any Reaper.

"You have your choice, scythebringer," said a second hat,

in a thick Russian accent. "Turn around, and survive as best you can in fiction. Or try to come through us, and feed Ammut. We'll get what we're due, either way."

The last basket-hat spoke in Latin.

"*Nec experiri, stulte,*" it chuckled. "I'm gonna reeeeeeally enjoy this, right?"

In reply, Khatri tapped the heel of his staff against the ground. A blade hinged out from its tip, all quicksilver and cold. The light glinted off it as it locked in place, with a sound like ice forming on a polar lake.

"Why don't you just call it a day, lads? You can tell him you tried. Honestly, you can tell him whatever you want. So long as you tell him that I'm coming for him, next."

Hands moved inside those red robes. Weapons swung free. *A pair of daggers, inlaid with gold eagles gripping swastikas. A spiked censer on a length of sharpened chain. A Roman gladius inset with jewels.* The middle basket-hat twitched, inviting him to start the dance.

Dangerous, dangerous, dangerous. These three were all wrapped up with stories, and this was still fiction they were standing on.

"Let me tell you how this is going to go," grated Khatri. "You're going back to the asylum. I'm going back to the Clock Tower. And your boss is going down the Reject Chute, about ten minutes after."

The hat tipped up. A tiny, prim little grin flashed, beneath a comically small black moustache.

"Then for you, Captain Khatri, *ze war is over!*" snarled Adolf Hitler.

As he, Rasputin and Caligula leapt to the attack.

They may have been shadows of their real selves, these things born of hate and history. But they were long, dark shadows indeed – stronger than the villains who'd cast them. Steel blurred silver as Khatri jumped back, sweeping low with his scythe. Its blade moaned through the air, narrowly missing Hitler's ankles, and he jumped over it, stabbing underhand.

Khatri blocked high with the scythe-blade and low with the handle, fouling Caligula's gladius. But this left Rasputin's censer, which hissed past his face on its serpentine chain, cracking like a whip at full extension. It came looping back in an arc that should have snared the Reaper's neck.

It would have, too. But Jaghtaran Khatri was quite a hands-on Reaper-Captain of PostMortis.

Now, China and Japan often get their own pages at the front, whenever the big book of martial arts is opened. But India – being a subcontinent of boiling, melting, colliding cultures, with a history more tangled than a tornado of spiderwebs – had its own arts of battle, many of them developed for weapons so specific, odd and strangely formed that their number of practitioners could be counted on a single digit.

In that big book we just mentioned, it had its own separate volume, with pictures you'd often have to turn upside down and squint at.

Khatri unleashed a tight flurry of blows using a modified *Gatka* technique, driving the three possessed souls backward in a shower of sparks. But they rallied. It was three-to-one. Here came Adolf again, daggers making a wicked scissor-cut. Caligula's gladius speared in, scoring a line across Jaghtaran's shoulder that burned with pain.

He'd once travelled to Kerala to learn *Kalaripayattu* swordplay in dusty seaside courtyards. He'd wrestled with *Malla-Yudda* masters under monsoon rains in the mud. He'd sailed to Ceylon to study the form of *Silambam* stick-fighters and even dared to practice with the Urumi whip-sword, losing a tiny sliver of his left ear in the process.

Now he improvised. An elbow smashed into Rasputin's nose, flattering it in a spray of blood. He reached out, dragged Caligula in close, and tossed him over one hip, flipping him in the air. But that left *Der Fuhrer* in the open.

Khatri blocked Hitler's dagger-thrust, and used the shaft of his scythe to trap the dictator's arm, drawing him across his body. He spun, just as Caligula swept low with his gladius. The Roman sword sliced through Hitler's dusty red cloak – then through his black SS uniform, and into the flesh beneath, carving a long and vicious gash. Scrawls of bright blood burst out, hanging in the air, as Khatri rolled his hip and threw the Nazi aside, parrying Caligula's backswing and ducking under another sweep of Rasputin's morningstar.

The censer hissed past, chain snapping taut, and Khatri reversed his grip, smashing it with the flat of the scythe-blade. It rocketed back toward the Russian monk, thudding into his chest and driving the breath from his body.

"Give it up, all of you!" shouted the Reaper-Captain. "You're mythsick, and you need help! If you don't give up those evil echoes, you'll be cursed forever."

Rasputin wiped a long, sticky streak of blood from his beard, gasping.

"*Forever*, my dear Captain, means we never die. Immortality! It's well worth the price of forgetting who I really was, back in Stalingrad. Better to be a monster from an earlier age. A glorious one!"

"I thought you'd say that. Too bad. Because you've all died once, already. It's time to remember."

Khatri planted his stance. He folded up his scythe between two hands, ending in what looked very much like an attitude of prayer. He bowed, then beckoned the three lost souls on.

They needed little encouragement. Caligula, Hitler and

Rasputin were intoxicated with power. Like addicts, they convinced themselves they could stop whenever they wanted.

But here's the thing about the office of the Grim Reaper. It's *all about* stopping people, whether they want to or not.

Khatri caught Caligula first, leaning back to let the point of the gladius whisper past his neck. He grabbed the back of the man's head with one hand, then splayed the bony fingers of the other and wrapped them around his face.

There was a burst of purple light. There was a sense of cold, and of falling, even though everyone stayed perfectly still.

Then Caligula dropped, boneless, to the ground. His sword clattered from his grip. Curiously, his eyes had gone utterly black, speckled with stars.

Hitler was next. He attacked from the right, and Khatri had no choice but to let one of the daggers go ripping through his cloak, narrowly missing his ribs. The other he blocked with a deft twist of his wrist, tucking the Nazi's forearm under with his own, so that he could press his palm against the man's face.

Once again came that pop and flare, all chilly ozone. This time, Khatri felt the death-hex flow through him, unlocking memories.

In that frozen second, Hitler remembered the sound of Russian tanks, rumbling through concrete. *The taste of gun oil in his mouth, and the barrel of the pistol scraping against his teeth, as he screwed up his eyes and his courage...*

The sharpened chain of Rasputin's morningstar whipped around Khatri's arm as he stood there, Hitler's body hanging ragdoll-limp from his palm.

"What did you do to them?" rasped the mad monk, one eye swollen shut, blood matting his unruly beard. "Tell me! Or I'll pull this chain, and have your arm off. *Snick,* just like that!"

Khatri smiled, and it was a terrible thing to behold. Even behind his impassive bone-white helmet, you could tell the smile was there, hung like a body on barbed wire.

"I gave him the memory of his death. Both of them. You see, the *real* Caligula was stabbed by a mob of Roman senators, after he left a list of murders on his desk for everyone to see. I made him feel all sixty-five stab wounds. He's still feeling them now."

The erstwhile God-Emperor twitched on the ground, drooling. His hands waved feebly, as if staving off invisible knives.

"And we all know what happened to *Der Fuhrer*, don't we? Took the coward's way out, at the end. Didn't want to end up hanging from a lamp-post, or worse, torn to bits in a courtroom, having to justify his madness."

There was only night in Hitler's eyes, as he whimpered in a fetal ball on the gravel. But there was a certain angle where, horribly, there was a suggestion that you should be able to see daylight through them.

Rasputin laughed, twitching the sharpened chain. Khatri felt it bite into his skin, prickling up a line of blood.

"Ha! Then I'm safe, aren't I? They couldn't kill me! Poisoned, stabbed, shot, bludgeoned, frozen, drowned, and I still came back!"

There was a flicker of confusion there, for a moment. The monk's bushy eyebrows furrowed.

"That is how it went, wasn't it?"

Reaper-Captain Khatri sighed.

"That's how it went, for the real Rasputin. For you, it just means that this is going to take slightly longer."

He moved before the myth-sick monk had time to react, stepping in close, slackening off the chain, and flicking a loop of it up and around Rasputin's head. In an instant he had him; the Russian couldn't pull the chain tight without cutting his own head off.

"Fool," he hissed through his beard. "The Cardinal has already replaced you! You'd have been better off going into nightmares, or staying in fiction. Death has no place for you. Not any more."

Khatri contemplated the palm of his own hand, then. He looked into the violet light welling up, and he nodded.

"Wherever I am, that's a place for death," he said, with utter, coffin-lid certainty. "What can I say? I love my work."

Those skeletal fingers wrapped around the side of Rasputin's bald head, and a sizzling blast knocked the reason from his skull. His eyes welled up black and starry as Khatri let him fall.

The scythe came out in a blur, telescoping and clicking into place before the mad monk hit the ground. *Snick* – and the tethers of his soul were cut. Just like that. A spin on one heel, a figure-of-eight whisper of silver, and the other two were done.

They peeled apart like burning paper, those lost souls. A dust of glowing motes blew away across the vast face of the mirror behind them. Then came the spirits of the dead men who had ridden the power of stories. Or been ridden by them; Khatri made no distinction.

A sad and doughy-looking skinhead, with a bad swastika tattoo on his cheek. A thin, shifty-eyed old man in a knitted vest and tweed trousers. A grizzled-looking soldier, with his lip twisted up into a sneer by a scar healed wrong.

They struggled to rise from flesh gone cold and pale. They got part of the way clear before something began to tug at them, plucking at their corners and edges. One by one they felt the pull, and turned huge and horrified eyes on something Khatri couldn't see. One by one, they saw the sun rise over a desert made of tiny black gems, and stared into the dripping jaws of Ammut...

Three screams were cut off, with a sound like a ruler a billion miles long, twanging across the edge of some cosmic desk. And then there was nothing left on the mountainside, except a few strewn boulders which might, with a long look and a squint, appear to be three huddled human bodies.

Because this was fiction, and because of all that had just unfolded, the far-off tones of a Japanese *shakuhachi* flute blew in on the breeze. Jaghtaran Khatri shrugged, folded up his scythe, and stepped through the mirror.

Twelve
The Pits of the Duat
vs
The Panopticon

SEPTEMBER HAD NEVER been locked up inside a paddywagon before. She was aware, of course, that you weren't really allowed to call them that these days. But that was all just games with words. The reality was a big, cold steel box on wheels, with thoroughly uncomfortable seats and a faint smell of urine.[28]

Cedric seemed to know about the back end of police vehicles all too well; he slumped defeatedly in the corner, groaning to himself when he thought September wasn't listening.

But she was oddly optimistic. She was certain a plan would suggest itself. And, after all, she was in the afterlife. Another world!

Even the most determinedly normal people sometimes entertain the notion that they're meant for magic. Blame children's authors if you must. But the fact remains that a little whiff of destiny is a potent drug. It explains, amongst other things, horoscopes, gambling and no small number of marriages. It makes people behave as if they were in their own fairy tales, even when they aren't.

Right now, September was lost in her own, staring out of the tiny barred window of the not-paddy-wagon. Uncarnadine, wrapped up in its eternal midnight, was like

---

28. These days, they were called 'suspect relocation vehicles', and Little-Mean-on-the-Average didn't have one. Constable O'Dwightly spent quite a lot of his time leafing through exciting magazines with names like 'Total Enforcer' and 'SWAT Hardware Enthusiast', but the Borough Council had not seen fit to fork out for the list of matte-black tactical things he so desired.

a reef of neon corals, teeming with a whole nation of the dead.

They may have been deceased, but the people of this town were very much alive – getting in one last drink before the ultimate closing time. There were even ghostly zeppelins cruising between the skyscrapers, their gas-bags glowing and transparent. Some of them were quite conventional in a 1930s art-deco way. Others had yachts and tugboats swinging underneath them, complete with the holes in their hulls where they'd been wrecked. One even boasted an entire thatch-roofed cottage as a gondola, with window boxes full of flowering vines. Broomsticks were ranked up on its porch.

Now, knowing what Kolslaw had said, September could see that it was terribly crowded out there. People were living on top of buildings, bridges, skyscrapers, construction cranes and under railway arches, statues, monuments and scaffolding. However, mostly they were living on top of and underneath each other.

No wonder space was such an obsession, she mused. Even magical worlds, it seemed, had civic council issues, and probably stupid Standard Academy schools as well.

The sound of Cedric's voice jolted her from her reverie.

"They took the scythe, and the Tarot, even though I hid them," he groaned.

This was actually an improvement. For a while there, September had been worried that the sounds he was making might mean that he was sick, or at least very constipated.

"I don't know why they didn't search *you*," he went on, "but just those two things alone are enough to get us both in serious trouble."

"How serious can it really be?" asked September, stepping away from the bars. "I mean, compared to being arrested in the afterlife, in he first place?"

Ced fixed a pair of runny, poached-egg eyes on her, and slumped even further back on his seat.

"Bad enough. For example, we're not going to the Clock Tower, which is where we should be headed. I know the streets here very, very well. I did ten years as a community constable before they'd even *think* of letting me be a Reaper. I've got a map in the soles of my feet, and all that. *We're going the wrong way."*

September didn't find out just how wrong until the paddywagon slowed, and she felt the road angle downward. Outside the window, the skyline of the city was eclipsed by concrete. They went rumbling under a vast, monolithic gateway, at the bottom of a canyon of billboards. Every last one of them advertised a company called Gravesend Consolidated.

**Rehabilitation starts
with the right attitude!**

Enthused one such neon-lit canvas, the size of a football pitch.

**Gravesend – Delivering
Synergistic Outcomes!**

Shouted another, next to a cartoon of a happy skeleton in an orange jumpsuit, breaking rocks with a sledgehammer.

September heard a clatter and thud, and she turned to find Cedric at the bars on the other side of the wagon.

"Crime doesn't pay, but Gravesend secured investments do," he read. "This is bad, Miss. Very bad. Do you think you could... you know?" He mimed wiggling his fingers, in the universal sign for 'weird magical hokum'.

September frowned, ready to make a cutting reply, but then she felt the metal of the bars under her fingers. She felt how easy it would be to let the Endarkenment flow over the steel, and creep around the entire paddywagon. No sooner had she pictured this than an awful sensation blurred through her brain; she was, *at the same time*, a red-haired girl in a long white lab coat, and a slightly beat-up 1968 Dodge truck.

But no.

She had to see this through, and get to the bottom of this Repo business, and Dark Lazarus, and – she supposed – save the world. It's what her great-great-granddad would have done, and it was going to require a certain amount of cunning.

"We have to get inside, wherever we are," said September. "For one thing, they counted Arbourdale and Virgil as evidence, and banged them up in a big plastic box. Then there's whatever that vulture Kolslaw is up to. When I mentioned the Repo trade, she looked about as sick as someone who's just noticed half a caterpillar in their salad."

Cedric turned away from the bars, as the old Dodge rumbled into shadow.

"Getting inside's no problem," he said. "This is the Ghost Trap. The new prison. What with the city getting overcrowded, the Mayor gave in and privatised it, see? Gravesend built this place, just like they built the loony bin and the hospital. When you're not alive, *every* sentence is a death sentence."

She looked at him quizzically, with the head-tilted-to-one-side frown she didn't realise she'd inherited from Septivarian.

"I mean, if they give you 400 years hard labour, it's not a euphemism!" he said. "Look, the reapers still work for the Clock, and Transit do too, but Enforcement is all recruits and rentals these days, and they hand down *completely mad* sentences for the smallest things. To get people off the streets. To get them in here. This isn't just a prison,

Miss. It's a *slave factory*. If they're not taking us to the Clock Tower, they're going to try to bury us."

It wasn't six feet of graveyard earth they'd thought of, either. It was paperwork.

Brakes squealed. Boots thudded on concrete. Doors clanged. And pens scratched, scribbling and scrivening a path down into oblivion.

The long and horrible route through the intestines of Gravesend's prison was greased by yellow forms, in triplicate. September and Cedric were manhandled onto a little rubber-wheeled electric cart by two goons in full-face gas masks, then driven down miles of identical concrete corridors, every last one painted a drab shade of green.

There were little cubbyholes at every intersection, in which lurked a range of cobwebbed and mummified clerks. Each one was distinguished from the last only by the obvious ways in which they had died; here, a missing cross-section of a head, there, a garden fork through the chest, and there again, a scalp still burning blue with acetone. At every stop-off, a shuttered window rattled open and one of these spectres peered out. They compared Cedric and September to a black-and-white picture on a little beige monitor, then each one added a thick, musty wad to their official paperwork. Soon, one of the masked goons was carrying a cardboard box full of files.

September tried to ask questions. The goon driving the little cart held one rubber-gloved finger up to where, he presumed, his lips were. *Shush.*

There was no sound in the bowels of Gravesend's prison. Only the oppressive silence which comes from a billion tonnes of concrete squatting right on top of you. The scuttling of a cockroach across the ceiling sounded like tap-dancing. The drip of condensation, from the great lagged and steaming pipes overhead, was like the

Azraeon's clock itself.

Presently, the cart squeaked into a lift, and a zombie in a bellboy's uniform threw a lever. Grated doors rumbled closed, and the cart rose, to the sound of opera played on rusted speakers. Then, as they came clattering up into empty air, September saw what this prison for the dead was really like.

In 1791, animal rights activist, founder of the Thames River Police and liberal philosopher Jeremy Bentham devised an idea so horrible that it made the politicians of the day shiver in their powdered wigs.

He'd been asked to design the perfect prison, to replace the tottering, rat-infested, black-dog-haunted and allegedly cannibalistic old pile at Newgate. What he came up with lacked moats full of crocodiles and reams of razor wire. Instead, he envisioned a prison where there was simply *no privacy*; one where everyone had to assume they were spied on every hour of the day or night. Internalised guilt would beat down the urge to be wicked more effectively than any amount of truncheon-wielding guards. Or so Mr Bentham thought.[29]

At least, thought September, *he'd had the good grace never to bloody build it. Gravesend had.*

The lift juddered to a stop, and a cold wind rattled the gates of the cage. They squealed back on their runners, and rough hands bundled Cedric and September out of their cart, and out onto a colossal concrete pier, jutting from an encircling wall as pale and huge as the surface of the moon. It was all art-deco and grim, stained and weeping rust, and it described a bowl as wide around as the biggest asteroid craters. Football stadiums would have

---

29. September knew all about the prison he'd designed – the Panopticon – because of an essay she'd written in school about the novel '1984'. An essay about how shrill, hand-wringing internet experts kept referencing it, but had almost universally *never actually read it.*

been swallowed whole, with room to spare.

A domed sky loomed above, all dirty riveted metal. Below it a wall curved away, like the glacier-front of an ice age. But it wasn't just a wall. It was an endless grid of tiny, open doors. Every last one of those doors was the cut-out back of a tiny cell, and in each one was a single hard little plank bed, a single stained porcelain toilet, and a single light bulb hanging on a wire. They were all empty.

There was a sound to this vaulted space, and a smell, too. The sound was the rattle and bang of construction, of rivet guns and jackhammers, trucks reversing and cranes swinging their loads into position. The air reeked of concrete dust and welding rods, stale sweat and misery.

But what were they building?

This was something September pondered as they trudged out across the massive arch of the bridge, too far from the tall steel parapet to look down. The only other thing to focus on was a kind of twisted lighthouse, squatting at the centre of it all.

It was ugly, as only prison architecture can be ugly. A kind of Soviet version of Sauron's tower, holding up a mad collection of bulbs and lenses, all welded into a sphere. They clattered and moved, according to a whole astrolabe of pistons, motors, drive-chains and rings, and magnified in each one was a bloated, bloodshot eye.

September had a lot of time to consider this as they made their way toward it. And she fancied that she recognised that jaundice-yellow eyeball. When the doors of the tower were thrown back and a tongue of red carpet unrolled, she found that she was absolutely correct.

On a rotating throne, set in a birds-nest of brass and steel steampunkery, sat Sharon Kolslaw, head of Transit, a gloating smile plastered across her face. She fussed with her tiny dark glasses as she rose, tucking her eyeball monocle back into her top pocket.

"So nice of you to join us!" she grinned. "You're just in time to join our happy little family, and complete the construction of Stage Three," Kolslaw rubbed her hands together briskly, all business. "We're going to revolutionise *everything* you think you know about dying!"

"This whole deal is a pretty big surprise already," shrugged September, who felt that this was no time to appear impressed. "You know most people think you just rot in the ground, or that your soul goes to play a harp on a cloud, right?"

Kolslaw grimaced.

"I know it all too well! That's why this stupid, inefficient system exists in the first place! Woolly thinking, muddled beliefs, new-age woo-woo and a general lack of backbone. No offence, Gerald."

This last was addressed to one of the monitors of the panopticon, who hung from strings suspended from the ceiling. It was clear that all of his bones had gone missing somehow, leaving him a human sock-puppet. He winked and smiled, flashing a floppy thumbs-up.

Kolslaw nodded, and stalked down a steep set of stairs toward them.

"No! Too long has this foolish city accommodated the *silliness* of humanity! Transit used to *mean* something – my lads and ladies met every soul at the gates, and had them ticketed, processed, and out to the right afterlife before you could say 'existential crisis'. Now Khatri and complete muppets like your boyfriend there just shovel them in, and never mind the consequences! That's why it has to *stop!* That's why Gravesend, bless its balance ledgers, has invested in a solution."

Kolslaw's hands flicked out as she strode past September and Cedric, gesturing to her goons. They bundled the pair along with her as she strode to the rail. And it wasn't just September's imagination – the Transit boss really *was* getting taller and thinner, her arms attenuating out of her sleeves, and her fingers becoming long and knotted, like the roots of sunless trees.

"Look! Look what we're building here! For those who refuse to choose an afterlife, we're making one that works. These lost souls have been given the *correct motivation*, Miss Normalsson. See what we can achieve when we allow the free market to guide us!"

They reached the edge, and Sharon Kolslaw's gesture took in a full third of the great Panopticon. It was a concrete world, lit by the fires of industry below. There were millions of people at work in the pit; orange-jump-suited prisoners and guards in uniforms and gas-masks, wielding long whips. Machines cobbled together from dead excavators prowled like spiders, and spindly cranes lifted huge pipes, girders and slabs of concrete into position.

They were building Hell.

Not in any metaphorical way. Not allegorically, or as a snide little jab at corporate architecture. No; this really was an industrial-style copy of the Inferno. And it was *huge*.

Circantrates had been hacked into the bedrock. Pipes like great metal maggots gushed with propane flames. Lakes and vats of bubbling acid lapped shores of spikes. There were machines made for torture on a grand scale, ziggurats of sadistic madness, forests made for impalement, and great ovens yawning hungrily for flesh. All were surrounded by gothic cathedral architecture, carved with demons and skulls. Three huge, tilted towers speared up from amongst the red rock and fire, all pale marble and black iron. Each one was bigger than the biggest skyscraper September had seen on television. All three appeared to be built inside pentagrams paved in onyx and gold. Just looking at it, empty, sickened September to the bone. The thought of it full and fully operational was nauseating.

For once, she was at a loss for words. Even the black aura which was scribbled around her fingers flickered like bad neon where she gripped the rail tight. Cedric managed to speak first.

"Why?" he gasped, turning to their captor.

Sharon Kolslaw had fully transformed, now. She reached up and plucked away her little black glasses, revealing a pair of dark and sunken sockets where her eyes should have been. Two sockets, into which were screwed a pair of shiny copper coins.

"Because by not choosing, they're still making a choice," she hissed. "And because, for hundreds of years before that fool Dante made his move, this world was *mine!* Mine! I was the Psychopomp Supreme! Before humanity replaced me with some agricultural metaphor done up in bones, things were *efficient!* **One** afterlife, **one** way to get there, and **one** authority. Me! Ohhh, yes. It's time for what you humans call a 'regime change'. And this time, I'll be able to enjoy everything the living world has to offer, as well. This is going to make us rich and powerful, beyond all our dreams. Up there *and* down here!"

Something September had read about as a child, long before it had been mentioned in school, came bubbling up to the top of her mind.

"Two pennies a time wasn't enough for you, then?"

Kolslaw chuckled again, with the rasping sound of a nightmare predator. Her parking-warden's uniform had become a long and flowing robe, and her haircut, all shiny and domed, had attenuated into a cowl. She hunched over and tilted her head, like some great stalking heron, with a monstrous curved blade of a nose for her beak.

"You know, they even forget those, most of the time,"

she spat. "And adjusting for inflation, it should be more like... never mind. This new regime is going to be *ever* so profitable. A church that can prove Hell is real? That can send you there, and pluck you back out again, to tell everyone all about it? We'll be *rolling* in it. Which is why I wanted to give you a chance, September. Repo made this possible. But we need that card your granddad squirrelled away. The last one up his sleeve. We need Dark Lazarus. We've built him a throne. What do you say?"

September had expected, perhaps, the threat of immortal, undead slavery. She'd anticipated being thrown off the edge of the Panopticon, and down into the depths of Kolslaw's ersatz Hell. She hadn't even remotely prepared herself for a job interview.

"You want *me* to help *you?* **Me?** The one who you've been trying to *kill* this whole time? And the one who, by the way, has figured out that you're not Sharon. You're *Charon.* The ferrym... um... ferryperson. Of the underworld."

"Oh, indeed! Charon, the harbinger of equal opportunities in the workplace," the apparition chuckled. "And I was never trying to kill you. Those horrible Elvi, *they* wanted you wiped out. They see infinite futures, there in their little nuclear-fried time loop. They know that in a lot of them, you'll shake my hand, right now, and change all our worlds for the better. Just as your great-great-grandfather intended."

"He intended to work with your mate the Cardinal, did he?" asked September, a little skitter-crack of anger spiderwebbing across the ice of her mind. "He *intended* to push a drug that makes people go mad, and get possessed?"

The look on Charon's face turned like the flip of a coin, light into shadow. It went from vile cheerfulness to abject pity in a heartbeat.

"You mean you never worked it out? Smart girl like

you?" The ferryperson's face was a perfect mask of tragedy. "He *invented* it!"

"Repo?" asked September, in an ashen little voice.

"*Of course*, Repo! He had to have some leverage, if he wanted to bargain with the dead. A regular seance doesn't cut it, when you want something as twisty as the true identity of the Devil! All the crocheted doilies and patchouli oil you could muster wouldn't help! It was your old grandpa who found out what the dead really want. *They want to go back to the land of the living.*"

September didn't want to believe what she was hearing.

"Back to reality? Back to pollution, and economics, and crooked politicians, and war and famine and the 6 o'clock news? Back to the pop chart 100, and fast food, and 9-to-5 slavery until your brains dribble out your ears? It looks better over here!"

"Really?" chuckled Charon. "You know the problem with Uncarnadine? The one that grinds your soul down like a rotten tooth? It's a *fake*. A faded watercolour. A photocopy, with the toner almost run out. Air like a stale old inner tube! The flowers look lovely, but they smell like a grandma's attic. Every hamburger is the ghost of someone else's hamburger, and every meal is the memory of someone's indigestion!"

"Does that mean they're farts?" asked Cedric. "Umm... honest philosophical question. Not trying to lighten the mood."

Charon grinned, with a set of teeth like the staved-in planking of a shipwreck.

"He thinks he's being funny, but they might as well be. This place is a tomb of regrets, September. We *all* want out. And by possessing humans, we can do it. That's why your dear old grandpa invented the stuff. Silas Rosewood got him the funds, and he used a machine called B.I.S.H.O.P to work out the alchemy. Have you heard about the Voodoo *Loa*, miss Normalsson?"

September had, because it was a wonderfully gruesome tradition. She didn't get a chance to say so, however, because Charon was ever so keen to elucidate.

"Spirits, riding the bodies of humans, and becoming gods, after a fashion. For a little while, at least. If you were researching how to create a new, useful manifestation of Satan, you'd have to give that a poke, wouldn't you? And he did. A more evil, mad, twisted scientist I cannot recall. It was a pleasure to match wits with him. So, what do you say? Keen to get on board with the new firm, girl?"

She pretended to consider, for a second.

"I could be convinced. I am, after all, the great-great-granddaughter a supervillain, right? But what about the others? What about reaper-boy here, and the little fuzzy one, and the berk in the lamp?"

Charon shrugged, balancing her dark glasses back atop her huge beak of a nose.

"Do I care? The Cardinal didn't say anything about them, though you'd better believe he wrote you up a contract already. You can have the lot, so long as we get that Tarot. After all," she leered, pointing one long and gnarly finger at Cedric. "It's thanks to *this* idiot that poor old Captain Khatri is missing, and his own bloody Death-card with him. Without that, or the scythe, he's no threat to me. Transit are staging a bit of a hostile takeover right now, with Gravesend's rent-a-cops to help them. I'd be a right onion not to show a little gratitude."

September risked a glance at Cedric, who returned it. A flicker of hope snapped between them.

They hadn't found the scythe, or the tarot of Death. Even though Cedric said he'd hidden them. Even though he was sure they'd been taken. Which meant...

"You know what, Miss Kolslaw? Actually... *really*, Kolslaw? the Charon part, I get, but..."

The ferryperson of the damned shrugged.

"You needed a surname on the application form. It was what I had for lunch that day."

"What I was thinking was this. Give me back Arbourdale, and Virgil, and I'll keep this handsome little moron as my henchman. A mad scientist ought to have brainless henchmen, don't you think? The stupider the better. It's traditional."

Cedric looked suitably gobsmacked. Charon grinned, as only a creature with a smile like a pair of splintered matchbooks could. A snap of those long, loathsome fingers, and a pair of gas-masked thugs trotted off to fetch a plastic evidence box, with a very irate living teddy bear and an unlit hermit's lamp inside it.

"See? The Cardinal had all kinds tedious torments planned for when you said no. But of *course* you're going to be reasonable! Septivarian Quintimegistus Archimedes' successor, I said, is not going to be some sentimental drip." She rustled around inside her robes, and came out with a long and spidery scroll.

"Right! Here's your toys, here's the keys to your toy-boy's handcuffs, and here's a bloody huge long contract on a scroll, because our boss, bless his little ecclesiastical socks, likes things to have a certain amount of gravitas. Sign *here*, and *here*, and initial *here*."

A lackey proffered an entirely black peacock-feather quill pen, and indicated several places on the scroll.

"Don't you want to know what changed my mind?" asked September.

"Well... I suppose, if we're going to be in business together..."

Charon leaned in horribly close. The effect was like

watching a furled umbrella wilt, to the sound of popping vertebrae. September stood on tip-toe.

"You think you're the bad guy here, but that's not how the story works. Here, you're *Authority*. And I'm a supervillain. Which means that *you* get doublecrossed. Thanks for monologuing your whole evil plan."

September's smile was prim and sweet, and utterly terrifying. She heard Cedric shucking off his cuffs. She heard the top pop off of Virgil and Arbourdale's box.

By comparison, Charon's picket-fence grin had gone all wobbly.

The boss of Transit saw September's hand come out of the pocket of her too-big lab-coat, all wrapped up in the chromed steel and black rubber of the Befuddler's gravitonic manipulator, and she knew she was in trouble.

Exactly the thing she'd needed, right now.

He'd built it to throw tanks about, and dismantle cruise missiles in flight. When you're a supervillain, that kind of thing is your bread and butter. With a gesture, September ripped through the metal plating between Charon's feet, coiling it up like a length of carpet. The Ferryperson tottered, shrieking fit to burst. A guard raised his gun, but September gripped the metal nib of that absurd peacock-plume pen and sent it corkscrewing across to plug the barrel.

Then she reached past Charon, and grasped the iron frame of the Panopticon. Wyrd forces ran through her fingers in a shimmering surge, flux lines warping.

"I'm a Keen and Curious young scientist, Miss Kolslaw. And you know what? I think I'd like to try a little experiment."

September plucked all of the lenses away, spinning them through the air. Another snap of her wrist and they snicked into place, biggest to smallest, in a cone which pointed straight down at Charon.

Up above, through the iris of the Panopticon's dome, hung a sunless sky. But September wasn't trying to focus light. The moon which beamed down from above wasn't a moon at all. It was the face of the Azraeon, the original Angel of Death, and she'd concentrated the trillion-year stare in his eyes.

"You wouldn't dare," croaked Charon.

"You're the second person who's guessed that wrong, today," said September.

And she let the Endarkenment loose.

A beam of turquoise energy lashed out, turning every drop of moisture in the air to frost. Where it splashed against the walkway it threw off tiny inverse rainbows, in every shade of black. Steel turned instantly to powdered rust, and Charon scrabbled backwards, like some monstrous cockroach.

"*Tell me you were lying!*" shouted September. "My great-Grandad wasn't evil! He wasn't crazy! He was just. Very! **Misunderstood!**"

Prison lackeys looked upon the face of September, and trembled. Things that had been dry bones for decades suddenly felt a pressing need for fresh underwear. She was levitating now, magnetic fields sizzling around her, and her hair floated like deep-water seaweed on the currents of it.

"It's... it's a *m-m-m-mad scientist!*" stammered a huge undead thug, his gas mask dropping off to reveal a mummified skull with yellow eyes. "Run for your unlives!"

Stooges and lackeys fled the Panopticon's central platform as September wielded the stack of lenses, dicing machinery and scoring gouges across the concrete dome. Tiny, empty cells detonated. Toilets full of dire home-brewed liquor ignited like far-off fairy lights, all up one wall.

"Mad doctor! Every ghoul for himself! Sound the alarm!"

A little laugh escaped from September as she sheared the warning klaxon in half. The stitched-together apparition who had been reaching for it curled up in a ball, and began to cry, sucking its thumb.[30]

"Mad? She shouted. *Mad?* They all called me mad! *Me!* Whose only crime was creating a frog more perfect than the sum of its sad little dissected parts! Mad! For daring to go to a birthday party my parents didn't approve of! I'm a Smart and Curious Young Lady! I'm not mad, for... for having no friends except old, dead scientists, and elderly supervillains, and..."

September only realised she'd gotten a little carried away when the turquoise beam decapitated the Panopticon, sending its ball of gears and lens-frames crashing down. Charon scuttled back to her throne, which telescoped up like some nightmare barber's chair, out of the severed neck of the tower.

"Do your duty, probationary officer Welbourne!" she shrieked, in a voice which had hollered 'all aboard' to a billion plague victims. "You brought this maniac here! *You* stop her! Or it's the Reject Chute for you both!"

Her hands hauled back a set of levers, like the ones which switch railway tracks, and a slab of concrete rumbled open.

In the purple glow which blasted up from beneath, September noticed Cedric's face. It was all twisted up with fear and guilt – everywhere except his eyes. Those were fixed on September, and they were resolute. For the first time, she got an inkling of why he'd been chosen to be a Reaper. There was iron in that look, and ice, and duty.

He held Captain Khatri's scythe out in front of him. It

---

30. Well, *someone's* thumb. There were a lot of stitches, and it seemed to be the wrong colour. But it was firmly attached to the thing's hand, which is really nine-tenths of the law, where thumbs go.

wobbled, just a little, but it was pointed at her. September's toes touched the ground again, as the black aura around her sizzled low. He couldn't *really*...

"Miss Normalsson? Are you in there? I'm afraid I'm going to have to get you to stand down. Turn it off. All of it. Ummm... I'm not exactly on Commander Kolslaw's side, exactly, but... I think she might be right."

"Right about what?" asked September, with a little tremor in her voice. Being threatened by Cedric Welbourne, even when he was armed with the Blade of Ultimate Entropy, was like being menaced by a dachshund. But it was one that remembered that it was just a tiny bit wolf.

"Ced? Come on! I, erm, got a bit carried away, there, but *what did she say?*"

September looked past him now, at the many fires still burning, the holes punched through the great perimeter wall of the Ghost Trap, and the palls of smoke rising from the New Hell below them. A construction crane chose this moment to buckle at the waist, toppling down to ruin.

"She asked what really happened to your granddad," he said, in an ashen voice. "The one who never turned up here, even though I tagged him. The guy who was trying to cheat PostMortis. She thinks he's *possessed* you, September. He's hiding in your head. After all, he invented the Repo. And, well..." He looked left and right, at all the devastation. "You just did *that*. With the big monologue, and everything."

"Cedric! Come on! It's *me*," began September, taking a tentative step forward. The stack of lenses crashed to the ground and shattered. Cedric and Charon recoiled at the same time.

They were afraid. Both of them.

More afraid of her, in fact, than of the pit which now yawned in front of Charon's throne. A pit which exhaled the smell of boiled dry air, and glowed with a purple light.

September remembered that smell, and that crepuscular glow. She edged forward a little more, and looked down into what appeared to be a throat of swirling clouds. Beneath them spread a foreshortened little desert surrounded by pyramids. In the middle, the vast and horrible face of Ammut looked back at her.

Snap, went a set of jaws big enough to swallow whole nations. A set of beady little eyes glared from three kilometres down, and narrowed.

September felt a tug on the hem of her lab-coat, and looked down to see Arbourdale, carrying the hermit's lamp under one furry arm. Inside, Virgil was sound asleep, curled up with tiny cartoon 'z's circling his head.

"This don't feel right at *all*, Miss," said the little bear. "Any second now, someone else going to get betrayed, you mark my words."

September's eyes flickered from Arbourdale, back to Cedric, and then to the gloating cadaver-grin of Charon.

"Yes, but is it going to be *me*? Is he right? Is my great-Grandad trying to possess me, Arbourdale? I can't believe I actually had to ask a talking teddy bear that question!"

The ferryperson lurched forward on her throne. Its telescoping stem bent over so she could step right off.

"Give me the name, September! Tell me where we can find the Devil's tarot! We're just trying to build a world that makes *sense*, girl! All the really interesting parts of the bible could finally come true. Think of how comforting that'd be, for so many people!"

"Never!"

"Then you leave me with little choice," growled Charon. Quick as a snake, one of her long, knotty arms lashed out, and her fingers wrapped around Cedric's neck. The scythe tumbled from his fingers and fell – down into the purple glow of Ammut's realm, spinning end over end until it stuck blade-first into the huge monster's snout.

It must have hurt; Ammut roared, pawing at her muzzle. Yellowed claws the length of windmill blades came perilously close to hooking into reality.

"There it is..." muttered Arbourdale.

Charon flexed a set of ropy muscles, like shucked oysters on a broom handle. Cedric swung out wide, gurgling in terror.

"Oooh, yes! Nothing like rowing to build up your stamina. Great cardio, too. Now, September – let's do this again. Give me what I want, or he's going down the Reject Chute. The poor little sod actually *believed* me! And to think we wanted to make him an officer!"

September tried her hardest to appear cold and uncaring. Her black aura forked and sizzled.

"*Go ahead*. He turned on me, at the end. You dead things are all the same. Just remnants and echoes, that a scientist like me can use. I'll be taking the Devil's tarot, and completing Dark Lazarus, so I can rule the world. The *real* world. The one that you'll be locked out of, forever."

After all, a desperate bluff is what Septivarian would have done, in my situation, she thought. *Right?*

"You're a *much* worse liar than he was, girl," hissed the ferryperson. "I can see you, down to the bone. I know where you all think you deserve to go to, after all. And that's how I know you still think you can be...*ugh... good*. Despite the power, and the isolation, and the bitterness already growing inside you. Ahhh, yes. You still feel *mercy*. You still feel *gratitude*. It's **disgusting!**"

She let Ced slip between her fingers, and he lashed out, swinging wild. His fists didn't even reach past Charon's elbows.

"Come on, then! You know how this ends, September!

Give me the name, and you can have him back."

September sagged. She couldn't let the poor stupid boy die. Not like this.

"We never had a name!" she shouted. "But we had his exact time of death. We thought we could get into PostMortis, and scan through the records and find out who came through on June 12, 1666, at 1:03 am. That would be your ex-Devil. He'd have the card."

Charon cackled. It was a proper witchy one, that could have etched diamond glass.

"Ohhh! Clever, clever! Of course, your great-great-grandad could seek out all the clues, there in the realm of the living. Let me just see, then..."

The hand not clutching Cedric reached out, and hooked a screen on a long, jointed arm down from the Panopticon's throne. A few finger-taps, and a wash of green light – then Charon's grin stretched so wide it should have detached the top of her head.

"Right there, all along. All we needed was the bloody digits, eh? And, of course, we had a deal, didn't we? A little bit of information, and you and your boyfriend here could be back together?"

Arbourdale gripped the lamp tight to his chest, shaking his fuzzy little head.

"Awww, no, no no! Not after I've had a bloody folded-up scythe hidden somewhere very uncomfortable, and all..."

"Well then. I wish you every happiness together. *For the rest of your lives!*"

Now here came the double-cross. Charon uncurled her lean and gnarly arm, and hurled Cedric at September, hard. The young reaper grabbed her instinctively as his feet scrabbled on the edge of the pit, and September leaned backwards, trying to beat gravity. They spun, and she saw Ammut far, far below, licking her gigantic chops in anticipation.

For a second they teetered on the brink, tiny chips of concrete cracking off and skittering away into empty air. Then September lurched back, and staggered, holding Cedric up in an awkward hug.

She looked back over his shoulder. She saw the horrible, oily smile spreading across Charon's face. She saw the long black thread which stretched from the ferryperon's fingers, all the way across the pit, to where it had unravelled from the hem of Ced's uniform.

"Bye bye," chuckled Charon, pulling the string.

And then she was falling, tumbling down through purple light, with Ammut's jaws creaking open to meet her.

Suture Seven
The Red and the Black

HE'D COME ACROSS the border like the leading edge of a Monday hangover; a black figure scrawled onto the dust. Every mote was a single fragment of regret, because this was the Azraeon's country – and Jaghtaran Khatri was finally home.

The border guards had been from Transit, and that hadn't tweaked him. Not at first. It wasn't much of a surprise to find them out in the badlands, where the cold wind sifted between the rocks and wrecks. The road was a whip-scar in the moonlight here, and they'd sat right in the middle, next to an old Indian Scout with a sidecar, both of them smoking cigarettes that couldn't kill you, this side of the veil.

Both carrying guns, too.

That tweaked him. That make the memory of his fillings itch, where the silver they'd put in his teeth hadn't made it through to the afterlife.

Jaghtaran Khatri had a thing about guns. He had a history with them, and a hole in his ghost-flesh to match, there under his regulation black robes.

More importantly, Transit cops weren't supposed to go armed. They were meant to see to it that souls who'd outlived Uncarnadine got to where they were meant to go, or at least where they believed they should be headed.

Call it caution, then, the way he sunk down into the gloom, quiet as ice melting into ink. Maybe call it something a little bit more. He was thinking about the Cardinal, (and Gravesend, and the sad predictability of betrayal) as he crept up on the pair, easing from darkness to darkness.

There was a second, as he emerged from the shadow of the vintage motorcycle, when the pair of them turned. Pupils pinholed down, and eyes went wide. Hands fumbled with oily metal, and curses got stuck sideways in a pair of throats.

Mr Khatri was good at reading people. He'd seen a lot of them, at that point in their lives when masks were set aside. He smelled the treason boiling off of those Transit boys like rank sweat, and noted that they made no attempt to talk.

Their guns came up. The brace of them were silver, stolen from someone's dying memory of a Spaghetti Western. But the scythe – it was a poem hammered out of endings, a song in flight, a swallowtail's flicker in its apprehension.

Two hands tumbled through their air, knuckles tight around a couple of pearl handles. Two sprays of arterial blood painted the dust, black as Chinese calligraphy. The guns hit the ground, and both went off; the bullets were made of metal he could taste in the air as they flew.

Wedding-ring gold and christening silver, pieces from birthday jewellery and Valentines-day gifts. Things which people used to forget about death, and push it back into the shadows. Things that would put holes in a Reaper, for certain.

He supposed that was meant to be ironic.

The scythe spun in the air. At the top of its arc, the blade reflected what looked like a wink in the Azraeon's eye.

"*I need your clothes, your boots, and your motorcycle,*" Jaghtaran Khatri said, an echo of Fiction still clinging to him, like smoke on cashmere. Then came the sound of a crisp piece of paper being ripped in two, and four separate thuds, and a patter that absolutely wasn't a shower of summer rain.

He'd really appreciated the bike. *Something like the one*

that Cedric kid had tried to put through a wall, he recalled. And what should he make of *that* little situation?

He'd put it aside. He'd slid on a pair of black sunglasses, as though everyone was watching. Because some things, you just have to do *right*, if you want them to finish the way a story should.

Then he went to finish it.

Which came, at last, to *this*. A headlong, full-blast motorcycle assault on the great marble steps of the Clock Tower, scattering Transit lackeys in his wake.

Ironically, Jaghtaran Khatri felt more alive than he had for decades. He stood up on the foot-pegs and whirled his scythe around his head, one giant bat away from a classic album cover. Goons in black ducked and scurried across the marble, as the Reaper-Captain took a row of skeletal statues off at the knees. And roll, and tumble, and crush, and *scream!*

The bike juddered up over the broad steps, pistons thrashing, wire-spokes gleaming chrome. Up, and through a knot of Kolslaw's thugs trying to set up an old Maxim machine gun, bowling them down in a tangle. Up further, rubber peeling sideways across the marble, and he was at the doors of the citadel.

These were quite deliberately impressive – slabs of black marble the size of football fields, wrought with a confection of skulls and bones and curling vines in copper. They could have stood against an army, but as the commander of PostMortis, Jaghtaran Khatri was famously scornful of locks and doors. The gleam on the edge of the scythe took wing ahead of him, and the chains Charon's rebels had looped about the death's-head handles were shattered. The marble slabs cracked open, just enough.

Then he was through, and a snarl of engine noise went clattering away before him. Inside, the cathedral-vaulted hall of the Chronauspexion was flooded with moonlight.

Well – *a sort of moonlight.*

The Azraeon, huge and impassive, loomed over Khatri's shoulder, all inevitable. Under his silvery glow, the sanctum of PostMortis was cast in brushstroke monochrome.

The bike skidded to a stop. One bony foot slammed down the kickstand. The butt-end of the scythe rang against the ceramic tiles, each one imprinted with the signs of infinity and the omega.

There had been a battle here.

No – not a battle. A massacre.

Seeing as this was the other side, the *Immateria Aeternus*, there was no blood, and there were no bodies. Sad little piles of clothes and patches of frost told their tale; that of twice a hundred PostMortis officers sent to oblivion.

Here and there, the tattered remains of Transit Authority uniforms proved that Khatri's boys and girls had given almost as good as they'd gotten.

But this wasn't the worst part of the scene which greeted the Reaper-Captain, there in the great barrel-vaulted hall of the Clock Tower. His officers were scattered, his desk, up high on its central dais, was smashed in two. But worse; the Chronauspexion was silent.

It crouched in the half-darkness. A cresting wave of spidery, oiled machinery, snap-frozen. Nobody knew who built it – or if indeed, it *had* been built and not grown, or hatched, or something even weirder. But everybody knew that it never stopped.

It was a machine, in the same way that a hive of bees or your intestinal tract is a machine. Slickly organic, bulbous and curved, intermeshing and spiky, it rose up to form one entire wall of the Clock Tower's base. Some of its pipes carried little chrome ball-bearings around to a toothsome whisper of cogs, metres deep, stacked up like doric columns. Others were filled with mercury, or with fluorescent gases, or with slivers of rainbows and shadow.

The whole thing was lit by a brace of furnaces, boiling four cauldrons of molten glass, each big enough to drown a colossus. The sand which went into them, poured down from twisty funnels set high amongst the buttresses, came from the Possible Desert. Like the dust which puffed from Khatri's clothes as he strode across the hall, it was made of dead futures.

Because that was what the Chronauspexion made. *Dead futures*. Those pipes and nozzles and spills of sand all came together to produce hundreds of little hourglasses, all with a very finite amount of time in them. Conveyor belts led from the ice-blue mouth of the machine, stretching the width of the hall, to a row of sorting stations. From there, a spaghetti of pneumatic tubes shunted them to the personal lockers of a thousand Reaper-Operatives. It was rumoured that the Chronauspexion was plumbed directly into the spinal cord of the Azraeon himself. It told them who was about to die, and where to find them.

For centuries, since Dante's working, when it came into being (having always been in existence forever, from that time on), it had never once been wrong.

Now, Cedric Welbourne said that it had been... 'hacked', he believed was the modern term. And worse – it was broken. The molten glass had solidified in its cold cauldrons. The pistons were silent, and the cogs were still.

The reason why was poised on the wreckage of Reaper-Captain Khatri's desk, perfectly aware of the gravitas of the moment. He sat in a pillar of his own private midnight, and his robes were the crimson of a cut you've only just noticed, raw and deep.

Khatri didn't wait for him to speak.

"It's over, your Eminence. They couldn't stop me. Do you

still want to bother with the whole big villainous speech, or do we just fight, here, on *my* ground, and see what's left of you afterwards?"

Now Cardinal Syn deigned to incline his head. His face was a blur of features, in which only a very smug smile remained constant.

"Ahhh, yes. How very *heroic*, old son! But, you see, this isn't about you. Not anymore. This is about the Azraeon being rather in two minds about this whole arrangement. He's an angel. You're basically breeding agnosticism. It was easy to be, as it were, the conscience standing at his shoulder."

Which couldn't be true... could it? Khatri fought the urge, like an itch up his spine, to turn and look the skull-faced moon behind him in the eyes.

"You're lying," he grated, knuckles flexing around his scythe-grip.

"Of course," purred Syn. "Would you expect anything else? But feel the seduction of *doubt*, O righteous man. Isn't it delicious? I've managed to make the Chronauspexion doubt, just like you did, just now. Every time one of those poor Repo fiends up in the *Materia Mortalis* dies, the machine glitches. Order those glitches just right, and you can tell it who to kill, and when, and even... who gets to make the call."

"Like assigning Septivarian Archimedes to some poor sod on his first day?"

"*Exactly* like that. I wanted a screw-up who'd botch the job, and send the old charlatan scurrying for his lab. That, or put him in a hospital which I control. Either-or."

"You've perverted the course of mortality? You admit it?"

Now the Cardinal got angry. He slammed his fists against the rail, up there on the dais.

"You think there are still consequences to be had? *Come on!* I've already won! Gravesend got the best of both worlds. We used your reapers to murder our opposition in the *Materia*, and when they came down here we *hired* the ruthless bastards! We own the property, the technology – even the *theology* we need to reign, both here and there. You're a has-been, Khatri. You should have stayed in fiction."

"And you should have gone on to some bijou afterlife, Your Eminence. There are hells for people like you, you know. Places where you could be happy."

This time, the Cardinal's smile was a sneer, hitched up at one corner as if by hooks.

"People like me? There *are* no people like me! I'm not even *people* at all, Khatri! Let me tell you a little secret, Mister Ex-Reaper Captain; the 'Syn' in my name stands for **Synthetic Intelligence**. The reason I was able to become a ghost in your machine, so very easily, is because I'm the ghost *of* a machine. A machine which cracked the para-psycho-genetic code for Repo. A machine which was supposed to bring back the Devil, for people too short-sighted to see the potential of owning Him. No, Mister Khatri. I'm not people, and I don't *have* people. But I do have *customers!*"

Up on the platform, the Cardinal threw a switch, and for an instant a great billow of hellfire wreathed him, shot through with circuit-board diagrams. Now the pistons and wheels of the Chronauspexion began to turn again, but the glass tubes which threaded across the walls pumped with neon-green ooze. The cauldrons fired up, huge rings of propane flame glowing bright, and molten glass began to bubble. What came out, as the cogs chattered, and the whole great edifice sweated oil, was a steady stream of little hourglasses, filled at the top with Repo.

"*Customers*, Mr Khatri. Not clients like yours, who expect to be shepherded into the great hereafter for nothing, and who still think you're a monster. No! I'm talking about the living who envy the dead, because of the rotten system of the world above. And the dead who envy the living. We're going to show them that there's life after death! We're going to do it for fun and profit! And we're going to show them that Hell is very real, for those who don't obey! Do you have the *slightest* idea how much the politicians up there are going to pay me, when my bum's on the papal throne?"

"Speaking of bums," snarled Jaghtaran Khatri. "It sounds very much like yours is overdue for a kicking. That was a villainous monologue."

"That scythe is nicked from a fictional peasant, you berk," sneered the Cardinal.

"Yes," replied the Reaper-Captain. "But on my way here, I've made people believe in it. Quite hard, in fact."

The weapon in question shivered in his hands, twisting as if the wood of its handle remembered the tree it had once been.

"But..."

Cardinal Syn, for all he claimed to be the ghost of a dead machine, looked all too human at that moment. In fact, he looked like he'd polished off ten pints of extra-strong lager, then poured a triple-hot curry down on top of them, and felt, as the mini-cab pulled away from the kerb, the first rumblings of apocalyptic intestinal distress.

"*Charon told me you'd lost the tarot...*" he stammered. "*It can't be...*"

But it could.

"I'll bet you slit someone's throat for the power you're carrying," said Khatri, as the scythe became transparent as glass, then as solid as an idea, then folded up along hidden lines until it was just a one-dimensional memory.

"No!"

"The Hierophant, isn't it? Gutted some priest, with a snarky one-liner about the mercy of God? Something like that? Well, I *earned* mine. So long as Cedric Welbourne still thinks of me as his boss, the Card's more in here–" he tapped his chest, which suddenly looked, from a certain angle, like a bony ribcage, "than drawn on some piece of Florentine pasteboard. And the scythe, *wherever it is*, will come when I call it."

He opened his hand, now a skeletal claw, and let the memory fall. It was a single black line, like a pencil-stroke in the air, but when it struck the ground it crazed into a thousand cracks, shattering the tiles.

"*No!*" snarled Syn, as the darkness around him blazed. "It's my turn to win! *Mine!* I'm going to finish what my creator never had the courage to imagine, and not you, or that pitiful human great-grand-niece of mine are going to stop me!"

Two things happened at the same time, then. Things which, if the afterlife had insurance assessors, would have been pored over to find the tell-tale fingerprints of divine intervention. Because you don't have to pay out for acts of God, even if they're very tough acts to follow.

Cardinal Syn's face froze in a rictus of hate as he drew forth a sceptre from under his robes. The jewel at its tip had a very odd number of sides, and burned with a negative flame.

The cracks at Khatri's feet merged, and met. The sound of a hammer crushing a crystal champagne flute rang out, clear and bright.

Little pieces of reality fell away, down into a jagged-toothed gap of purple light.

Then the Cardinal spoke a Word. Something from the Hidden Key of Solomon, or the *Arcanum Maelifica*, or the shabby back pages of those newspapers which sell x-ray specs and levitating boots. Something twisty, all covered in hooks.

A bolt of black lightning corkscrewed up from his sceptre, up into the shadowed space above the Chronauspexion. Jaghtaran Khatri staggered back, as he realised exactly where his scythe was returning from. He saw, for a tottering, mad instant, the crater-sized eye of Ammut beneath him, its pupil narrowing down to a slit you could swim in.

Then something shimmered across that huge and limpid eyeball, raising ripples across the liquid on its surface. It arrowed up, through the crack in reality, and slammed into Khatri's hand, with a smack that sent him bowling over backward. It was a rod of steaming cold darkness – the Last Word in Lawn Care. The Trimmer of the Edge of Forever.

He caught it – just in time for Syn's blast to strike the huge glass bulb full of Repo which swung from the chamber's rafters. The one which was supplying the machine, and churning out doses for all his 'customers'.

The glass didn't just shatter. It *exploded*. A vast volume of mind-bending, arcane narcotics hung there for an instant, in a great wobbly sphere.

Then down it came. Down, past Khatri, who would have been slapped out of the Aught and into a human addict's brain so fast that his skeletal toes would have curled. Down, through a crack in reality that was healing up, far, far too slowly.

Down, falling though the cold dry air of Ammut's realm, to splash against the great beast's eye like the world's most ill-advised hit of LSD.

Khatri rolled to his feet, letting the scythe's blade hinge out with an oily little click. Frost traced fern patterns across the steel. Cardinal Syn looked down at his smoking crozius, then locked eyes with the Reaper-Captain.

The word they both said at once is thoroughly unprintable here – if only because these pages are flammable.

And beneath them, the pillars that held up the undercroft of reality shifted...

Thirteen
The Soul Eater
vs
Community-Based Policing

IT USED TO be easy being Ammut, the devourer of souls.

Slurk about near the cosmic scales that Anubis and Thoth took care of, make big puppy-dog eyes for the odd human heart or two, gnaw on the corpses of the unredeemed until they dissolved into regrets and memories... those were the days!

But the smorgasbord just couldn't last.

A few tasty dynasties and one big leap for civilisation later, and the food dried up.[31] Belief shifted, and theology frayed, and new afterlives opened for business. The old firm were part of Fiction now – if they showed up at all – and Ammut had curled up like a disgruntled cat, tucking her own tiny pocket reality around her.

Now the only food that came through was thin stuff, weak and tasteless. The doubly dead, mostly. That's why the scent which prickled in her gigantic nostrils was so very sweet. There was no sense of time in the tiny handful of desert which Ammut had coiled around herself, but it hadn't been so long ago that she'd smelled exactly the same delicious aroma.

The living! *Bloodgush and bonecrackle and slippery red panic!*

A group of tiny figures fell from the sky, and toward her open mouth.

One of those figures was September H. Normalsson, and she was having a bad day.

---

31. This might have been because most of it was mummified.

No – scratch that. She was having a *total disaster*, which had frazzled its way clear through twenty-four hours, and into that hot, prickly place where even black coffee ceases to work, as the brain recoils like a blow-torched slug from the whole concept of reality.

She was falling into the maw of a mythical monster, tumbling end over end until concepts like 'up' and 'down' made as much sense as a custard trombone. September reached out and grabbed the lamp which contained Virgil, and brought it up in front of her streaming eyes.

"This is going great!" enthused the little man inside.

"Great?" shouted September, her words sliced to ribbons by her own slipstream. "I have a *very* hard time accepting your definition of 'great', even if you are the world's greatest poet! We're about to get digested!"

"Awww, no we're not," said the tiny toga-wearing figure, tapping the side of his nose in a conspiratorial fashion. "You've worked it out, haven't you? I mean, this, this, *gravity* nonsense is all just to make the scene a little more suspenseful, isn't it? Super-villainous stuff, and all that? After all, I got a look at what Charon brought up on her screen. It'd be a shame to die now."

"You what?"

"I'm a *security system*, in case you didn't catch all that malarkey back at the lair. That ferry-paddling pillock was wearing dark glasses, and her computer screen was reflected right in them. All I had to do was zoom in. Now, come on, we've got a world to save!"

Down below, Ammut opened her jaws even wider, her tongue lolling out amid waterfalls of drool. There wasn't just a flock of birds down there to clean the monster's teeth; there were *colonies* of them, their nest-holes drilled into each colossal peg of enamel, and they swarmed around the soul-eater's blackened gums in a twittering cloud.

Focus! Virgil thinks I'm just showboating, which means Great-Grandad would have already been out of here, and on the trail. If only Newton's laws were a little more negotiable!

September looked down at her hand, which was still clad in the jointed metal gauntlet of the gravitonic manipulator.

"The pyramids!" she shouted, as she arrested her spin, reaching out toward Cedric. By instinct more than anything else he grabbed onto Virgil's lamp; September noticed that Arbourdale had attached himself to the junior Reaper's back like a fuzzy rucksack.

"What about the pyramids?" he wailed, sneaking a glance down toward the toothy chasm below. "I mean, it's hardly time to enjoy the view, Miss, even if it *is* geometrically interesting!"

"They can sharpen a razorblade!" shouted September. "Even my dad knows that one, and he's been avoiding anything remotely Fortean since I was a toddler. It's all something to do with" – (and here, she flexed her fingers inside that big metal gauntlet, feeling it fizz and crackle) – "their magnetic field!"

She had no idea how to really use the manipulator. But the Endarkenment whispered instructions right into her nerve-endings. She levelled her palm at the biggest pyramid she could see, clenched her fingers, and...

The world turned ninety degrees sideways.

There was a smell like burning roses and barber-shop hair, the taste of peppermint, and a wistful nostalgia for something September couldn't quite remember having actually experienced...

She was vaguely aware of her companions screaming, as her brain rotated slowly in her skull, and the desert blurred to the left. There was just time to take deep breath.

Then they hit the side of the pyramid, with a sound like steak slapping a chopping block. A radial shock-front of dust billowed out, as magnetic fields met and decided that they really didn't like each other. Luckily, this slowed September, Cedric, Virgil and Arbourdale down from the kind of speeds where the coroner needs a squeegee, to the kind of speeds which merely hurt.

September wheezed a very unladylike curse. Then she wished she'd saved it, because, even as the pain faded to a stubbed-toe blur, she began to slide.

As any student of ancient civilisations will tell you, pyramids are pointy. This one was slippery with antiquity, buffed smooth by time. Hieroglyphics scrolled upwards, offering no purchase for September's fingernails.

Somewhere, far away, came a snap, then a howl of confused, betrayed agony. What was perhaps the biggest tongue in the universe had just been bitten, and Ammut was not amused.

"Buggerbuggerbugger ohnooooo!"

September looked up just in time to wish she hadn't. Because Cedric, Virgil and Arbourdale were sliding just a tiny bit faster than she was, and they'd hit the pyramid above her. They swept her up in a tumble of lab-coat and school tartan, a tangle of curses, bumps, limbs, expletives and dust which finally splashed down in a sand dune made of tiny black gems. Cedric was the first to unfold himself from the pile.

"Well, at least I got hold of the scythe," he said, brandishing that gnarly cosmic weapon. "You really left it until the last minute to pull us out of Ammut's jaws, just so I could grab it! Right?" He smiled at September, a smile which was wobbly around the edges and fraying fast. "*Right?*"

She couldn't do much but groan. When they'd struck the pyramid, she'd broken the Gravitonic Manipulator, and it sparked feebly as she shucked it off her hand. There were bruises the colour of an angry sky all up her arm, and something sticky in her hair that she hoped wasn't blood.

"Of... ummm, of course. Yes. A strategic delay, definitely." September levelled a finger at the scythe, and a little spark of darkness popped from its tip. "Though that thing's got a mind of its own, you mark my words."

It certainly seemed so. Because just then, some force wrenched it out of Cedric's hand, leaving a nasty friction burn.

"Hey! Come back here!" wailed the young Reaper, jumping up and down with his injured fingers between his knees. "That's only on loan!"

The pair of them watched the scythe curve away, whipping upwards past Ammut's great craggy face, to disappear through a tiny hole in the sky.

"Does that normally happen?" asked September. But she didn't hear Ced's reply, or the yelp of fright which came from Arbourdale, or the cursing in Latin which issued from Virgil's lamp, as it rocked its way back to upright.

Because at that moment Ammut recoiled, stumbling backwards to land on her scaly rump. The ground trembled, and then the air did too, ripped asunder by a howl of utter animal outrage.

"That sounds bad" said Virgil. "Come on! Pick me up! You've got a plan to get us out of here, don't you?"

Six very mismatched eyes looked at September imploringly – two teddy-bear buttons, two tiny holographic pixels, and two belonging to an ex-junior-Reaper well out of his depth.

"Because it looks like big ugly over there has just gotten a nasty shock, and we're the only ones she can blame for it," said Arbourdale. "Oooh-errr. If looks could kill, folks, then all those teeth wouldn't be necessary!"

September looked to where Arbourdale's purple fuzzy

paw was pointing, and saw Ammut roll back onto her feet, shaking her head like a bee-stung rhino. A huge pair of eyes turned on the little party, and narrowed. One of them was glowing radioactive green, and seemed to be dripping fire.

"Any minute now, Miss," said Cedric, with a gulp.

September was quite surprised to discover that she *did* have a plan, after all. She deliberately took her eyes off of Ammut – miles away across the cold, black sand, but sorting out her huge limbs to get a real nostril-snorting one-monster stampede going.

"Cedric, when we were here last, and I opened up the Doom Clock, what did it say?"

"Well, that's the thing. See, you said you didn't want to know, but it was just flashing the time, back in the mortal world. It had stopped, because you were dead. Sort of. Temporarily."

September shook her head.

"No. It stopped, because there's *no time in here*. None at all. The only time that this place has experienced, for hundreds, maybe thousands of years, was the piece we brought in with us. So, what was it?"

"Four forty-four PM," said Cedric. "Exactly when the Chronauspexion told me your hourglass would run out," he shrugged. "Except that it didn't."

"And this is going to help us *how?*" asked Arbourdale, who was still staring off over September's left shoulder, at a rapidly approaching mountain of scaly death. Massive footfalls rumbled up through the desert beneath them. Tiny black gems jittered like poppy seeds on a hot plate.

"*Because time and space are the same thing*, you numbskull," said Virgil, who was grinning madly. "She gets it. Just like her old Grandad did."

September nodded.

"The Doom Clock doesn't measure time by observing the universe. *It measures how long you have left to live.* Seeing as we're in here, and we're alive, we've used it to bring time to a place that's timeless. I'm pretty certain that's a paradox which the universe doesn't like. We're going to make it *itch*. And if we set the Doom Clock to four forty-four PM, we'll create a loop back to the other time when it was here. We'll create a weak point that will want to spit the damned thing out, exactly like it did the first time around."

"Wouldn't you end up appearing in a hospital room with yourself?" asked Cedric. "I mean, in basic training, they said that if you ever met yourself, it could get *very* messy. There'd be some kind of cosmic disintegration thingy, with a big blast radius. Insurance got mentioned."

"That's the thing," said September, letting the wild, dark confidence of the idea build its rickety rails out into the unknown. "The universe is big and tangly and weird enough to be paradox-proof. We should, if I'm right, end up in the Little-Mean-on-the-Average Hospital, in whatever passes for 'now', back in reality."

Cedric pulled the little gold travel clock out from inside his leather jacket, and held it out to her.

"I don't even begin to understand all that super-science stuff," he said. "But I trust you. I reckon it's worth a try."

"You *think?*" asked Arbourdale, with a rising crescendo of terrified sarcasm. Ammut's shadow rose up and over them like a cresting tsunami, megatons of furious bulk behind it. The soul-eater's crocodile jaws were hinged wide open, so that a broad swathe of black desert was being ploughed up in front of her lower mandible, like rubble before a bulldozer blade.

"Do it quickly, and if we get disintegrated, at least it'll be over fast!"

September hardly even had to look down. There were

two tiny little plastic dials on the back of the clock, inside its clamshell golden casing, just like the ones on the back of her alarm clock, back at home.

In her pale blue room, with its pale blue bed, and its pale blue curtains, in a pale blue world that seemed far less real, in that instant, than the tiny little dimension she was trapped inside, with a mythological horror bearing down on her like a meat avalanche...

Click, click, click.

All the fours lined up. September remembered the observer effect, and looked down into that row of blinking LED digits, collapsing the waveform into particles, which were snap-entangled with this bijou afterlife's only other memory of time.

It wasn't as if the janitor's closet in the Little-Mean-on-the-Average Hospital appeared before them in a swirling portal of sparks, or anything fancy. It's just that certain shadows and lines – *which had always been there* – suddenly revealed that they had been the other edges of things like mops and buckets and tubs of bleach, all along.

When September turned the clock in her hands, *just so*, those edges twisted around so that they gained all three conventional dimensions. And the spare one – the one she only saw out of the corner of her eyes – became the planes and angles of an ersatz Egyptian purgatory.

"Quickly! Hold onto me!" she shouted. Cedric scooped up Virgil, and Arbourdale made a dive into one of the pockets of her lab coat. Then she grabbed the junior Reaper's hand, stepped over an invisible threshold – and snapped the clock shut.

A sensation twisted through September Normalsson on an atomic level, like someone plucking a single great gossamer guitar string, light-years long.

She opened one eye. Then, based on the fact that she was

still breathing, and that nothing had swallowed her soul, she opened the other. She was standing under a flickering fluorescent tube, in a janitor's closet, with a teddy bear, a hermit's lamp and a boy from the 1950s arranged all around her, amid the wreckage of several shelves worth of boxes, bottles, bins and buckets. A clattering of assorted brooms and a groan proved that Cedric was still alive.

"We did it! We made it back!" she said, reaching out for the door handle.

Just as the lights went out.

Just as something horrible shivered through the hospital, from its foundations to its rooftop helicopter pad. Something vast, and gnashing mad, and undoubtedly alive.

They had indeed, made it back.

But something else had come through with them...

Detective Chief Inspector Rupert Crimble climbed out of his E-type Jag in the rain, and strode across the damp black tarmac, hands stuffed into the pockets of his coat. Red and blue lights reflected off the puddles, and the quicksilver slosh of the overflowing gutters, and glittered off the ranks of police cars and paddywagons lined up all along the main street of Little-Mean-on-the-Average. It created quite a festive effect. Until you realised what it meant.

As an old-fashioned police inspector, he was *definitely* permitted to say 'paddywagons'. He was also allowed to smoke – a vice which he'd been giving up, continuously, for the past eight years.

Not now, though. Health concerns had gone out the proverbial window when he'd seen the things inside Elvis Presley's face. He popped open his zippo and torched the end of a Pall Mall as he approached the big tent that had been pitched in front of the library, secure in the knowledge that death was no longer the end. Not when you could think a sentence like *that*, in all seriousness.

Need it be mentioned that this grim-faced, soggy apparition, with its haggard grey face, dripping moustache and thousand-mile stare, was having a bad day? Oh yes.

Because not only had poor old Rupert been granted visions of things not meant to be known by mortal man. He'd also been informed, on the drive up from London, that his boys had apprehended Jack the Ripper, who had been found testing out a shiny new Husqvarna chainsaw in Madame Tussauds wax museum.

Normally, this would be a feather in his cap, what with the case having been open for more than a century. However, he'd been told, in no uncertain terms, that he was to keep it all a secret. And one did *not* go against the word of a nuclear-powered robot Margaret Thatcher, if, (he had been reminded), one wanted to keep one's testicles in pristine condition.

He pushed back the flap of the tent, and was welcomed in by a sluice of ice-cold rain down the back of his coat. A uniformed officer passed him a cup of tea just in time for most of it to get tsunami'd away by this downpour, utterly soaking one leg of his tweed trousers. For an instant, the Chief Inspector simply stood there, immersed in horror.

For even when this passes, he thought, *I'm still dying, right now. Every second I'm alive, it's getting closer. And from what I now know, the afterlife is just a whole eternity of more of the same...*

Then someone clapped him on the shoulder, and he opened his eyes, watching CFO Lesley Bellingham recoil from whatever was reflected in them.

"You all right, mate? Jesus, I hope I don't look like you right now, Inspector!"

It was probably meant to be a joke, but Rupert managed

nothing more than a twitch of the corners of his mouth, in imitation of a smile.

"Is the perimeter clear?" he asked, pushing past the fire chief and up to a folding table covered in maps. He throttled an anglepoise lamp and pointed down at a big schematic of the town centre. "*Please* tell me that the perimeter is clear. I very much need one thing to go right, this evening."

His bloodshot eyes twitched up, looking across the table.

"Uh, huh, that's a big ten-four," drawled an overweight 'Viva Las Vegas' Elvis, all in monochrome. "My boys started by evacuating the hospital, and we've co-ordinated with the fire brigade and local law enforcement to enact an all-points curfew."

"Local law enforcement?" asked Rupert, sceptically. He'd been told by Mrs Goosegarden that there was just one fairly dim bobby up here, for the sake of appearances...

"Yo!" enthused a voice from the darkness beyond the lamp. The green glow of two pairs of night vision goggles at once lit up the face of Constable O'Dwightly, who had slathered on what he thought was tactical camouflage, but was in fact a trio of sachets of tomato sauce. Someone had told him that this massive mobilisation, with its helicopters and mounted police and paddywagons, was to stop a terrorist plot.

"I'm ready to kick arse and chew bubblegum, and I don't really even like bubblegum!" burbled the uniformed berk, who had availed himself of every piece of paramilitary equipment he could strap to his body. He looked like a combination of the Michelin Man and a badly-built cyborg. "Let those scum try anything in *my* town, and they'll find out that I eat scum for breakfast!"

"Really?" asked Rupert. "Do you put it on your cereal, or is it more of a hot cuppa kind of situation?" O'Dwightly looked puzzled – or more so than usual. "Never mind, lad. The important things first, eh? Have we secured our three key targets?"

Elvis nodded, with a ripple of extra chins.

"Hooo yeah. baby. Wrinkly Acres is locked down by my most experienced veteran Elvi. Ain't a-nobody gonna get through that line, thankyouverymuch. As a follow-up, we've put the body of the late, lamented Septivarian Archimedes to rest. He's very dead, mister policeman. No encores for him, at least without a lot o' voodoo." The Elvis winked. Somehow, even its eyelids contrived to be fat.

Lesley Bellingham whacked the map with a handy ruler.

"And the fire brigade's special interdiction units, one through three, are in position at Bleachwood Scours. No loonies are getting out of that old pile tonight."

Rupert harrumphed, which, as a tweed-suited old-fashioned police inspector, he did fantastically well.

"Well, my boys have cordoned off Saint Pewtred's Academy, and we've made a thorough search, just in case this Normalsson girl was hiding out there. No such luck. As to the hot-spots for paranormal activity – well. CFO Bellingham, your teams were very efficient indeed. One of the, umm, 'terrorists' you captured has been transferred to the mobile intelligence centre, along with the asset we apprehended in London. Both are definitely connected to the Repo trade."

Rupert wasn't going to utter the word 'vampire'. He felt that his head might hinge open like a boiled egg tapped with a spoon, if he acknowledged the fact that Count Dracula was currently remanded in his custody. Little details like those tugged at the unravelling ends of his sanity, all bright, brittle and fluffy.

"Which brings us to the hospital," said Elvis, gesturing for a sandwich the size and shape of a paving slab.

"Baaaad juju, pardner. After your girl September ripped through there we discovered trans-dimensional scars in three places, and enough raw Repo to drug-out a dozen Woodstocks."

"What's the status now?" asked CFO Bellingham.

"A clear perimeter. Full evac. Until this September situation is taken care of – uh huh – we can't get a Bureau Innominandum haz-mat team in there to dispose of the stuff. Patients have all been sent to the nearest army base hospital, with a little something to help 'em forget, awright?"

Rupert shuddered. The Elvi still made his scalp try to crawl down the back of his neck, after what he'd seen behind their master's face. This one took a moment to fart spectacularly.

"Did he say *trans-dimensional scars?*" asked Constable O'Dwightly. "Cor! That's some sci-fi, high concept stuff!"

"I'm sure our American friend meant to say 'yellowcake uranium, for making a nasty bomb'," said Rupert, patting the young policeman on one shoulder. He jingled. "These buggers are pretty serious, you know!"

O'Dwightly shook his head sadly. Laser pointer beams scribbled across the inside of the tent, from where they were strapped to his policeman's helmet.

"And to think that September Normalsson is working with them! I mean, she's been in some pretty weird trouble at school, like that business with the frog yesterday, but *this?* It's a whole new level of naughtiness. I think it's a cry for attention."

"And her parents?"

"I've brought them in. They're over by that mobile intelligence thingy we're not meant to look at, if you want a word."

Rupert took a swig of his cup of tea, realised that it was

mostly rainwater with twigs floating in it, and grimaced.

"I believe I do, in fact. Now – do you happen to have, among the several tonnes of ordnance strapped to your body, such a thing as an umbrella?"

The constable shrugged, causing an array of grenades to sway alarmingly.

"Sorry, Inspector! I…"

But Rupert was already halfway out of the tent flap, and in the process of being doused for a second time by a sluice of freezing water. This time it went right down his back.

A helicopter came beating its way through the curtains of rain, spotlights tap-dancing across Little Mean's chimneypots and roofs, and its downdraft lifted the surface of several puddles, soaking Rupert with a sheet of stinging spray. That would be the lads from Section W, and that nasty little doctor with the green teeth; he'd been *very* keen to see what could be excavated from under the library.

It had been a strange phone call, filled with sentences that chewed on their own tails, and phrases like 'I can remember why I don't remember this all being predetermined not to happen again'.

Bloody weirdness! Huh! If this whole stupid situation could be made to go away by filing actions and checking CCTV cameras and nabbing a single trouble-making teenage girl, then he'd fix it all with old fashioned police work.

That meant talking to the parents.

Norma and Norman Normalsson looked very small, under a pair of huge black umbrellas held up by black-visored riot cops. The wash of spotlights sketched both of their worried faces in monochrome as the Chief Inspector strode over to them, icy fingers of rainwater trickling their way into places beneath his tweed suit that he'd very much rather they hadn't.

He took a second to quell the frustration which bubbled inside his head; these two weren't suspects. If the records he'd listened to on the way up here were any indication, they'd tried harder than most to be utterly, absolutely boring, despite the handicap of being related to...

"Have you found her?" asked the other figure in the little group – the librarian. "One of your lot said something about September being a suspect! Blowing up the hospital, and being a drug baron, and such nonsense. *Please* tell me you're all mental, or perhaps just very stupid."

Miss Rummage delivered this question with a kind of brittle brightness at odds with the hangdog expressions of the Normalssons.

Now they, thought Rupert, *actually believed that their little girl could have done it. Here are people who know there's a supervillain in the family...*

"I'm sorry, but we haven't managed to find your daughter yet, Mr and Mrs Normalsson. As to any charges, well – it's early days. We very much believe that all of this could be to do with the death of Professor Septivarian Archimedes, and that September's involvement is, ummm... coincidental? Or at least, merely a case of bad luck. Wrong place at the wrong time, and all that."

"Well, obviously!" said Miss Rummage. "I told you berks, there was a vampire trying to kill her! The girl was running *away* from something, not toward it. In any case, supervillainy isn't something you inherit, like a set of embarrassing paintings, or a silver tea set!"

Norma and Norman shared a look, then. It was one which made Inspector Rupert's left eyebrow raise of its own accord.

"Sadly, no," said Norma, wringing her hands as if she was washing them under an invisible tap. "But it might be something that you inherit, like blue eyes, or the ability to wiggle your ears. Or a tendency to certain... *illnesses.*"

"Now, dear, you know we don't talk about..." began Norman, but his wife shut him up with a razor-edged glance.

"Oh, grow up, Norman. It's no time to play all coy. We knew this day might come. You knew it when you married me."

Norman nervously fumbled for his pipe and tobacco pouch, looking just about as sour as Rupert felt.

"We did nothing wrong! *Nothing!* Twenty long years, and not a stitch of spandex in the house, not one comic book, not a single little doomsday device or alien power crystal! We played your game, Inspector. So if anything's failed here, it's *you.* The Bureau. Oversight. We..."

"Hush, dear," said Norma, putting a hand on his shoulder. She turned to Rupert, and there were tears in her eyes. "You say my great-grandfather is dead. I don't really know how to feel about that. He was... difficult to have in the family. There was a time when I could have gone that way, too, but when I met this one," – she squeezed Norman's shoulder – "I chucked it in. We had a shot at a normal life. We *had* to do it, for her. So you tell me straight, mister policeman. Do you really think our little girl has taken up the black cape?"

Good gods, thought Rupert. *Usually, it was parents asking why they hadn't seen the signs that their kids had started puffing on the old devil's lettuce, or why they'd wanted to join a gang, or steal a car.*

"We've got video of her inside the professor's secret lab, utilising certain proscribed technologies, and in collusion with the Doom Commission," said the Chief Inspector, in the same tones he would usually use to tell someone that their cat had been run over. "I know you did everything you could. The Bureau won't accuse you of anything, ma'am. Septivarian Archimedes was—"

Norma cut him off.

"He was a *lot* of things, Inspector. He was a hero, and he helped us win the war. He was a mad scientist, when you lot needed plausible deniability. And he was my grandpa. But he's not September. She's at that awkward age, I'll admit. But she's not the type to monologue, or try to destroy the universe. A mother knows."

"A father too," said Norman. "Especially one who was a Boy Detective."

There was something there, in the man's eyes, as he lit up his pipe. Something more than the reflection of fire from the match he struck.

"Can you find her, Inspector? Without these paramilitary types shooting first?"

It was there in Norma's eyes too – the flash of a steely tripwire in long grass. There was a quality there, beneath the determinedly middle-class respectability of this pair. Something which was like the glimpse of a determined triangular fin, cutting through midnight water.

"Investigations are proceeding," he said, biting back on a momentary, unreasonable panic. "But you're welcome to stay here at the command centre, so long as you keep out of the way."

Miss Rummage bristled. The pencils stabbed through her hair rose like hackles.

"And that's it? You've got an army of thugs, and *you-know-what-else* from the bloody Bureau Innominandum out there, hunting a scared teenage girl with itchy trigger fingers? I suppose we're supposed to believe you if you say she's not already attending a certain get-together of Elvis impersonators, eh?"

Norma folded up the accusatory finger which the librarian was waving under Rupert's moustache, and gently steered her hand away. Miss Rummage must have caught a glimpse of that look in September's mum's eye as well, because all the anger drained out of her at once, leaving her looking frazzled and small.

"No thank you, Inspector. My husband and I would like to cope with this terrible news in our own way."

It was said softly, and with no small amount of quiet desperation. But once again, Rupert picked up a certain harmonic beneath September's mum's words. It was like the high, faint, incoming whistle of a very large bomb. And after the day he'd had, the Chief Inspector was not about to try to comfort anyone. He was about as good at that kind of thing as he was at blindfolded topiary.

"Very well. Thank you for making a statement. I know this can't be easy for you to deal wi... *oh, sodding hellfire, what is it now?*"

Sirens wound up to a full-throated wail. Searchlights, which had been criss-crossing the clouds with random sweeps, all pointed in the same direction. There came a roar, as of an oil refinery with severe gastric issues. Then a far-off explosion, and the sound of screams.

Rupert looked up, and watched, open-mouthed, as the helicopter he'd seen before came cartwheeling across the sky, bent in he middle like a banana. It arced over the central square of Little-Mean-on-the-Average and disappeared behind the construction site of Denver Gas, exploding in a great oily fireball. As is mandatory in these situations, its whirling rotors detached at the last instant and decapitated a whole row of poplars, along the riverbank at Monkston's Green.

That roar came again, shuddering up through Rupert's oxfords and making his spine tingle. He turned back to make his apologies to Norma and Norman, but they were gone. Only the librarian remained, and the look of horror on her face was enough to make the Inspector turn around, his eyes following hers to a point high above the library rooftop.

"Bugger a duck," he managed, his policeman's lexicon of rude words utterly failing him. "We're going to need a *much* bigger paddywagon."

Before we proceed; a little note about Genius Locii.

These are the spirits of places, of buildings and sacred groves and rivers, which develop from the collective imprint of human belief down the generations.

Say there's a gnarly old oak in the forest, where the druids always find good mistletoe, and where the mushrooms grow which make the strangest potions. Say there's the insinuation of an old, frowning beardy face in the knots and twists of it.

Now, local people may very well start to make up stories about the glade where this old tree stands. The druids might help this along, so as to gently steer people away from the place where they like to have a bit of a sit-down and a quiet roll-up, away from the problems of spiritually shepherding a tribe of iron-age nutters in a world where wars can start over which way a sheep is facing in its paddock.

Stories like:

'The mossy oak was a wizard who was turned into a tree in olden times,' or 'goblins live under its roots and come out to put curses on those who stray there at night,' or 'there's a doorway to fairyland there, and if you fall asleep you could wake up in the future.'[32]

32. Like the legendary idiot Parp Van Wonkle, who, by carefully calculating how long he should nod off in a very fae-cursed glade, managed to pop up in several future years, and gather all the scores for every major football international between 1831 and 1977. The only problem was, his plan for returning to the early Victorian era involved going back to the same glade and drinking too much coffee, on the reasoning that being very, very awake there would send him back in time. In 1978 the glade was paved over

The thing about stories being, of course, that no matter how hard you bend the narrative to make people stay away, there's a kind of terrible gravitational attraction to weirdness, forged into the human soul. A place would have to be *properly* creepy, like that dark and horrible wood Dante found himself in back in the 1300s, to really keep people away.

So they come to poke around. And they amplify the stories, like a feedback loop turning a single guitar note into howling echoes. A connection tunnels through, from the seething alternativity of the Aught, using the kind of entanglement that scientists would probably love to try to describe to you in detail. The fictional becomes real, in a way which Septivarian Archimedes was trying to achieve for the government, back in the 1980s.

In short, there are those who say the first invention of humanity was the wheel, or fire, or the pointy stick. But it's not. What we're good at making, better than anyone else, is *gods*.

Genius Locii are little gods. Sometimes *really* little, like the ones who summon you to the fridge in the middle of the night for no reason, with their siren song humming to the light inside the dairy compartment. Others are merely trivial. Some are old and cunning enough to become real people, like the many aspects of the Green Man, or the manifestations of rivers and sacred groves and standing stones. At least one that the Bureau Innominandum knows of makes a living by giving tourists a guided walk around its own sacred megaliths, which is a bit of a cheek.

Now imagine a building – thousands of tonnes of concrete and rebar and linoleum and glass – that's the focus for the whole entire wireless bandwidth of human

---

for a new roller disco, and Parp ended up becoming a rather successful photocopier salesman. Who knew *far* too much about vintage football.

emotions, turned up to eleven. A place of grim news and raw joy, utter sorrow, sad partings, massive relief, quiet triumph, grace in agony and brave determination.

Pour all that through a place for forty years, and you'll get little superstitions, and stories, and weird feelings up the back of your spine. You'll get a place which either has its own *genius locorum*, hiding in the spaces between here and the Aught, or one in which it's marbled through the entire great structure, making it *live*.

Now imagine the Little-Mean-on-the-Average general hospital, built in 1958. There's not a rational mind there, but there's something dreaming inside those walls. The sum total of ten thousand first breaths and last ones, fed by decades of poorly aimed prayers.

It's enough. Enough, when whole oil-drums worth of Repo have sloshed through the basements and dripped through the pipes, thanks to Gravesend's distribution plans. Who'd look for drugs in a hospital, after all? Better to look for sand at the bottom of the ocean.

For an instant, all those trickles and splashes and drips strained upward, as if gravity had been reversed. They glowed green. Something connected, shuddering like a car struggling to start on a cold morning...

And Ammut, the Eater of Souls, opened eyes which were, inexplicably, a bank of mirrored windows. It was the right size, this new form. But it was the wrong shape entirely.

Not to worry. Millennia spent holding up the pit-props of belief had made Ammut strong. The soul-eater had no trouble at all commanding a brute tonnage of concrete and metal.

*Ammut yawned. Ammut shuddered. Ammut **made some changes**.*

Angles and geometries spun in and out of parallel

spaces, as if matter was light, and light was imagination, bent around an armature of nightmare. All at once, this great pile of pale-green concrete and red brick *had always been* a squatting, squamous sphinx of a thing, snorting smoke from chimney nostrils. Leftover planes and vertices snapped closed like origami fans.

Ammut raised a head the size of a battleship, on a neck now made of grinding slabs of masonry. A mouth cracked open, with jagged triangles of glass for teeth. Rows of them regimented back into darkness, where a huge black-and-white linoleum tongue slithered. Perspex-bubble eyes glowed from within, lit by neon.

Now, that chequer-board tongue licked out, tasting the air. Rain hissed against it, puffing to steam. *And oh, the flavours which came in on that night wind!*

Drool made of firefighting foam slicked the creature's mouth. For thousands of years, Ammut had fed on regret and despair, and now here she was in the middle of a medium-sized British town. Some of these people were called Colin. Some were even *Keiths!*

Ammut called this kind of situation 'dinnertime'. Silas Rosewood, on the other hand, used words which sliced the air like fish hooks, all arcane and nasty. They were far more accurate.

He'd just lost one of Her Majesty's very expensive top-secret black helicopters. Well, 'lost' wasn't really the word, because he knew exactly where the wreckage was. He'd leapt out of the machine as it hovered low, and the pilot had stared into the glowing eyes of a hospital possessed. Silas legged it. Some weaselly survival instinct told him that to stay out in the open was to quickly become a sad little *crunch* and *squeak.*

He'd caught one last look at the stealth chopper, as a paw made of concrete and rebar swatted it from the sky. He'd forgotten his mission – to discover the source of southern England's Repo supply – and his dignity too, crawling down the gutter on his belly and into the shadowed doorway of the Floating Chrysanthemum pub.

"Well, there's something you don't see every day," said Hiro Mulcahey, popping his head out the door. "Some sort of kaiju, is it? Big radioactive beastie like that, I'd blame the Americans. I knew they was squirrelling away toxic waste down at the old airbase, you mark my words!"

Silas turned his head, with a creak of well-oiled leather. He grinned a green-toothed grin at the little man in the kimono and the bowler hat.

"Heavens, no! It's nothing of the sort. You've just been overdoing it, is all. All of this is a terrible hallucination, brought on by stress. There's no such thing as kaiju, or atomic monsters, or even the very real likelihood that old Ronnie Reagan ordered his lads to bury several tonnes of glowing alien goop underneath RAF Chestnut Hill. No, you just go and have a nice cup of tea and adopt the duck-and-cover position, and it'll all be over in the morning."

"'Ere – what's up with your teeth, mate? You really ought to see a dentist about…"

But Silas Rosewood had already produced, from about his person, one of those little silver pen-like devices so beloved on the Men in Black. Men who, on closer inspection, usually looked a lot like a certain King of Rock and Roll.

A bright flash lit up the doorway of the Floating Chrysanthemum, and Hiro collapsed backwards. Silas snicked the door shut, and peeped out around the corner.

Ammut was in the process of tearing its final paw clear of the hospital's foundations, severing a tangle of cables and pipes. The creature took a tentative step forward, utterly crushing Mr Stanhope's tobacconist's, then turned its massive snout toward downtown, into the glare of searchlights. It bellowed, and a plume of propane fire belched from between its jaws.

Damn and blast! Just exactly where he'd meant to slip away to! There was a hollow in Silas Rosewood's memories, centred on the civic library. He was certain there was something there which he should recall, but when he'd tried digging for information about it, he'd found out two things.

Firstly, that Mother Goose retained a whole vault of files about this seemingly innocuous little book repository. And secondly, that they were so top-secret that they were for the robotic Margaret Thatcher's beady little eyes only.

Something had happened there. A project called Dark Lazarus. Something which had scooped out whole months of his memories, as if his living brain was a tub of runny ice-cream.

He'd reconstructed what he could, of course. For example, he'd been working with The Befuddler, Septivarian Archimedes, on something important. The word BISHOP lurked behind the net curtains of his subconscious. But then came the suture-stitch of altered memories; and suddenly Archimedes was a retired criminal. Silas could dimly recall fire, as well, and the fact that he'd lost his name-tag; the one which went with his old code name, PROPHET.

No. Not lost. He'd left it behind. He'd left it there on purpose, for his future self to find...

There'd been no chance of slinking away to investigate all of this, in the years between. Section W was a harsh mistress, and Mother Goose kept him on a very tight leash. He was certain that shadowy figures in bell-bottoms followed him, and that he'd often spotted Elvi lurking at the corners of his vision, sneering from behind upside-down newspapers and skulking in unmarked black cars.

Now, a six-storey-tall monster was loose, and the policeman who Mrs Goosegarden had chosen to ringmaster this circus was *well* out of his depth. It was time to have a little skulk, and take care of that nagging void.

Only one problem. There was no way he could use his personal helicopter, now that it had been swatted like an insect. And obtaining a vehicle from the Dead Elvi would mean *talking* to them. He shuddered. Silas knew that there was a hive mind oozing behind all of those oily Elvis eyes. What one of them witnessed, the Supreme Aaron would feel as a pang of intuition. And *that* fat bastard had always been suspicious.

Doctor Rosewood sidled out from the doorway of the pub, and almost tripped over old Wilf Handisides, who was having a very interesting evening. He'd decided, on the balance of the evidence, that the world had gone completely mad, thus putting him (for once), on exactly the right frequency. Even better, he'd gotten himself fifty pounds, which was good for a bottle of whisky as well as a new second-hand bike. The fact that the old Raleigh Chopper had been pulled out of a skip behind the nearby Burger Slave by that scurrilous local wheeler-dealer, 'Cowboy Dave' Flynn just meant that it was cheaper, if a bit on the rusty side.

Wilf saw it as a perfect compromise; a nice back-rest for while he supped on Glengonnagle's Old Non-Euclidian single malt, and watched the fireworks.

Silas Rosewood, however, saw potential in the hastily rattle-canned old bicycle.

"I say, old chum," he said, grinning his peas-in-a-pod grin. "How would you like to make an easy hundred pounds?"

At the same time, the person who had bought Wilf's last bicycle was holding on to a very flimsy aluminium aerial, high atop the great rugged head of the Little Mean hospital. She didn't notice a tiny figure in a black trench-coat pedalling furiously in Ammut's wake.

A part of September quailed before the immensity of what was happening all around her; the lashing rain, the searchlights, the wail of sirens, and the steady crump and rumble of Ammut's progress. *This was not*, screamed that little voice, *behaviour befitting a proper young lady!*

The vast majority, though, told it to get stuffed.

September's mind thrilled to the howling feedback of the Endarkenment. Sometimes people have second thoughts, and regret the things they've done. Some manage first ones, and avoid disaster. September, perched atop a concrete behemoth, was having *zeroth* thoughts; whole limbic arpeggios of them, they made her mind whirl like a snow-globe, juiced up on savage voltage.

She could reach down, here and here and here, and twitch some wires, and cross some connections, and take control of the beast. Sure, there was a distinct chance that raw feedback would strip her soul like thin paint under a blowtorch, but hey! This was living, folks! This was the real stuff, with your toes just above the spinning blades, and your kite lofting right up into the thunderheads!

She almost did it, too – and would have, if she hadn't heard her own laughter.

"Oh dear. Cackling during a thunderstorm. That's a bad sign," said Virgil. "The old master was always on the lookout for those kind of mental tics. He had pills for them, and all."

Now came those second thoughts. They must have shown in her expression, as she turned to squint through the rain at the poet, swinging in his lamp from the television mast.

His expression was dour.

"You were thinking that you could do great things, with a behemoth like this. Better yet, you could do great things with the principles that made it exist, eh? Right wrongs, squish horrible politicians, generally tidy up the place, yeah?"

She couldn't lie to the little hologram. Not with Cedric standing there, looking all wary and brave at once.

As if, perhaps, the real monster here wasn't six storeys of brutalist architecture with teeth...

"Maybe," she conceded. "Maybe I was. And maybe that's something Septivarian had to worry about, too. But I'm September Hyacinth Normalsson. I'm not some kind of mad tangle of powers, just wearing her skin. I've *got* this."

She took a deep breath, and hoped like hell that she was right. Third thoughts now – she still *felt* the same; still, like all of us, balanced at the point where inner musings met outer experiences. *The pinch in the hourglass...*

"Speaking as the only one who's got this, then... how the heck do we get down from here?" asked Cedric. He was clutching Arbourdale to his chest, and the little teddy bear had wrapped himself up in a fold of the young Reaper's leather jacket. "I only ask because, see, this thing isn't supposed to exist. And that means, if all's going according to plan, PostMortis will have a response prepared."

"That sounds *very* civilised," said Virgil. "This would be the same PostMortis that might very well be under the command of a bitter, omnicidal ferrywoman, seeing as you locked their real boss inside a children's picture book?" He adjusted his little wreath, and stuck out his chin. "Do you think they're going to send the diplomatic corps with cucumber sandwiches?"

"Virgil! You'll blow out your sarcasm circuits!" admonished Arbourdale.

"I didn't mean response, as in a polite letter. I mean response, as in 'nuclear'!" wailed Ced.

"Literally?"

"Quite possibly!"

Below them, the massive back of Ammut rose and fell like the swell on a concrete sea. Huge limbs swung ponderously, and the beast ploughed its way through a row of duplexes, making a desultory snap with its jaws at the little figures who ran before it, screaming. Virgil winced.

"This is our stop coming up, anyhow," said the tiny poet, knocking on the glass of his lamp. "If I believed in luck, instead of the carefully nested interlocking shells of causality which make up the multiverse, I'd say it was a stroke of good fortune that we ended up here at all."

"What do you mean?" asked Cedric, clinging to the aerial and looking ill. "I thought we were supposed to hunt down the devil, or something? Wouldn't he be some place warmer?"

"Like the Seychelles?" hazarded Arbourdale, hopefully.

"Or at least more evil," interjected September. "I mean, it's not paradise, but Little-Mean-on-the-Average isn't exactly the abode of the damned."

Virgil, swinging in his lantern, gave a meaningful blink. His clothes changed from a toga and wreath to a natty yellow uniform with a blue and white striped apron. A tiny paper hat, like a parody of a sailor's cap, appeared on his head.

"Yeah," he said, gesturing with an inch-long spatula. "But *that* place is. And that's where Sharon bloody Kolslaw's computer terminal said we'd find him."

September peered down through the rain, toward a very familiar glowing neon 'BS'. The cartoon face of Beefy Roger leered and winked on an endless loop.

"I suppose you're right, at that," she conceded. The look

on her face was all determination, and both Virgil and Arbourdale felt a little thrill of anticipation; it was a look that came right up from her DNA. It was the spit and image of her great-great-granddad.

"I saw some fire hoses in there. We can use them to abseil down. The trick will be missing those feet – don't want to get stepped on, do we?"

Cedric sighed. The number of things he'd done today which he really never wanted to do was ticking over faster than the dial of an elevator in free-fall. But there was no countermanding that look. It reminded him, with a pang of guilt, of Jaghtaran Khatri.

If he'd known just what his erstwhile boss was going to do next, perhaps he wouldn't have felt quite so bad for him...

PART THREE

THE DIVINE SLAPSTICK COMEDY

"Step right up, come on and try your luck, find the red card and double your money, it couldn't be any easier!"
– Jesus of Nazareth

Suture Eight
Jackal of all Trades

Across the Aught, through the chasms and cathedrals of human imagination, rang out the sound of mortality collapsing. It was the echo of vast engines underground, burning their bearings down to molten steel.

Half-forgotten saints heard it, and prayed. Bloody urban legends heard it, and trembled, clutching their axes and machetes in little loops of midnight. Fictional characters heard it, and their ink-and-paper souls shivered.

The Chronauspexion shook. Gears jammed and sheared through, teeth grinding and screws unthreading. The tremor of it rocked the great Clock Tower and was felt, Reaper-Captain Jaghtaran Khatri was certain, all the way up the Azraeon's skeletal arm to the shoulder. He stole a look out through the open doors of the Chronauspexion chamber, up into the star-dusted heavens, where the First and Final One's face hung huge as a harvest moon. He fancied, with a thrill of terror, that he saw a flicker of annoyance in those world-swallowing eyes.

The vision gave him a kind of doomed, reckless hope.

"It's all for nothing, Cardinal!" he bellowed, over the sound of tonnes of machinery ripping itself apart. "I'm just a shadow of him, up there in the sky. Him, with this whole world in his palm. Kill me, and there'll be another one, and another, because he's got entropy on his side. Nobody knows it better than me. Run as far as you like, but you'll end up with one of us standing right behind you."

If there wasn't a gaping hole in reality between them, he was certain Cardinal Syn would have gone for him, then. The creature had claimed to be the ghost of a machine, but he was beyond calculation now. His face, ever indistinct, blurred like a film strip on fire, all inkspatter and madness. Eyes boiled in that scatterslash of images, and teeth. Not all of them were human.

"Where has it gone? What have you done with it? You can't bring the Soul-Eater here! It'll chew its way through all of Uncarnadine!"

Jaghtaran stepped back, confused.

"I thought all of this was *your* plan. All that Repo, just to enslave the beast, and then..."

"And then *what?* I want to **rule** this rotten city, not bulldoze it for a multi-storey carpark! The Repo was for *Sapiens Humana!* The Pre-deceased! Ammut was just supposed to stay at the other end of the Reject Chute and deal with inconveniences. *You* were the one who opened the gateway!"

Above them, something terminal sheared through, sending a shower of sparks cascading. Hourglasses filled with toxic green sludge were piling up on the conveyor belts, and Repo was dripping and spreading from shattered tubes.

"Not I," mused Khatri, almost to himself. "But the scythe did. The one which Cedric Welbourne stole from me. Him, and that stupid girl from the *Materia Mortalis*. Ohhh, empty fate!"

"So, her and that stubborn old goat who made me, eh? Them all along!" raged the Cardinal. "Imbecile! Ammut's stupid little stump of a world was here before *everything*. Before those fool *Sapiens* could even dream properly, it was. Now it's going fractal, and it's all your fault!"

"Shut. Up." said Jaghtaran. And such was the authority stamped into the walls of this place, by generations of Reaper-Captains, that the scarlet apparition was silent. A blur of frustrated faces tried to pry their lips apart, but they were welded shut.

With a gesture, Khatri summoned down a great bone-framed projection screen, hanging from a jointed arm of femurs.

"Show me what the Tarot can see," he said, in a voice not much louder than a whisper. "First shadow of the Azraeon, bound by Dante's hand – lend me your eyes."

What the screen showed, as it flickered into life, was enough to freeze Cardinal Syn's face in a mask of horror. Jaghtaran was certain he'd look just as stricken, if he wasn't wrapped up in his skeletal uniform.

The view swung loose and dizzy, from up high above a searchlit town. Rain came down in curtains, sliced up by a score of huge spotlights, and Reaper-Captain Khatri could see a pair of hands reaching out in front of him, gripping a length of fire hose. The wind caught the tarot card, where it hung on its chain around Cedric's neck, and the view skittered and flipped, alternating an expanse of concrete and glass and the rooftops of a suburban street.

Then Ammut's great rebar-clawed paw came down, crushing a Ford Fiesta to ruin. Perspective swooped. Rain sheeted down the pebbledash flanks of a beast made out of government-issue building materials. There was no sound – no screams, no sirens, no crackle of sporadic gunfire, but Jaghtaran knew a war zone when he saw one. He'd been to quite a few, on business. In fact, he'd been to all of them, eventually. On both sides.

The Cardinal had found his voice, now, but all the bluster and hellfire had gone out of him.

"Oh. That's bad, isn't it? That's very, very bad."

The Reaper-Captain nodded.

"We'd call that a class-nine cross-dimensional containment breach, there. Hasn't been one quite this bad since Krakatoa in 1883."

"A lot of paperwork?"

Khatri sighed.

"Friend, there's not enough ink in all of Fiction to cover it. It's a destabilising cascade, is the problem. People start to believe in whatever's causing the breach, and that feeds back. It distorts the entire Aught. We could be looking at five thousand more years of pyramids, if people get it in their heads that Ammut the soul-eater is real."

He swore, later, that he could actually hear the wheels turning in Syn's head, or the blur of hacked-up faces he used for one. Spinning like the gears in the poor doomed Chronauspexion, as he slotted these new developments into whatever plan he'd concocted, there on the dry seabed of his madness.

Perhaps, thought the Reaper-Captain, *that was his disease. Plans and schemes and evil doublecrosses were all he was made of, after all.*

On the screen, Ammut ploughed through another terrace of houses, jaws snapping. Cedric was, for reasons unknown to science, trying to rappel down the creature's side.

"Yes. Yes, indeed. They're seeing something supernatural. Something numinous. Something staggering and portentous." The Cardinal leered, a series of grins colliding. "I can use that! I can work with that! We just have to bring it all forward. We need to go live, right *now*. Then it's part of the revelation. Their own minds will make the story work, when they see what's at the end of it."

Jaghtaran Khatri didn't like the sound of that, one little bit. But he could feel the rumble and shriek of the Chronauspexion shifting, all around him. Lines of fate came skeining in from out of nowhere, and wove tight around the central axis of inevitability, right here. *This was where the death of everything else killed uncertainty.* Futures were collapsing. Things were growing sharp, along invisible edges. He could feel the choice taking shape, before the Cardinal gave it words.

"It's up to you, then. You can try to stop me, and leave that thing out there, in the *Materia*, doing who-knows-what kind of damage to Azrael's work. "His smile, this time, was like a razor-thin knife wound. "Or you do your duty. And you leave me to mine. We'll still have a job here for you, Charon and I. Under the new regime."

Khatri hesitated for an instant. Because, underneath it all, he was still human. He was human enough to want to erase that smug, grinning face, hashed in between Syn's red collar and his crooked mitre.

The scythe twitched. Just a wobble. Inside the Chronauspexion, speculative universes blossomed in imagined phase-spaces, burned, and feathered away to pure mathematics.

But he was also the embodiment of his duty. God had once been said to see the fall of every sparrow. But with *deus in absentia* since the middle ages, the Reaper-Captains of PostMortis had had to arrange each one, personally. It took careful scythe work, and, these days, a baseball catcher's mitt.

New regime. Huh. If he didn't do this now, and right, there wouldn't be anything left to regiment.

The pair of them broke apart, then, and until Jaghtaran moved, he hadn't noticed just how thick and tight the tension had become. This was a place where the story pivoted, all right. The thing was, it could only bend one way.

"I'm going out there, then. I'm going to put Ammut back in her box. But when I'm done..."

"Spare me," chuckled the Cardinal, with a wry little twist of his lips. "By then, I'll have finished, for better or worse. You know, you could always just let us both burn up. Right here, right now."

"No." replied Khatri. "If you were me, then *you* could. But I can't. I'm going to stop that thing, and you're going to do what's in your nature. It's not going to make you happy, I assure you."

Once again, that little smile that wasn't a smile.

"What ever will?" shrugged Syn. "I'm more about bringing the rest of you down to my level, anyhow."

With that, he was gone – leaping up and over the railing to land, sure-footed, among the broken-glass wreckage of the Chronauspexion's conveyor belts. In a blur of red he was at the great double doors, darkness flickering around him like his own pool of spilled ink. Then he vanished, off down the marble stairs, off into Uncarnadine.

Jaghtaran Khatri looked down at the scythe in his hand. He looked up at the bone-edged screen, where Cedric Welbourne was now staring up at the titanic rump of Ammut, slowly lumbering away. The tarot around his neck would have made this a whole lot easier, but the scythe remembered. There was an idiom for this, deep in the helix of myth which twisted through its handle.

Ammut's realm had been formed by human minds, unable to grasp the finer points of theology. They'd made gods with the heads of beasts and insects, and made them fight and fornicate like the cast of some mad soap opera. That kind of thinking was catching. Left unchecked, it would topple the Aught back into centuries of credulous darkness.

No time to meditate. No time to prepare his mind. And about as much hope as a tadpole in an arc furnace...

Jaghtaran focused on the scythe. He felt it begin to hum, a colossal tuning fork in his hand. Its outline melted, blurring, and it changed colour and shape, contracting and curving until it was a battered old sickle-sword made of bronze, carved with eye-watering hieroglyphs.

He felt the resonance spreading. Through his fingers to his palm, then up his arm, down his spine...

What was the Azraeon before he was Grim? What was the shadow of the reaper, when His harvest had first conceived of a thing with the body of a hippo, the paws of a lion and the head of a crocodile?

After a moment or two, Jaghtaran Khatri gripped the edge of the screen with both hands, and tore it open into the gateway he was absolutely certain it was. Those hands had claws. They had fur.

As the searchlights over Little-Mean-on-the-Average eclipsed the skeletal moon he'd left behind, Khatri had to fight a terrible, visceral urge to howl...

Inside a copy of *Jolly Dormouse Jim and the Little Bad Wolf,* a picture of a black felt canine gave in, and did it anyway.

Fourteen
The Prince of Darkness
vs
Public Health Regulations

THE AMERICANS *GET* fast food.

It's no coincidence that all of the big, successful chains of restaurants which pump the arteries of the world full of delicious cholesterol hark from the Land of the Free. It's because they understand something fundamental about what the public want, when it comes to dining.

Here's the secret – *it's not actually about the food.*

It's all about the *illusion of dining.* The best fast food joints offer you flavour without taste, convenience without substance, and pop you out through the swinging doors at the end with the feeling that something culinary must have happened.

The Americans get this. Their great fast food icons are all showmen, with a wink and a nod and a little sleight of hand. This works extremely well, all wrapped up in primary-coloured plastic and plonked down in the middle of a Californian suburb.

It worked considerably worse in Little-Mean-on-the-Average.

September, who thought a lot about these kind of things, put it down to the well-developed British sense of irony. You couldn't, in all earnestness, have a sign under the menu saying that 'smiles are free' in a place as stark and joyless as Burger Slave. Not unless you chalked it up to the kind of pitch-black humour which should only exist after several years of relentless trench warfare.

September would admit that she was partial to the odd

Big 'Un with cheese and bacon, especially during those devil-may-care bouts of ennui which can assail a person upon a lonely two a.m. That's why Burger Slave had a 24-hour drive-thru, after all. But was it the domain of the Prince of Darkness? She didn't think so.

"Are they even open?" asked Arbourdale, peeking out from behind one of her socks. "It looks pretty dead in there. Pardoning your presence, Cedric."

The ex-grim-reaper leaned up against the glass, and peered through, into the neon-lit aquarium tank of the fast-food joint. It was, indeed, an empty and sterile place. White tiles, beige plastic tables, and huge, backlit menu boards dominated. On posters all around, Beefy Roger and the other Burger Slave characters, like The Hamterrorist, Cannibal Chicken, and Grumbles hawked great greasy sandwiches, packed with industrial quantities of meat.

"It's deserted. Then again, I suppose the town being attacked by a giant, mythical soul-eating monster is bad for business."

September looked up over the roof-line of the restaurant, toward the centre of town. There were explosions, and screams, and searchlights criss-crossing the clouds there, as Ammut ploughed a furrow directly toward her destination. September could guess what it was. No matter whether the Doom Commission had collapsed it down on top of their heads, Septivarian's laboratory was a beacon which would attract the beast like... well, like the aroma of sizzling lard which came wafting out of the Burger Slave itself.

"Oh, you think so?" asked Arbourdale, all sarcastic. "I *did* note a general trend towards fleeing in horror. Not much call to make a pit stop and pick up a family feast bucket when you're wetting your pants with dreadful insanity!"

"Here! Hold me up!" said the Electric Virgil. "I can see

something moving back there. In the kitchen. Do they have a Beefy Roger mascot working here, all the time?"

September lifted the lantern, and the little poet inside leaned forward, up against the glass. He'd produced, from somewhere, an ornate brass telescope.

"Naw. False alarm, I'm afraid," he said. "Looks like one of those inflatable things with the flailing arms made of tubes. Now, why would someone put one of those in between a pair of deep-fryers?"

The answer came from behind them. It was the unmistakable sound of a pump-action shotgun being chambered.

Funny, thought September, *she'd never heard such a thing in real life before, but her body knew exactly what it meant.* Her hands went up before she even had time to curse.

"Because it makes a truly *excellent* diversion," oozed the voice of a man with a radio-perfect accent. "No, don't turn around. There's a good bunch of, I assume, chaps. And Chap-esses, pardon me, miss. We're just going to step indoors, and then we can talk about the massive, twisted, supernatural aura that's on you all like stink on a very fine cheese. Alright?"

This time when September stepped up to the glass doors they sighed open, sliding apart to let a wash of grease-fried air waft out into the night. Very aware of the muzzle of the gun at their backs, the little crew hustled inside. Soon they stood before the plastic counter, like supplicants in search of an all-night breakfast bagel with extra bacon.

"I sent the team home early," said the man who now stepped around behind the cash register, cradling a big, black Mossberg model 88 in his hands. "Not a lot of call for a takeaway dinner, when Ammut the Soul-Devourer is ravaging the countryside, is there? You lot wouldn't know anything about that, now, would you?"

The surprise and guilt writ large across the faces of Cedric, Arbourdale and Virgil was probably mirrored precisely on her own, thought September. *Busted smuggling a ten-thousand-tonne monster into reality, without a license!*

"You... you know what that thing is? And you're not, you know, running around in little circles weeing yourself?"

The restaurant manager (for such was proclaimed by the little plastic tag which he wore on his shirt) wrinkled his nose.

"I'm not certain that would help, young lady. I mean, that's a cross-dimensional incursion, that is. PostMortis will have to take care of it. And, before you ask, yes, I'm well aware of the bureaucratic hierarchy of the Other Side."

"Is that something *all* Burger Slave managers have to know about?" asked Arbourdale, very suspiciously. "Only I hear rumours about where the meat comes from, and..."

"Oh, that's all nonsense!" grinned the manager, clacking his big oversized shotgun down on the counter. "Grade-A horseshit, the lot of it. That's the stories, not the burgers, you understand." He waggled his eyebrows. "Head office starts those rumours to pique a bit of morbid curiosity, and to give us an excuse to loudly protest our innocence. Gets you on the television news for free, that does. Lots of nice footage of sizzling hot burgers gets 'em through the doors, even if the news article started out about cannibalism."

"Then how do you know about Ammut?" asked Virgil. "Are you a student of Egyptology, on the side, kind of thing?"

"Oh no," smiled the manager. "I'm the Devil. The great adversary. The enemy of mankind. And you're here to complete the unholy bargain your great-great-grandfather began, back in 1984. But don't worry," he said, to their shocked expressions. "I'm retired."

Now, this would have been somewhat fantastically

unbelievable, even considering the day's other events, had September not seen him, at that moment, remove his silly, oversized Burger Slave baseball cap, to reveal a pair of tiny little horns.

Overall, they didn't entirely sell the impression of a cruel and haughty prince of darkness. September had been expecting someone more like Tim Curry. But this fellow was short and stocky, fair-haired and frankly chubby, with a cheerful face and a little pointed blonde beard on the end of his chin. He was dressed, as per the guidelines scribed down in Burger Slave's sacred three-ring binder, in yellow pants, a blue short-sleeved business shirt, a stripey blue and yellow tie, and sensible non-slip shoes. The horns budded out from his forehead like those of a cartoon satyr, all of three inches long.

"*You?* You're Lucifer?" asked Cedric. "And you work at a *hamburger restaurant?*"

"Shh!" shushed the Scourge of Christendom, his eyes flickering left and right. Something shuddered below them, in the pipes. "Not the L-Word. Not him. Different franchise. I'm the Dante edition, me. Just like you, mister reaper. And, as I told my mate Milton, back when we used to sink a pint or two together, 'wheresoever I am is Hell'. This is my retirement gig. Got to keep one's hand in the game of ultimate evil, right?"

"The Prof said you quit," put in Arbourdale. "said the puritans were getting you down."

The Devil smiled, a too-wide grin showing a lot of enamel. The light seemed to fade all around him, and the ghost of flames licked across the shiny white tiles and yellow plastic of the Burger Slave's counter.

"Professor Archimedes was *very* good at keeping things compartmentalised, my fuzzy purple friend. Like you. Made for his great-granddaughter, to keep her life far removed from all the complications of his own. Oh, my word, yes. *There* was a man who could have taken my job, if he'd been in the vicinity of Florence back in the 1300s."

September didn't like the oily, arch tone of that, at all. Septivarian may have been a supervillain for a time, when the times demanded it, but he was never, well... *this*. He'd never consider a polyester tie, for starters.

"A job you quit, as soon as Newton started chipping away at the edges of your power, right? So this is what the Enemy of God has come to? Manager of a small regional hamburger dive?"

The erstwhile Devil arched one eyebrow. It was a perfect little curve of disdain, sculpted over centuries.

"Please. Call me Charles," he drawled, with just a slight aristocratic chuckle as a chaser. "All this Prince-of-Damnation stuff is so *very* late medieval. And yes, I built this franchise from the ground up. I'm the manager of *all* of them, thanks to some very nifty phase-space knock-throughs, courtesy of your great-great-granddad. I was Roger Hoffenmeyer, Junior, back in 1952. I wrote the three-ring binder, and I command, between these walls, an artificial world which is a theatre of sloth, greed, envy, rage, entitlement, pettiness and gluttony to rival the court of Caligula."

The light had drained away from the whole restaurant now, as neon tubes flickered and died. Charles' face was underlit in red, and his shadow rose jagged and huge on the wall behind him, eclipsing the posters of capering cartoon mascots. His voice was getting deeper, too.

"My staff damn themselves for minimum wage, and they find that my employee-of-the-month club, and being constantly on-call, are more subtle tortures than the keenest of agonizing knives. My customers bloat and seethe and ooze cholesterol, and the merest issue – a single slice of tomato out of place, or an errant onion ring in their fries – rips back the scab of all their dissatisfaction, lays bare their insecurities, and gives them an excuse to be their true, revolting selves. I tell them they can cram happiness into their reeking maws a quarter pound at a time, I assure them that they are 'always right', then I leave them feeling dirty, and ripped-off, and *oh so very hungry for more!*"

Red light blazed in Charles' eyes, then, as he crooked his fingers into claws, and let loose the kind of evil laugh which really demands its own thunderstorm and pipe-organ solo.

"The Hell which Dante sealed up was a crude and simple place by comparison! I'm ploughing rain forests under, racking up the extinctions and foreclosing on family farms – and people nod and smile and call me a captain of industry. I fund studies which prove my food kills people, then pay to have them ignored, while also paying money-grubbing commentators to call being brainwashed by my advertising a kind of 'freedom'! When I was the Devil, I tempted one person at a time, and the world hated me. Now, I do *children's birthday parties!* In a place like *this!* Do you have any idea the repressed trauma which... but ahh, forget it! That's not what you're here for. You're here to complete Dark Lazarus, whether you know it or not."

He seemed to deflate, then, as the light came rushing back, and the neon tubes fizzled and popped overhead. His smile, reconstructed, was a soulless as that of a great white shark. His shadow was plump and middle-aged again.

"In the end, old Septivarian was the real arch-manipulator," he said. "I owe him. And the Devil, as they say, loves a bargain. That is, unless you kids are up for a bit of a violin contest, kind of thing? Double or nothing?"

September had once tried to play the violin, as part of a half-formed plot to be a more normal and boring child. The sounds she had managed to wring from the music teacher's old practice instrument had been the kind which, it's said, haunt the dreams of Azathoth, the blind god at the centre of space and time. The poor old music teacher had doused the violin in lighter fluid and ritually burned it, right on the Normalssons' front lawn, chanting in Aramaic. That sort of thing *really* got the curtains twitching. September hadn't tried again.

"Perhaps not," she said. "Look, it's been a long day for all of us, and you have a milk shake machine right there. Let's whip up a round of double chocolate malts, and talk this through. There's a lot about this whole Dark Lazarus situation we don't know, and I'm not certain that completing it was what the Professor had in mind."

She deliberately turned her back on the Devil, whose name tag did indeed say 'Charlie', and stalked over to a plastic table, where she slumped onto one overstuffed bench.

"Oh, he wanted it complete. Just not for Mrs Thatcher," said Virgil, gesturing for Cedric to pick him up. "He said that once you figured out how to create a perfectly tractable God, you'd get one. Actually doing the work and putting the pieces together was a mere formality. Like that Doom Clock he made, right? The computer he built, the B.I.S.H.O.P, could work out how things had to go, to make a satisfying story. Narrative Causality, and all that. That's why Charlie here is gonna give us the card. To see what happens. He wouldn't be the Devil if he didn't want to know."

"No," said Charlie, slamming his fists down on the counter. "*It's because I owe him.* Septivarian Archimedes made me the Perpetual Patty, the single archetypal frozen disc of beef which made all this possible. It enabled me to build my empire of evil. Still, there's no time to reminisce. Because *they're coming.*"

Charlie twisted the screen of the restaurant's cash register around to face September and her friends, and at the same time the menu boards hanging above him all flickered with static and became grainy security-camera feeds, centred on the outside of the Burger Slave.

The parking lot was alive with Elvi. Rock 'n' Roll royalty, tooled up with assault rifles and rocket launchers, crept through the plastic topiary, and between the hideous fibreglass cartoon characters of the children's playground.

"How did they find us?" yelped Ced, turning to face the glassed-in front of the restaurant. The darkness outside meant that he could see nothing but a distorted reflection of the neon-lit interior. "I thought we'd seen the last of them, back under the library."

For some reason, Charlie didn't answer him, but looked right at September instead.

"I don't know where you found this one, but you'd better bring him along, right sharp. I can hold the illusion that this place is empty for about twenty more seconds, okay? Then we'll be knee-deep in suede."

"To be fair, we probably lit up their thaumic scanners like a solid plutonium lighthouse, as soon as we dragged Ammut through into the *Materia*," said Arbourdale, jumping down from the counter to follow the Devil. "So come on, kids. I've been wanting to see how this whole thing turns out since hair-metal was a fresh idea. Chop chop!"

An overenthusiastic gas grenade clonked off the sliding doors, and spun hissing on the concrete outside. September briefly considered how to fortify the serving counter against a small army of cosmic horrors, and then shook her head.

"What about that milkshake?" she asked, forcing herself to smile.

"Young lady, even *I'm* afraid of what's in the milkshakes. There's no cows involved," said Charlie, poking his head back around the corner from the kitchen. "Now, hurry up, and bring the sacrifice! We haven't much time!"

September noticed a word sitting crooked in that previous sentence, like a turd on the green baize of a billiard table.

"*Sacrifice?*" she hissed, grabbing his arm. A tingle of something prickly and supernatural jolted through her fingers. "What do you mean, sacrifice?"

Charlie shrugged.

"You're about to use techno-sorcery to raise a new Prince of Darkness. More than my job's worth for there *not* to be a sacrifice, really. I mean, you know. *Someone to become the new Devil.* You didn't think *I* was going to do it, did you? I've got things just how I like them, and burger sales are up! Plus, at my age, with me dodgy knee and wobbly ankles, and all..."

September's eyes went wide. She pulled her hand away as if Charlie's polyester work-shirt was suddenly electrified.

"You don't mean... with the blood, and the pentacle, and the big black dagger, and all that?" she asked, making a slicing motion across her neck with one thumb. "A bit old fashioned, isn't it?"

Charlie rolled his eyes.

"Positively medieval. Which is when I'm *from*, young lady. But no. Your great-Grandad wasn't having it. Said that all the theatrics was unnecessary. But that you'd definitely need to bring someone who was up for a change of career. I used to be a wandering minstrel, you know. Which explains a lot about old Hieronymus Bosch's paintings, and the, ummm... instruments in various places." He looked slightly sheepish for a moment, then shrugged. "Can't blame a man for seeing off a few of his enemies in the musician's guild, when he gets to be Prince of Damnation, right?"

September got the very real impression that he was sidling away from the issue at hand.

"You mean Cedric, don't you? You think I brought him along just for that. *You total bastard!* I'm not that kind of..."

"We're here," interrupted Charlie. "And for the record, 'total bastard' is the nicest thing anyone has ever said about me, that was even remotely accurate."

They caught up with the rest of their little party in front of the door of a huge and shiny-white chiller. Frost glistened on its chrome fittings. Under his breath, and just for September, he said –

"*And of course you're that kind. When it comes down to it, everyone is. It's my job to know it.*"

"Glad you could make it," drawled Arbourdale. "You know, it's not like there's an army of evil Elvises trying to break in and murder us all. Why not stop for a bite to eat?"

Cedric was peering through the tiny fogged-up window of the chiller, and an icicle had formed on the end of his nose.

"There's something in there. It's glowing, and spinning. Is that what we're here for?"

September took a long look at his old-fashioned face, and his slightly worried expression. *There was just no way she could go through with it, was there?*

She wondered, somewhere in her second thoughts, who Septivarian had considered for the job of the New Satan, back in the 1980s.

"Ermmm. Well, it's like this. We sort of have to..."

"I can feel it," he said. A dreamy look spread slowly across his face as he turned back to the window. "The tarot is in there, and it's calling to me. Probably because I was silly, and channelled the other one, back at the library. There's all *kinds* of belief flowing into it, and he's using it to... using it, ummm..."

Charlie threw open the big chromed clasps, shouldered past Cedric, and opened the door.

"I'm using it to keep Professor Archimedes' Perpetual Perma-Patty cold." he said, as chilly fog boiled out around them all. "Which is why nobody could find it, for all these years. Come on!"

They stepped into the chiller, which suddenly seemed a whole lot larger, especially when the door slammed closed. It was arctic white within, and racks of metal shelves marched off into the fog-shrouded distance, all rimed with ice.

"This thing's not even plugged in, is it?" asked Virgil, being carried in both paws by Arbourdale.

Charlie chuckled.

"Saves a fortune on electricity, that. No, the tarot's still connected to the original Lucifer, the fallen angel. Dante froze him in the middle of Cocytus, the bottom level of Hell. Hence the winter wonderland you see before you. It's done wonders for keeping the Patty fresh."

September wasn't waiting around. She pushed past and stomped off down the corridor of shelves (which was much longer than it had any right to be), toward a little hill of snow, above which rotated a pinkish, lumpy disc. She stumped her way up the hillock, and squinted at it with the furious concentration of a Keen and Curious Young Scientist.

"It's a burger patty, with a tarot card stuck to it," she said. "About a quarter pound of what you're supposed to think is beef. Frozen solid. It appears to have forgotten about gravity, too."

Charlie rubbed his hands together and smiled.

"Your great-Grandad's finest creation, at least in terms of fast food," he said. "The Perpetual Perma-Patty. It's the absolute archetype of a slab of ground beef. Every atom in it was compiled from the perfect ideal of the taste of a burger, in the mind of someone imagining one. I heard he refused to eat for days, to make himself very, very hungry, before he extracted the image of it from his own brain."

"So it's a fake?" asked Virgil.

"Oh no!" The little restaurant manager looked shocked. "It's more real than any other burger patty ever made. You know the allegory of Plato's Cave? How everything we see is actually just the shadow of a perfect archetype, that exists in the collective imagination of the universe? Well, this is *that* one."

"Wait! You mean Septivarian managed to steal *the perfect theoretical hamburger patty*, from a purely allegorical phase-space outside of time?"

"Exactly. And then he applied a bit of quantum entanglement, so that the exact same patty appears in a little stainless-steel box, in all of my restaurants, every time one of my fry-cooks needs one. *All of them are one. All of them are imaginary*. Which explains why they taste exactly like you expect them to, but don't really fill you up."

"How do they make you fat, then?" asked September.

"That's mainly the fries," shrugged Charlie. "And the shakes. Pure, abstract obesity. Don't tell anyone."

He snapped his fingers, and the spinning patty stopped, leaving the tarot card of the Devil hovering just inches from September's face. She heard a strangled shout, and as she turned she saw Cedric being dragged across the frosty metal floor of the chiller, upright, the card around his neck on its chain pulling him behind it. His boot heels carved two grooves in the snow behind him.

"Would you look at that! They recognise each other!" grinned Charlie. "How wonderfully appropriate! Now, September, do you want to explain the situation to your young friend, here, or can I do it?"

Cedric grappled with the tarot of Death, and finally got it under control by tucking it down the front of his leather jacket.

"Explain what?" he asked, all red-cheeked and puffing. Something all tangled up and painful squeezed inside September's chest.

This wasn't who she was, and definitely not who she wanted to be. *Oh well. Time for honesty.*

"He thinks I brought you here to be a sacrifice," she said. "The only way to finish my great-great-granddad's plan, was for someone to..."

Cedric's old-fashioned little smile was quite unexpected.

"Take the card. Become the new Devil. I mean, yes. Of course! It stands to reason. I mean, it'd be just like using Captain Khatri's one, wouldn't it? But, erm... perhaps a bit more sinister, and all that. I'd sort of assumed I'd have to give it a try. After all, Virgil here's just a hologram, and Arbourdale is a teddy bear. He'd either be the silliest devil ever, or the most terrifying."

September caught a little glimpse, out of the corner of her eye, of Charlie's smile. It was the fat, contented grin of a cat who's just swallowed the family budgie.

"You don't have to," she said. I could always..."

But the provisional ex-Reaper had that look about him again. The one that was all duty, and damn the expenses.

"No. I volunteer. If it means saving the world, and everything."

"Bloody fine sentiment and all that," whistled Virgil, who had been put down in his lantern beneath the levitating patty. He squinted up at it, hands on his hips. "But don't you rush into anything now, Cedric. The Professor never said that there was any coming back from the transformation. He ran all kinds of calculations, with his chum Rosewood, but even *that* green-toothed little weasel wasn't keen to put on the big daddy pants, when it came down to it. The tarot of Death knows it's part of a uniform, and part of a duty. The Devil is exactly what it says on the box. They're not the same."

"But it's not, is it? What it says on the box?"

That was September, who had plucked the frozen meat patty from the air. She turned to Charlie, and whatever he saw in her eyes wiped the grin off his face immediately.

"It's all in the picture, isn't it, Charles? The man and woman, chained to the Devil's throne. Dante wasn't telling us that humanity was enslaved. That would be like saying that dogs are in charge of humans, because they're both on opposite ends of a leash."

Cedric looked her in the eye as he reached out for the card. His fingers bloomed white with tiny ice crystals as he pushed them through the field of energy around the Perpetual Perma-Patty.

"Hey! Steady on! Don't let's be hasty!" shouted Virgil.

The sound of shattering glass, and the first shuddering chords of 'Heartbreak Hotel' rang out, from somewhere outside the chiller. More bangs and crashes followed, along with a clatter of gunfire.

"Bugger that!" said Arbourdale. "You *go*, my lad!"

Charlie looked avid and transfixed. September's eyes went wide with horror. The card peeled away from the surface of the meat patty with a sound like scissors through spiderwebs, and flew the last couple of inches between the frozen theoretical beef and Cedric's hand, all in slow motion.

There was a sense of hot oil, and summer lightning, and the sound of fingers running down a long, long fretboard, as magnetic pickups hummed.

All the things which made up Dark Lazarus; all those tanks of Repo, with their records and twenty-sided dice and fifths of moonshine and ripped denim inside them, were buried under the rubble of Septivarian Archimedes' laboratory. But what the old Professor had been creating wasn't a physical thing. *It was an idea.* An image, seeded in the Aught, nourished by newspaper headlines and fevered imaginations, and the smoke from pyres of burning records and books.

Metaphorically, it came sizzling down the chains which bound *Sapiens Humana*, that little naked man and woman, to the Devil's throne, right there on the tarot. But with a whacking great charge of Endarkenment behind it, 'metaphorically' was real enough.

Cedric closed his hand around the card.

And the music of creation rang out – not some celestial hymn, but its opposite. The sound of a crackly old vinyl record meeting needle with groove.

One.

Two.

A-One Two Three FOUR!

Fifteen
The Past
vs
Sanity

Of course there was a secret back entrance.

When you build the ultimate clandestine lair, in which to create a tame version of the Prince of Darkness, and a drug which can open up a gateway between the living and the dead, you pretty much have to have one, don't you? It was only because Little-Mean-on-the-Average was situated in rural England that it wasn't hollowed out of a skull-shaped volcanic island. Septivarian had toyed, briefly, with the whole thing being built atop a giant Zeppelin.

At least, thought Silas Rosewood, *they'd put some proper skulls and crossbones on the door.*

It was down under a span of mossy concrete; the Memorial Bridge which carried the high Street over the boxed-in River Average. Willows hung low into the oily water, where shopping trollies lurked half-submerged, like chromed-wire crocodiles.

It was, in fact, the spot where a tiny otherdimensional Elvis had met its demise, just yesterday afternoon. The frog which had done the deed now perched on the banana seat of an overturned Raleigh chopper bicycle, its tiny little head cocked in puzzlement. A man had dropped the bike here, then pried open a metal cabinet set into the wall, puffing and muttering all the while. The frog had watched him dial a number on an old rotary telephone inside the cabinet, and then the brickwork had cracked open along hidden seams, accompanied by a great exhalation of dust and dried-out pigeon poo.

The door was still open a crack. The frog plopped down onto the slimy flagstones, and scented the air with weird senses, stitched into its skull by September's black-nail-polished fingers. Something familiar wafted up out of the dark. Something which ignited a deep and improbable yearning, all out of proportion to the tiny amphibian's brain. It had so very many questions, and none of them could be adequately summed up by the word 'ribbit'.

Perhaps its creator could help make sense of it all.

Deep below, down a spiral staircase all rust and chipped yellow paint, Silas Rosewood leaned up against the kind of door which was usually only found on submarines. *Nuclear* submarines, to be precise; it was blazoned all over with dire warnings, skulls, atomic trefoils and the health-and-safety equivalent of medieval curses.

Silas was the one who'd written the warnings. He crouched up against the steel, listening intently, because the first two doors he'd tried had nothing but millions of tonnes of rubble behind them. Opening this one to discover a short, fatal, horizontal landslide would be a bit counter-productive, he felt.

Rosewood tapped on the metal. A slow, treacly grin spread across his face – in pea-green, of course. It seemed that this room, of all rooms, was still intact. This stood to reason; he couldn't really remember why, but he recalled building it to survive a medium-sized nuclear apocalypse.

Those memories, in fact, were exactly why Silas was here.

He spun the wheel, and stood back as the blast door swung open, hinges groaning. Inside was all blackened soot and charred concrete, burnt wire, and that peculiar electrical smell which informs you that it's time to hunt for the warranty card.

Silas didn't need to scrabble through excised memories this time. Oh no. This was the room where they'd built the B.I.S.H.O.P. – the Bio-Intelligent Silicon Holistic Operations Processor. Or rather, Septivarian Archimedes had built it, while Rosewood passed him screwdrivers, as well as a selection of ham sandwiches, shortbread biscuits and cups of tea so thick and sugary that they'd lost several spoons inside them.

Silas drifted over the threshold of the room like a man in a dream, eyes wide, feet puffing up little clouds of charcoal dust. He couldn't recall what the damned machine had done, or what had happened to it, in the end. But he could feel the edges of the holes he'd cut out of his own memory, using a device like the one which now bumped against his hip, in his trench coat pocket. Those edges traced out things like cans full of gasoline, and a furnace wind, and the deep, deep knowledge that he'd cheated.

Quis custodiet ipsos custodes, eh? Who guards the guards? Who oversees Oversight, the Bureau Innominandum's internal affairs wonks? And who, except the man who'd built the first memory-slicer, knew that it didn't just erase – that it could cut and paste, too?

He'd put the clues in feelings, and half-supposed intuitions, and things which would never bubble to the surface, even if he was tortured. In the Bureau, that wasn't just paranoia. Mother Goose could make you profoundly uncomfortable, in ways which horrible little men with rubber truncheons and jumper cables could only dream of. He knew, because one of his jobs was to monitor and randomly review the dreams of those horrible little men.

Silas Rosewood had pretended to accept losing a large part of his mind back then. But what he'd never accepted was the loss of all that he must have learned, working alongside Septivarian Archimedes. Now that the old man was dead, *he didn't have to be second best*. Not any more. Oh no! He'd reclaim all of that knowledge, earned at the elbow of true mad genius, one ham sandwich at a time.

He let his eyes unfocus as he opened a second, more normal door, and stepped into a railway ticket booth. The metal grille which covered its window was buckled inward, with concrete and reinforcing steel forced halfway through the gap, but the mannequin was still there. Rosewood's mind worked on autopilot, guided on rails that had nothing to do with thought, and he plucked the name tag from its chest.

PROPHET, it said, stamped into plastic that was just a tad too thick, and a touch too heavy. The safety pin which backed it caught a gleam from the neon lights overhead as he held it up. Then, in one swift, unthinking motion, he plunged the entire needle into the meat of his palm, like a tiny crucifixion nail.

Silas staggered, gasping, as information exploded through his hand. It rose up his spine, urgent, churning like spaghetti on full boil. He made it as far as the blackened room where the B.I.S.H.O.P had once stood, before he keeled over like a felled tree, down into the soot and ashes, his mouth opening and closing without words.

This was where Rosewood had stored his memories. In a bio-chip, a sliver of artificial brain, hidden in the little name tag. Now they burst out from his eyes, flickering like an old-fashioned cinema projector's light, and painting the wall with moving images, all turned sideways.

The scene they showed was chopped up, as real memories so often are. It was a storm of impressions, out of time, out of phase, but so vivid that they even came with their own smells and tastes.

They showed a nude Septivarian, covered in soap suds, writing something horribly complicated on a two-level chalkboard. Then they skipped to a conference room, in the height of 1960s military chic, where a trio of dour, suited men delivered a very serious speech to both Silas Rosewood and Professor Archimedes.

Rosewood's breakthrough invention, the memory redaction machine, was projected on the wall in schematic form. Then came images of a young woman wearing the costume of a super-hero, complete with a lightning-bolt-and-question-mark design. Next to her was a lad of a similar age, dressed in what appeared to be a boy scout's uniform and a Sherlock Holmes deerstalker hat. The pictures had been taken candidly, out of sight, their subjects all unwitting.

The dour, suited men smiled. it was not a pretty sight.

Archimedes' expression turned dark for a moment, and he leaned forward over the table, things moving unnaturally under the fabric of his lab coat. Then the dour man in the middle spoke, at length. In the memory his voice was like the noise of a muffled trombone, but by and by Septivarian's expression turned from anger to resignation, and then to weary acceptance.

He held out his hand. It was barely trembling when the suited man shook it.

Now came a rush of images. Of military bases and linoleum-floored corridors, of generals whacking maps with hammers and sickles splashed on them in red, and of nights spent tinkering with circuitry and drawing up plans. Septivarian knew people on both sides of the law, it seemed; there were clandestine midnight meetings with supervillains and scoundrels. A sit-down with the Confectioner in '62, at a patisserie off the Rue Bac in the Seventh Arrondissement of Paris. An assignation with Penny Dreadful, while a full moon hung over a graveyard in New Orleans. A discussion with the Doom Commission, all young and full of costumed malice, and still led by Omegabrain on that jasmine-scented night in

'64, in the courtyard of an abandoned monastery in Chile.

How did you create a new God? That's what they talked about, because that was the business they were in, back then...

You repurposed one that was already there. You relied on the semantics of the treaties, which talked about 'all extant deities'. You delivered two suitcases of unmarked currency to Anton Szandor LaVey, in a hotel room in Vegas in 1971, interrupting a game of poker between him, Hunter S Thompson, The Suede Spectre and what turned out to be, (after a moment of exquisite terror and awkwardness), the real, actual Elvis Presley.

You seeded the fertile soil of the Bible Belt with stories of the new Satan. You started record companies, and shipped crates of weapons to cocaine cartels in the misty hills of Colombia, and you penned yellow headlines about Dungeons and Dragons dementia, backwards song lyrics, and biker-gang sacrifices conducted in the Sonoran desert. You staged music festivals in telluric places of power, making the ley-lines shudder like bass guitar strings.

All this, they did. All this, and more. While at the same time they built a machine called the B.I.S.H.O.P, to hack the Aught. It wasn't enough, both Silas and Archimedes saw, to just fix things on the living side of the veil. They needed to build a framework, over in the *Immateria Aeternum*, to hang their new creation on. They needed to build a machine that could dream.

In the end, there was only one way. They'd replicated brain tissue, in silicon. They'd ginned up a rudimentary intelligence, but it always fell apart before it could bridge the gap. The hardware was right, but the software would require a copy of a human mind, and one so powerful that it could expand into all the super-cooled memory banks of the B.I.S.H.O.P at once, becoming the soul of the machine.

Silas had suggested necromancy. Spade-and-scalpel work. Archimedes had said no.

They were tantalisingly close. The Bureau held up their end of the bargain. Memories of a wedding painted the blackened wall, back in 1978. Those same two kids from before, but without the superhero get-up or the detective's hat. Grown-ups, now. Kissing under a rain of tiny white petals, in a ray of sunlight. The aisles of the church separated factions; heroes and government types on the left, villains and super-creeps on the right, all unaware of the non-proliferation pact which was about to upend their world, so very soon.

Silas saw his hand, shaking the blue rubber glove of Omegabrain. Slipping him a card, all unseen. Septivarian sat alone at a table, staring blankly at a slice of wedding cake. A brochure for a planned town called Little-Mean-on-the-Average was open next to his plate, fluttering in the breeze through the church doors.

And then, this place. This room, decades ago. There was a poster on the wall, behind massed banks of clicking, whirring computer towers; a kitten clinging to a washing line by its paws. *Hang In There.*

Silas watched, in the wash of images spilling from his own eyes, as his ghost entered the frame. The lights came on, neon buzzing and popping. He set down a case, and opened it up, and took out something which, when assembled, looked very much like the dome-topped hair dryers you'd find in a high street salon.

He was alone. The rest of the lab was silent. Archimedes – now reinvented as the Befuddler, Quizmaster of Chaos – was busy tonight, stealing Mozart's unknown book of sheet music from the catacombs beneath Vienna. But here came a knocking at the secret back blast-door of the lab. And here came Silas Rosewood, in the height of late-70s fashion, to open it.

Omegabrain strode in, and though the film was silent, you could see that he was giving it the full nickel-plated evil laugh. Silas joined in. *Oh, this was a doublecross for the ages, right? Here was the acme of nefarious swindling! Decades of government research, and the genius of the only mad scientist who could out-think Omegabrain himself, all served up on a plate, thanks to Rosewood's treachery.*

There was the big suitcase full of cash. There was the handshake, and another evil laugh. Omegabrain was a slightly chubby middle-aged chap, with a big silver Spartan-style helmet, crested in blue. His claim to fame was his status as the world's smartest bastard, with an IQ that ran to four figures, cranked up by his helmet's alien technology. He was the leader and grand strategist of the Doom Commission, the brains to their brawn.

What Silas knew, and millions didn't, was that he could only keep the helmet turned on for a few minutes at a time. This was enough to design clever technological toys, or plan heists of Machiavellian complexity. But it wasn't any use in spotting the dart gun Rosewood had tucked into the waistband of his bell-bottomed trousers. In the end, he was just like most narcissistic arch-manipulators; pathetically certain that he was three steps ahead of everyone else.

He watched the lights go out in the poor supervillain's eyes. He smoked a cigarette as he waited for the paralysing poison to do its work. Then he cranked the dial on Omegabrain's helmet up to eleven, socketed his entire head, helm and all, into his specially built mind redactor, and copied his whole brain. *Sucked it dry.*

There was a brief period of editing, of cutting and splicing memories. A whole lot of Omegabrain stayed on the cutting room floor. There was a short, nasty, messy interlude with a black tarpaulin, a hacksaw, and an oil-drum full of acid.

As dawn broke, somewhere up above, kissing the television aerials and chimneypots of Little-Mean-on-the-Average, Silas Rosewood stubbed out one final woodbine, and uploaded some fresh, new software into the B.I.S.H.O.P.

Now the crescendo unfolded. The great work. He watched the celebration turning sour, even as the secrets of the Aught were unlocked, and Dark Lazarus rushed towards its conclusion, with the fall of Communism and the rise of Mrs Goosegarden making it both irrelevant and horrific.

You couldn't keep a truth that big, and that horrible, from a mind like that of Septivarian. He never knew what Silas had done. He had no idea who he'd done it to. The poor bastard even swore he'd avenge Omegabrain, and he took over the Doom Commission himself, in blatant contravention of the non-proliferation pact.

Silas carefully worked his cutouts. He implicated the Silver Sorcerer, and then the Atomic Samurai, and the Animator. All has-beens, and stooges, and fall guys. The Commission flouted the Pact to snuff them. Rosewood tidied house.

But Septivarian suspected. And he was the kind of person who picked away at things, worrying at threads, unravelling coincidences. He certainly knew that, while they'd built a hollow place in the Aught for the New Satan, the rock 'n' roll rebel angel, to inhabit, the B.I.S.H.O.P had been running counter-programs of its own.

It was Silas who convinced him that it had to burn. Not just because the thought of the Neoliberal, post-cold-war hollow men having their own tame devil was abhorrent. But because Septivarian was too close to finding out why

Rosewood's supposed artificial intelligence seemed so effective, and so un-artificial.

They swore an oath. They shook on it. Septivarian was thinking of his great-grandkids; somewhere up above, they were living a normal life. There was no telling what the government would do if he didn't make this look convincing.

The fire killed B.I.S.H.O.P. In a very real sense, it finally finished off the remains of Omegabrain, tangled up in silicon. The pair of them watched the fire catch, and turned, and shook hands one last time, and aimed a matched pair of mind redactor pistols at each other's heads.

It had looked like an accident. They'd *made* it look like one, up to and including the terrible burns, and the broken bones, and the horrific memory loss.

The experimental supercomputer had gone critical, and when it blew, it had all but destroyed Septivarian Archimedes. He'd thrown himself between Rosewood and the explosion, Silas has told them, with very real tears in his eyes, even though both had been blinded white and half cooked in their sockets. He'd sacrificed himself, and given up huge parts of his genius. There was no way to rebuild the B.I.S.H.O.P, or salvage Dark Lazarus. Better to mothball it all. Better that poor old Septivarian got sent off to Wrinkly Acres, and a government pension.

It was the least they could do.

Of course, the Bureau had their suspicions. But how could they ever find out? How could Silas Rosewood ever slip up, or say the wrong thing, or dream the wrong dreams, when he was only now, in this moment of drooling paralysis, learning the truth again?

Too bad, then, that he hadn't been the only one to witness it.

The light from Rosewood's artificial eyes flickered

and died, in a blur of security warnings and stencilled numbers. He found that he could move again, though it felt as though he'd been pushed downstairs in a skip bin full of hammers. Silas wiggled his toes, groaned, and rolled onto his back.

Just in time to see a group of very bruised, angry, and above all, very *old* faces looking down at him. They materialised from behind some sort of invisibility field, which seemed to be projected from the tiny crown that one of the geriatrics was wearing.

"Zneeb G'tharg Blorp Blubble," said this long-bearded apparition, narrowing its eyes.

"Exactly, yer highness," said another of the heads, this one dressed in the charred remains of a stoat costume. From somewhere about its person, the mystery head produced a half-smoked little roll-up, which it proceeded to light.

"There's only one question, really, isn't there, guvnor?" asked Stoatman, who looked like he'd had the worst day at the office since Generalleutnant Dietrich Kraiss had sat down at his desk in a bunker above Omaha Beach in Normandy, on what appeared to be a lovely sunny morning in June of 1944. "Did he know?"

Now normally, Silas Rosewood had all kinds of countermeasures at his disposal to deal with this sort of thing. Fingertip tasers were just one of the options. But the aftermath of being hit in the prefrontal cortex by a wrecking ball of pure reminiscence was taking its toll. His vision blurred, and he felt something cold, metallic and very, very strong pinning down his arms. Realisation icepicked into him, right between the hemispheres of his brain.

"You... you're the Doom Commission! But they said you'd died! Crushed under tonnes and tonnes of rubble!"

The Red Mobster leaned in, from where he was casually restraining Silas Rosewood's legs with a single one of his huge claws.

"What's the line, Medusa? Rumours of our deaths 'ave been greatly exxagermerated."

Stoatman leaned in, hands on his bony knees.

"Yeah. What the big fella said. We was doing a proper redemption arc, right, and the whole ceiling fell in. Too bad for those Bureau boys, but then again, henchmen know what they're signing up for. Bugger me if the old Prince here doesn't have a force field generator in 'is little crown, to match the whole see-through thingy. So we retired to a safe distance, like. And that's when we met *you*."

Silas licked his lips, and felt little beads of sweat breaking out across his forehead. They must have seen everything. Which meant...

"I have money! he squeaked. "Loads of it! Big bags and bushels and boxes. It's all yours if you let me go!"

Medusa Oblongata scowled.

"And you think we don't? Sonny, at a certain age you realise that there's nothing left to spend it on, even if you *have* stashed thirty years of loot under some chocolate cuckoo clock factory in Geneva. Some things are just worth more."

Stoatman took a drag on his horrible little roll-up, his face once more underlit with red.

"See, I reckon it's what the old Prof used to talk about. The Aegis of bloody Destiny. Ha! I thought it was some kinda Greek clobber we were gonna steal one day. But it turns out, it's just the nature of stories. *We're* here, and *you're* here, and wouldn't you know it, we're all in the room where you backstabbed poor old Omegabrain."

"He was never a good judge of character, the silly sausage," sighed Medusa.

"Hence the question. Because I'm comfortable with what I am, mister Rosewood," said Stoatman. "I'm a horrible old supervillain, who'd stab you in the danglies as soon as look at you. But I reckon you still gotta have a code. So, I'll ask you again. Did. He. Know?"

All four of the surviving Doom Commission stared down at him, grim and implacable as old age itself. Silas swallowed, hard.

"Septivarian? No. He would never have... but we *had* to. You don't understand! We unlocked the secrets of life and death! What was Omegabrain doing with all that grey matter, anyhow? Designing silly death-traps for secret agents, and stealing the Mona Lisa over and over again? You know he always just sold it back to the French government when he was a bit low on pocket change!"

He spit it out, reckless, and lay there panting, his mouth full of the taste of soot and burned wire. Almost immediately, he regretted it.

Not because any of the Doom Commission did anything nasty. Not just then. It was the look they all got on their faces, as Stoatman shook his head and sighed. He stood up, with a great clicking of knees and rubbing of his bent old back.

"Seems that's it, then. Aegis of Destiny, see? It weren't a redemption arc, sort of thing. It was the bloody anti-heroism, all along. Looks like some horrible, merciless vengeance then, lads and lady. Anyone up for a bit of the old ultra-violence?"

Silas contemplated that look. It was in all their eyes. It was the look of people who'd sat through a hundred funerals, for friends they'd known and loved. Those eyes had seen innumerable after-service platters of ham rolls, and little sandwiches with the crusts cut off. Those eyes, looking down at him, saw him as already dead.

"You think it was just me?" he shrieked, straining upwards against his bonds. "It was the whole damned committee! Mother Goose! The Supreme Aaron of the Elvi! Mister Blank, and the rest of Void Chamber. You can't beat them all. Not on your own. Not at your age!"

"Gnaarg Blap Zporp!" chuckled the Invisible Prince.

"Exactly," said the Red Mobster. "Age is just a number. Like, you know. A casualty count."

Medusa Oblongata frowned.

"And we ain't alone, sonny. Oh no! I know where there's a whole retirement home full of people who would very much like to know what happened to Omegabrain, and that you government bastards did Professor Archimedes wrong as well."

"But... but there's *monsters* out there!" shouted Silas, in one last attempt to stay useful.

Stoatman shrugged. The tip of his vile cigarette glowed red. From somewhere in the rags of his costume, the bandy-legged little man had produced a switchblade, of the old-fashioned kind Cedric would have remembered. He popped it open.

"See, that ain't quite your concern, Mister Rosewood," he said, with a voice that was all the more terrifying for the fact that it was full of regret. "*Your* problem, for a very short while longer, I might add – is that there's monsters *in here*."

Chief Inspector Rupert watched a fireball rise up over the rooftops with a grim scowl. He lowered his binoculars, and turned to the officer on his right, who, unfortunately, turned out to be Constable O'Dwightly.

"Bring up the tanks. Tell the mounted police and the riot squads to fall back – that monster is going to require some serious ordnance."

"Are you *certain* we shouldn't try to arrest it?" asked the constable. "After all, I've listed about four hundred and thirty different offences that it's committed, and a few more that I've had to make up, like jaywalking through buildings, and illegally stepping on a vehicle in a disabled parking space!"

Rupert pinched the bridge of his nose, in an attempt to make the headache go away. This was all so far out of his wheelhouse that he was, metaphorically, standing on the pier as he watched the boat sail away. But he'd been given a job to do, and he didn't much like the thought of reporting back to a homicidal robot Margaret Thatcher that he'd failed. The image of those eyes, like the grinding mechanisms of two electric pencil sharpeners, still haunted him. He shuddered.

"No, the tanks it is. And I take it that Rosewood's lads have deployed the super-secret informational warfare jamming thingummy-bobs, and the big electronic security doo-dads? Where *is* that slimy little rotter, anyhow?"

Constable O'Dwightly (who, it must be said, was having the time of his life), had seen the mysterious trailers full of aerials and dishes being wheeled into position, by government types in yellow space-suits. He saluted, perhaps a tad too sharply, and his oversized night-vision goggles slipped down over his face again.

"Doo-dads deployed, and thingummy-bobs activated, sir!" he enthused. "Gosh, do you reckon it knows you're here? I mean, it seems to be coming right for us..."

This wasn't something which Rupert really wanted to think about. But he *had* noticed that the huge, impossible monster was making a bee-line right for his position. Surely it couldn't be that smart? Surely... but then again, *surely* Elvis Presley wasn't the leader of an army of cosmic horrors, and *surely* the former prime minister wasn't a nuclear-powered robot who lived under Westminster.

The Chief Inspector would never find out.

Because at that moment a ripple passed through the weave of the world, as reality was stretched in every direction at once. Rupert experienced a horrible moment when he saw everyone around him in four dimensions, with all the fractal ghosts of their possible pasts and futures splayed out. Most of Constable O'Dwightly's, he noted, (as he watched the young berk's face melt and blur) involved a career in village idiocy, not law enforcement.

A line of Egyptian hieroglyphs flared into existence over Little Mean, sliced stark across the clouds. It separated into two, then hinged open into four, directly in the path of Ammut. Runic eyes blazed at its corners, and the skyline beyond it was obscured by a rectangle of dusk-purple, shimmering gently and edged with pyramids.

Gosh! Lucky I've already gone mad, thought Rupert. *I'll beat the rush!*

Because the gateway was immense. *Impossible.* Phantom pillars carved with stern, ancient faces flanked it. The Chief Inspector could already feel hysteria bubbling up inside his chest, even before he glimpsed the moon which rode that otherworldly sky, borne up on a foam of starlight. *It was a huge and skeletal face, on a planetary scale.*

Then something far worse rose up to obscure his view, all sleek and black and gold. Rupert gibbered slightly, just to try it out.

Oh, excellent! he told himself. *It appears to be one of those animal-headed gods they sold little statues of in foreign airports! The doggy one, wasn't it?*

It was of course Anubis, Lord of the Necropolis, He Who Stands At The Gates of Eternity. And somewhere behind those void-black jackal's eyes, Jaghtaran Khatri's sanity was failing just as fast as Rupert's. His mind was a dying sun, and memories spun from its orbit and burned. *Sparks cast into an abyss...*

Anubis raised a muzzle flecked with blood toward the heavens, and his howl rattled windowframes all the way across Little Mean. It would have warmed the Little Bad Wolf's tiny, felted soul.

From those windows, thousands of people watched; most of them slack-jawed, some of them gibbering, some praying. *Anubis had their attention. Now he had to use it.*

Rain lashed down, saturating the black fur of the death-jackal. His black eyes blazed violet. His immense paws stepped through the gateway, claws clicking against the wet tarmac.

Ammut's eyes grew wide. When the soul-eater saw her master step through into the world, the look on her face was one of pure canine guilt.

"Who's been a naughty personification of oblivion, then?"

The sixty-foot armoured jackal-god held out his hand, and a golden staff materialised in it. It was all cobras and thunderbolts, meshed and glittering. Ammut cowered, covering her scarred old snout with both paws.

"Bad soul-devourer!" scolded Anubis, in perfect ancient Egyptian. **"You know you're not allowed out into the mortal world! Now, get back beyond the veil like a good cosmic monster!"**

He spun the staff, and brought it hammering down across the high street in front of Ammut's face, cracking the surface. Water mains blew, sending geysers spouting up. Car alarms shrilled for blocks in every direction.

It looked as though it was going to work, too. Ammut shuddered and sighed, and something began to bleed out of all the concrete and steel which made up her body. The possession was fading.

Right up until a high-explosive shell exploded against the jackal's helm.

The huge death-god staggered, snarling. He fell hard against the high street shops, splintering the facade of the Tao Maharajah takeaway. That shot had rung his bell, and he shook his head to clear his vision as he rose. Bricks and shards of glass avalanched.

"*Concentrate fire! Bring the blighter down!*" shouted a very twitchy tank commander, who had rolled in across the Memorial Bridge with a trio of Challenger IIs.

Rupert made frantic motions for him to bugger off, but the tank commander had no time for semaphore. Deep in his withered little heart, he would dearly have loved to have been General Patton, but he lacked the backbone, the shiny boots and, sadly, a chin.

"*Give that thing hell, by thunder, like it's the Russians coming through the Fulda Gap!*"

Rupert thought back wistfully to his days in police training college, and how fast he used to be able to run back then. It probably still wouldn't have been fast enough. Because the God of Death was out of his sarcophagus, and back in business.

Anubis leapt, much higher than a thing that size should have been able to, and much faster as well. He landed atop the first tank, and his staff hammered down to impale it right through the turret, like a butterfly pinned to a corkboard. The ammunition inside the tank exploded as a pulse of violet light blasted every bolt and rivet from it at once. The crew within were reduced to blackened skeletons.

The Challenger to the left (just outside of Mrs Blixby's specialist magazines and art-house photography store, for the discerning gentleman) tried to traverse its turret, but it was far too slow.

Anubis spun his staff, wrenching it clear from the burning husk of the first tank. His huge back paw slammed into the war-machine's main gun and stopped it dead, gears shrieking as they were stripped smooth. Then the staff hammered down into the middle of the high street like a foundation piling. Anubis flipped forward, planted his paws on the front and back of the tank, and ripped its turret off. Then he held it up over his head, muscles straining under his glossy pelt, and shook it.

Dangling wires sparked, and the gunner hung on by his fingertips, a horrible warm sensation trickling into his boots. He was brought up eye-to-eye with Anubis, and surveyed a mouthful of razor-sharp ivory, bared in a rippling growl.

When the Death-god flicked him with one clawed finger, he cleared the horizon.

The last remaining tank was crewed by veterans. It was a credit to their training that they managed to get a shot off, as Anubis crushed reinforced steel between his palms. It was velocity and mass, rendered as a deadly equation.

Unfortunately, the Jackal of Eternity was not at home to the laws of physics.

He tossed the crumpled remains of the turret over his shoulder, then blurred forward and gripped his staff, wrenching it loose in a spray of concrete. Then he spoke a Word. It was uttered in a forgotten tongue, hinting at eyeless statues buried under sand, and scuttling scorpions, and the suffocating weight of time.

The armour-piercing shell stopped in mid air. It was webbed in a violet halo, spinning gently, while Anubis peered at it, narrow-eyed, then tapped it with one claw.

"Erm... ahhh, sorry about that!" shouted the tank commander, fiddling with his binoculars. "Orders, and all. You know, umm, how it..."

Anubis snorted. You didn't need a degree in Hieroglyphics to comprehend, in that great exhalation of breath, whole oceans of contempt.

The jackal-god struck so fast that he was simply a blur. His staff came slicing through the rain in a great overhand swipe. When it struck the artillery shell the world rang like a church bell, right down to the atoms. The shell flew on a flat trajectory right through the engine of the tank, as pistons and gears and fuel exploded in a blazing fan.

"Now run away, little man," rumbled Anubis, leaning over the trembling figure of the tank commander. The driver and gunner had already popped open their own hatches and taken his advice. None of them would stop running until they were as far away from Egypt as humanly possible.[33]

Some of the people watching from their windows applauded. Some of them even cheered, and didn't wonder if it might have been for the wrong team entirely.

Ammut, however, watched all of this with narrowed eyes. Lips made of linoleum pulled back from rows of jagged metal teeth.

The soul-eater was the Jackal's creature. Whole entire dynasties had imagined her crouched, subservient, at the foot of his throne. But now, here, in this shoddy latter age...

Well, things were different.

Strange rebellious thoughts fizzed inside Ammut's mind, which ran on the copper cables woven through the Little-Mean-on-the-Average hospital.

These thoughts made the monster's hackles rise, with a thrill of disobedience. This could be her last, best chance to break free of the black desert, with its freeze-dried air and its purple sky. *Here in the Materia of Humana, death*

---

33. The trio eventually set up a small kebab shop in Mataura, French Polynesia, a country which has no tanks at all.

meant *something.* *Here,* *incarnated* *as* *a* *hospital,* *she* *understood that it was an option for everyone.*

Ammut saw Anubis take off his helm. There was a jagged dent in the side, where that first anti-tank shell had struck. He reached up with one huge hand and swiped at the side of his head, just below one ear, jangling with gold hoop earrings.

His fingertips came away bloody. And Ammut snarled, with the sound of chainsaws in darkness.

This was the moment when Jaghtaran Khatri died. He'd been holding on, thanks to Anubis' popularity among heavy metal fans and gamers. It was thin stuff indeed. But it was enough to give Khatri's soul a fingerhold.

But as Ammut pounced, arched in the air like a concrete rainbow, the Jackal drew in every echo of himself that he could.

It was instinctive, and it spanned realities, tapping deep into the Aught and sending wyrd harmonics jangling through the world. Cedric Welbourne, who was experiencing his own supernatural problems at that exact moment, didn't feel the lanyard around his neck part with a sad little 'twang', or see the tarot of Death disappear in a burst of red-shifted light.

Gravestones in the Little-Mean-on-the-Average civic cemetery went blank, the memories of the dead worn away to smooth marble. Condolence cards in the supermarket and stationers lost their messages, and Little Mean's three-man outlaw motorcycle club, (made up of Surly Albert, Grease-Pit and Derek-the-properly-hard-sounding-nickname),[34] found that every last skull on their

---

34. The so-called Hell's Inland Revenue Service – named, (in a fit of what could have been genius, or intoxication) by Derek-the-properly-hard-sounding-nickname himself. "Angels, see, dey ain't scary, right, or else they'd not be up on toppatha Christmas tree, and all hanging out wif Jesus and that," he'd reasoned. "You know what's terrifying, though? The bloody tax department!" The HIRS brotherhood had cornered the local market on drugs which only the three of them were daft enough to want to snort.

jackets and bikes had turned into a picture of a hamster. In Miss Rummage's locked-down library, all the books by swooning gothic men in lace shirts and black nail polish suddenly turned into self-help manuals about business excellence.

As Ammut rose up, a concrete wave with teeth, Anubis' staff blazed violet. He twisted at the waist, graceful as a dancer, and brought it around in a blurring arc. Its cobra head scored a groove in the tarmac, showering sparks. And as it came, a blade shimmered into existence at right-angles to it.

It began as a mere suggestion, but it took on solidity and the very essence of sharpness as it came around to meet the soul-eater's head, right behind her open jaws.

THUNK!

The blade went in, right up to the haft. It slid out the other side of a face which suddenly lost all animation, and became, instead of the slavering maw of a crocodile, a mere assemblage of concrete and metal. Anubis held his pose for a long beat, as people all over Little Mean craned out of their windows to see, or stood in darkened suburban gardens, watching the two titanic figures on the skyline. Flickering lightning obliged the drama. Grumbling thunder followed.

At last, the whole terrible tonnage of Ammut remembered that is was, in fact, simply the ruins of a hospital. Great slabs and cross-sections of masonry obeyed the pull of gravity, and came undone.

"**Bad puppy,**" said Anubis, rolling the kinks out of his neck. A puzzled look stole over his face, which is quite an achievement when you are a sixty-foot-tall black jackal in armour. With crossed eyes, the god tried to look up at his own forehead, where the Tarot of Death fluttered, stuck to his fur.

Someone had put that there, hadn't they? Someone to whom it must have been important. Surely?

Somewhere, deep within the tangle of old myths, half-imagined fragments, tatters of dreams and ancient memories which made him up, the last of Jaghtaran Khatri feathered away to nothingness.

There are reasons why the Reaper-Captains of PostMortis spend hours each day in the meditations of balance, saving up borrowed seconds. To summon a god five thousand years dead had taken more than he could give.

His last thoughts, as his ego unravelled into an afterlife beyond Uncarnadine, were of the smell of saffron, and of hot concrete after rain.

Anubis, suddenly untethered from reality, blurred like a badly tuned black-and-white TV signal. A shuddering ripple passed through the jackal-god, and he fuzzed around the edges, going all transparent. Then, with a final, fading howl, he was gone. All that was left to prove he'd ever existed was a trio of ruined tanks – and a memory, burned into the minds of hundreds of people.

Little-Mean-on-the-Average had seen miracles and nightmares walk. For a very short time, they *believed.*

Not in anything in particular. Not in that old-time Egyptian gospel, that's for sure. No matter what happens right before people's eyes, the stories furrowed into people's brains stay the same. It's a defence mechanism, really.

They just *believed*, in a numinous, fuzzy way. They believed, and it was like a slug of raw grain moonshine. *Mix it with any flavour you like, and it'll still hit you like a sock with a hammer in it.*

Miss Rummage believed, as she looked up into clearing clouds, and saw what she thought was a skull on the face of the moon. September's parents believed, and the power of it broke something brittle and hard inside them, so that they turned and clasped each other's hands, and nodded, once, with a certain sense of finality.

Wilf Handisides believed, and Hiro Mulcahey too; they'd seen the Kaiju, and they knew the world was weirder than anything they could dream though the bottom of a bottle.

Constable O'Dwightly believed, as only a grown-up berk deep inside a boys-own adventure can.

And Chief Inspector Rupert believed, down to the tassels of his leathery little soul. He watched a fighter jet come swooping in over the chimney pots, rattling the windows of the main street as it completed its run, and then he watched it dip its wings and curve away. He saw the pilot, who was most definitely Elvis Presley, throw him a mocking little salute as he turned and disappeared into the east.

And he saw what was slung under the plane, all bulbous and shiny, blazoned with a yellow nuclear trefoil. One of the bombs which the Elvi had caught, frozen in their little doomed time loop, and brought with them as a final deterrent.

They wouldn't be needing it this time. Or at least, not at this particular moment.

But belief is power. Not so much in the *Materia Mortalis*, where all it usually inspires is dodgy cults, warbly hymns and a vague idea that crystals and dolphins are important.

In the Aught, belief can make ideas **live**.

While the Chief Inspector was busy looking up at the sky and imagining a terrible roiling mushroom cloud of flame, a motorcycle rolled in across the bridge. It slipped between the ruins of three Challenger tanks, idling low. It was a big black Buell X-1, and its rider was dressed in road-worn denim and leather, with a silver helmet and a big round patch on the back of his jacket. This patch, reflected in the shattered windows of the Tao Maharajah takeaway, was of a red crucifix and crossed swords. A *real* sword – five feet of no-nonsense battle cutlery – was strapped to one saddlebag, sheathed.

The rider stopped, reached down, and picked up a scrap from the asphalt. He held it up before the mirrored visor of his helmet, and turned his head to one side, like a magpie contemplating something shiny.

It was the Tarot of Death.

The rider tucked the card away inside his leather vest, and prodded at a boxy, green-screened unit bolted to the Buell's handlebars.

Under the eyes of a dozen very nervous policemen and soldiers, but all apparently unseen, he looped the big bike around in a circle and blipped the throttle, disappearing into the smoky haze toward the west.

Suture Nine
Heck on Earth

THE RED CARDINAL felt faith explode across the streets and houses of Little Mean, even as he hurried by secret ways toward the Ghost Trap. It earthed itself through the place where he'd used to sit, down under the civic library, back when his body was five tonnes of 1960s hardware. It hit him like a savage dose of something wickedly illicit, so that his feet barely touched the floor.

His mind, such as it was, was filled up to the edges. It seethed with the piston-hammer of purpose.

"*Now*, Charon!" he shouted, bursting into the Panopticon. He didn't even notice that it had been torn apart. "It has to be now! The Reapers are headless, and there's ten thousand pitiful humans up there, right where we need to strike, all scorched on pure, directionless FAITH!"

Charon was sulking on her throne, in a tangle of long, black-robed limbs. There was a box of tissues balanced on one armrest.

"*What* has to be now? Have you lost your tiny little silicon mind, Larry? Or have you lost someone else's?"

He blurred across the intervening air, all raw and vivid.

"No. Oh no no *no*. I've *found* it. Events have moved past us, Ms Kolslaw. We risk missing the tide, if you need a metaphor more ferry-adjacent!"

Charon sniffled.

"But... but we're not ready! And that girl, that *September*, will ruin it all! She was here! I could feel the story flowing through her, Syn! It's her bloody great-great-grandfather, working the angles. I can feel it in my bones."

The Cardinal snarled.

"Oh, climb down off it, you sad old fairy tale! It's *time!* If we raise the towers now, it'll become part of the mythos. Too bad if they're still a wee bit under-construction. The little details fade into the big picture, you know. And... think about it! What a bloody masterpiece we've painted!"

Charon reached out one long-fingered hand and caressed a row of big, chromed levers. Wistful. Craving.

"Are you certain? Our tame nightmares are ready, are they?"

The Cardinal nodded, slow. *A hunter, willing a tender neck through his snare...*

"Can't you feel it? This is our chance! We bring forward the launch, and the mortals will swallow it all like bad advertising. They'll *have to*. Their minds don't work any other way."

"We'll make it all make sense again," nodded Charon, uncurling from the throne a little. "Neat and orderly. Predictable. *Sane*."

The Cardinal grinned, serpentine, as he heard the little note of hope in her voice. His own was a razor on velvet. 'Sane' didn't even touch the sides.

"*That's riiiiiight*. You'll get the respect you deserve. All of it. Even a crown, my dear. And for me, the silliest, most gold-encrusted hat the Vatican can afford."

The levers were labelled. Tags spun in the brimstone-scented breeze. They were inked up – *Gehenna Tower, Sheol Tower, Dis Tower*. Charon's fingers spider-walked them.

"And no doublecrosses?"

The Cardinal's smile extended, right up to his ears. There were *far* too many teeth crammed into it. He made the sign of the cross over his chest, keeping his head down, so Charon couldn't peep at it.

"My sister, I assure you. There will be enough power, and enough riches, to satisfy us both. Come. Our destiny awaits!"

The moment stretched. Charon's eyes flashed copper, behind her tiny sunglasses. He had her.

One swinging slap hammered all three levers down. The ground began to rumble. Red lights began to strobe, frantic. Capacitors thrummed, and crimson lightning crawled, slithering up the skeletal armatures of three big, black gantries.

"Here we go!" shouted Charon, reaching for a final, skull-topped lever. This one was festooned in black and yellow caution tape.

The Cardinal took her hand. He bent over and kissed it.

"*Mi amore!* Do it! I'll see you on the other side."

He grinned, as a set of pale fingers reached out.

Charon cackled – "Wait until they get a load of us!"

Charon pulled the lever.

Down below, engines bellowed, and clouds of smoke and spark belched out. Cogs the size of buildings meshed and thundered. Chains pulled tight, rust sloughing from links that could shackle gods. Lightning arced above, sketching out a gigantic pentagram across the dome of the Ghost Trap. A million lost souls howled in counterpoint.

As the three huge towers they'd built, all skull-cherub'd and cathedral-twisted, began to rise...

Elvis Aaron Presley – or at least, a nasty, other-dimensional copy of him – rewound the VHS tape and pressed play again. He had to be absolutely sure, because what he was seeing in this little piece of betrayal pried out of the Aught could be Earth's death sentence.

The monitor blurred with static, and wobbled to a view of Cardinal Syn's back, facing a huge screen shaped like a stained-glass window in a gothic arch. His voice crackled into focus.

"I'm aware that you had your own timetable, Madam. I'm prepared to offer concessions. But this *will* work. Trust me."

Dolly back. Pan the view. Cut to widescreen. The figure on the stained-glass screen leaned forward, into the light of a stuttering naked bulb. She sat at an otherwise empty table, set up to accommodate eight. Thrones carved with sinister eyes and ravens gathered dust.

"I can't say I'm pleased, but neither am I surprised," said Mrs Goosegarden, her artificial lips set in a bloodless scowl. "The benefits to all of us outweigh the risks. When all is said and done, humanity will go back to what they were before Dante ruined everything. Herd animals. But not for some fractious divinities, be they ever so false. *Ours.*"

"And September Normalsson?" asked the Cardinal. "Charon still has worries. Personally, I think the old man was overrated, and his descendant is even stupider. She's a tourist in all this. Out of her depth."

The robotic Margaret Thatcher smiled, as precise and cold as cryogenic ice-sculpture.

"See to it that she drowns then, your Eminence. Dark Lazarus is a loose end, and we need it tidied up. We need it under control, for long-term operations."

The Cardinal nodded. One of the chairs around the Void Chamber table was carved up with angels and crosses. The place-card in front of it said 'The Antipope'.

"Hence the schedule change," he purred. "Everything has come together in Little Mean. It's almost as if Dante's banished God has been meddling after all. *This* way, we have forces on the ground. *This* way, we have momentum. One teenage girl can't possibly hide from all the devils of hell."

Mother Goose frowned.

"There's legends about that kind of thing," she said.

The snare. The wire in the grass. The little smile. He had her.

"Madam, the only legends being made today are being made about *us*."

He gave it all the veracity he could scrape up. He sold it. He was too artificial to sweat, but his eyes were bright and black, avid with need.

The robotic Margaret Thatcher nodded. The tension cracked.

"Proceed," she said. And the screen went black.

The Elvis switched off its television, lit up a cigarette, and reached for a big black rotary-dial telephone, inscribed with Abdul Alhazred's favourite Elder Sign.

The boss wasn't going to like this. Not even slightly.

But anyone left alive in Little Mean was going to like it a lot, lot less.

Somewhere out over the North Sea, a jet fighter-bomber crewed by a bloke with incredible sideburns got the order to turn around for another loop...

Sixteen
The Star of
Blue Hawaii
vs
That Star Called
'Wormwood'

REALITY TAPPED GENTLY on the side of her headache, and September cursed in her sleep.

The second time it didn't tap. It knuckled up and swung for her jaw.

"Hmmmhhhrthfrkmshn*bastard!*"

Tiny ice flakes exploded from her eyelashes as the world came rushing back. So, too, did the horrible realisation that she'd been lying in half-melted hamburger water and that she couldn't feel her fingers or toes.

Which meant, at least, that Dark Lazarus hadn't sucked them into hell. Or perhaps that it hadn't really worked at all.

She shivered, and sat up, and checked her fingertips for frostbite. Just in time to see the far-off door of Charlie Wickham's chiller crumple inwards, burning as bright as the sun around its edges. It fell with a sad little pop, trailing smoke.

Ahhh, excellent! Waking up just in time for imminent death. It had become a bit of a bad habit recently…

It was the Dead Elvi, and they'd come mob-handed. Sneering, fantastically hairstyled and clanking with guns. They trooped into the chiller by the dozens.

"Now see here!" growled Charlie, stepping forward between the Elvi and the flash-frozen shape of Cedric, where he'd collapsed to the floor. "This is neutral ground, you sons of the Nameless! Want to explain all this to a commission of enquiry, do you? The Unmanifest Accords are very clear!"

"Who's the spatula jockey?" asked an Elvis dressed in a natty lime safari suit. The fat, tasselled specimen next to him shrugged, an uzi clenched in each pudgy fist.

"He's the manager. Hamburger boss. Got a little badge, see?"

Safari Elvis grinned.

"Hah! We eat hamburgers for breakfast!"

A small Elvis at the back put up one hand.

"Ummm... we sort of eat hamburgers for *every* meal, chief. Still don't explain who this guy thinks he is."

"Please allow me to introduce myself," began Charlie, in a voice that was like the purr of oiled and sharp machinery. His shadow slithered up the wall behind him in the frost-light, growing horns.

He never got to inform them that he was a man of wealth and taste. Because an Elvis dressed in full Admiral's whites grabbed him by the tie, levelled a pearl-handled Colt 1911 at his face, and pulled the trigger seven times.

The noise racketed and echoed in the white immensity of the chiller. Blood blew wide, vivid on the crystal frost. He collapsed, and crumpled, smoking from his sheared-off neck. Arterial patter landed after he did, frozen to little chips and flakes.

"Uh-huh huh. Thankyouverymuch. The ex-devil has left the building," chuckled Admiral Presley, spinning his Colt on one finger and slapping it back into its holster. "No Tarot, no protection, baby."

He smiled, and mushroom clouds boiled across his sunglasses.

"Now, Miss Normalsson, you're coming with us. Playtime is *over*, little lady. There's things a'happenin' out there which are not at allllllllllll groovy, and we think you know too much about 'em."

September put out one hand, almost absently, and stopped Arbourdale from charging at the Dead Elvis. The Endarkenment flared around her, and the Elvi flinched back, as chains lashed and clattered, aisles deep.

They saw the look in her eyes. It was the kind of thing which even monsters from beyond reality are afraid of. But there was no arguing with their firepower. A wall of silencers and suppressors, muzzles and laser-sights hemmed September in. She sensed that she could shear off a spring there, jam a receiver here, cross wires and cook bullets... but not all of them. Not all at once.

So she put her hands up, with her heart hammering at the back of her throat.

This isn't a game, girl. This is real. You aren't in a comic book, and you might not even be the main character, if you were...

But something made her pause, just as a look of trepidation washed across the faces of the Dead Elvi. The sun seemed to have risen behind her, indoors, at night.

"Are these jerks bothering you, babe?" asked a voice all cultivated drawl and rebellion. "These grandpas? That's quite unrighteous. You know, I reckon they think they're some sort of *authority*."

That last word was out of harmony with the rest. It was spit with all the bitterness of hate. It was a word with it's fists up; the kind that throttles the frontal lobes while grinning.

Admiral Elvis was unimpressed.

"Stand down, little buddy. There's twenty of us, alright, and only a-one of you."

A chuckle. September couldn't see who was standing behind her, but he'd brought a summer afternoon with him, along with the smell of hot tarmac and the back stairwells of rock-concert dives. That chuckle was something else, as well.

"That's right!" A slow clap. Another little fragment of a laugh. "There's only one of me. Only ever one. And you'd loooove to think that all of you, together, could ever be a fraction of what I am. But you're not. So sad, buddy! Get the man some tissues! It's because *you* need numbers, that I'm number *one*."

Admiral Elvis snarled, all black gums and monochrome teeth.

"I don't have time for this shit! Grab the girl, and kill the rest of them!"

He reached for the gun swinging from his other hip, but he was far too slow. The presence next to September stepped past her, moving with the hum and jangle of guitar strings in another room. She caught an impression of ripped denim and spiked leather, and a face haloed by perfectly feathered long blonde hair.

Then discord sliced the air. Admiral Presley had just enough time to look shocked, before the sound itself wrapped around him like a brace of wires, all glassy and shimmering. It plucked him from his feet, dimpling and slicing his skin until black blood welled up.

"*Orders, orders, orders.* Always with the *rules*, man. You have to lighten up," said a voice full of horrible mirth.

And then space folded in on the Dead Elvis. There came a series of sick, snapping, popping sounds. Parts of the Admiral folded the wrong way, and flattened, and folded again. Limbs twisted and compacted. Black ichor dripped.

With a final click of his fingers, the denim-clad angel collapsed the mess down into a tiny cube, no bigger than a kid's puzzle. He spun it on one finger for a moment, then made it vanish. His laugh was absolutely pure, utterly bright and beautiful – and it chilled September to the bone.

"What a drag! Right, babe? Come on. These clowns aren't stopping us. Let's go find some fun."

He held out a hand and September took it, not knowing if she was relieved or terrified. Not really thinking at all, actually. It was only when their fingers touched that she realised, with a little static shock, that this was the new Devil. This was Cedric Welbourne.

It wasn't the neon lights which made him a blur. Radiance seemed to flow from his great shaggy mane of hair, and ripple over his skin like the pattern of sunshine through water. There was a very strong suggestion of Cedric's old-fashioned face still there, but over the top, Dark Lazarus had sketched something from the worst nightmares of a million bible-belt parents.

He was lean and tattooed, with a folded black paisley bandanna covering his forehead, dipped low so it obscured his eyes. He wore ripped-up Levis, and hi-top skater shoes, and his leather jacket would have been the envy of any Ramone you care to mention. His hair was long and blonde, surf-bleached, and a single golden earring flashed behind it. His t-shirt was bright yellow – imprinted with a smiley face, and the words 'laugh, you'll live longer'.

There were no horns, and no tail, and no pitchfork. There was a battered old cherry-red flying-V guitar slung across his back, and when he smiled at her, September could see that every one of his perfect teeth came to a predatory point.

"I know what you're thinking," he drawled. "But this... this is someone else you're talking to, right now. The Morningstar. The Lightbringer. Little Sunshine, you dig? Your pal Cedric was too hot on the rules, and some kind of duty. So *I'm* driving. And I say we should go light up this town. You and me."

September could hear the jangling hum in the air. Unplayed notes, scored for the human brainstem. They had very particular ideas about what she was meant to do next, and most of them involved kissing. This was a troubling development.

But –

Would that be all so bad? It had been a very trying couple of days...

You'd have to get past the fact that he wasn't real, said a second thought, which was probably actually a ninth or a twenty-third. This creature was a *weapon*, built for Ronnie Reagan in the days of leg warmers and the cola wars.

Maybe that alone wouldn't have been enough to stop her from taking his hand, as he held it out to her. But the guilt that twisted through her next was.

He used to be Cedric Welbourne. And apparently, there was no coming back. Charlie Wickham had died trying to hold onto a fast-food version of evil, and *he'd* stopped officially devilling when Blackbeard was still a cabin boy.

"I don't think we've got time for fun, Mister Sunshine," she said. "Really? Morningstar is better, but it still makes you sound like the kind of person who wears ponchos and plans to juggle hacky-sacks professionally."

The new Devil pouted. It was devastating.

"Look, it doesn't matter!" said September, ignoring the kicked-puppy look on his face. "Because we really have to save the world right now, you know. If you're not too busy."

"Hey!" put in another of the Elvi. "hold it just a minute, pal! Nobody's saving anything without our say-so!"

The Devil leaned in close, and September smelled cinnamon and motor oil, and the scent of ozone you get before a lightning strike. It was all a bit too much, really. Like Vlad Dracula's silly attempt at seduction.

"Well, we could have a problem there, babe. You see, I could do that origami thing maybe once, twice more? Then we'd probably get shot full of holes. Now me, I'd get better. But it'd mess up your pretty face, and that's a sin too far, even for me."

September felt something fuzzy push between the two of them, at knee height. *And that was all she felt*, said thought number one hundred and sixty-two.

"Break it up, Romeo. Yeah, yeah. You smell like the 1960s, and you've got moves like an 8-bit fighting game. But these slimy Elvi have bigger problems right now than your supernatural hormones."

It was Arbourdale, and September wondered, not for the first time, why her utterly normal mother would ever have needed an extremely violent talking teddy bear.

"Big words, fluffy midget. Too bad you're too short to back 'em up." sneered an Elvis in blue denim dungarees and a straw hat.

"You can kiss the stitching *right* where my arse would be," snarled Arbourdale. "I wasn't talking about me, or even Virgil, if he's awake yet. I was talking about the guy with the sword."

Morningstar looked up. September looked up. Arbourdale gestured with one stubby paw. A chorus line of Dead Elvi spun on the spot.

"And *that's* how you make an entrance," said the bearded, heavily muscled medieval knight who stood in the doorway of the chiller.

He pretty much filled it, at least horizontally. The knight was wearing a black motorcycle jacket, under which he was clad in chain mail, denim jeans, and a white tunic with a blood-red cross. "It's only taken a few hundred years to get it right, but it gets them every time!"

The neon light glinted off of his perfect teeth – *TING!*

It glinted, too, off the massive cruciform battle-blade he held over one shoulder, carrying it with the casual grace of somebody who could probably use it to carve a toothpick out of a dining table.

"Who the hell is this rube?" asked comeback-special Elvis, hefting his uzis.

"Oh, sorry about that, all!" beamed the knight, slinging a silver motorcycle helmet underhand, to hang on an empty meat-hook. "I'm Brother Jacques, Vacant Acquisitions. Knight of the Temple, freelance monster-slayer, and biscuit factory shareholder.[35] Among other things."

"What you are, is *dead*," snarled Safari Elvis, who appeared to be more bold than his brothers. "Come on! Sir blabs-a-lot here shouldn't have gotten in our way!"

Brother Jacques shrugged.

"I'm not here for *you*, creature of the Outer Darkness. I'm here for the Magician, and the Devil, and the former bearer of Death. They've got some explaining to do."

"Enough!" ranted the rock 'n' roll monster, adjusting his pith helmet. "I've always wanted to say this, especially with a big, villainous shriek. I thought I'd get to do it *years* ago." He took a deep breath.

"*Destroy them!*"

Brother Jacques sighed, as all those guns came up. He took a slow and steady breath, as muzzle-flashes erupted all around him. Only then did he move.

September was certain she could only see what he did thanks to the Endarkenment, and even then, it was a blur. His broadsword moved like chrome lightning, a shimmer

---

35. Astute readers (or hungry ones) will be able to note, at their next earliest opportunity, that a certain cookie, said by some to be the world's most popular biscuity snack, contains on its surface the images of the Cross of Lorraine, several Maltese Crosses, and the letters O.R.E.O., standing, of course*, for Ordo Rex Ecclesiarchus Orientis, the order of the king of the eastern church. The 'eastern church' is another name for the Templar fortress in Jerusalem, long said to have been built over the laboratory of Solomon. *Allegedly

which intersected with barrels, suppressors, stocks and magazines, and with the hands, arms and fingers of a score of Elvi. Blue sparks flickered where metal met metal, and sprays of inky blood hung in the air, weightless. Time held its breath as the Templar did his work, and when it exhaled, a ruin of monochrome flesh and gaudy polyester hit the floor. Dissected armaments clattered down.

Black arterial spray on white plastic.

"There's a technique, known to some of those venerable old monks in China, that lets you trade time from the end of your life for time in combat," said Brother Jacques, casually wiping the blade on a fluttering tatter of Hawaiian shirt. "Your own personal time – which you, Cedric, if you were properly with us, would know all about. The stuff the Chronauspexion measures. It's just that for each second you gain with your sword out, you take a week off your old age. That can put a crimp in your retirement, if you're a magnet for stroppy bastards, like me."

"But... you don't look a day over forty!" said Arbourdale, all incredulous.

"Ahhh. I cheat, you see," said the Templar, with a raised eyebrow. "I'm immortal."

September picked her way carefully across the ice to pick up Virgil's lamp. Inside, the tiny figure of the poet was just waking up, stretching and yawning.

"What'd I miss?"

"Well, a medieval Templar who claims to be immortal just arrived, and Cedric is now an immensely powerful eighties hair-metal godling. The former devil is headless, and about two dozen Elvis Presleys just got turned to black ooze all around you. Sleep well?"

Virgil bristled.

"Hey! It's not my fault! It's how I'm built. Thaumic overload does horrible things to my batteries, and –

wait? Did you say a Templar? Is he, I mean even slightly... ummm... French?"

September turned back to Brother Jacques, clued in by his name.

"How about it, Sir Knight? Do you have a preference for croissants, fine wines, and being rude to American tourists?"

The brother shrugged, in what was clearly a very Gallic way.

"Well, I do have a weakness for a nice Cabernet sauvignon, and those Elvi were all technically tourists. You saw how it worked out for them."

Virgil jumped up and down inside his lamp, all sleepiness forgotten.

"Then he's one of *them!* Those two buggers Dante himself set up to guard the tarot! The old master was very keen to never see them. Ever! Some things were said about getting chopped in half, and all that."

September raised an eyebrow at the Templar. He frowned.

"Oh, yes. All that business. I'm afraid your great-Grandad was meddling with forces he knew not how to control, miss Normalsson. The problem is, he was just so damned good at it! It's been six hundred and eighty-five years since old man Alighieri hired us to guide his wagon through that forest darke, long since we had left behind the straight and narrow path. I've never seen anyone try to mess it all up with such panache."

Now it was September's turn to get angry. It had been a long time coming, but all the weirdness of the past few days had frayed her nerves down to sparking wisps.

"So where were *you* then? Swanning about eating snails while we've had to try to save the world, were you? Do you even know about this red priest bastard from the Aught, and how Charon is actually Sharon, and the prison they're building a new hell inside? My granddad told me that I have to fix it, not phone some kind of leftover remnant of the middle ages. So if anyone's been messing it up, it's been *your* people. We were knee-deep in Elvises before you even put in an appearance!"

To September's astonishment, just when she thought she'd gone too far, the knight bowed his head and sighed.

"It's this town, really. We didn't realise just how efficient all the wardings were. It wasn't until Ammut the Soul-Devourer turned up to take a stroll through the suburbs that we even knew what was happening here. Bloody Bureau Innominandum! In any case, it's not about the professor. Not now. He's transcended. Gone. *Somewhere.* It's..."

September let the Endarkenment flare up around her, sizzling like propane fire, all in black.

"If you're here to arrest me, we'll just see how that works out. I didn't like my chances against twenty Elvi, but one Frenchman's a different story."

Brother Jacques sighed again, wiped the black ooze from his sword, and scabbarded it. He pointed past September, to Morningstar, who was rummaging through a shelf full of frozen curly fries, and stuffing them into his mouth two-handed.

"Oh, no. Not even *you* are that important, miss Normalsson. It's *him*. Well, the fellow who he was, up until a few minutes ago. I told you, I'm from what's called Vacant Acquisitions? That means, ages ago, that Dante Alighieri charged me with the duty of finding people to carry his tarot. For example, I've just picked up the tarot of Death, from where it fell out of the pocket of Anubis, Lord of the Gateway. And this lad... well. He's not just got the Devil card, burned right into his chest, somewhere under that very risible t-shirt. He's also got the Knight of Staves in his pocket."

September recalled how Cedric had stolen it from Vlad Dracula, what seemed like an awfully long time ago.

"Oh. Is that all, then? Not here to heroically save the day, when a young damsel such as myself is beset on all sides by monsters and – what's worse – the government?"

Jacques smiled.

"Miss Normalsson, you look like the kind of damsel who'd make a dragon turn vegetarian. It'd be hardly worth rescuing you, 'cause then I'd miss seeing what you do to any poor bastards who thought they had you captured. No, I'll just take the card, and prevent a possible colossal, worldwide rubric collapse, thanks."

"A what?" asked Arbourdale.

"Oh, he means the end of the Rubric of Dante," said Virgil, in a schoolmasterly tone. "Right? The end of the working enacted by the Divine Comedy, and a return to the credulous darkness of medieval times?"

The Templar nodded.

"That's the bunny. He had to put a catch in it, just to satisfy universal probability. *Human greed*, it was. If one person ever possesses three of the tarot, the first seal is opened. Then, if the other ones go, boom! God or Lucifer will be back, or maybe both, and I can guarantee that they will be pretty pissed off. Spoiling for a fight, as it were."

"A fight like the one at the end of the bible, perhaps?" asked Arbourdale, sounding worried. He was picking at a loose thread on one of his paws.

"I reckon it might make all that Revelations guff seem a bit like a slumber party dust-up with pillows, at this point," grinned Jacques. "Although it'll never happen. What are the odds that one person could ever have three of the Tarot on him at any one time? The fact that this Cedric had *two* was enough to give me the willies, and that's an achievement!"

September felt a horrible little suspicion begin to scrabble at the back of her mind, like the one which tells you that you've left the oven on, just as your plane taxis onto the runway.

If he'd had the Knight of Staves in his pocket this whole time, and he'd carried the Tarot of Death right up until the moment they found the perpetual patty, then...

"Soooo, ummm... just what *exactly* is needed to break those second and third seals you mentioned? Asking out of pure scientific enquiry, you understand. Just theoretical, abstract Bright and Keen Curiosity."

Jacques frowned, concentrating.

"Let's see. Well, first, someone would have to build a mighty cathedral, dedicated to either Jehovah or Lucifer, somewhere with plenty of ley-line convergences. A real big bugger. Something to concentrate Earth's telluric power, like the capacitor in a stun-gun. That's the second seal."

"Aaaaaand?" asked September, now feeling horribly certain of what was unfolding.

"Well, the third one's the charm, isn't it? The bearer of the three Tarot – the chosen, as it were – would have to renounce all of them, cast them aside, and then anoint the altar of this cathedral with his blood."

"Hang about!" chimed in Virgil. "If you're the one who flies about handing out these tarot cards, haven't *you* had more than two of them on you at once?"

"Ahhh... *touché*, my tiny Roman friend! But of course, Dante was not *le muppet total*, was he? Part of the power of the Page of Swords is that it makes me immune to the rule of the Three Seals. And for the record, I can't fly. It's either weird supernatural teleportation or the motorbike, for me."

He chuckled, but noticed, suddenly, that nobody else was laughing. In fact, September, Arbourdale and Virgil were sharing a look of profound and unsettling gravity.

"Oh, *bugger*," said the little bear.

"Perhaps we should just get very, very far away from here," said Virgil. "I hear Mars is nice. Fresh start, no pollution, lovely red landscape..."

"You know how you said I don't need rescuing, Sir Knight?" asked September. "What if, ummm, *everyone else does?* Is that sort of in your mission statement, or whatever you have? Code of chivalry, perhaps?"

"Oh? Well, I suppose I did swear an oath, very long ago, to protect the weak and uphold justice. What it really came down to was bashing a whole lot of very angry blokes with banana-shaped swords. I recall a lot of sand getting into everything, too."

He tried his big, moustache-bracketed grin again, spreading his hands wide.

"But come on! Why so glum? The crisis is over, I've got the cards back, and in any case, there's no huge cathedral of ultimate theological dominance out there! I mean, you'd have to be utterly mad to build one here, and nobody's going to!"

It's funny how things happen, in situations like this. It's almost as if Dante hadn't quite gotten his Rubric sealed up tight. As if some kind of all-seeing God really *was* peering down through his telescope, looking for moments of irony to prosecute with the single-minded fervour of a personal injuries lawyer.

The ground began to shake. A rumbling sound shivered through the air, and screams rung out, above the crack of immense slabs of concrete. At the same time, the air became greasy with the fizz of unreality, and the temperature dropped, even inside Charlie Wickham's impossible burger chiller.

"Ooooh errr! That's not right. That's very, *very* wrong indeed," said Arbourdale.

Morningstar had stopped scarfing frozen chips, and turned his head toward the ceiling. He sniffed the air, in a peculiarly animal gesture, baring far too many pointed teeth.

"Oh yeah! Rock 'n' roll!" he said. "Now *that* tastes familiar! Now that, kids, is what I call some serious fun!"

September grabbed him by the arm, and dragged him toward the door.

"Come on, then. My great-Grandad made you to beat the Russians, so you're probably useful in a fight. You too, Mister Templar. It's time to sort this out, like Septivarian told me I'd have to. If you want to help, get moving."

They followed in her wake, as the sound of tectonic upset rumbled and grumbled all around. Out of the chiller, down a corridor, through a door marked 'service technicians only', and up a flight of dingy stairs to the roof.

They looked out upon Little-Mean-on-the-Average, and beheld the beginning of the end...

September saw the beams of searchlights scissor-walking across the clouds. She heard the screams, and the rumble and thump of huge machines underground. Little Mean blurred around the edges, windows cracking in their frames, as something huge and horrible began to push up through the three empty construction sites dotted around the centre of town.

A petroleum company's office block, they'd said. A huge, retro video games arcade. *A Dutch grocer's. Denver Gas. Nerd Vegas. Anders' Veg.*

All of them, of course, silly anagrams for GRAVESEND. The company run by the Red Cardinal. He must have gotten his marketing ideas from Vlad Dracula, who used to think that re-arranging the letters in his name would conceal the fact that he had the dentition of an anglerfish, and didn't show up in mirrors.

Possibly, thought September, *the crimson bastard had thought he was just too clever, and that nobody would ever get it.*

Which made it all the worse that she hadn't – right up to the point where all three worksites were growing twisted towers of evil. Then again, it *had* been a rough couple of days.

Hell rose up over Little-Mean-on-the-Average, with the clank and grind of huge cogwheels underground. Sparks fountained, and flames belched from the screaming mouths of gargoyles. As they grew, the huge edifices unfurled buttresses and arches like insect legs, plunging them down through other homes and buildings to leech onto power cables and gas mains.

To the south, the Tower of Sheol loomed jagged and gothic, a melted pile of cathedrals twisted up into a spike. Light beamed from its red and orange stained-glass windows, all of which depicted experiments in proctology using medieval weapons, farm implements and musical instruments.[36]

To the west, the Tower of Gehenna rumbled skyward, wreathed in poisonous vapours. It was wrought of slick and dripping bone, dominated by great lumpen skulls, cracked and diseased. Each one was caught in the act of vomiting segmented copper worms, maggots crafted from white marble, and blasphemous images of the human form, all looking distinctly uncomfortable.

To the East, out of the site for Denver Gas, rose the Tower of Dis, a citadel of iron and anger. Its battlements were crenellated with blades, glowing furnace-hot. It was

---

36. These last ones were compliments of Charlie, RIP.

all riveted metal, studded with swords, hung with chains, and sizzling with the kind of runes which didn't just hurt to look at; they beat up your eyeballs from the inside.

Now girders and spans of twisted steel unhinged from the crowns of each tower, clanking and unfolding. Now they formed a great triangle of metal above the centre of Little Mean – right over Saint Pewtred's, Wrinkly Acres, and the asylum of Bleachwood Scours.

"Tell me," asked September, of the utterly gobsmacked Knight Templar beside her. "Does that look like a cathedral of ultimate theological dominance to you?"

"By the burnished brass buttocks of Belial!" blasphemed Brother Jacques. "It would certainly appear to be, and no mistake!"

"And how about you, Mister Morningstar?" she asked. "Feeling any pangs of demonic homesickness? Perhaps a bit of the old call of apocalyptic destiny?"

The smile had slid right off of what had once been Cedric's face. All the cheerful, sun-dazed confidence had dropped out of the new Devil, as he looked upon something far more biblical and dire. His voice, when it came, seemed to echo up from a bottomless chasm in his chest.

"Look ye, mortals, and witness the throne of he who came before," intoned Morningstar, in voice which sounded horribly like Cedric's. "Behold, for my dark Father is with us."

Virgil was all but jumping up and down inside his lamp.

"The one who came before? Look, sorry to derail your little funeral train, matey, but your predecessor is downstairs, spread over two weeks worth of frozen hash browns."

"And as for your daddy issues... I thought the Professor kind of made you out of religious zealotry, loud music and green gloop," added Arbourdale.

Brother Jacques got it, though, just before September did. A boiling mist of brimstone radiated out from the towers, where they now encircled the centre of Little Mean, and with it came a horrible rasping wheeze, rumbling up from underground.

"Ohhh, *that's* not good. Last time I heard that, we were standing at the gates of Hell. The real one, you understand. The one Dante made to put the demons in."

"You have built it," said Morningstar, in that same iron-chisel and gravestone voice. "And now He comes."

"My Father, who shall tear down Heaven, unhallowed be thy name. Thy kingdom come, dark will be done, 'til Earth burns alongside Paradise..."

"The mystic chanting is never a good sign, really," observed Virgil. "Neither is the eyes rolling back until they're all white, or the drooling and foaming."

September did the only thing she could think of, at that perfectly awful moment. She hauled off and slapped Morningstar across Cedric's face, as he made a lurch for the edge of the roof.

"Hey! Come on! I know you're in there! Time to wake up!"

But there was no recognition on that horribly, subtly altered mug. The thing which wore Cedric's skin smiled, mindless, and a tiny dribble of blood trickled from the corner of his mouth. September was so fixated on his eyes that she never saw the sword come down over her shoulder.

Brother Jacques held it steady, though September could see the tremble in the silvery steel when she turned.

"Step aside, please. His blood must never be spilled on the altar they have built for him. This must end, here. **Now.**"

And it would all be her fault. She'd brought him to this

place, to be a sacrifice. Just like Charlie Wickham had said. She'd told the old Devil that wasn't who she was, but how could she be so sure? *He was already dead, after all. A fascinating specimen. A monster, to be used up by mad science, and spent in the pursuit of... what?*

Victory over the USSR, a failed empire that had imploded ten years ago? Revenge, for a great-great-granddad who had lived longer than two normal people put together, and who had gone to his grave smiling a bit too knowingly? Her own horribly self-conscious need to be a Smart and Curious Young Scientist?

To prove to the world, and the part of herself that still, wretchedly, cared about its opinion, that she was able to be what they wanted?

September stole a look into her own eyes, reflected in the blade, and decided that she *was* sure, after all. She reached out, placed a finger on the ancient Damascus steel, and stepped aside.

"Good," said Jacques, "Now, I take no pleasure in this duty, but..."

$$\Sigma_{\;}^{\vee}\{\$\text{-X+0}\;*\;\text{Ʊ}\;(((?\geq|\text{⊙}\#.4\;\text{ᙅᗴ}))\}[x\;/x])\;+\;0\;=\;42.5$$

— said September, in a voice that was all ink and imminence. It wasn't a word. It was a *formula*, in the mathematical code which made up the sheet-music of the universe; the Endarkenment, expressed.

It wasn't the characters you see here on paper. Not any more than $E=MC^2$ is the blinding oblivion of an atomic explosion. Not any more than the calculation of the rotation of the Earth is the sunrise, watched for the last time with someone you love.

It came out as a tangle of calligraphic lines pierced through reality, curling up on themselves to describe ratios and curves of disharmony. It found the metal of Brother Jacques' sword, and suggested to the carbon and iron that they had other options.

Before the knight could draw back his blade to strike it turned entirely to powdered rust, and blew away in a puff of ochre. September was almost as surprised as he was – though from the expression on his face, not quite.

"Witchcraft!" he breathed, eyes wide, as he dropped the hilt of his sword, sending it clattering across the concrete. "What they always said *we* could do. Just like that, that... that *Doris*, all them years ago."

"There's no such thing, you fourteenth-century fruitcake," said Virgil. "That was the formula of the ultimate equation! Just a piece of it, mind, but more than old Archimedes ever summoned up, in all his decades."

"Huh!" said Arbourdale. "If that's Hell down there, then maybe it was the voice of the Almighty. He's probably knocking about in all this mess as well, you know. And he takes a dim view of people incarnating the Devil. I'll be pleading witness protection, if you see a big bloke in sandals and a toga steaming our way. What do you reckon, Mister Morningstar?"

But the final product of Dark Lazarus wasn't listening. As Brother Jacques crossed himself, and September tried to forget the feeling of electricity tap-dancing across her back teeth, the thing which had once been Cedric Welbourne winked, rather salaciously. Then he stepped backwards off the Burger Slave rooftop, and was gone.

"Gah! Why did you have to do that?" groaned Jacques. "Ooohhh, Martin's going to be here any minute, and you'll have a whole lot of explaining to do!"

"One – who's Martin? And two – why me?"

"Because the fluffy one is quite correct, Miss September. That's *Hell* down there, and, magic words aside, we need to stop your boyfriend before it's everywhere else as well."

"He's not my boyfriend!" said September, perhaps a bit too quickly. "Even if he was still the boy who was, I'll admit, actually one of my friends. Which he's not. And, by the way, neither is *that*."

September realised that she might have lost her audience as a tiny Roman poet, a truculent teddy bear and a medieval knight all looked at her with varying degrees of incomprehension.

"I saw you giving him one of those looks humans have, when their eyes go all big and wobbly..." began Arbourdale.

"I mean, *that's not Hell!* It's only a model. It's fake. Ersatz. Phoney. A mock-up. It's window-dressing. It's a silly place, like Camelot." September took a deep breath. "We saw that horrible Ferryperson building it, for some kind of scam they've got going. So, before anyone starts quoting The Omen, generally chanting in Latin or telling me to woe betide anything, I say we go down there, find the bastards who've ruined my town, and *kick their supernatural arses.* Right?"

"Do you think you can do the, umm... thing again, then?" asked Virgil. He mimed bad stage-magic with his fingers. "You know. The Equation, and the Endarkenment, or whatever it was?"

"Witchcraft," nodded Brother Jacques, utterly sure of himself.

"Science," countered Arbourdale, balling up his tiny purple fists.

"We call it the Way of the Ultimate Word, actually," came a voice from down below. "The most secret praxis of the Baal Shem, largely because the book it's in is fantastically dangerous. It's been sealed in a plutonium box, inside a lead box, under the New York Public Library's Stephen A. Schwarzman Building, since 1897. It was Von Leibniz's reply to Sir Isaac Newton, the *Principium Tenebrarum Lux*."

September recognised that voice.

"Good evening, Miss Rummage!" she shouted. "I don't suppose you can get me a copy via interloan?"

"No. But I think you could probably write a few new chapters. I heard that incantation, three streets away!"

The librarian had come prepared for some heavy-duty post-apocalyptic shenanigans – she was astride a big off-road Honda motorbike with knobbly tyres, and carried a cavalry sabre, a pump-action shotgun and a selection of potent grimoires in her saddlebags. She wore a long brown wild-west trench coat, a second world war paratrooper's helmet, gold-rimmed mirrorshades, and camo pants with the cuffs tucked into a pair of steel-capped boots, all painted with daisies. A card stuck into the webbing of her helmet read – 'born to shush'.

"Now, it's been an awful time all round since you left, your parents are worried sick, the police would like you to help them with their enquiries, Anubis just smashed up the curry house, and I just passed a young man who looks like one of your travelling companions, levitating a foot off the tarmac and muttering in Aramaic. He appears to be drifting towards the nearest of those towers, and he has a crown of cold fire wreathing his brow, kind of thing. What would you like to do?"

September considered this for a moment, as that was the kind of thing she felt one ought to do, when making momentous, reckless, foolhardy decisions. But the sizzle and pop of the Endarkenment was still there, coiled up around her brainstem. Like a certain talking snake around a very particular apple tree.

"You. Sir Knight. I saw a helmet, earlier. Did you come here on a motorcycle?"

Brother Jacques nodded, looking just a little bit frightened.

"Well, yes, but it's a big one. I mean, heavy and all. I reckon you'd be better off..."

September looked him up and down. The Templar had not felt so thoroughly eyeballed since the day when he'd stood in a too-big hauberk before the Sergeant-at-Arms in Lyon, and been asked (as is traditional in armies across time and space), if he was, indeed, a worthless maggot.[37]

"I'll just fetch the keys, shall I?" he asked, remembering all too vividly the sound of that terrible Word, which had shuddered through him like glass wires.

September held up her hand, and let the black flame of the Endarkenment caper across her fingertips. Right now it was as clear in the *Materia Mortalis* as it had ever been in the Aught.

"I don't think that's going to be necessary," she said. "And, at the risk of ruining the perfect opportunity... I don't think your clothes or boots will fit me, either."

---

37. Except for the armed forces of the planet Parplezag Theta, who represent a civilisation of six-foot sentient maggots. Their drill sergeants, all shiny and bulbous, gesticulate at new recruits with their six little arms and ask them if they are worthless bipedal primates.

Suture Penultimate
Scenes From a
Flat-pack Hell

HELL CAME LURCHING and staggering onto the streets of Little-Mean-on-the-Average, in the form of a legion of the dead. Some were ridden by the spirits of history's greatest madmen, while others, driven insane in the Aught, had been cut and crafted by the Red Cardinal's plastic surgeons, tattooed by renegade shamen, and turned into demons. The majority, however, were Gravesend prisoners, let loose with fairly crummy costumes and a license to commit mayhem from Sharon Kolslaw.

They spewed forth from the gaping maws of the three towers, and if nobody noticed that there weren't really enough of them to constitute a real Damnation Army, it was because they were busy running for it, in most cases with soggy trousers.

It was no contest really, even though several of the residents of Little Mean put up more of a fight than the Cardinal and Sharon had expected.

Mrs Malorbian, the school cook, faced down a gaggle of demonic Mongolian horse-archers, led by what appeared to be Genghis Khan. She was armed with a ladle in one hand and a meat cleaver in the other. Half of a demon steppe pony was jammed into the upper spout of her huge, industrial-green mince grinder, and the Conqueror of the Heavens and Earth was torn between stark terror and frank lust for this stout vision in her hair net, non-slip shoes and rubber apron.

Mrs Seeply and Mrs Cludge found that they were utterly immune to the hypnotic powers of a vampiric Lady Elizabeth Bathory, and were busy battering her with a pair of furled umbrellas, for trying to turn all the tea in the Gilded Doily to boiling blood.

Joseph Stalin, 'Papa Doc' Duvalier, Idi Amin (and that bloke from the scary films with the hockey mask on) were hidden behind an overturned desk, recalling the warning of their master *not to mess with the librarian*. In this case, they'd mistaken Mrs Dearborn for Miss Rummage, and though the keeper of the school library was not a magical practitioner of the Order of the Baal Shem, she *was* a complete psychopath when someone threatened her cardboard cutout of Sir Isaac Newton. Poor Stalin had a cake fork through his forehead, and Mrs Dearborn stalked the darkened aisles, armed with the blade from her big laminating guillotine and a rubber stamp which said 'discarded'. Not one of them would see the sunrise.

Headmaster Mackleduff was awoken to the sound of swearing in Welsh, and ran downstairs in his nightgown and terrycloth bed-mortarboard, to find his lodger, Groundskeeper Hackforth, belting ten bells of shite out of a trio of Japanese *oni*, copied from a popular anime. The oriental demons had smashed up the kitchen, but were faring terribly against the enraged groundsman, who wielded twin cricket bats in the style of the dreaded Miyamoto Musashi.

An entire unit of SS Death Troopers, complete with skeletal faces and black uniforms, burst into the bakery of Mr Patel, only to find him wide awake and armed with a little something he'd built for himself, in imitation of his hero, the Confectioner.

"Say hello to Sugar Daddy!" cackled Mr Patel, as the hot-pink sci-fi cannon in his hands began to hum and shudder. A blast of sickly-sweet fuchsia lightning haloed the demonic Nazis for an instant, before every last one of them was mummified in candy floss, banishing them instantly.

And it's best not to dwell on the horrible misfortune that befell the 'demons' who kicked down the antique doors of the Little Mean-on-the-Average fire station, only to find themselves confronted by Assistant Chief Fire Officer Bixby Meldrew and a full turnout of the special provisional auxiliary brigade, proton accelerators crackling with barely-harnessed power...

Others, however, weren't doing so well.

'Unpleasant occurrence discomfits editor...' typed Wilmsloe Busby, as a pair of zombies dressed in American football uniforms dragged him shrieking from his office.

Wilf Handisides and Hiro Mulcahey had been forced to flee with unseemly haste, absconding in the Japanese-Irish publican's Nissan 'Godzilla' Skyline-powered Riley Kestrel roadster, ahead of a horde of Roman legionary ghouls. The Floating Chrysanthemum was in flames, as, in the words of Mulcahey;

"No rotten old centurion and his gang of corpses are getting their hands on my vintage whiskey. And if I can't bloody have it, neither can they!"

Nurse Valerie had discovered that it was impossible to run in twelve-inch platform heels, but had run out of ammunition after throwing both of them at an axe-dragging apparition of Witchfinder General Matthew Hopkins, who had come back from the 1600s to terrorise her.

Just as she'd thought it was all over, and that the mad puritan was going to burn her at the stake, Hubert Ableton (bachelor of the parish, appreciator of 'art' magazines, and current owner of an exploded potting shed) had appeared, screeching to a halt in his old Triumph Dolomite Sprint. He lugged a big heavy weapon up to the passenger window; the Dead Elvi's General Electric minigun, recovered from where their van had so spectacularly disintegrated.

"Come with me if you want to live," said Hubert, just as Nurse Valerie slid across the hood of the Dollie, her PVC nurse's uniform making a sound like a finger down a soaped whiteboard. He raised a single eyebrow at Hopkins, and then proceeded to utterly destroy the puritan ghoul with a withering stream of bullets.

Unfortunately for Nurse Valerie (who looked upon Hubert Ableton – for some reason dressed as Mel Gibson from *The Road Warrior* – with sudden and burning passion), the blast also shredded her letterbox, wherein lurked a letter from a major Mexican television company. If she hadn't peeled off into the dawn with Hubert, to a new life somewhere in the wilds of East Anglia, Valerie could very well have become the newest star of the critically acclaimed telenovela, *La Pasión y la Lujuria de los Completamente Estúpidos*.

All across town, people stuffed suitcases, loaded loot into wheelbarrows, packed pillowcases with pounds and pence, and fled. The roads were snarled with cars, and this was made even worse by the logjam of military vehicles, police trucks, black unmarked vans and things which were definitely allowed to be called paddywagons, which turned the centre of the town into a gridlock.

Some families abandoned their vehicles and hared off into the countryside on foot. Some appropriated horses from nearby farms, or resorted to other larcenous shenanigans. Mr Hicks, the proprietor of the main street fish and chip restaurant ('we'll batter and deep fry anything of less than a cubic metre in diameter') was seen heading for the hills atop Groundskeeper Hackforth's trusty lawn tractor, Gertrude.

Such was the panic that few people noticed a curious fact. None of the horrors spawned from Hell were *actually killing anyone.* They menaced, and they roughed people up, and they stole and smashed and dabbled in a bit of light arson, but when it came to bloody dismemberment, the severed wobbly bits were thin on the ground.

A second clue could have been the number of demons, complete with horns and tails that were, on closer inspection, actually Halloween costumes and props, who had chosen to assault the land of the living armed with video cameras.

But such was the terror, and such was the panic, fuelled by a sizzle of utter, credulous belief in the air, that nobody stopped to think. Most of them didn't even stop to use the toilet.

"Bugger this for a game of soldiers!" wailed Police Chief Inspector Rupert, as his trembling fingers tap-danced across a series of keyboards. "Every approach! Every screen! Mrs Goosegarden never said anything about Hell on Earth! Just one very naughty teenaged mad scientist!"

The CCTV footage which flickered across the Chief Inspector's screens was a veritable double-feature matinee of horrors. Historical nightmares, comic-book ghouls and gibbering mad devils rampaged through the streets of Little Mean, and his stout-hearted bobbies just weren't up to stopping them.

This wasn't a bunch of long-haired labour unionists or pot-addled anti-nuclear hippies, after all. This was worse than having to shut down a football riot on half-price lager night, and it didn't help that the armies of Darkness included several nasty deceased senior policemen.

Even the hardest-headed modern recruits knew the stories about old 'barbed wire' Banbury, leader of the most bent armed-robbery squad in history, or the doings of Nobbler Hempwick, Mad Murphy Staples, DCI Angus 'the thumb chopper' McTavish, or the original Victorian-era bad-apple copper, Archibald Scroad, who used to interrogate suspects by biting off their noses.

Pictures of these loonies had glowered down on generations of policemen from old photos, high up on the walls of station houses. And now they were out there in the flesh, routing his boys with a pants-wettingly menacing 'allo allo allo'.

"We're pulling out. This is one for the special forces now, or maybe bomber command. No! The orbital nukes. It's the only way to be sure!"

Rupert was white as a sheet as he turned to find that everyone else in the command tent had already taken his advice. The only other soul remaining was Constable O'Dwightly, who was still, inexplicably, almost quivering with vim and enthusiasm.

"Golly, Chief Inspector! My notebook's almost full. Do you... do you think those big giant towers are compliant with the county building code?"

A whole phalanx of mounted police went thundering past the tent, like the Charge of the Light Brigade in reverse. Rupert took a hold of himself for a moment, and narrowed his eyes.

Yes. It wouldn't exactly be *desertion*, if he just up and followed all those gallopers, now, would it? Not if he left someone else in charge. Someone who knew the lay of the local land, as it were. Someone young and keen, and able to make best use of regional resources...

That would just be *delegation*. Chain of command, sort of thing. Leaving Rupert to appraise the situation from a more tactical vantage point. Such as somewhere in the Bahamas, behind a bucket of vividly-coloured strong liquor.

"Lad, I think it's about time you had a promotion," said

the Chief Inspector, raising a wobbly smile.

Robot bloody Margaret Thatcher was frightening, after all. But a good copper always knows when it's time to sidle off and leave the paperwork to someone else.

An even better copper, mused Rupert, as he ducked out of the tent, catching one last sluice of horribly cold rainwater down the back of his neck, *also knew when to admit that he was actually a pretty bad one.*

All the doors had slammed open, deep in the nightmare asylum of the Aught. All at once, with the clang and rattle of Hell's ovens, and the rancid smell of an Everest of mouldy socks on fire.

The sound reached down into the darkest places beneath the Gravesend Unmerciful Hospital. Some of those places were inside people's heads. Some of them were deeper still.

The echoes rumbled off into the dark, complaining to themselves. And down inside it, they found Doctor Cliff Hunkstrong.

Doctor Cliff hadn't been quite right since some time around 1994. He suffered from egomania, delusions, blood pressure like the interior of a top-fuel dragster's piston head, and a penchant for noshing mood-enhancing drugs like cereal. He'd made a deal with unhallowed things, and started a career in illegal drugs, and heard the whispers of ghosts.

Dying had not done wonders for his outlook on life. Neither had being locked up in Dracula's tomb.

Some might say that he'd even gone a teensy bit mad.

Mad? Thought the good doctor, swivelling one eyeball up to where the padded door suddenly lolled ajar. *I'm not mad, surely! I'm as healthy as a cowboy walrus! In the pink of... of being pink, or some such! No, the brain of Doctor Cliff Hunkstrong is cast iron, mate, with wonderful green lacy frilly bits, and a statue of a fetching little strontium penguin called Mabel on top!*

The sane part of him, (the part we might still call Reginald Spudley, in fact) registered this. It gave a little whimper of despair. But he heard it. And a kind of realisation dawned.

Oh my goodness! What was this sticky stuff he was lying in? What was that smell? And... more pointedly, more urgently... *who had done this to him?*

Cliff pulled himself gingerly to his feet, using a whole wall of impaling spikes as handholds. Little mummified bat and mouse skeletons, desiccated spiders and the husks of cockroaches fell away.

Oh, yes. *His horrible boss. His pet vampire. The madhouse!* Of course! His mother had always said he was a very sensitive boy. *This place had made him forget. But now...*

"That bastard," hissed Doctor Cliff. "That utter *bastard!*"

Slowly, the clarity that comes from leaving one's limbic system behind took hold. Cliff realised, in the time it took him to furtively pop his head outside the door and note the lack of guards, that he had been stitched up, betrayed, and left behind.

By that supernatural, *monumental* anus, the Red Cardinal.

As Doctor Cliff H... *no, as **Reginald Gary Bloody Spudley*** became more angry than he'd ever been while alive, the thought of revenge presented itself. Certain unrealities meshed together in his head, with the dreamy inertia of supertankers colliding in the English Channel.

He was a doctor. This was a hospital. People had to do what he told them, here.

Señor Ricardo De Palma, the fellow who had so recently sent Nurse Valerie a letter about the popular soap opera *La Pasión y la Lujuria de los Completamente Estúpidos*, would have marvelled at his transformation.

In an instant, Reg was clad in immaculate surgical whites, crisp and pure as a snowdrift of cocaine. He stood tall, and his hair developed a plastic sheen. His teeth gleamed, like a rank of brand-new refrigerators in an appliance store window.

"Right!" said Reginald Spudley, in a voice which could have launched a thousand prime-time radio careers. He rubbed his hands together, and strode off down the corridor, doing a remarkable impression of someone with an important mission in mind, and every right to be exactly where he was.

It was time to find some coffee. And then it was time for some mayhem!

As Hell unfolded at the heart of Little-Mean-on-the-Average, every single person who had ever enjoyed a taste of the designer drug known as Repo suffered a violent and synchronised flashback.

All across the nation people dropped coffee cups, took their hands off of steering wheels, slumped backwards in easy chairs, toppled from behind office desks and sprawled across factory production lines.

All of them, without exception, caught the frequency, broadcast from those three huge supernatural towers, using the telluric power-grid which centred on Little Mean. All of them opened their eyes wide, rolled all the way back until only the whites were showing, and began to intone a fell chant, in fairly bad Latin.

Scholars of theology would note, later, that it was actually just the theme song from the movie *The Omen*, but scholars were in short supply as events unfolded. What was plentiful was panic, as a large proportion of the population made a rather good impression of demonic possession.

Television news stations picked it up. Evangelical types got naked and ran out into the streets in anticipation of the Rapture. The usual percentage of opportunists decided that this was the perfect time to smash a window and take home a wide-screen television. Several megachurch televangelists were seen to suddenly repent, and promise to give all the money back.

Amid all this came images of Little Mean itself, its location undisclosed but the mayhem on screen showing, (oh so vividly) what the talking heads behind the news desks read on their teleprompters. Burned-out tanks, crashed helicopters, ruined buildings, policemen running away screaming, and a stream of terrified refugees. Above it all, the trio of looming towers, all horrible and haunted – a vision of the nasty bits of the Bible, made suddenly real.

Pundits drivelled. Presidents dithered. Generals seethed. *What was the use in bombing it, even with the biggest A-bombs available? Didn't the devil live in eternal fire anyway? What could an army do, against supernatural forces that almost certainly numbered under their banners some of the finest military strategists who had ever lived – bastards, the lot of them?*

Half an hour into the panic, Mrs Goosegarden issued an order to every major news channel in the developed world, of which she and her Void Chamber colleagues owned controlling shares. A ray of hope beamed out across the airwaves, as the scene cut to the Vatican. Or at least, to a very nice replica of what people thought it should look like.

"We go live now to Vatican City, where we can report both a tragedy, and a possible solution to what people are calling the End of Days crisis. Stephanie?"

A perky female news anchor appeared on screen, standing in a throne room packed from floor to ceiling with gilded cherubs, renaissance masterpieces and white leather furniture. In just thirty minutes, someone had managed to manufacture a 'Hell On Earth '99' button for her lapel.

"Yes, Tom, it looks like the shock of the imminent biblical apocalypse was just too much for the incumbent Pope, Callixtus the Third, who died of a suspected heart attack while watching news of the demonic incursion in the papal hot tub. It seems he may have also choked on a spicy chicken wing at the same time, though the theological implications of this gastronomical misadventure are unclear at this point. The two bikini-clad nuns who were with him in the hot tub are receiving counselling."

"Yes, it's a sad occasion, Stephanie, as Catholics everywhere will never again be able to enjoy a delicious bucket of hot wings without reflecting on this profound tragedy. But you mentioned a possible silver lining, on this day of unprecedented strife?"

"Indeed I did, Tom, because now I'm joined by the senior cleric who's picked to be the next leader of the church, his, ummm, extreme eminence, Cardinal Larry Sinibaldi. And he claims to have a solution to the strange and unsettling scenes afoot in Great Britain."

It wasn't a real person who wobbled into focus, as the camera panned around. There was something a bit too perfect and shiny about his face, and something utterly chilling about his smile. It was like looking into an industrial-sized mince grinder, all scrubbed and wicked.

It was Cardinal Syn, the ghost of the machine, dressed up in the technology which had rebuilt Margaret Thatcher. He looked about as smug as an overweight cat floating down a river of gravy on a Christmas ham.

"Do not fear, people of the world! My flock. My children," he said, spreading a pair of hands all heavy with golden rings. His red satin robes shimmered under the television lights. "Hell is real. Hell is upon us. But have we not said so, all along? The church is the very rock on which God has built his earthy kingdom, and we know how to deal with the naughty one and his misguided angels. Oh, yes indeed we do."

"So... you're saying that the Vatican has a solution to the scenes of horror now unfolding in England?" asked Stephanie, trying very hard to look serious and professional.

'Larry Sinibaldi' gave a little chuckle. A chuckle! No, the coming of the Dark One and the potential End of Days were, to him, a mere trifle, or perhaps some other inconsequential sponge-cake-based dessert.

"Of course, my dear! After all, it stands to reason. If the power of Satan is real, then so is the power of God. Exemplified, right now, by an ass-kicking holy son-of-a-cleric – me! Trust in your pope, heed your pope, *obey* your pope, and most of all, send him whatever ready cash is just sitting about, and we'll put the lid on this kerfuffle."

Stephanie rallied magnificently, as the Cardinal tried to hog the camera.

"But why England? Why has the Devil chosen to make the Home Counties his base of operations, instead of somewhere warmer?"

Syn nodded. As if this was a good question, and not just the next card he'd written out for her.

"And did those feet in ancient time, walk upon England's

mountains green? And was the holy Lamb of God, on England's pleasant pastures seen?" he asked, shrugging. "*Nope*. It's a very naughty country, really. Quite sinful. Don't get me started on Henry the Eighth, who might be a little bit to blame, with all his head chopping and divorces and his *big fake church which is stupid and not even a proper one*."

The Cardinal exhaled, making an attempt to get himself under control. But one of his eyes twitched open, as a sound that wasn't part of the script grumbled in the distance.

"Now, what the *made-up Hell* is that?" he muttered. The sound came again, louder now, and an aide came rushing in, wearing a Weasel News Network blazer and a worried expression. He went to whisper something to Stephanie, but Syn grabbed him by the collar and yanked him close.

"I'm paying for all of this, sunshine, bloody muggins that I am! So you'd better sing a tune I like, or the whole jukebox is gonna be playing sweet goodbyes, right?"

The aide, (who was very American) understood the words, but not the order they'd come in. He reverted to nodding like a novelty dog in the window of a speeding rally car.

"Ummm, it's *motorbikes*, your holiness, sir. Big ones. It's kind of like they..."

The Cardinal cursed. Because they weren't really inside the Vatican at all. The camera crew had been brought in by secret means, through corridors knocked up out of plywood and painted white, to a room that actually lurked near the narthex of the Tower of Sheol.

He pointed at the camera, and this time he was smiling. It was not an improvement.

"Tell 'em we're experiencing technical difficulties. And erase the last few minutes of tape. What do you *mean*, it's going out live? You ignorant, accursed bunch of *useless motherf...*"

The cameraman shut down the feed. Stephanie, the sound man and her aide quailed back, as the man who would be Pope drew all the shadows in the room around him, bending the light in ways which caused an instant migraine.

"Get out. Leave! I will take care of this unholy mess myself. And then—" suddenly he was all beatific brightness again, turning a beaming grin on the news team. "We'll try this all again. Without the interruptions. Perhaps there will be cake!"

He didn't wait to see them all scurry away, pleased, in that instant, to be out of his presence. Instead, he composed himself, gritting his teeth as the sound of motorcycles echoed through the vaulted halls, getting closer.

Not now! Not when he was so very close. Not when power lay just beneath the skin of reality, and the scalpel was in his hand...

Carinal Syn had, of course, planned for this eventuality. He stopped at a huge and saint-encrusted door, took a deep breath, reminded himself he didn't have to, and stepped through, into the nave of his cathedral.

To end this, once and for all.

Seventeen
The bridal march
vs
The funeral chorus

WHAT WAS IT like for September Normalsson, riding into the jaws of Hades?

Valkyries could well have been referenced, and the more lurid kind of comic book covers, and certain guitar solos as well. But the sensation, as September twisted the throttle, was of unreality.

After all, a part of her put in its not-so-gentle reminder, *she was still just an ordinary young lady, who happened to be having a rather difficult day.*

Well. Perhaps not 'ordinary'. Not actually very close to 'ordinary' at all, even with a tailwind and a squint. She left an imprint of tyre treads across acres of gaudy red carpet in her wake, all flickering with black fire.

It was all deeply suspicious.

And it was too late to stop. She could feel the story unfolding, just as Miss Rummage had said it wanted to, as the Endarkenment crackled across its metaphorical pages.

Now the cavernous nave of the cathedral opened up before her. She roared down between two aisles of crowded pews, then slid the big Buell to a standstill. There was a crowd here, evil bastards all of them, and they all held their breath as the kickstand scraped the flagstones, and September's boots slapped down next to it.

"Sorry. Can I park here? You know what? It's fine. You can keep it."

Before her, the altar crouched atop a pile of black marble steps. If funerals had their own kind of deathday cake, this would be how it looked; iced with red velvet and topped with an inverted cross.

And that wasn't all.

Cardinal Syn lounged amid the skulls and candles, posing with malice aforethought. He was propped up on one elbow, and he gave a little wave with the tips of his fingers, like a celebrity hairdresser. His face – or the horrid plastic simulacrum he was wearing – split into a grin full of aluminium teeth.

"And finally, we're all here," he oozed. "I've been expecting you, in a James-Bond-villain kind of way, young lady. Haven't you just caused just *so* much inconvenience? Dear *me* but you have! What would your parents think, eh? And where's our librarian friend? What's become of her, and that insufferable teddy bear?"

September leaned back against the bike, and unhooked Virgil's lamp from off of the handlebars. The tiny hologram looked more than a little seasick, but he gave her the thumbs up, and a wobbly little smile.

"She's back there, finishing off a few of your b-grade demons," said September, trying her very best to sound nonchalant. "They're about as convincing as the rest of this place, actually. Don't think I haven't noticed all the cardboard and spray paint. Cheap."

There was a murmured 'ooooh' from the assembled nasty bastards from the Aught.

"Have you heard the saying 'build it, and they will come?" retorted Syn. "It only has to look good enough for my television audience, love. And because they're just brainless humans, that doesn't have to be very convincing at all." He shrugged. "Did the redoubtable Miss Rummage give you a bit of the old 'leave me, go on without me', eh? A bit of the heroic self-sacrifice, or some of that clichéd rubbish?"

"You'll never get away with this!" shouted Virgil, rallying magnificently.

"Oh, and *speaking* of clichéd rubbish, listen to the world's greatest poet here! Of course I'll get away with it, you banana. I already have. If people think Hell is real, and I can send them there to prove it, the world will fall into line. Theocracy, my electric friend, is the natural state of the human flock. And wouldn't you know it, you even managed to bring me a fake devil, to help sell the sizzle!"

The Cardinal made a grand gesture, that even the most flamboyant opera singer would have found a bit gauche. Lights slammed on, bathing the throne behind the altar in a smoky glow.

And there was Cedric Welbourne – Dark Lazarus, the new Devil. His face was plastered with a beatific smile, and his brain was somewhere down the garden path with the little snot pixies. For reasons which September didn't even want to think about, he was dressed in an all-black version of David Bowie's costume from the movie *Labyrinth*, huge haircut, painted-on trousers and all.

She'd be lying to herself if she didn't admit he looked fantastic. But the Endarkenment shouted right over the rest of her mind when she noticed that he was perched on a very familiar throne. The one from the Tarot of the Devil, in fact.

"Whosoever believeth in me shall have eternal death, and be sustained by darkness made radiant," he burbled happily to himself, with his eyes rolled back to nothing but glowing whites.

"Look out!" shouted Virgil.

September had been distracted for a heartbeat too long. Syn slithered down the stairs faster than humanly possible, to loom up beside her, fingers steepled. He was too smart to try to touch her, with the Endarkenment sizzling around her like chainsaw teeth. But he turned a blackened fingernail on Virgil's lamp, and blasted it with a bolt of lighting that made it spin and clatter, then go dark.

"*You can shut up too, you little berk,*" he snarled, before composing himself with a whir of hidden servos.

"Now you know, I've wondered precisely what to do with you, young lady," he said. "Your great-great-granddad made me, so I can see that he's marked you, oh yes. Stamped and sealed you are, missy. 'Damaged goods, property of the family Archimedes'. He's a tricky bugger, and I've known it since *well* before he set me on fire. So I thought to myself, what are we really dealing with, here?"

He arched one eyebrow, walking around September in a tight circle. The air tingled, with the charge before a thunderbolt.

"*Heredity. Family. Tradition.* Dante was a smart little hamster, oh my word, yes! But he was *very* mediaeval indeed. Product of his time, and all that. So I put my thinking cap on, and had a little cogitate. I thought... how does one make an alliance, by his dirty old Florentine way of thinking? And it came to me. One of the powers of my office, in fact." His smile was silicon-shiny, face-splittingly wide, and totally self-satisfied.

"**A wedding.**"

Now the underpinnings of the world trembled. Now September was suddenly afraid. Because when she'd just tried to punch Cardinal Syn in the nose, nothing at all had happened.

She was unable to move.

Candles lit up in the vault of the cathedral, spluttering to life with a shower of greasy sparks. September saw a whole choir full of history's villains, ranked up on the pews. Napoleon was at the pipe organ, and he struck up a mangled version of the bridal march, leering like a cartoon weasel.

"It's never going to happen," she said, through gritted teeth. "You know I'd take half of your head off in the divorce. And anyway, you're hardly my type. About forty years too completely insane, I'm afraid. Try a dating agency."

"Ooh, nice try, petal! Wrong answer, though. I was looking for 'I do.'"

A gesture. A slicing cut with one hand, heavy with ruby rings.

A sickening lurch shuddered through the world, then, like a twist of nausea. Huge banners unfurled, waterfalls of ink plunging into icy water. Black flower bouquets bloomed and exploded, trailing ribbons.

September looked down, and realised that she was wearing a long black dress, of the style favoured by Stevie Nicks – or perhaps run up for some lacy, fey-sworn witch-queen. Its neckline plunged like the graph of a stock market implosion, and it trailed a train of black satin roses, each with a human eye at its centre.

"Oh, I think you'll be whispering the vows and some sweet nothings beside, my little treasure," crooned the Cardinal, in a voice like a finely tuned hacksaw. "Because it's not *me* that's got designs on your luscious hand. Oh no. I'm not born of the flesh, like you primates. I'm not possessed of lusts and urges of the kind you'd find... familiar. Or particularly wholesome, to tell the honest truth."

His eyes were plugholes, draining down to nothing.

"Oh no. You'll marry *him*."

One finger stabbed out toward Dark Lazarus, sprawled across his throne.

"And then, as they say, what's mine is yours, what's yours is mine, September Normalsson. You'll be the queen of my little bijou Hell, and all of your great-granddad's wild ideas will be mine for the taking. This is what Septivarian wanted, see? I worked it out. Not his final rest. His final restitution! But I'm the one who controls Dark Lazarus here and now, in this pretty cage of mine. Come on! Don't you want to just give him one. Little. *Kiss?*"

The words spun past her like sparks from a bonfire. Part of September's mind registered the fact that she was walking up to the altar, and that, yes – there was a tug on her soul, deep as drowning, which had Cedric Welbourne, transfigured, as its lodestone. Thoughts, from second down to twenty-third, screamed that this was all wrong. That something much worse lurked beneath the surface. Something squirming away from the light, as if the Cardinal's words had cut it deeply.

"How the hell are you doing this?" she managed to ask, while Cedric, all radiant in black, came stalking down the marble steps toward her.

The Cardinal put a finger to his lips – *shhh – it's a naughty secret!* He reached into one voluminous sleeve, and brought out a little knitted doll, dressed in September's tartan dress and white lab coat. Its pale skin and red hair were stained green with Repo.

"Proper voodoo, actually. Easily done. You left one of those bloody tangly copper-wire strands of hair in the Aught. And of course, you're full of a very special dose of old Septivarian's wonder drug. A brand new mixture, it seems. Fine-tuned, to a very specific frequency."

"What! When? *How?*"

Cardinal Syn winked, as he swept back behind the altar, and cracked open a huge, dusty bible. It probably wasn't the one with Jesus as the main character.

"Did the old bloke ask you to drink any mysterious potions, along the way? Any valuable family heirlooms you were oh-so-innocently requested to keep on your person?"

September remembered the little phial which had broken the unlucky curse. Which, if she thought a bit more critically about her current predicament, may not have been broken at all. *If it had ever existed.*

Then there was the strange icon of Dagon on the cross, which had been both a key, and the carrier for a captive hologram. It was still there, and it suddenly felt very heavy on its chain, biting into the back of her neck.

"I told you, the old feller had a plan! Sharon Kolslaw told you, too, didn't she? You think he was going to let it slide, what the government threatened him with, back then? That it was just water under the bloody bridge, a twist of the arm so vicious it made him make *me?* Not on your fondest memory, miss. Not in your wildest imagination!"

Now Napoleon struck up the tune, and the skull-faced organ pipes belched fire and smoke. Now a choir full of ghouls opened their hymnals, and began to mumble in that sort-of-pious way which people do in churches, (even ones which are consecrated to ultimate evil), when they don't want the people next to them to realise they don't know the words.

"The problem with old Professor Archimedes," said Syn, "is that he didn't do half-arsed jobs. So he made me just a bit too smart for his own good."

"I won't do it!" hissed September. "You can't make me!"

"*Of course I can*," stage-whispered Syn, behind one hand. "Have you got any idea what's going to happen to your parents if you don't? What's going to happen to *all* the people in this stupid little town? I need the world to believe that this is Hell on Earth. But as you've so insightfully mentioned, it's looking a bit of a fixer-upper. A few dismembered bodies ought to do the trick, of course.

Unless, that is, we can give the cameras a proper 'Bride of Lucifer' moment, instead."

September thought, briefly, about saying *you wouldn't*. But of course, he would.

And that's when she discovered something else about herself. Because, for all that she knew, deep down, that society was rotten, she still wasn't prepared for the actual, real people who made it up to get murdered.

"So... if I marry him? What then?"

The Cardinal waggled his eyebrows suggestively.

"Well, surely they teach you about all that sort of thing in school these days..."

A spark of Endarkenment sizzled the end of his nose.

"Bloody hell! No sense of humour, your sodding generation!" He fussed with the bible, licking a finger and flipping through the pages. "What happens, see, is that you'll be the brains of this operation, for me. I'm gonna be Pope, and sit with the Supreme Aaron and old Mother Goose and Mister Blank and the others, on the committee that runs the world. You'll herd the few lonely brain cells of my devastatingly handsome but mentally deficient new Devil here, and be a very photogenic adversary. Not a bad life, really. So long as you do as you're told."

September nodded once, grimly.

"*Fine*. Let's get it over with."

The Cardinal beamed.

"See? Logical, rational, and scientific. Septivarian would be proud. No; not really, what with you losing and all. But he'd *understand*. You might just get to ask him about that, if Sharon was right..."

Now the music swelled, and the shadows streamed out past the trio at the altar, painting the cathedral in stripes of monochrome.

"Deadly departed, we are gathered here today to celebrate

the union of science and the supernatural, mortality and the numinous, innocence and evil!" intoned Syn. "Let any who object to this union keep their bloody mouths shut, or risk having them stitched up in a twinkle, right? Because, by the power vested in me – by myself, mostly – and in defiance of a God who apparently doesn't feel like turning up, I am about to wed September Normalsson, bearer of the Endarkenment and heir to Septivarian Archimedes, to the Morningstar, the Devil of Dante's Tarot, cypher and scion to Lord Lucifer himself."

September realised that she had one hope, at this point. And she could see it, struggling deep inside the eyes of the new Devil. It was Cedric Welbourne, trying to get out.

It was at that moment that Silas Rosewood, ex-PROPHET and former member of the Void Chamber, crashed the party.

It was a literal crash – one which shattered the great stained-glass pentagram high up above the altar. And it was just his head. It landed right in the baptismal font, lips drawn back from a ghastly set of pea-green teeth.

Assorted ghouls, demons and horrible historical figures turned to look, scandalised. Not so much because of the decapitation; for most of them, that was barely impolite. But the beam of pale dawn sunlight which came streaming in behind it was another story.

Outside the tower of Sheol, morning had come. The storm had broken. And now, with light bathing the frankly tawdry movie-set of Cardinal Syn's cathedral, things of a redemptive and violent nature were starting to unfold.

"Do you bloody mind? We're trying to have a wedding here!" screamed Syn, with the discord of dial-up modem noise echoing behind his words. "Didn't I just tell you lot that any objections would be met with *intensely* personal brutality?"

The doors slammed back. More light blazed in, around a throng of shadows.

"Funny you should say that, squire," said a familiar voice. "Because my oh my, aren't *you* overdue for a face full of boots."

The shadows shuffled forward, and September saw why. Shuffling was their usual speed. For some of them, it was a way of life. Because here were the denizens of the General Crowley Memorial Home, Wrinkly Acres. In all their super-heroic and villainous costumes; most of them still reeking of mothballs and lavender fabric softener.

The Confectioner was there, and the Dread Panda, and the Holy Roller, the Groundskeeper, the Purple Paladin, Snorr, Neopatra, The Septic Seven and Doctor Defenestration. The Suede Spectre, Rough Justice, Short Temper, Captain Captain, Midget-Mooseotaur, Professor Cramp, Robobabushka, the entire Fungus Force, and many more. Even some of the fearsomely efficient special-forces nurses had come along, one of them pushing the dessert trolley.

Front and centre were the Doom Commission, all looking battle-scarred and grimly determined. It was Stoatman who had spoken, and he hobbled forward with bandy-legged inevitability, a one-man geriatric ice age.

"Now, I'd like to say that if you let go of the girl, and whoever that glam-rock feller is, we'll go easy on yer. But that's a load of bollocks, and we all knows it. It's back to the Aught for you, in so many pieces they're gonna need a picture of you and pair of tweezers to even *start* putting you back together."

Cardinal Syn snarled, and it was a sound like the gears of some bladed, gristly engine grinding themselves to pieces.

"Begone, you ancient muppets! This is consecrated ground, in case your cataracts deceive you. Both of these fine young people have agreed to be wed, and I have sealed the circle about them, with all the runes, and all the sigils, and no small amount of quite expensive beaujolais. In the words of that manky old wizard, YOU SHALL NOT PASS!"

He wasn't kidding. A triple-circle of crimson blazed up from incisions in the floor, smoking with brimstone. The altar, the throne, and all those within its bounds wavered for a second, as if behind translucent walls.

Stoatman put his chin in his hand. He crossed his arms, then uncrossed them. He extracted and lit another of his atrocious roll-ups.

"Fair enough. But, see, there isn't gonna be a wedding. I know that girl, and she's not the type to say 'I do' under duress. Especially when you'll have to come outta that circle at some point, what with there being no food, no water, and rather importantly no toilet in there with you. And us out here. With as I just recall, a Mistress of the Dark Arts among our number, who can probably banish your little handicraft project in a trice. Penny?"

And this is where it went all wrong. Completely arse-backwards, in fact.

Because Penny Dreadful, evil mistress of necromancy, may have been seventy-seven years old, and supported by a sinister, skull-encrusted mobility frame. She may have had a face which looked as crinkly and rosy as a very embarrassed dried apple; the type that was one lace-trimmed bonnet away from trying to put ducks in waistcoats. But she was still, for her multitude of sins, a very powerful witch indeed, and witches don't forget a face.

Even when it's been back-combed, feathered and suntanned to within an inch of its afterlife.

"*Cedric Welbourne? Is that you?*"

Penny's voice used to be sultry, but after decades of sinister incantations and censers belching smoke, it had a bit of sandpaper to it. She plucked a pair of spectacles on a mauve plastic chain from around her neck, where they'd been clattering with a whole lot of bat-themed jewellery.

"Blimey, my lad! Haven't you aged well? I... I don't suppose you recognise me, what with the several decades, and all. I heard you got yourself dead. But I never could find you, even with all the... you know."

She gestured vaguely at the occult trappings of her trade, including the spider-web-themed satin evening dress she still wore under her black dressing gown.

September had already been staring into Cedric's eyes, and hoping for some kind of miracle. So she saw the spark which flickered deep down inside them, even if she couldn't move.

She remembered him mentioning a certain somebody, from very long ago. Somebody who would have had a whole life, between the night he rode away from an argument with her, into the rain, and never came back. And now...

Didn't time work differently in the Aught, he'd said? *Oh dear.* September's thoughts, never finely tuned to social situations, finally informed her that she might be standing at the marriage altar with somebody else's boyfriend. Now would be the perfect time to be able to explain how this was entirely unintentional.

"Penelope?" asked Morningstar, the new Devil, in a voice which was not at all wicked. "Penelope Ann Simpkins? Of... of number twenty-three, Isambard Avenue?"

His mouth hung open afterwards, and he closed it with both hands, looking very, very surprised.

"The same," answered Penny, and with a gesture of one hand she banished the Cardinal's magic wardings. They crumbled as if they were nothing – because nothing in the universe could possibly have stopped the two of them coming to stand hand in hand before the altar. September quickly moved out of the way.

"You know, I heard about what happened that night. For all these years, I've wondered why I had to be so stubborn about you meeting mum and dad. He was a crusty old bugger, but he'd have seen the good in you. I tried to get in touch, you know. Got a whole stack of books about the witching, 'cause I wanted to say I was sorry. Not a lot of good it did. But here we are."

"No!" hissed Syn. But now *he* was the one who couldn't move. Wyrd energies went warping and seething through the whole cathedral, centred around Cedric. The face of the new Devil, Dark Lazarus, began to blur and shift, turning back into that old-fashioned vintage mug with it's swept-forward haircut and slightly runny eyes.

"Here we are," he said, and his voice had lost the supernatural, sardonic edge of the Morningstar. "You know, I became the Grim Reaper there for a while, just to get back to Earth. They guessed I'd try to see you again, and they talked me out of it. But..."

September could only watch, as the kind of forces which mash two entire stars together to create a supernova unfolded three feet away from her. It was the kind of thing which she'd been determined not to believe in for most of her life, but there was an inevitability here. *I might as well be happy for them both*, she thought. *Because they're going to be. Any minute now, she'll say...*

"And you don't mind that I've gotten old, then?"

And look suddenly shy, in a way that made all those years of supervillainy seem like a triviality. And *he'll* say...

"Well, I'm the Devil at the moment, actually. So if you like, I can make one or two dark desires come true. It's kind of my thing, I suppose."

The power which flooded out from him, then, was the kind that feels like a very concentrated springtime, all in one place. The kind which makes every one of your teeth feel as if it's been rotated by a quarter-turn, and electrified.

When it faded, jangling off down the empty corridors of Sheol, what it left behind was an image from a living photograph. One taken, it seemed, on that early colour film they used to develop in little kiosks in shopping centres. All over-saturated and sunny – a memory bled through into reality.

Penny Dreadful was still dressed in black, because witchery goes deeper than the bones, and no amount of anything can make it hide. But she was young again, and it was no illusion. Her hair was long and black, held back by a band inset with silver spiders, and her dress was a vintage masterwork of layered petticoats, over long black and white striped socks of the kind you'd usually see sticking out from under a Kansas farmhouse. Young Penelope Ann Simpkins was the kind of pretty that knows there are other things more important, and bends the whole room around her with a smile because of it.

Cedric was back, too. His shadow might have been huge and horned and wearing a crown, splashed across the floor of Syn's cathedral, but he was a 1950s rocker again – just more so, in this moment, than ever before.

"It's real, isn't it?" asked Penny. "I used to be able to do the old glamour, pretty well, you know. Saved a bundle on hair and makeup. But this is different, isn't it?"

"Technically, it's evil sorcery," said Cedric, who was still clasping both of her hands in his. "And there's supposed to be a cruel and ironic price, kind of thing. But I don't have to be the Morningstar any more. Neither of us has to be anything, except what we want to."

September could feel the sheer force of circumstance, welding the moment together. But she felt two other things, with a sudden thrill of disquiet.

The first was the distinct impression of Septivarian Archimedes, her great-great-grandfather, gurgling silently in horror. Finally confronted with something so inexplicable it derailed the clockwork juggernaut of his mind.

The second was of huge inhuman eyes cracking open, in some subterranean place of darkness and heat and utter pressure. *The feeling of something speeding through magma, down in the depths, churning molten rock in its wake as it rushed closer...*

She turned to look at Cardinal Syn, and saw that he'd felt at least part of it too.

"Can't you stop them?" he croaked, almost unable to move his lips. September shook her head.

"Erm..." she managed, as Cedric and Penny gazed into each other's eyes. The Doom Commission and their assorted geriatric hangers-on applauded. Most of the ghouls and demons packing the pews did, too.

Now here was a *proper* wedding – the kind that Doctor Cliff Hunkstrong would have totally approved of, if this whole scene was televised in Spanish.

"Dearly beloved," intoned the Cardinal, in a voice which definitely wasn't his. "We are gathered here today to witness the shattering of the seal of Dante." He'd managed to get his hand around one of the big ornate black candlesticks, but something had a hold of him now, and it was determined that he was going to officiate over *something*.

"Penelope Ann Simpkins, as a witch, you're already colloquially a Bride of Lucifer – care to make it official?" he continued. His mouth opened and shut like a ventriloquist's dummy's, totally out of his control. Penny nodded.

"I do."

"And Cedric Welbourne, ex-provisional junior Grim Reaper, ex-human, former bearer of the Knight of Staves and of Death itself, and pretty passable temporary Antichrist... do you renounce the power of the Devil's tarot, and cast it aside? As a cheeky bonus, that'll keep Miss Simpkins looking about sixty years younger."

The whole tower was shaking, now. Random notes began to moan and whistle from the pipe organ. Napoleon swore blisteringly in French and abandoned his post. September remembered what Brother Jacques had said, and raised a hand to object. But something tugged at the black nimbus of the Endarkenment around it, and dragged it down. She staggered back, almost losing her footing on the slippery marble.

"I do," said Cedric, and the Devil's Tarot appeared on his chest, bleeding out through his cotton shirt. He gripped it with two fingers and peeled it away, dropping it to the altar.

Three things happened at once.

First, the rumbling stopped, and the world held its breath. The card fell end over end, in fluttering slow motion.

Second, Cedric and Penny snapped back into reality. Their feet, which had been hovering an inch from the floor, touched down with a crackle of static discharge. This let Cardinal Syn go, and, (too late!) he swung his candlestick, blurring it around to clock Cedric right in the temple.

It was a poorly timed blow, and only a glancing one. But one of the sharp corners of the candlestick's base scored a cut across Cedric's face, and a drop of bright blood fell next to the Tarot of the Devil, as it landed face-up on the altar.

Which preceded the third thing. The important one, as it

would turn out. Looking back, September would wonder just how much of all this had been planned, and how much was just down to cold, infernal patience.

Because as soon as Dante's card landed, (and the blood splashed across the picture of a now-empty throne, and Penny caught Cedric before he could fall), everyone in the cathedral heard a voice from below. Echoing up out of the sub-basements of Sheol, or somewhere deeper.

"**AT LAST**," it said, in tones of vast, gloating hunger and awful satisfaction.

Then the shadows pulled tight, peeling off the walls and spiralling in, like a ragged flock of bats. They raged around the great throne above the altar, coalescing into a cloud of darkness, even as chains lashed out, with spiked collars attached, and snapped shut around the necks of Penny and Cedric.

This time September *did* fall backwards, because the presence which came rushing up into that teeming cloud was immense. She saw Cardinal Syn go down as well, and a scattering of elderly supervillains, too. Reality itself creaked and groaned with the weight of it, as something settled its dark aeonic bum onto the seat of power.

Now she could move. Now, when it was too late. A pins-and-needles ache tingled in her hands and feet, and she pushed the hair back out of her eyes, dragging herself up to her feet against one of the pillars.

September caught a glimpse of what was seated on the throne, and bit back the kind of language that a keen and curious young lady shouldn't even know about.

She saw a face which would have been achingly beautiful, if one side of it hadn't been burned and melted to a charnel-house ruin. A single black-feathered wing, so dark that it scattered into deep purple and green around the edges. A nifty combo of white robes and golden armour, defaced with horrible runes.

And the eyes. Eyes which were filled with the terrible comedy of cruelty, forever.

"Well, I'm back," said Lucifer, the Fallen Angel, Adversary of God. "Do you mortals still have such a thing as pizza? I could absolutely *murder* one of those."

Bonus Suture
Deus In Absentia

EVEN TRAVELLING AS fast as an angel can fly (which is fast enough to get speeding tickets from the arbiters of physics themselves), Nathuriel took a long time to reach the edge of the visible universe.

There are some who said that this frontier existed because of the time it took for light to reach the Earth, and that an infinity of spangled, gaseous, exploding wonder awaited beyond that veil of a billion years. But Nathuriel knew the truth. Which had not been the truth five minutes ago, but was now the whole and eternal quill of veracity.

God was painting new galaxies. He was seated on absolutely nothing (or rather, on a fat, overstuffed Turkish cushion, perched on absolutely nothing) and he was wearing a jeweller's loupe and a big shapeless paint-spattered smock. A few minutes ago, in an alternate trouser leg of time which was quickly unravelling into having never been sewn, he hadn't been here. In fact, He'd been locked out of the universe altogether, in a sealed-off little loop in the Aught.

Now, he was wiping a particularly nice shade of aquamarine on his long, bushy beard, and peering at a fresh nebula. And that's what he'd been up to for the past several decades. Both of these things having happened at once made reality squeak like two balloons being rubbed together, but you had to be very supernatural to sense it.

"Sir! Good morning, sir! I've got some news from Earth!"

Nathuriel hovered near the shoulder of his Lord. By comparison to God he was a tiny figure in white robes, with six eyes and six wings, as befitted a messenger of the Almighty.

"Do you think that this globular cluster looks wonky around the edges?" asked the Alpha and the Omega, gesturing at a smudge of airbrushed rosy gases. Blooms of nuclear-furnace glow lit it up from within in a very pleasing manner. "I don't want astronomers to know I'm doing this, you know. It's just, they've put up a new telescope which for some reason I was unaware of. If they peek over here, it all has to look natural, hmmm? Can't be letting the side down by confirming my existence, hey?"

Nathuriel took a deep breath. The fact that he was afloat in hard vacuum did not help. He reminded himself that this manifestation of God was, like him, not strictly real. He was the human idea of an angel, his boss was the archetypal universal creator, and that this far-flung existential edge (where he had set up his planet-sized palette, rimed with comet ice), was actually a complex brane-like manifold of interwoven Aughtic pseudo-reality interacting with consensual spacetime.

In short, this was what people *believed* God was, now. A big, mysterious fellow who lurked on the edges of science, creating wonders and then slinking off for a quiet cigarette.

"Yes, my Lord," he ventured. "Very nice, ummm, magnetic vortices. And the colours. Ummm. Yes. Spot on."

Despite only having been back for a few minutes, Nathuriel was far less complicated than God. People believed in two kinds of angels, and he wasn't the type who blessed fluffy kittens on get-well-soon cards. He had been imagined, and thus created, as a ruthlessly efficient prosecutor of the War On Evil. A flaming sword was belted at his hip and all, which, if he paid attention to things like thermodynamics, would have played merry hell with the dry-cleaning bills. He cleared his throat.

"I think you should know that your immortal enemy, the Betrayer, Enemy of the Light, Scourge of the Righteous,

The Morning Star, Lucifer Satanas, has enthroned himself on Earth, due to some spectacular silliness on the part of the humans. Did you, I don't know... want to perhaps muster the legions of the light's wrath, and descend upon them like the wolves upon the unshriven flocks of the Malachianites?"

God dipped his brush, and the thing about it was this. Each of its bristles bifurcated an infinite number of times.

"Pretty sure it was the Midianites, young lad. Mmmm. Or perhaps the Molochorianites? Both were pretty slack about shriving the old flocks, eh?"

Carefully, he dotted a new star into existence. It flared with hydrogen flame, churning a disc of scintillating dust which would one day become planets.

Nathuriel wrung his hands. The people who had believed him into existence had given him an itchy trigger finger, when it came to smiting the unholy.

"Are you quite sure? I mean, we've been locked out for a good few centuries, Sir. Could be about time for the big one, if you take my meaning. The prophesied antipope has turned up, Satan is enthroned, a thousand years of darkness looks like it might be on the cards, and all that."

The messenger angel's voice was a pitch-perfect simulacrum of the one used by junior managers everywhere, who have to manage senior managers who went to expensive schools but who could not, in point of fact, find their own buttocks with a torch, a shaving mirror and a copy of the Ordnance Survey.

God looked unperturbed. He mixed up a pigment of things from the explosive and colourful end of the periodic table, and spread them across the darkness of eternity in a pleasing ripple.

"Hmmm. I think you'll find it all works out, m'lad. Evil sows the seeds of its own destruction, and all that."

Nathuriel frowned, which was as close to disobeying the divine will as his little circuit-loop of a mind could get. But there was no changing things. *This* was what people believed, now, apparently. Not like the good old days, but then, what was?

"Moving in mysterious ways again, Lord?" he asked, with a small sigh.

"That's the bunny," said God, smiling to himself. "Now, do you think we should have more green galaxies? Apparently ionising oxygen has quite a lovely tone..."

Eighteen
The Rebel Angel
vs
Parental Supervision

IF YOU'VE NEVER witnessed a horde of geriatric super-beings going to war against the Devil, you should start by imagining the smell.

There's hot iron, and brimstone, and the scent of liniment and eucalyptus ointment, foot balm and lavender soap. There's the acrid smell of boiling blood, mixed with that baldy slaphead tonic your great-uncle swears he's never heard of.

The nose tends to shut down in horror, really, but that leaves several more senses to appreciate the utter madness of it all. The sound of energy beams and coughing, wheezing war-cries. The dark, unhinged laughter of the Lord of Evil, as he gathers himself up from his throne, wings of shadow flaring wide and ragged...

Then the blur of images which assail the eye. The razor-strokes of impossible light, clashing and swirling with darkness made sentient. The flying fists and maliciously swung walking sticks. The levitating electric scooters and the flashing blades, which were certainly against the matron's rules. Solid rods of force, jam and cream, ectoplasm, superheated lava and dark sorcery met, blurred together in an expanding bubble – and then broke.

The blast-wave was perfectly spherical and utterly silent. In fact, it created a deafening anti-noise, centred on Lucifer as he screamed a Word. It was a naughty bit cut from the marginalia of God's hymnal, and it was in the exact same language which September Normalsson had used to frame the Ultimate Equation.

It blew two-score superannuated heroes and villains back from the throne like chaff before a cyclone. And then it stopped, blurring static-soft around the edges. September had felt the blast rush past her, but it had kept her on her feet; now Stoatman, the Doom Commission, and a rouges gallery of other supers twitched and moaned in the air above her, pinned like spandex moths. The air shimmered around the Evil One's hands, and heat-haze boiled over his head.

"Oh, I *like* you! Little angels and demons, playing out little versions of my story, over and over again. '*You created me, so I defy you! You hurt me, so I'll hurt everyone!*' Love it!"

Lucifer grinned, and here was the thing about it – you knew he was laughing at you, but you wanted, so very much, to join in.

"I'll keep you all for later. I can see how you'd be entertaining."

A gesture, and the superannuated horde were plucked from the air, and slotted neatly into a row of empty pews. In their prime, this pack of spandex-clad superhumans had swung more geopolitical power than the a-bomb, but Lucifer had just folded them up like fresh laundry. Now his attention turned to the Red Cardinal. A single wicked finger pointed.

"And what do we do with *you*, hmmm? You summoned me from that infernal prison Dante trapped me in. For that, I should thank you. But of course, sending people a nice muffin basket isn't really in my nature, is it?"

Syn licked his lips. September could see the mesh of arch-betrayals haloing his nasty plastic head.

"Well of course, my Lord, this was my intention all along. I've always been a devout follower, and I'm ready to serve as your Antipope on Earth, making sure that the, ummm, tedious administrational duties of global rule don't cut into your schedule of evil…"

He wound down slowly, realising that none of this was working.

"Oh, give it up, you manky appliance," chuckled the Prince of Darkness. "You think I can't see those weasly sad thoughts of yours, clear as damnation? More to the point, don't you think that I might be just a *little* bit leery of the oldest story in the book? The one about a conniving but wildly ambitious second-in-command, with a thing for sedition? Ring any bells?"

Lucifer leaned forward on this throne, and Cedric and Penny, chained, quailed back from the sudden flames that erupted around him.

"*I could accept the slimy, scheming, monomaniacal plans, Cardinal.* I could enjoy the intricate chess-match of sharpening my wickedness against a cruel adversary. But you're a screw-up, Syn. All of this was a *mistake*, and that's **unforgivable!**"

For an instant, his eyes blazed with the furnace-heat of the rising sun.

"So, if you want my job, I have just the place for you. Frozen, in the middle of the fictional Hell I've endured for all these tedious centuries!"

Lucifer clenched one fist, and then opened his fingers, palm up. The ground beneath the Cardinal yawned open, marble and granite screwing clockwise to become a maw fanged with icicles. A freezing blast of air flapped around Syn's robes, in the fashion made popular by the late, great Marilyn Monroe, revealing that he wore satin love-heart boxers underneath.

"No! My lord! I can…"

But that was all he had time for. Because an immense and

spindly hand of pure ice came up out of the hole, wrapped its transparent fingers around him, and then snatched him away down to Cocytus. The pit slammed closed behind him.

Lucifer leered, rubbing his hands together.

"All of you wicked bastards in the pews, don't worry. I've got work for the lot of you."

There was a half-hearted cheer from the historical villains and madmen in the choir. They could see which side their toast was buttered on, and no mistake. Then the Evil One turned his gaze on September Normalsson, and it was all she could do to meet it without screaming.

"Now. You. The only one here I might actually be afraid of. You're just not quite evil enough for me to get a handle on, are you? And this power that's all around you is nothing to do with God. Tell me, girl – who do you serve?"

This is Lucifer, the fallen archangel, talking to me directly, thought September. *Usually, just thinking that sentence in all seriousness makes you a candidate for an extra-long-sleeved coat that does up at the back. But he's not as scary as he should be. And did he just say he was afraid of me?*

Once again, she felt a weird disharmony inside her mind. There was the terror she ought to feel. And there, looming over it like a wave about to break, was sheer affront that this kind of nonsense should be happening to her at all.

She planted her feet, like she did on the hockey field when she was about to cause a major concussion, and lifted her chin defiantly.

"Who do I serve? Nobody! If you really have to know, I'm pretty much an atheist. I don't believe in you, or the other fellow I'm guessing you'd rather not hear the name of, or his son with the long hair."

"**Atheist?** *I'm right in front of you,* child! And there is another, who works through you..."

"Atheist. Yes! Because you look like an evil deity and talk like one too, but it's all a bit too fictional, isn't it? I've been to the Aught, Mister Lightbringer. I have a fair idea of how it all fits together. And this power, which I notice you're not keen to come any closer to, is the Endarkenment. Science that doesn't play by the rules."

She took a deep breath, and arched one eyebrow, in a way that Septivarian would have fully appreciated.

"You know what people believe in, these days? They don't waste their faith on big, bombastic cartoons like you. They don't know how their clock radio works, but they trust it'll get them up in the morning. They have no idea what makes their car start, but they pray that it will. They sit around and worship a television most nights, with no concept of how it's tethered to satellites whirling through space over their heads. So yeah, you might be right here in front of me. But I'm not about to believe in you, just for your convenience! In fact, you can come and have a go, if you think you're hard enough. We'll see what people believe in. A manky old villain from Sunday School, or whatever keeps the lights on."

This seemed to genuinely delight Lucifer, which was, September thought, far better than any of the other alternatives. In retrospect, she had no idea where that whole speech had come from.

"Oh, *yes!* You'd weaponise their dim credulity with humdrum little miracles, eh? Devious! But when I said that another worked through you, I didn't mean some kind of new god. I was talking about..."

Discussions on theology would have to wait, however. Because at that moment, possibly the single most embarrassing thing which has ever a happened, happened.

In the middle of her big, climactic showdown against the Enemy of God himself, September Normalsson's parents showed up.

The big cathedral doors crashed open, and the first which September knew about this moment of pure horror was the sound of her mother's voice.

"*September Hyacinth Normalsson!* Are you trying to pick a fight with the Devil, young lady? That's not the kind of behaviour we expect from you!"

"Yes, your mother and I are *very* disappointed," put in her dad. September turned, in skin-crawling mortification. Even Lucifer cringed on her behalf.

It could have been a horrible dream. But it was exactly as real as all of the madness which had dropped on September in this last couple of days, like a skip-bin full of dead fish dropped from orbit.

Norma and Norman Normalsson advanced down the aisle of Cardinal Syn's theatre-prop cathedral, with Miss Rummage and two fully armoured Knights Templar behind them.

But what really made September do a literal, cartoon double-take, was what they were wearing.

Gone were the tweed suit and the pale pastel twin-set with pearls. September's dad was dressed in what appeared to be a boy scout's uniform, quite a bit too small for his middle-aged belly. It was topped off with a Sherlock Holmes deerstalker, and a pair of bright yellow boots and gloves. A stylised magnifying glass was stitched onto his chest.

Her mum was got up in pink spandex, white knee-length boots, white gloves, and a white cape with a question-mark-and-lightning-bolt motif. A domino mask covered half of her face, in one of those vapid comic-book attempts at concealing her real identity.

"Mum? Dad?" croaked September. "Ummm..."

The anger had washed out of her. The strange, insistent

feeling that this was somehow destined went, too. Even the black flame of the Endarkenment faded. Because nothing is ever as real, in all your life, as getting told off by your parents.

"Yes," continued Norman. "We're disappointed you didn't tell us you were having trouble with supernatural bastards like *this* sad example. We could have been kicking his arse as a family."

"You're... both of you... with the... I think I even..." stammered September.

"Yes, that's right, dear. It's our shameful secret. We were super-teens, once. Timmy Tenacious, Boy Detective, and the Quizmistress. It's, ahhh... well, it's something we tried to put behind ourselves. *For your sake.* But it seems to keep coming back."

September didn't know quite what to say, but this was her mum. This was Professor Archimedes' great-granddaughter, who he'd raised as his own. There had been dark intimations of some kind of tragedy in he family, during the War. So she had to be told.

"Mum, he's *gone*. Grandpa Septivarian's dead. He gave me some kind of quest, and all this started to happen, and there's a grim reaper, and a robot Cardinal, and..."

"I know," said Norma. Septerina the Quizmistress, who'd been part of the Unstoppable Force, and then one of the Teen Terrors, and then, well, just *vanished*. "Arbourdale told me. I hadn't seen the little guy in years, but he was my teddy bear, once. Granddad made him for me, and all..."

"That's why we decided we had to come out of retirement," said Norman. "We've got no regrets about trying to keep you out of this madness, September. But now that it's come to find you, we're not going to let you make the same mistakes we did."

"Would those mistakes include rudely interrupting the

literal personification of evil?" asked Lucifer, who was feeling a bit left out. "Because, I assure you, touching as this little reunion is, *I've just defeated the entire Doom Commission and all their friends.* You two, if memory recalls, were little better than sidekicks."

September's dad didn't look afraid. If anything, he looked wistfully sad, then, despite his two-sizes-too-small boy detective costume.

"You don't get it, do you? Yes, we were sidekicks, and on different sides, too. Then we were quite inconveniently head over heels in love, so we decided to run away to the real world. Leave this whole circus behind."

"My Grandfather arranged it all for us," said Norma. "This whole town was his idea. This entire place is a trap, because the Endarkenment isn't just about science. It's about madness. *It makes these kind of things happen.* If it wasn't you, Mister Devil, Sir, it'd be things with bat wings and tentacles, or a giant alien god with a knife and fork, or some sort of lizard people again. Reality's thin here, but it's not a door in. *It's a garbage disposal.*"

Lucifer's face changed, then. From smug amusement to actual, abject terror. He saw the black flames of the Endarkenment billow into life all around September's mum, not as a flickering line, but as a teardrop-shaped hole torn in the world. It tapered up above her like a candle-flame, dark as hard vacuum.

"No! The Magician's power is finished! Dante's rubric is broken! *My time has come!*"

"Bollocks, mate. Your time is up," said September's dad, cracking his knuckles. "Miss Rummage?"

The librarian, secret master of the Baal Shem, stepped forward, unrolling a very official-looking black scroll.

"*Lucifer Morningstar, manifestation of human belief in radical evil! I find you guilty of crimes against reality, and sentence you to be banished to Fiction for all eternity, to be the antagonist in hackneyed supernatural thrillers, and to be played by a suave British actor on television, time without end! I hereby invoke the Gatekeeper to banish you, with the praxis of the Ultimate Equation."*

September's dad hauled out a key from on a chain around his neck, and it was no surprise that it looked almost exactly like the alien crucifix which September still had around her own. A jag of black lightning curled away from Norma's fingertip, and became a huge dark keyhole, through which September was sure she could see tentacles.

Then the two came together, and a bolt of unreality slithered across the air, sizzling like oil on black iron. It leaped from September's mum's fingertips, viciously whispering the numerics of the Ultimate Equation, and arrowed toward Lucifer, who reared back against his throne, his one wing curled over to protect his ruined face.

But the bolt never struck. Instead, it curved in the air, wavered...

...and earthed itself against September, who swallowed up that living darkness with her own black aura. The smell of ozone and burnt rubber was all that remained.

Norma shook her fingers and frowned.

"Ooooohhh dear! Well, *that's* not supposed to happen. September, you wouldn't happen to have become the mortal incarnation of Dante's Magician while you were at science camp, would you?"

Now Lucifer was grinning. Now, his fear had turned to cruel amusement. He stood from his throne, and hellfire boiled in his slitted eyes.

"Triple sixes, I'm afraid. The house wins!"

"Mum, I *told* you!" shouted September. "Arbourdale told you! Septivarian's dead. And he willed the card to me. I didn't get to ask him why."

Norma stared up at the huge, triumphant figure of Lucifer, and then at her daughter. There was a look on her face which it took a moment for September to decipher, but it was hurt. It was loss. And it was disappointment.

Not for September, and the fact that all of this was behaviour unfit for a nice young lady. But because the mad genius who'd raised her, and then kept his distance for two decades to protect her, had chosen someone else.

"But you don't know how to…" began her mum, once again looking decidedly un-super, despite her costume.

She never got to finish. Because the Prince of Darkness was not about to be kept waiting.

"Very nice. Very touching. Very fitting, even. The old man cut you out of his will, eh? Well, allow me to be the first to say I know how *that* feels. My father was a total bastard too!"

Lucifer held out his hand, and the air itself creaked and popped with cold. A lance of blue-white energy blasted out from his palm, wreathed in a shroud of ice crystals. When it struck, a radial blur of mist exploded from September's mum and dad.

As it cleared, she saw that they were frozen solid, trapped in a jagged pyramid of ice. A look of betrayal and hurt was still on both of their faces. That, thought September later, was the worst part of it all.

In the moment, though, there was nothing but rage. In the moment, she remembered what her mother had said about this town being a trap, and what the fallen archangel had said about being afraid.

September turned, very slowly. The look on her face was the equivalent of several major wars, with a minor nuclear exchange for dessert.

"*Right*," she said.

"No!" shouted Cedric, chained to the throne.

"No!" shouted Miss Rummage, who had run forward to smash her fists against that steaming block of ice.

"No!" howled Arbourdale, who was trying to shake the Electric Virgil's lamp back to life.

"Non, ne le fais pas!" shouted the two Templar Brothers, who were facing the pews full of history's monsters, swords drawn.

It was too late for advice. Good or otherwise.

September took off from a standing start, ran up the two steps to the altar, then up onto that big slab of black stone, pulling back one fist as spiky, jangling darkness exploded around it. She may have been screaming as she leaped from between the two great gold candlesticks, kicking off with one boot squarely and sacrilegiously in the middle of Cardinal Syn's bible.

If she was, she couldn't hear it over the chainsaw sound of the Endarkenment pulling cause and effect apart at some sub-atomic level, ready to make whatever her knuckles connected with cease to have ever existed. A massive, shredding heavy-metal riff unfurled in her head, and echoes of it bounced around the pillars of the dark cathedral.

There was no way that Lucifer could block her, or withstand that blow. All the momentum of both fiction and reality was behind it.

So he didn't.

Just before September swung her fist in an apocalyptic haymaker, aimed right at his jaw, the Fallen One unleashed a minor cantrip – and banished her.

The world went into a flat spin. But it wasn't a blur of black banners and stained glass and flames. It was grass and water and sky, tumbled over each other, with a terrible sense that the grass (and mud with it) were coming closer...

September hit the soccer pitch behind Saint Pewtred's

Academy at a dangerous velocity, and only the spitting, arcing fire of the Endarkenment stopped her from being smashed to ruin. As it was, she dug a trench in the midfield which would give Groundskeeper Hackforth quite a headache. Mud and smoking divots of sod rained down, as she lay there considering, for a moment, how it would make a very comfy grave, if she just decided not to move.

But there were questions to be answered. And parents to save as well. And more than anything else there was a horrible suspicion, just beginning to open black petals in the recesses of her mind, that all of this had been some kind of setup.

"*Right*," she said, again, to someone who could hear her, even in the privacy of her thoughts. "It's time you told me exactly what you had planned. And then we'll see if we can salvage any of it, at all. And perhaps the world, too."

In a tremulous voice, something answered.

Last Suture
Bad Morals

SUSPICION IS A terrible thing.

It's a worm which devours itself, once it's finished chewing through the certainties of the mind. It's the borer in the antique furniture of trust, turning relationships to damp and fungal rot.

It's also a perfectly natural response, when you've decided to partner up with the most devious bastard ever kicked out of reality for bad behaviour.

Charon – AKA Sharon Kolslaw, AKA the current de-facto boss of Uncarnadine's secret police – had let it get the better of her. She should have been in the Panopticon, with her hands on the levers, ready to shut off the Aught from the *Materia Mortalis* if something went wrong. Instead she'd watched on live television as her supposed partner orchestrated a wedding. During which there had been no mention *at all* of her glorious role in the new world order.

Suspicion is a terrible thing, but that ravenous grub of an emotion is nothing, when compared to the huge and squamous tarantula of jealousy. You see, Sharon Kolslaw quite fancied the new Devil which old Septivarian Archimedes had created, and she reckoned that she, with all of her evil experience, would make a much better witch-queen than September.

That's why she crept into the Red Cardinal's hidden secret sanctum right now, deep inside the Gravesend No Mercy Hospital. Betrayal!

And that's why she was unpleasantly surprised when the lights came on, and a voice purred, in a thick Spanish accent –

"Ahh, Miss Hospital Administrator Sharon, si? Are you,

perhaps, looking for these?"

Charon turned, claws out, just in time to watch the big padded-leather chair in the corner of the Cardinal's office spin dramatically. Seated there, and clutching a handful of manilla folders, was none other than Doctor Cliff Hunkstrong.

"You! Mortal! What are you doing here?"

It was meant to be a menacing hiss, but it came out... well, 'sultry' was the only world for it. Something about the good doctor was curdling the warp and weft of reality around him. Something which crackled and bipped like old VHS tape playback, and filled the room with unnatural heat.

Cliff laughed, and it was badly dubbed.

"I could ask you the same question, señorita. But perhaps you were interested in what our hospital's so-called benefactor has been up to, hmmm?"

He held out the top manilla folder. In big, printed letters, it read:

MY PLAN TO BETRAY
SHARON KOLSLAW

The ferryperson of the damned recoiled, putting her hand to what could only be called her décolletage. She was most disturbed to discover that after several thousand years of possessing an anatomy like a wind-blasted olive tree, right now she actually *had* a décolletage. And considerable cleavage. In fact, whatever charismatic magic Doctor Cliff Hunkstrong was radiating had warped her image completely.

"Surely not! Señor Cardinal is an honourable and sexy man!" she said, and then wondered why.

"Oho! Then what about *this?*" asked Cliff, flipping the next folder.

YES, I'M ABSOLUTELY GOING TO DOUBLECROSS THE HECK OUT OF SHARON KOLSLAW AND HERE'S HOW

Sharon tottered backwards on what were now four-inch stiletto heels. They matched the pencil skirt and low-cut suit jacket she was now wearing.

"*Madre de dios!* It cannot be! That sort of treachery is just not his torrid, passionate style!"

Yes it was! Howled a little voice in her head, jumping up and down. And *passionate? The Red Cardinal was about as sexy as a chainsaw lobotomy!*

Doctor Cliff looked grave, as he flipped the final folder.

HORRIBLE TREACHERY – IT'S MY TORRID, PASSIONATE STYLE,
By
CARDINAL LARRY SYN

"That's why I have come here, my dear," breathed Cliff, all husky and intense. He stood up, and Sharon noticed that the top buttons of his lab coat were open, exposing a swathe of hairy chest and a big gold medallion.

Ooooh err! Thought that little voice in Sharon's head, as big parts of her neural switchboard, unused for millennia, came clunking back online. *He looks almost as hunky as that new devil feller, and no mistake!*

She knew that it was wrong. She knew that something weird was happening – probably even something wyrd. But, even as the cynical, bitter part of the Dark Ferryperson realised that she was trapped inside a hackneyed Mexican telenovela, the part of her which used to be a river naiad, in those carefree days of ancient Greek mythology, decided to go with it. It had been a very long time since she looked *this* good, after all.

"Then let us escape, back to the living world. Together! That crooked old bastard Syn has a Reject Chute right here in his office, that goes direct through the realm of Ammut. That's our way out, and he'll never know."

Cliff swept her up into his arms, his hair blowing back from his face in an invisible breeze.

"Wait a minute. Isn't that, like, some kind of huge soul-eating monster? I remember hearing about it in school once. Egyptian thing, like a big taxidermy accident at the zoo?"

Sharon laughed, the carefree laugh of syndicated televised love. She reached out for the hidden button which would open the hatch below them – the one Syn had used to get rid of unwanted visitors.

"Yes, but it's gone, see? That wretched brat September Normalsson managed to vanish it somehow. I tied to feed her to it, you know."

Doctor Cliff laughed too, his teeth gleaming in invisible stage lights.

"Ha! I tried to kill her once, as well. We should look her up, once we reach reality."

"I don't think so," said Sharon. "I've managed to embezzle quite a lot of money from this Gravesend scam. We'll be on the beach in Barbados with bucket-sized cocktails before you can say 'no comeuppance!'"

The button clicked. The floor swung open.

And Ammut, Devourer of souls, who had just pulled herself together after the kicking Anubis had given her, was delightfully surprised to see two very tasty treats come dropping in from above.

Snap.

Snap.

Gulp.

Belch!

Oh dear.

Me temo que nuestro programa de televisión está experimentando dificultades técnicas...

Marjorie Goosegarden was having a very bad day, deep beneath Whitehall in the darkened, wood-panelled cloisters of the Void Chamber.

"You've lost control of the situation!" raged the Supreme Aaron, slamming his greasy fists down on the table. "My masters absolutely forbid this kind of nonsense! Lucifer is a Type-One Infernal Deity, of a kind we were assured was gone for good. Now there's people out there *believing in him!* They're supposed to believe in booze and football and bad politics, not fallen angels! We had *assurances,* dammit!"

The robotic Margaret Thatcher's eyes twitched, as her withered old soul scrabbled against cold circuitry.

"I assure you, Mr Presley, the matter is in hand. There's been a slight deviation from our internal plans but this remains, at the heart of it, a human matter."

"Then you'd have no objection to a little diplomatic aid?" asked the huge and doughy creature. Nuclear fire boiled across its sunglasses as it sneered. "After all, we have a sizeable presence in the affected area. Are you *sure* this isn't the work of that troublesome professor of yours?"

This time, Mother Goose snarled. It was like the sound of rotary pencil sharpeners chewing up fingers.

"We reclaimed his body as soon as he died, you ungrateful sack of cholesterol! Cremated him! Soaked the ashes in lye, and then in acid! Entombed that mush in concrete! He's currently on the back of a lorry, waiting to be dumped in the North Sea. And your men – or whatever they are – can stand down too. I've heard about you flying over British airspace with a bloody nuke, you mad fat bastard, and *I'm not having it!*"

But *she* was having it. With a side of deep-dried mars bars.

Because one thing which the Supreme Aaron of the Dead Elvi had learned from humans, early on, was how to lie. More recently, he'd learned that Marjorie Goosegarden had betrayed her own government, his masters, and himself with blithe abandon.

So, no sooner had he sweated and fibbed his way out of the Void Chamber than he was on his two-way communicator watch to Long-Lost Vegas, summoning up an army of Elvis impersonators such as the world had never seen.

Them, and the shoggoths, and the creeping claws, and the abyss spawn. The Black Goliaths, and the blank-heads, and the sizzling clouds with teeth. Even... yes, (whisper it) even *Francis the Duck!*[38]

Sometimes you had to burn a world to radioactive cinders to save it, after all. Sometimes, thought the Supreme Aaron, you got to have fun while doing it.

Other times, you caught a glimpse of what that bloody duck did to people's insides, and you had to have a bit of a lie down, afterwards.

In a cell, in a trailer, in police custody, Vlad Dracula sat and felt sorry for himself.

He did so with the darkling angst which only a Victorian gothic novel character could muster; you could just about hear the choir and harpsichords if you leaned in close enough.

Nobody did, of course.

Dracula was banged up in the Bureau Innominandum's ironclad portable nick, specially designed to hold the worst

---

38. Look, you don't want to know about Francis the Duck, all right? You just don't.

kind of supernatural offenders. It had been put together by Silas Rosewood, who knew a thing or two about these matters.

"Failed!" groaned the Father of Vampires. "Oh, woe and worry! Horrible ennui, and that feeling you get when you stand in front of the open fridge at two AM for no apparent reason!"

Deep in his despair, a voice answered him.

"'Ere! Is that you, Count Drac?"

It was a nasty-sounding cockney voice, raspy enough to tickle the eardrums of anybody listening. The kind of voice which oozes villainy; or perhaps just respiratory illness.

"Come on! I'm 'ere to get you outta here! Cor blimey, I'm yer biggest fan, and all! You can call me Jack."

Dracula sat up against the wall as the door swung open. He'd been down in the dumps and no mistake. Deflated, certainly. But the scent which now filled his oh-so-sensitive vampire nostrils was one that sent sparks sizzling through his brain.

Raw, undiluted belief. Jack the Ripper blazed with it, like a horrible broken-nosed little cockney pulsar.

"Come on, guv! They can't keep you down! Not you! Not the scourge of Carpathia! Why, I took such inspiration from you, sir! I based my great work very much on your own, and so when the Cardinal hung me out to dry, I thought..."

Dracula's fist entered Jack's ribcage right over his heart, and burst through his back in a spray of shattered ribs and gore. In that horrible instant, as the Whitechapel murderer's face became a mask of confused horror, he slid forward down the vampire's arm, gurgling. When Vlad spoke, his outrageous accent was gone, replaced with a tone like carbon-steel wire.

"We are nowhere *near* alike, you petty little butcher," he

snarled. "Mutilating a few innocent women doesn't make you anything but a monster. So you can go back to the Aught, and tell the cardinal that if he wants Hell on Earth, he's got it. I'm going to ruin his day, call-me-Jack. A world full of humans is my hunting ground. A world ruled by demons makes me rather obsolete, hmmm? And slightly peckish, too."

He let the corpse fall. He took a bite out of Jack's heart, like munching on an apple. He felt, for the first time in a long time, quite ready to ride into battle like the knight he once was.

A police horse, cropping the grass outside, caught his eye and remembered, from somewhere in its horsey DNA, the rumble of cavalry charges. It snorted.

"Exactly," said the vampire.

It was time to fight back.

The forecast for Hell included snow, sleet, hail, and slush, not to mention the kind of absolute, bollock-numbing cold which goes with them. While flames raged and brimstone bubbled high up among the other circantrates of Dante's pit, its heart was a sheet of grey-green ice kilometres thick, blasted by dire supernatural winds.

At its very centre, a great jagged fissure split the crust, its edges toothed with wicked spikes of ice. Here, something immense had hauled itself free, shattering the glassy surface. Here, like the world's most unfortunate bus-stop commuter, a tiny figure sat on a mound of snow, and waved a mobile phone in the air.

At some point, it appeared that the figure had built a snowman, then kicked its head in.

The phone was one of the big, plastic, bricky jobs you got in the 1990s; the kind that you could famously use to concuss the paparazzi, with a green and black screen and a set of big rubber keys. This was not the odd part about the phone. Neither was the fact that, in this snowy hellscape, it was registering no bars at all. The futile waving of the primitive mobile, in a motion like that of a very useless druid attempting to pop off a weather spell, was accepted practice for the era.

What was odd was this. The phone was plugged in, via a little black cord, to a hole in the sad and tragic figure's wrist, just below the rolled-up sleeve of a red cassock.

In a fit of piqued desperation, the man in red jumped up and down on top of the ruined snowman, and extended his arm as high as it would reach. The screen of his phone flashed green, and a chorus of discordant beeps rang out. For perhaps the first and only time, someone danced a triumphant little jig on the blasted ice of Cocytus.

A short, terse conversation followed. There was a lot of shouting. There was a little bit of shameless wheedling. There was a very large amount of money mentioned.

Presently, the figure in red unplugged his phone, tucked it away beneath his robes, and got to work.

Any of the demons which Lucifer had left behind here, pending his imminent conquest of the Earth, would have seen a curious sight if they'd looked down where their master used to be frozen. Cardinal Syn spent the next half-hour building a monolith of snow, packing it into bricks and stacking them up as if he was building the most ambitious igloo ever, and starting with the front door.

When he was done he stood back, slapped the ice crystals from off of his fingers, and drew a knob on it with one finger. Because that's exactly what it was.

The light dimmed. The rattle of chains of paper clips haunted the very edges of reality. A bright, merciless light burst out around the outlines of the door, like the hard white radiance under the lid of a photocopier.

And with a grinding sound, as of several tons of granite, the door opened. The Sybarites of the Order of the Papercut had arrived.

"Hello, *Ralph*," said the Cardinal, as a grim figure in a long black leather coat approached across the ice, his face studded with memo spikes.

"Hello, *your eminence*," sighed Ralph. "Couldn't find anyone else sort of Hell-adjacent to come and pick you up? The bloke with the knives for fingers and the awful sweater washing his hair, was he?"

Cardinal Syn shrugged.

"I always choose the best, old son. Oh my, yes! After all, you've got a handle on the situation out there. I know you never wanted to be part of my little enterprise, but a real devil, and a real Hell? He might have a bee in his bonnet about lads like you, from a fictional one. Might think you was taking the piss all these years, sort of thing. Then there's the money, of course."

Ralph, the Grim Harbinger of Workplace Injury, gave a prissy little sniff.

"In a very real way, he's as fictional as we are. Bloody prejudice, if you ask me."

Syn nodded.

"And us boys from the Aught have to stick together, eh? Can't have the big religions muscling in on our space in the human subconscious, can we? So, shall we cut to the bit where you get me out of here?"

The gathering of Sybarites looked at each other, and nodded. Ralph sighed.

"You *do* have a plan to fix this mess, don't you?" he asked.

Syn's wide and artificial smile may have been, for just an instant, the most horrible thing in Hell.

"I know where there's a very official scythe going spare, that can kill anything it touches. Fancy dropping me off at the Chronauspexion? I'm late for a job interview."

They found Detective Inspector Rupert in a hedgerow, as the army rolled in to make a perimeter around Little-Mean-on-the-Average. In the bright dawn of a new and horrible day, the three towers which now crowned the town were far too real.

He was baboon-jugglingly mad – or at least, that's what the soldiers who found him thought.

But in the streets of Little Mean, every dark portent he gibbered was coming true.

Doorways had yawned open in the angles of shadows, and stained concrete had ground open along hidden fault-lines, allowing an army of Dead Elvi to step through, tooled up for war. They gathered near the site of the old hospital, bringing with them all the weaponry they could scour and steal from their own version of Long-Lost Vegas. This included a huge pink 1959 Cadillac Eldorado Biarritz, with its aircraft-carrier-sized boot lid torn away and replaced with a trio of nuclear warheads. Poured into in a throne where the back seat of the Caddy should be, the Supreme Aaron marshalled his forces, decked out in a super-sized jumpsuit sparkling with rhinestones and lit up with glowing neon in baby blue.

Another army gathered in the shadow of the Tower of Sheol, on Monkston's Green.

They were a rag-tag bunch, made up of denizens of the Aught who could see which way the wind was blowing, the possessed, the mad, and no small number of people who had stayed behind when Little Mean was being evacuated. They rallied to a banner made from a bedsheet, spray-painted with a black dragon. Mounted-police horses, dirt bikes and foot-soldiers milled, in a motley assortment of medieval armour, sporting pads, crash helmets, hard-hats and Halloween costumes.

Holding up that banner was a man in red-lacquered plate mail, riding a black stallion. In this moment, from this distance, it was hard to make out his expression, as a little group of three motorcycles idled through the crowd to approach him. But one could imagine it was a wry little smile.

"You brought Templars," said Vlad Tepes, the warlord of Transylvania, addressing Miss Rummage. "Excellent!"

While at last, inside the cathedral of darkness, from his throne of agony, where two terror-struck humans knelt, chained, Lucifer addressed his congregation.

"So, you wanted to take over the world, did you? You wanted power, and horror, and dominion?"

The assembled monsters of history, Syn's murderers and madmen, mumbled their agreement. Lucifer stood from his throne, his half-burned face contorted into a rictus of fervour.

"I can't hear you!"

He levelled one black fingernail at a small Klansman, evaporating him with a brief and horrible shriek.

This time the response was louder.

"YES, LORD!"

"Well then! That's all right, isn't it?"

Lucifer spread his arms wide, and his wings, too. One was a glossy fan of dark feathers, shimmering with green and purple. The other was a blasted stump, complete with a shattered nub of bone.

"Let me show you some *real* demons, then! Let me show you how Armageddon begins! And with my Father as silent as always, the only one who will hear the prayers of a tortured world... will be ME!"

PART FOUR

THE BOOK OF RENOVATIONS

"Each had four faces, and each of them had four wings; the legs of each were fused into a single rigid leg, and the feet of each were like a single calf's hoof; and their sparkle was like the lustre of burnished bronze."
— Ezekiel, describing the Cherubim

"The CB-81 tactical air-to-surface nuclear munition features a quad-core visual and satellite telemetry tracking system, four steering vanes, and a single solid-fuel rocket booster, all finished with an easy-to-clean metallised low-drag coating."
— Sales brochure from Aegis Arms International

"Jacob! Jacob, call the bloody city watch! That loony bastard neighbour of ours won't shut up, it's three in the morning, and he's been at the funny mushrooms again!"
— Sarah, wife of Jacob the Corinthian,
Neighbour of Ezekiel

Nineteen
The Endarkenment
vs
The Lightbringer

IN A HOLE in the ground, in the clammy embrace of several metres of good, stolid English football-field mud, September Normalsson was talking to herself.

Usually, this was just a convenient way for her to have an intelligent conversation. Something along the lines of:

Hey there September! How's it going? Not being able to relate to any of the people around you really hitting the spot today? How's that sense of isolation coming along? Is it turning into narcissism and delusions of grandeur, do you think, or just making us into a curmudgeon well ahead of your time? Tell us – when we inevitably become a crazy old lady, what are we going to call all of our seventy-three cats?

'Intelligent' was not the same as 'cheerful', when it came to internal conversations. But then again, it rarely is.

This time, however, September wasn't checking in on herself. In fact, she hoped that she was just being paranoid. But of course, she knew that she wasn't.

"Great-great-granddad? Septivarian? Professor Archimedes? I know you're in there. Now, are you going to tell me what your mad, convoluted plan was all along? Or are you not quite the supervillain I thought you were?"

Silence unfolded inside her head like a cold and fragile origami sculpture, as she stared up at the pale belly of the morning clouds. But only for a few heartbeats. And then a pair of cherry-red Doc Martens boots clumped down on the side of the hole, one of them held together with electrical tape. They were September's... but they were several sizes too big.

She didn't move her head, or even her eyes, but she twisted her vision around nonetheless, to take in long black-and-white striped socks and knobbly old-man knees. Then the hem of a tartan school uniform skirt, a big, shapeless cardigan all patched up with leopard print and heavy metal band logos...

And her great-great-grandfather, not at all either ashamed or surprised to be dressed as a schoolgirl. Not after the weird supervillain costumes he'd rocked in the sixties. He was contemplatively smoking a pipe, and gazing out over the sports fields toward the little river Average.

"You know," he said wistfully, as a little curlicue of smoke trickled out of his nose. "I was almost certain that we'd have to have this conversation, but not exactly in these circumstances."

"You didn't foresee the real devil crashing your party?" asked September.

"Oh no. That kind of thing is right on the edge of the probability curve, which means that it's not uncommon at all for a place like this. No. I meant *inside your head* and all. I thought things would have gone slightly differently. Variables and such."

September realised that there was something a little different about Septivarian, now that he was a phantom co-habiting her brain. His voice seemed more steady; sharper and colder. He'd lost the little mumbles and tics which come from operating on mental hardware that's the same vintage as a steam locomotive. She wasn't sure if this was a good thing or a bad one.

"But you did predict *this*," she said. "And you planned for it. Possessing me, that is. That's the sort of thing you really should have asked permission for, granddad."

The slightly puzzled look he gave her revealed not that

he was a rude, ill-mannered person, but that he'd *never even considered* whether or not it was polite to take up residence in someone's skull.

"I couldn't, dear. Because it wasn't you I was aiming for. It was Dark Lazarus. All that power and all that potential, in a naive mortal vessel? Under the command of the Bureau Innominandum, and their American chums? Not after what they threatened me with. Oh no."

There was steel behind his words, of a kind which September had never known. This was the voice of the world's smartest supervillain, not her eccentric old great-great-granddad.

"So all of it – all the weirdness, everything I've gone through, all the Endarkenment, all those little bits of revelation and insight, was just *you*? It wasn't even me at all?"

This time, Septivarian's smile was more genuine. Even a little bit proud.

"Heavens no, girl. I might have made some memories available, temporarily, but you did all the rest. We're quite alike, you and I."

September had gotten up a good momentum of being angry, though, and she wasn't about to waste it.

"Still! You *possessed* me! You fed me Repo! Which *you* invented, by the way! I've been trying to tell mum and dad for years that you weren't actually villainous, and then, then... you do something like this! Experimenting on your own family!"

Septivarian puffed out a little mushroom cloud of pipe-smoke, and his eyebrows crinkled.

"Not *experimenting*. No! I knew the possible outcomes. Nobody knew them better. It was the Bureau who brought my family into this, when they thought they had leverage. They weren't going to let your mother and father alone.

They strong-armed me into creating a perfect, tractable new devil. And they expected me not to use him? They expected there'd be no come-uppance?"

September propped herself up on her elbows, in the mud.

"How about you, granddad? Did *you* think there wouldn't be any? Did you think I wouldn't work it out, eventually? And how did you plan to get from my head to Dark Lazarus' body, anyhow?" A horrible suspicion exploded inside her head, like a black firework. "Oh *god*, granddad, you didn't think that we were going to... I mean, he was good-looking and all, but... and with you watching! Urgh!"

In all her eighteen years, she'd never seen Septivarian look embarrassed. But he did now. A blush – an honest-to-goodness crimson blush – advanced across his wrinkly cheeks.

"Well, erm, now, of course, there'd be no need for, ummm, with the probability vector transpositioning, and the narrative imperative state-changes, and... errrr. A kiss would have sufficed. But you couldn't know I was in here. He was built as the lord of lies, you see, and he would have scented out duplicity. We'd have been finished."

September thought back to the golden, hazy aura which had surrounded the new devil, and how something had urged her toward kissing him. It was bad enough when she had to work out if it was a good idea at the time, without factoring in the invisible urging of her disembodied great-great-grandfather.

"So that was your big plan? The silly, soppy girl can't help herself, and she kisses the rakishly handsome devil, and then... urrgh! Then, he becomes *you*? What happens to the person who picked up the card? Are they just so much meat and gristle, then?"

"Sacrifices always have to be made, for progress," said Septivarian. If September had thought he sounded cold before, now his words hissed with liquid nitrogen. "Have you any idea how wicked the Bureau really is? What they and their corporate masters had planned? I didn't beat the Nazis to usher in a new batch with less stylish uniforms. Whoever you chose to become Dark Lazarus was gone, in any case, as soon as he took up the tarot."

She thought of Cedric Welbourne, then, and how he'd broken free. Sure, it might have doomed the entire world – but he'd done it for love.

Hah! snided her extra thoughts. *Did thinking that was somehow noble make her just as soppy and silly as him?*

"Sacrifices have to be made? How can you talk about beating Nazis when you've got lines like that, granddad? Worse – this was a *stupid* plan. We're both smart people, even if you think I'm only useful as a swooning romance heroine. I can see that this scheme had too many holes in it, and it reeks of desperation. And if I can, you can. After all, you're freeloading in my brain! So, why did you *really* do it?"

Septivarian drew himself up, mustering his arguments, marshalling his reasons. She could see them slotting into place, like bullets into a magazine. But then his shoulders sagged, and his imagined face suddenly looked very, very old indeed.

"I was afraid," he whispered, in a smoky breath. "I faced the end, the very end, and beyond it *I didn't know what was going to happen.*" He took another drag on his pipe, found that it had gone out, and threw it back over his shoulder, where it vanished with a pop of sparks.

"I knew I was dying. I'd built the Doom Clock. And I knew about the Aught, but I knew it was an illusion. The collective subconscious of the species, made real. You've been to Uncarnadine, and it's just how we imagine death might be, those of us who don't cleave to any of the great religious stories. The Aught is an echo chamber. You only last *there*, so long as people remember you over *here*."

"What you are, there, is the collection of reflections left lodged in people's heads. The little bits of yourself you leave behind, every time you make an impression on a life. If you're just the ghost in the machine of your brain, imagine what the *images of you in everyone else's brains* can do, right? They can keep you alive, after a fashion. Until you fade, and hollow, and wisp away. Until even the people over there find a mythic excuse to send you on, into the deeper dark. Beyond which... who knows?" He spread his hands, in a little puffing, exploding gesture.

"I didn't. So I was afraid to die. I told them I was going to some scientific Olympus. But I wasn't sure at all. And... I made a plan."

September searched his face for the little tic of duplicity she was sure should be there. But it wasn't. There were no wheels within turning wheels inside Septivarian Archimedes' imagined eyes. Just a terrible, primal dread, of the kind that had lurked at the back of the earliest caves, waiting to mug the first upright ape who could imagine a future without them in it.

And, just like that, her anger fractured and fell away.

OK. He'd technically been trespassing in her mind, and he'd gotten her involved in a hugely dangerous adventure, and now the world was teetering on the brink of ruin. But... well, *was that really worse than being boring?*

Wasn't this what she'd often daydreamed about, while curling a strand of her hair around a pencil and studiously ignoring her maths textbook?

Wasn't this the kind of thing she wanted to do, and why her parents had tried extra hard to make her life as bland as a no-name breakfast cereal? But –

"Really? A *kiss?* You couldn't come up with something less... well, less stupid, and a bit less creepy, could you?"

She said it with a little quirk of a smile. The mordant look on Septivarian's face crinkled around the edges as his eyes sparkled.

"I thought it was very romantic. Kind of sweet, even. But then again, I'm from a different time."

"You're nearly as bad as that Count Dracula. He thought that being a total sleaze was romantic, too."

"I'm about the same age, young lady. And I... I do get a bit set in my ways. Convoluted plots, and all. See, the thing about dealing with the Aught is that it's made of human ideas. And human ideas, when you boil them right down to the gritty stuff, are just stories. There's a powerful urge to follow along the lines."

"Speaking of stories," said September, climbing up out of the mud, like a cartoon of evolution. "Was any of it true? Your wild ideas, and the curse, and all that? Or did you really choose me just because I look like the kind of person who'd find Dark Lazarus irresistible?"

The old professor nodded.

"Mostly true. There's no curse, of course. It's just that when you meddle with causality, things try to tap the flow of probability back into line. But the rest – well, I knew about the Cardinal, and I suspected where he'd come from. I knew about the Bureau, and the Elvi, and what they wanted from me. But as for why I picked you, well... it was because of things like *this.*"

Septivarian was probably only a figment of September's imagination, at this point. But he was the kind of imagination that she'd seen break out of the Aught and run rampant through reality. So it didn't surprise her at all when he held out his hand, with Frankenfrog nestled in his palm.

"Ribbit," said the tiny creature, looking upon its maker with religious awe. It was a pair of syllables which summed up so much.

"You've got that spark that I had, at your age. Not like your granny, or your mother, bless them – they always wanted to use it to be something shiny and famous and memorable. You just want to create things, for the sheer sake of seeing if you can. You think the rules were made to protect stupid people, so you ignore them, 'coz you aren't one. And that means you know what we have to do next."

And on closer introspection, she found she did.

It was that talk of stories which did it. Lucifer, the Lightbringer, the Fallen One, was just a very old story. A very powerful one, steeped in centuries of credulity and superstition, but as much a thing of the Aught as Tommy the Train or Jolly Dormouse Jim. Dante had trapped him with fiction, and the Templars wanted to hit him with big swords. But these days, people had different ideas about how you were meant to fight supernatural monsters...

"I don't think this ends with you possessing Dark Lazarus, Grandad," she said, tentatively edging out onto the surface of the idea. 'It might, in fact, end up with both of us blown to tiny little sub-atomic particles."

"But we'd save the world, wouldn't we? What my old chum Stoatman would call a big redemption arc, is it?"

"Could be," said September, holding out her hand. Frankenfrog hopped over, and rubbed the shiny top of his head against the heel of her thumb. "I know what we need to build. But we don't have enough time, is all."

Septivarian stood, smoothing down his tartan skirt and holding out a hand to help her up.

"*Time?* Is that all? Hah! I know a place where time isn't an issue, young lady. And if I do, so do you. We've got a high-powered biological capacitor, there in your hand, so all we'll need to get there is a certain kind of footwear. Right?"

And there it was. The last little piece of the idea slotted into place, and the cams and pistons and gears began to mesh and twinkle. September gave her great-great-granddad's hand a little squeeze.

"This has been a strange couple of days. But for what it's worth, I'm glad we had them together. Most people, you know. When someone they love dies, it's just..."

There couldn't possibly have been a little tear in his eye. Not the eye of the Befuddler, Quizmaster of chaos. Not in the eye of professor Archimedes, the super-genius who ran on pure logic, and bent the world around his brain.

But, just a small one, wiped away from the crinkly, 137-year-old cheek of September's granddad?

Perhaps.

"And for what it's worth, I'm sorry," he said. "I was a frightened old fool. I should have trusted you. Because I can see a bit of the future, girl, and you're it."

She grinned. The Endarkenment flared all around her, spreading to outline Septivarian's ghost.

"Not if we don't kick some fallen archangel arse! So, shall we?"

Septivarian snapped his fingers. His black mortarboard appeared in them, and he settled it atop the bald spot on his head. Then he threw September a crisp little salute, and clicked his heels together.

"Permission to come aboard, ma'am? I mean, back inside your brain, and all that?"

"Come and get a load of this plan," said September, as he faded, with an electric pop and crackle. "Notes appreciated. After all, this is my first time saving the world."

She stood up, stretching the kink out of her neck where

she'd hit the ground, and tilted her head to one side, listening to a suggestion from the elderly passenger in her brain.

"You're right. *Exactly* like we've been dragged through a hedge backwards. I reckon I know where to get a new costume, though. And then, to work."

As September walked into the school, the intelligent micro-fibres of her lab coat twisted, shucking off all the dirt and stains she'd picked up along the way. The hallways were cold and empty, all linoleum clatter and oak-panel gloom. But it wasn't far to the gymnasium, and to her locker there, where she kept the fitted white trousers and jacket of her fencing kit. The big, blank-faced mask wasn't needed, and in any case, a helmet would be no protection if her plan went wrong.

Saving the world was a bit like skydiving, in that respect.

"Is there any chance you can sort of turn around, in there?" she asked Septivarian. "I really do need to sort out a new body for you. Having to close my own eyes whenever I get changed is rather inconvenient."

As it turned out, he whistled an old 1920s vaudeville tune while she took care of her wardrobe. It looked like her school uniform had seen better days, and might have to be relegated to the compost heap. But the white, slightly padded fencing uniform was made for fighting in, and it thankfully came packaged with a freshly laundered set of athletic underwear. Certain small luxuries, she thought, made all this supernatural warfare stuff slightly bearable.

She checked in the mirror. And found that the overall effect was good.

White padded armour from neck to ankles, with the long, crisp sweep of the lab coat thrown rakishly over the top. A wild mane of coppery curls, scrawled in like cartoon fire, and twitching with the black outline of the Endarkenment. There were little round sunglasses, of the kind she associated with Ozzy Osbourne rather than John Lennon in the top pocket of the coat, of course. And for her hands, a pair of race-car mechanic's gloves; her feet were ready for war in her cherry-red docs.

Not so much gangly and awkward, she thought. *A bit more sharp and vicious*. It wasn't a bad change.

September briefly considered borrowing one of the school's ornamental pair of Napoleonic cavalry sabres, but reasoned that if you could beat Lucifer with a piece of metal, Brother Jacques would have done so centuries ago.

"You can open your eyes, now, umm... or whatever you have in there," she said. Septivarian made a small harrumph of approval, and she felt a little glow of pride radiating from somewhere just behind her right ear.

"One last thing, I think," said the voice of Septivarian.. "One which you are *more* than entitled to."

The Endarkenment sparked, and an outline began to grow across the chest of September's fencing doublet, little black lines sizzling into the white polyester. In the mirror, she saw it take shape – a big black question mark, with the dot below it shaped like a skull.

After that, It wasn't hard to find an Elvis.

One of them was smoking a cigarette in headmaster Mackleduff's office, his blue suede feet up on the desk, and a huge double-barrelled shotgun beside them. Two tied-up policemen were lashed to the headmaster's big wing-backed chairs, gagged and sullen.

The Elvis was on the phone when September peered through the little glass window set high in the door, and he didn't put it down when she entered. Instead, his ghastly face split into a too-wide grin.

"You all ain't never gonna believe what just mosey'd on

in here!" said the creature, to whatever was on the other end of the line. "Cancel the search parties, good buddy! We just scored ourselves some pretty young *leverage!*"

That was all that Mr Presley got so say, however. September was in no mood for mercy, and she knew it would be wasted on the spawn of the outer dark.

She crooked a finger, and Mr Mackleduff's desktop printer squirted a thick jet of black ink into the Elvis' eyes. She sliced her palm across, and the light fitting above him unreeled on its cable, smashing down to crown him with a tinkle of broken glass. September clenched her fist, and the Endarkenment sparked through the walls in an inverse strobe-flash, following circuits and wires. Then the big art-deco glass bulb stuck over the Elvis' head lit up from within, crackling and popping. A nasty sizzling sound and a rising scream were cut off by a final pop, and the inside of the light fitting was painted tarry black.

The two tied-up policemen looked at each other, and then at this apparition in white, her face haloed by coils of copper hair. There appeared to be a tiny frog sitting on one of her shoulders.

They both started trying to beg for mercy through their gags at once, bouncing up and down in their seats.

But September wasn't there for them. Once again, she tilted her head to one side, listening to the voice of her disembodied guest.

"And it doesn't matter that they won't fit? Allright. Here we go, I guess."

"Ywhhhh cmmmmh to stehhhhhr hsss *shuuuuuuuhs?*" asked one of the policemen, through his gag.

"Not just any shoes. Blue suede ones. He's got a whole song about not touching them, which was a bit of a clue."

September's hands were already moving, little traceries of Endarkenment unreeling from her fingertips to penetrate the telephone, the printer, and the school's ancient, beige plastic computer terminal (forged by elder nerds in a factory in Luton, with all the processing power of a twin-tub washing machine).

Bolts and screws all came loose at once, with a tinny little shriek. Then parts were airborne, and wires plaited together as September's fingers twitched, while motherboards and microchips were dipped quite deliberately in the ooze which was the late, unlamented Elvis.

The policemen watched, wide eyed. Everything came together at once, with a brief flash of ozone and sparks, and what remained was a mis-shapen plastic box, made from the computer's power supply. Two wires stretched from it to the dead creature's footwear, and two more dangled open-ended. Little LEDs flickered inside the box, and black goo bubbled.

"Now it's your turn," said September, holding out her hand to let a tiny green-and-orange frog hop aboard. "Yes, of *course* we're sure this is going to work," she said, to nobody apparent. "You helped with the maths, didn't you? And you're supposed to be a super-genius, right? So, all we need is a big, gnarly bio-capacitor, and a huge charge of electricity. Well, here's one I prepared earlier. Stanley?"

The frog looked up at her. It nodded. It *saluted*, which made both policemen gibber a little.

"Well, I think he looks like a Stanley. Don't you? Here, we'd better make sure we're inside the conversion radius. It looks like we're about to find out..."

Stanley the frog – who was in a state of religious rapture, having just received a Holy Name form his creator – had built up a massive charge of electricity during his short new life. He wrapped his tiny hands around the electrodes September had conveniently provided. Enough voltage to microwave an elephant went coursing through the box of arcane science she'd created, emulating the complex harmonic vibrations which the Dead Elvi used as a kind of fingerprint. Then into the blue suede shoes, which flashed actinic white.

A sphere expanded from the alien footwear. Everything inside it was cast as a stark black shadow, and then those shadows peeled away at the edges, and collapsed inward like a wave of midnight...

The two policemen blinked purple spots from their eyes, in the thunderclap aftermath. What they saw, when the smoke began to clear, was a perfectly circular bite taken out of Mister Mackleduff's desk, with a corresponding curved edge slicing through the filing cabinets behind it. There was a dished indentation in the floor below, and another in the ceiling above, and a perfect little segment had been razored away from the headmaster's aquarium, spilling indignant goldfish and greenish water out across the carpet.

Of September Normalsson, the Dead Elvis, its shoes, or the tiny frog, there was no trace. Just a small gold disc, spinning to a stop on what was left of the desk...

This was the emptiness of Long-lost Vegas.

This was the silent heat of its desert sky; cooked and bleached and shimmering over acres of tarmac and concrete.

This was the sound of oblivion.

It was a profound, sucking void which scrabbled at the eardrums, and it made September twitchy, like the prickle of far-off lightning. The sound of a single drop of sweat rolling down the slope of her shoulder seemed deafening, and the air tasted wrong.

Nothing lived here. Not even bacteria. Life had been severed from this place, as surely as if the Norns, or their

Greek counterparts, had picked up their massive chrome scissors and made a single fatal snip, on a city-sized scale. The baking-hot streets were empty, and the mirror-glass fronts of the casinos reflected each other, like an immense haunted circus funhouse.

It was what was up above, though, that was truly scary.

"Are you *absolutely* sure that it's stuck like that?" asked September, risking another glance up at the sky.

"There's no real time here, girl," said Septivarian, inside her head. "It's fine. That's why we had to leave certain things behind. The Elvi can't come straight from their master's domain to Earth; the stuff they're made of makes no sense to physics. So they found a place that was already doomed. Nothing anyone or any*thing* does here matters, because they made their little universe the exact size of the blast radius."

There were two suns in the sky. The first was familiar; a desert scorcher of a thing, but the same one which Jolly Dormouse Jim would have drawn a big smiley face on. September did not like to think about the cartoon face which the other sun would wear. It was a fist of seething light, misshapen and crackling with lashes and tendrils of energy. It was the unfolding of a terrible, erasing explosion, from the core of a missile that could still be seen sketched out behind it, cast in utterly black shadow.

"A Comrade-Stalin-Class thermonuclear warhead," sniffed Septivarian, inside her mind. "The biggest bomb the Soviets had. Every major city in the US got one. Of course, we don't know what they did to tick them off, but this *was* during the Nixon administration, so all bets are very much valid."

"So, no time's passing at all, outside? How do you explain that, anyway?"

Frantic shushing noises came from the disembodied old

scientist.

"You *don't!* Thinking about it is one thing you definitely *shouldn't* do! We're not meant to be here, because we're not nasty undead Elvises from another reality. Suffice to say that once we're done, we'll pop back just where we left off. Until then, you better know how to steal a car, missy!"

September didn't have to, because almost every car parked in the middle of the Strip had its keys in the ignition. The hard part was choosing the nicest one, and in the end, September settled for a cherry-red boat-tail Corvette Stingray that matched her boots.

"You know where we're headed, then?" she asked. Septivarian nodded, which felt more than a little bit strange. He knew.

The 'vette's angry growl echoed off the buildings as they clipped along the shoulder of the highway, headed out toward Nellis Air Force Base. It was still well within the lethal blast of the big nuke, despite being more than thirty kilometres distant. Along the way, Septivarian gave September a few driving tips, some of them rather urgently, and explained what they were going to do. It would take what *felt* like time, he explained, as they stopped off at the base commissary to stock up on cans and bottles and eerily well-preserved American snacks from the 1970s.

It would be an act of super-science impossible without the Endarkenment, he professed, as they traded in the Stingray for a big flat-deck Dodge truck, and piled welders and gas bottles and wrenches and batteries on board.

It was their best and only chance of taking on Lucifer, the fallen angel, because of what people believed, and what they expected. That's what September told him, as they raided the deserted warehouses of the 57 Munitions Squadron, forklifting missiles and automatic cannons and belts of bullets onto the truck.

Then he showed her the secret hangar, with the trick floor, and the ramp leading down below. Then they came to the vaulted halls where the naughty US Government had kept a selection of what could only be called flying saucers, surrounded by gantries and lights and cranes.

"This is where we'll build it," said Septivarian – and together they rolled up September's sleeves and reached for a blowtorch...

One of the policemen tied up in Headmaster Mackleduff's office had managed to cut his way free of his bonds by rubbing the ropes up against the sharp edge of the ruined desk. Whatever had sliced away a big circle of the time-hardened timber had done so with atomic precision.

"Like the Terminator, innit?" he asked his colleague, after both of them had removed their gags and had a bit of a rattle through the headmaster's collection of vintage whiskeys. "You know, when he turns up all naked, in that big ball of lightning?"

"Yeah, I never got that, right? Coz, OK, so, inanimate objects like clothes and shoes and guns and such, they couldn't come through the time travel dealy. But, see, the Terminator was a robot. He's a machine, too. So how did that work?"

"Maybe it was nothing to do with science. Maybe the big fella was just a nudist."

"A nudist robot?"

The policeman nodded.

"Exactly. How many other famous cinematic robots wear clothes? Johnny Five didn't have any pants. Robocop, even, technically a cyborg, right, but still – starkers. Optimus prime didn't own so much as a pair of y-fronts. I'm telling you, robots are nudists."

His colleague was about to make a very smart and

incisive rebuttal then, but the nature of multidimensional travel gave him an example, instead.

It had been a very interesting three weeks for September in the empty, timeless heat of Long-Lost-Vegas. Every one of the Dead Elvi was over here, on Earth, with a plan to literally nuke the Devil. So, while twenty days had passed under Nellis AFB, only one hundred and eighty seconds had passed in Mister Mackleduff's office.

Three minutes. Three weeks.

It had been enough time to really get to grips with the Endarkenment.

A circle of blackness expanded out from exactly where September had vanished, but this time, it didn't stop growing. The two policemen scrabbled back out the door and clattered down the hallway, slipping and sliding on the linoleum, pursued by the ever-growing edge of an onyx bubble. The staff canteen was swallowed up, and the first-floor sick bay, and the administration office, and then the black meniscus stopped. The terrified faces of two of CID, Rupert's finest were reflected in it, as frost began to crawl across its surface.

Then it flashed white.

Just like that, a massive bite was taken out of the side of Saint Pewtred's Standard Academy for the Determinedly Unobtrusive. A thunderclap rattled the big gothic pile to its foundations, and every window in the building shattered.

What was left behind, in the space where all that 19th century masonry had been, was a figure crouched for a super-hero landing; one clenched fist against the bedrock, the other arm held across its chest. It was the classic pose of a certain time-travelling Austrian cyborg, but there the similarity ended. Well, *almost* there.

"You see!" gibbered one of the policemen, chewing on the rim of his helmet. "No pants! No paaaaants!"

Because it was a robot. A nude one, as most of them are, having nothing to hide under a pair of boxer shorts except perhaps a humorously welded-on exhaust pipe.

And this one was *huge*. Not the exhaust pipe, because September hadn't had time for visual gags. But the rest... ohhhh, yes.

The entire machine stood taller than the school as it unfolded, its immense armoured-helmet face overtopping the aerials and chimneys. September hadn't had a chance to paint it, either, so the whole thing was very clearly made from parts of US Army ordnance from the 1970s. Nellis AFB had no shortage of weapons, a whole fleet of aircraft, a few handy tanks, and of course, a massive secret underground hangar packed with different models of UFO.[39]

An immense arm unfolded, and two fingers the size of telephone booths precisely plucked something from off the ground where it had fallen; something which had been utterly unaffected by the teleportation bubble.

It was a little disc of gold; the one which September had left behind on the headmaster's desk.

Now her creation stood tall, and took a step forward. It didn't move with the ponderous tonnage it suggested. The machine was light on its feet, which had been crafted from the landing skids of a 1950s flying saucer. The plasma-fusion core which had powered that vessel glowed purple, inset deep in the robot's chest.

As the two policemen cowered back, away from the cut-off edge of the building, the robot spun around, and leaned down to fix them with an immense and empty stare. Its face was covered by a visor, in the style of a motorcycle helmet, and this cracked open with a hiss, releasing a puff of air-conditioned haze.

---

39. Allegedly.

Behind the visor, in the light of a panel of looted aircraft controls, sat the girl who'd barbecued that horrible Elvis Presley. The one wearing the long white coat, who'd talked to herself in a most unsettling way.

It turned out to be considerably more unsettling when she spoke to *them*.

"Call your commander, or commissioner, or whoever's in charge. Tell him that it's very, very important that you all run away, right now. Because if this goes wrong, the blast radius is going to span about thirty or forty kilometres, give or take. You got that?"

The two policemen nodded, dumbstruck. Then the visor of the giant robot slammed shut and it stood, fresh welds glinting in the morning sun. It turned toward the great arching tripod-leg of the Tower of Sheol, and it slammed one huge fist into one huge palm. Against their better judgement, both coppers grinned wildly. As September strode away, leaving lorry-sized footprints in the football field, they shared a high-five.

Inside the cockpit of the robot, there was no time left to think. Thinking would have led to worries, and there were plenty of those lined up and waiting. This thing she'd built, with Septivarian's advice, wasn't just her first giant war machine. It was her first go at military super-science in general. It had all seemed so natural, like remembering how to cook a favourite recipe.

Wrap in reinforced titanium, drizzle with alien deuterium-plasma technology, garnish with air-to-surface missiles, and bake until bloody terrifying...

She'd called it the Revenginator, a name that she'd spray-painted across its massive chest in purple. Now it lurched up to a run, as her great-great-granddad cackled madly in her head. Every super-villainous shred of her DNA urged her to join in.

"You're absolutely sure this is going to work?" she shouted, as the wall of the tower came rushing up toward them, a great shattered stained-glass window right in the middle.

"*Of course not!*" replied Septivarian. "*We've done all the science we can, girl, mad and otherwise. Now it's time to surf the edge of chaos! Now it's time for the one-liners, and the big punches, and the explosions! Wheee heee! I feel like I'm eighty-six again!*"

September's supernumerary thoughts shrugged. At this point, there was no turning back. And anyhow, three weeks in the timeless, boiled-dust prison of Long-Lost Vegas had been enough time for her to get good and mad.

She pulled back one fist, and the haptic controls in her gloves mirrored its action, through an alien computer system jury-rigged to a 1970s fighter jet's controls. Huge pistons snicked and chuffed, and an arm like two articulated buses swung wide.

This was for her mum, and her dad, and Miss Rummage, and the Doom Commission, and... well, for everyone, really.

A wrecking ball of metal knuckles swung.

The frankly shoddy, prison-built walls of Sheol put up very little resistance.

Lucifer, the Lightbringer, the Morning Star, ex-archangel of music and current overlord of Hell-on-Earth, was very rarely surprised. But when a metal foot the size of a garbage truck caught him right on the arse, one might say that he was taken aback.

It kicked him off his throne and clear through the opposite wall, right in the middle of his big valedictory monologue. Faux-marble splintered to shards around him as he flew.

The Dark Lord wasn't about to go down without a fight, though. His single raven wing flared open, and opposite it a spectral counterpart unfurled from his shoulder. A swift cantrip arrested his flight, and he looked down upon Sheol, and at the bloody big hole in its side where he'd been used like a very evil football.

"Show yourself!" he shouted, and the sound alone, thrumming with the harmonics of the choirs infernal, stripped a layer of dust from everything below. "Come forth, coward, if you would face me! Who are you? Some trick of golemetry? A Templar artifice, dedicated to my absent father? *Come and be annihilated!*"

September was very careful not to tread on the giant block of ice which imprisoned her parents as she strode across the cathedral, knocking aside swinging chandeliers. She flexed her huge hands. She gripped the edges of the hole where Lucifer had made his exit – and she ripped the masonry apart.

"I think the phrase you're looking for," she boomed, through a stack of Marshall amps welded into her shoulder pauldrons, "*Is 'come and 'ave a go if you think you're 'ard enough.*"

Around her feet, monsters and demons scattered. She caught sight, through one of her many peripheral cameras, of Stoatman throwing her a jaunty little salute before he scarpered.

Lucifer laughed as the Revenginator peeled open the metal and stone of the tower, as easy as slicing through cardboard. Bravado? Perhaps. Prototypical villainy? Absolutely! He even had the next lines ready.

"*Pitiful mortal! You cannot hope to defeat me!*" he roared, and September could actually see Septivarian mouthing the exact same words inside her head.

"Now he's going to invite us to come and meet our doom," said the superannuated super-scientist.

"**Come forth then, and meet your doom!**" howled

Lucifer, manifesting a great blazing sword from between his hands. "This is the dark destroyer *Nox Aeternum*, the black flame of malice, archetype of spite, with which I have hacked the heads from a thousand angels of the Lord!"

September looked up, tracking him with alien targeting systems.

"Very nice. Good show and tell. Now *this*..." (and here, a pair of huge dark guns swung free, locking into place along the Revenginator's riveted forearms) "This is a pair of General Electric GAU-8A Avenger 30mm seven-barrel autocannons. You might remember them from the good old A-10 'Warthog'. Then again, perhaps not, seeing as you've been stuck in an Italian poem for the last few hundred years."

The massive gatling guns spun up. There was a sound – a glorious sound – as of a sheet of celestial bubble-wrap being rent in twain, right across the vault of heaven. Bullets flew, twin streams intersecting on the shape of the rebel angel.

...who brought his wings flexing up and over, forming a shield before his half-ruined face.

But who, nevertheless, had no argument for the sheer weight of supersonic depleted uranium that went hammering into him like fury. He spun across the sky, feathers both real and spectral flying free, and crashed into the Tower of Dis, making the whole edifice creak and wobble.

"We've got a saying, these days, about bringing a knife to a gunfight," smirked September, lumbering up to a run. Spent, the twin GAU-8A's sheared their explosive bolts and dropped. September let Septivarian take control of re-armament as she ran, and she felt the weird sensation of two Rheinmetall M256 120mm cannons locking into place on her shoulders.

Lucifer peeled himself from off the wall of the tower, broken limbs stretching out from painful angles to fuse back into shape. He was still grinning.

"We've got a saying, too, where I come from. From that holy book that I had *my* people write about half of, thank you very much!"

Now he dropped to the ground, right in the path of the onrushing Revenginator. Now he began to swell and grow, muscles exploding under his skin until it split. Now the rebel angel screamed, and that scream became unhinged laughter as he grew to the size of September's mad creation.

Lucifer had become a thing of raw, slick tendons and spikes of bone. A proper demon, at last.

"*So the Beast was allowed to make war on the saints and to conquer them! And authority was given it over every tribe and people and language and nation! It was given power to wage war against God's holy people, and to conquer them!*"

The twin cannons spoke. Two high-explosive shells went screaming in, each trailing a spiral nimbus of shockwaves. Lucifer's dark sword swatted them from the air, effortlessly.

"That's Revelation 13-7," he said. "Give me that old-time religion! Real hellfire and brimstone! Speaking of which..."

Lucifer extended one clawed hand, and flames roared out from it in a pyroclastic inferno, bathing the Revenginator from top to bottom. Inside the robot's head temperature gauges leapt into the red, and alarms began to yammer. September pulled a hanging chain, and extinguisher systems mounted on the outside of the machine hissed into life. At the same time, she tucked and rolled. Not away from the fire, but under it – coming in close like a prizefighter.

She rose to her knees, in a power-slide down the middle of the high street, steel grinding and sparking across the concrete. The 120mm cannons fired again as she turned the slide into a leap.

This made the Rebel Angel forget about sorcery whip his sword around, slicing one shell clean in half. The other, though, got through. It hammered into Lucifer's chest, detonating in a flash which sent him piledriving sideways through the King's Toes pub. Antique horse brasses, pool balls and uneaten packets of pork scratchings scattered.

September didn't slow down for a second. She sent the Revenginator charging in, feeling a hidden hatch on her upper arm unfold. It dropped a stubby silver tube into her hand, and Septivarian chuckled.

"I understand that this one's more from your particular vintage, girl. I don't know how it's going to fare against a hell-forged broadsword, but you'll get extra points for style."

Now Lucifer shook himself free of the ruined pub, sending plaster and timbers cascading off of his gigantic back. Now he screamed, utter frustration rending the air, and he brought *Nox Aeternum* around in a flat blur, holding it at low guard.

"Come on, coward! Match steel with your master!"

"Pretty confident, for a guy who looks like someone stapled half a vulture to Freddy Krueger."

"Ha!" spat Lucifer. "Do you want to fight me with pop culture references, or with blades, girl?"

September raised the chromed-silver tube in her hand to a salute, just like she'd learned in fencing classes. She thumbed a huge, giant-robot-sized button on its side.

"Why not both?" she asked, as a twenty-metre-long blade of purple light sprung out from it, with a hum of barely suppressed power.

It had been absolutely impossible *not* to make one of these, when she found out that the Americans' UFO had all the right force-field and laser bits. September had reasoned that if she didn't, then she wasn't worth the mad scientist's lab coat she stood up in.

Now Lucifer swung his blackened blade, coming up crosswise, and the thing which (for copyright reasons) September thought of as a 'plasma katana' blocked it. A shower of purple and orange sparks rained down.

She ground her blade down the edge of *Nox Aeturnum*, seeking leverage, or perhaps just to hack through its crosspiece and slice off the Dark lord's fingers. But he was quick, and strong with it – Lucifer twisted and deflected her away, turning the motion into an overhand slice. September was forced to bring her sword up over her head, catching the downstroke and rebounding it, then lunging forward into a stab which Miss Slugpounder would have been proud of.

Of course, the Fallen One cheated. He launched himself backwards into the air, laughing, and hovered there just outside of her reach.

"Oh, good try! Excellent effort! But you should know that I can do this all day, child. I fought on the front lines of the war in heaven. I can see from your style and from your posture that you learned swordplay as a game." He sniffed. "It's one that you cannot win."

"You want a fair fight, then?" asked September.

"I don't want a fair *anything!*" snarled Lucifer. "I want you dead, and what I want, I get! Now and forever!"

But September had seen the tell-tale glint of sunlight on glass, in her bank of monitors. True to the most primal instincts of *Homo Sapiens*, someone was filming all this.

"Can't you feel it, then?" she asked. "Surely you can, by now. Probability vectors collapsing. The phase-space tightening. That pressure-drop in future choices, leading to an inevitability?"

Lucifer looked nothing but arrogant and angry for another beat or two. And then a flicker of worry stole across his half-ruined face.

"What are you doing?" he asked, eyes flicking left and right. "What arcanum do you possess, girl?"

September grinned, deep inside the Revenginator's cockpit. She'd not been one hundred percent sure, herself. But it seemed as if Septivarian had been right, once again.

"You're a *legend*, Lucifer Morningstar. An absolute legend. And a legend is just a story people tell each other to make sense of being human. Thing is, you've been stuck underground in a medieval poem for the last few hundred years. So you weren't to know that the story has changed."

Something – either fear or desperate anger – took hold of him, then. The Rebel Angel attacked with all his skill and might, his blade cleaving apart the air itself, so a flaming nimbus writhed behind it. Orange and purple sparks showered, because now, in this new moment, this was true;

He wasn't quite as fast, or quite as mighty as he had been.

Amid the rubble, the camera crew that Cardinal Syn had brought in to record his triumph kept the signal tight. Other feral newsmen, who had rushed to Little Mean at the first whiff of disaster, sent out their own broadcasts. A web of satellites and invisible beams which Lucifer knew nothing about, wrapped the world in a cobweb of information.

Another flurry of blows. Another windmilling clash of blades – up high, down low, a sweep for the legs, a parried thrust for the face, a figure-of-eight blur with the grinding shriek of force-fields and plasma on iron. This time, as they broke, there was a tiny line of blood scored across Lucifer's perfect cheek.

Well – it *had* been perfect. The plasma katana had left a bloody slash.

"What have you done?" he hissed, all seething malice. His fingers came away crimson.

"I told you about television before, didn't I?" asked September, bringing her blade up to guard. It hummed like a neon tube in an empty underground carpark. "See, while you've been cooling your heels in Dante's hell, people have learned a few new things about giant demons and monsters. One of them's this. *You can go out and fight them with a giant robot.* Then again, they'd *never* even heard of Japan when you were knocking about in the middle ages, had they?"

Lucifer attacked again, shrieking like a burst tea-kettle, his sword describing arcs of utter darkness. Every one of them was met with a splash of purple fire.

"What madness is this?" he asked, reeling backward.

"Not madness. *Belief.* See, the giant robot always wins. The big monster looks like it's doing all right, but then the plucky pilot says something about the power of friendship, and *this* happens,"

September cocked back the arm of the Revenginator, and a rocket scavenged from a Hellfire missile roared into life. A missile-powered punch hammered into Lucifer's solar plexus, doubling him up around it. He barely managed to bring *Nox Aeternum* up to block the follow-up swing of the plasma blade.

"Activate Ultimate Special Destructo Beam Cannon!" shouted September. Millions of TV viewers nodded, and reached for the popcorn. That was how it went.

The chestplate of the Revenginator split open, revealing a spinning trio of magnets, surrounding the glowing purple eye of the UFO's warp core. September didn't know it, but it was actually quite an old and knackered example. The saucer which had crashed at Roswell hadn't been that of some alien overlord. The whole debacle had been the Rigellian equivalent of a few stoned teenagers nicking their parents' Volvo and cruising around shouting at pedestrians. Still, (as the second-hand saucer dealer had told their mum, slapping the side of the little spaceship and grinning), it was good for thirty times lightspeed, and really saved you money on deuterium at the pump.

With a bit of Endarkened super-science, it also made a fantastic weapon.

A rod of purple fire raved from the glowing eye in the Revenginator's chest, and millions of TV viewers knew what would happen next. Flickering beams of energy reflected from off of Lucifer's wings as he tried to shield himself, but it was too much. The beam widened, as September locked her stance, fists clenched at waist height, just as a hundred famous animes suggested. The beam phase-shifted purple to pink to white, and deep inside it, the face of the rebel angel became a mask of surprise and horror. He was cast all in black, in shadow, and little pieces at the edges of that shadow began to break and feather away, diminishing him.

"*Aaaaaaaaarrrrrrrrrrggggh!*" shouted Septivarian, inside her head. "That's right, isn't it? Just like the Atomic Samurai used to shout!"

Lucifer's heels dug furrows into the ground as he was pushed backwards. The tarmac melted, then the concrete beneath.

"Never mind that! Are you sure you want to go through with this? Are you sure we have to?"

All the screens blinked over, one by one, to the face of Septivarian Archimedes.

"Young lady, I've had 137 very interesting years. And I'm not afraid, any more. This little bastard can't be destroyed, not so long as there's religion out there – and he's the type who'd keep coming back. It's in his own book – 'none shall know the hour', right? So we follow the game plan. We do what he'd do, in our place, and then..."

His smile was sad, and wobbly around the edges. There was a 'goodbye' implicit there. But not just yet.

"**Nooooooo!**" shrieked Lucifer, as the beam went beyond white, into that weaving of infinite colours which forms the pigment of creation. The raw stuff that God's paintbrush, that one with the fractal bristles, lays out in cosmic strokes. Every shade at once.

There was a moment of weightlessness. There was a sense of choirs singing, a single note which was every note. There was the sensation of every atom standing apart from its neighbours, shimmering like still water struck by an expertly skipped stone, then locking back into place, rotated a quarter-turn.

Then, because tradition can't be avoided, there was an absolutely impossibly big explosion.

Millions of television sets flashed white. But the cameramen came out of cover one by one, as the echoes of the blast rumbled their way off across the sky. They took in a scene which was absolutely what the viewers expected. Of course. It couldn't be anything else.

When a giant monster fights a massive, heroic robot piloted by a plucky teenage girl, it always goes badly for the monster. After an exciting battle, usually with swords and lasers, the monster shrinks back to human size, and turns out to be an out-of-work actor in a rubber costume. There was probably a law about this in Japan.

Lucifer the Fallen One was not a bloke with an equity card, a week's worth of instant ramen in the pantry at home and a Halloween mask on. But he *had* been gone a very long time. Once, the terrible majesty of a rebel angel had been the benchmark for holy terror. But now the world felt that it knew where it stood with a giant robot.

Because, (everyone knew), the Government had already built things like that, but they kept them hush-hush, in case the Communists found out.

Now the Adversary of God found himself curled up around his pain, smoking gently, at the end of a trench gouged in the High Street. This was slowly cooling, with the *tink* and *plink* of hardening glass.

"You... you think that this is enough to stop me?" he wheezed, sounding a bit less than defiant. A couple of black, shiny insects crawled out from between his lips, split their carapaces and clattered away on transparent wings. "Foolish girl! I fell from Heaven itself, and into the lake of fire. I crawled out on that burning shore, and forged an empire!"

Crunch.

Crunch.

Crunch.

A pair of cherry-red Doctor Martens boots appeared, sideways in Lucifer's vision. One of them was held together by plumber's tape.

"I think this might be enough to make you think about it. Yes," said September. "Come on, now. We're all reasonable super-powered humanoids here, right? There's definitely a place for you in the modern world, which, let me tell you, is surely wicked enough to need a devil. There's a card for it, and all. But none of this 'immortal dark emperor' crap. Save it for the heavy metal album covers, which I can pretty much promise will be *right* up your alley."

Lucifer rolled over, and fixed her with a calculating glare.

"You want me to pose with Norwegians in make-up? Maybe appear in the odd burned quesadilla, as a frightful image? Kind of... semi-retire?"

"It's that, or oblivion, I'm afraid. And I *know* you. I know you're afraid to die. These are, after all, the 'strange aeons' the man was talking about."

Lucifer seemed to deflate, then. He hunched over, hugging his knees to his chest, as his robes gently smouldered.

"You're right, of course. Ha! The irony. That I could live on, as the image of myself painted by that hack Dante, on a little piece of pasteboard. A cartoon version of my former majesty." He sighed, and shrugged his shoulders. His single wing shrugged too. "You know me indeed, September Normalsson."

And there it was. That little sardonic half-smile. That glint of merry hellfire in his eyes. Here it came.

"*But not well enough, it seems!*"

It was a triumphant, braying scream, and it came as Lucifer surged to his feet, his burnt hand lashing out like a taloned claw to wrap around September's throat. The Rebel Angel lifted her from the ground with effortless grace – he was, after all, still a divine being, a Principality of the choirs eternal, first among the fallen.

"You threaten *me* with oblivion? Me? Whom God himself could not chastise? You humans have become fat and foolish in your hubris! You might believe in little machines of tin and wire, but the old fears are still there. I smell them. I *taste* them!

"Your bovine kind were *created* to fear, and to worship, because my Father is so very, very insecure. He could never count on love. Oh no. Nor respect. But terror... ahhh! *That* fills the pews. And they will know terror, your precious modern folk, when they see what happens to you, now."

"Lhhhh Dhrrrrnnn," said September, dangling by her neck. Lucifer's claws had pricked four bright points of blood from her skin, and now they trickled down across his burnt fingers. Across the raw wounds which had never healed.

"What?"

"Lrrrrrkk. Dwwwwnnnn."

Her eyes sold it. Lucifer glanced down, away from her face, all knotted up with pain.

And he saw the huge plastic syringe jammed into his belly. He saw the last little drops of glowing green liquid inside its barrel. He felt, at last, the six-inch needle deep in his supernatural flesh.

"Oh, *bollocks*," he said, letting his fingers come loose. September slipped to the ground, but she was laughing as he staggered back, literally transfixed.

"You know how you like to possess people, Lucy? The whole bit with the pea soup and the spinning heads and the lack of wear-and-tear on mattresses? Well, the more you use that kind of door, the less effort it takes to make it swing open. *The other way.* Welcome to introcism, you bastard. Say hello to Professor Septivarian Archimedes."

Lucifer staggered. He clawed at his throat, until one of his hands grabbed the other, and pulled it away. His whole posture changed, as he stood up, and rolled the kinks out of his shoulders, and turned. His eyes, once burning black, had become watery and blue.

"Hmmmm, quite singular! I didn't realise I missed being, mmmm, corporeal this much. I'd quite like one last cup of tea in fact, if that's at all possible Maybe a small Lamington cake?"

It was Septivarian's stance, and his voice. It was unmistakable.

"It's... it's really worked? There's no kind of trickery?" asked September, stepping forward cautiously. "Only, you know, he *is* the father of lies..."

"I, erm, think that the translation from the Sumerian was a bit off, there, actually," said the voice of Professor Archimedes, coming from the fallen angel's half-ruined face. "I think it was actually 'father of flies'. You know, the little buzzing things that make maggots? He was once just a minor plague deity, in the Euphrates valley area."

"But he's in there with you?"

"Oh yes. Nowhere else to go. My mortal remains are probably ten feet deep in concrete under a motorway support pillar by now, if I know the government. No, he's in here. And he's not happy. What a horrible little mind. Like a thousand little hamster wheels, all powering a torture chamber. Ghastly!"

"I'm just glad I didn't have to kiss this one. Can you keep him bottled up, granddad?"

The look on Lucifer's face – well, at least on the half of it that wasn't a mask of scars – looked pained.

"Only just. He's terrifically strong. After all, this is one of the most believed-in archetypes ever to spring from the human imagination. I'm running incredibly complex calculus equations with the part of his brain that he'd normally use to dominate others. If he'd paid attention during maths class, we'd both be in a lot of bother."

"So we're out of time?"

Lucifer smiled then, and despite using the cruel thin lips and sharp little teeth of a fallen angel, Septivarian Archimedes could not have looked more human. Proud, and tired, and determined. For the first time in mythological history, a tear ran down Lucifer's cheek.

"Then you know what I need to do. Being out of time is just what, hmmm, I need to finish this evil bugger." He held up his hands. "No hugs, I'm afraid. Not even a handshake. I can hear his thoughts, and he plans to try to possess you, if we come into contact. Just pass me the, mmmmm, items, and I'll do what must be done."

"Where will you go?" asked September, in a voice that ended up not being as strong and steady as she'd hoped.

"I don't have the faintest idea. And you know what? After

thirteen decades of knowing just about everything, that's rather a cheerful thought. I might try being reincarnated as an alien, perhaps. Or something made of magnetic fields, that swims in the corona of stars. It won't be the Aught, though. There'll be no memory of any of my wild ideas, I'm afraid. Not after this."

September resisted the urge to squeeze his hands between hers. Instead, she passed him two items from the supermarket carrier bag she'd brought with her from the Revenginator. The first was a pair of blue suede shoes.

"I'll come up with some of my own. They might be the same ones, too," she said, as Septivarian slipped them on. Lucifer's body trembled and shook the whole time, his toes curling as he resisted, all the way.

"I rather thought you might," said Professor Archimedes, standing to attention and throwing her a little salute. "I won't say goodbye. But I *will* say farewell. As in, enjoy the journey, September. I, hmmmm, am about to, as it were, change buses."

He picked up the other thing from the carrier bag. He clicked his heels together.

And, as Lucifer gained just enough control over the ruined half of his face to howl silently in terror, a sphere of blinding white expanded around him, trembled for a second in the morning light, then disappeared.

In the hot, dead silence of Long-Lost Vegas, Septivarian Archimedes stepped out of himself. He stepped sideways out of Lucifer's body, leaving the Fallen One gasping and patting himself all over, there on the gritty concrete of the Strip.

"*Bloody hell!* Is that how it feels to be possessed? I'm more of a bastard than I realised," said the Prince of Darkness. "But never mind that. Never mind any of that.

You!" He surged to his feet. "You are in a whole septic tank of the brown stuff, my elderly friend. You know you can't destroy me! No matter what dimension you try to trap me in, no matter how much damage you do with your silly super-science weapons, I'll *always come back.* I've got nothing but time, and I'll find you, and your wretched granddaughter, too!"

"You know, I'd sort of worried you might say that," said the Professor. "That's why you should look in your pocket."

Lucifer, who had begun to swell and change and grow, becoming something monstrous, paused. He felt a ticking coming from one of the deep pockets in his robes, and he slipped a hand in to encounter a smooth, slightly domed metal shell.

He pulled it out. It was a cheap, gold-plated travel clock.

"You see," said Septivarian, "I'll be utterly destroyed, the very first time. I'm just a normal human being, when it really comes down to it. But you... well. You can pull yourself together. Or you can use that mining-drill of spite you call a mind, and fold your way out of here. But you can't do both at once."

The Doom Clock popped open, there on Lucifer's palm.

The red LED numbers clicked over to letters, impossibly. Prophetically. They said –

-FOREVER-

And a little bit of time came to Long-Lost Vegas. About ten seconds worth, added to the one thirty-millionth of a microsecond which the Dead Elvi had looped, here in this doomed place.

They stretched the loop. They took it out to infinity. They gave it enough time to run those ten seconds on repeat, eternally.

Above Lucifer, in the desert sky, a fist of utter brightness expanded. A terrible, erasing power, held in check for decades, finally let go.

In that moment, it was not Lucifer who was the Lightbringer. It was 10,000 megatons of Soviet ordnance.

What choice did he have? He was utterly blown apart. In the furnace of that killing light, under that alien heat, Lucifer was stripped atom from atom. Around him, the road boiled, and steel melted, and buildings blew out in a scintillating wave of plasma.

Three seconds in, and a mushroom cloud was rising above the wreck of Vegas.

Five seconds in, and something began to re-form, amid the churning bouillon of hard radiation at ground zero. The agonized, furious scraps and shreds of an ancient consciousness.

Seven seconds in, and Lucifer was a tattered shadow, drawing in free electrons and little scabs of matter, building bones and teeth and muscles.

Nine seconds in, and he opened his eyes, prepared to spit curses at the place where Septivarian Archimedes had been.

Then there was a stutter.

Then there was a time-skip in the world around him.

The city didn't get any less ruined. The radioactive hiss and seethe around him didn't settle.

But up in the sky, another explosion blossomed.

There was just time for Lucifer to curse, and flinch, and realise that this was never, *ever* going to end.

And then the wave of light enfolded him, and his mind blew apart.

Twenty
The End
vs
Everything

ANOTHER PLACE. ANOTHER timeless city.

Uncarnadine, the Rotten Apple. The City That Won't Stay Down.

There was panic on the streets, under the eternal midnight of the Azraeon's watch. Transit and the Reapers had torn each other apart. The sky had been ripped open above Gravesend's prison, and the light of the *Materia Mortalis* shone through, cracking around the edges.

There was crime and chaos as sirens wailed, and the civic authorities scrabbled like ants in an overturned nest. Opportunities were taken – for a settling of ledgers, for sordid little acts of revenge, and for other minor sins. Refugees thronged the streets, but there was nowhere to go. Fiction? Myth? Fable? Nightmare? All the roads were closed, and most of them only went one way. Uncarnadine, nestled in the palm of the Azraeon, was the end of the line.

But there was another inevitability here, too.

In the great chamber of the Chronauspexion, all was silent. The machine was broken – though if you stood very still and watched it, you might notice, in the very corner of your eye, that the more organic parts of it were *healing*.

Nevertheless the vaulted hall was quiet, the fires snuffed, the cogs and pistons cold. The only sound was a single set of footsteps, making its way slowly across the marble, toward the very centre of the room.

Through a skylight wrought in the shape of bones, the aeonic eyes of the Azraeon looked down on a marble plinth, about waist-high. The plinth supported two silver rods, about as far apart as a person's outstretched arms. These terminated in little y-shaped bifurcations, and lying across them, presented, was the Scythe.

The one with the capital letter.

The last word in lawn care, pruner of errant lifelines, the literal edge of forever. Gently splitting the time which flowed over it into the past that had happened, and the ones that hadn't.

The footsteps stopped. A whisper of red fabric hushed against the marble floor. A pale white hand reached out.

It hesitated for an instant, as if fearing that the gnarled, smooth-polished wood would be burning hot, or perhaps electrified. Then it closed its fingers.

Then came the laugh.

It was not very nice at all. And it went on for a long, long time, before it was suddenly cut off by a small thunderclap.

In the silence which followed, the Azraeon looked down, impassive. Certainly not sorry.

Because while, for the past few hundred years the rules had insisted that somebody had to bear Dante's Tarot, the card was not as important as this.

Somebody always had to carry the scythe.

What people called them was far less important than what that meant.

In the aftermath of the thunderclap, Cedric Welbourne and Penny Dreadful stood in the middle of a charred crater, surrounded by burning robot parts. Scraps of red fabric fluttered down, smoking.

The young man looked up through the dome, into the eye of the immense skeletal figure which replaced the moon. For an instant – and just for an instant – as Lucifer perished, he'd been the only echo of any kind of Devil standing. And with that power, he'd chosen.

"I'll take the job," he said.

And he picked the scythe up from where it had embedded itself in the soot-blackened floor.

Outside, climbing the mountain of marble stairs in a kind of daze, came a small army of very sheepish-looking Elvis impersonators. Dead, one and all, with their private dimension blown apart.

"I think these guys are looking for some gainful employment, too," said Penny.

The Supreme Aaron, his mind freewheeling alone for the first time ever, looked up into the light between the huge doors of the Chronauspexion chamber, and beheld a young man in a leather jacket, with a swept-forward old-fashioned haircut and skinny jeans.

Now there, he thought, *was rock 'n' roll. **There** was someone he could follow...*

He fell to his chubby knees. His followers thudded down on the marble steps, all around him.

"Hail to the King," he said. "Uh huh huhhh. Thankyouverymuch."

It was a Thursday, and September Normalsson knew that the world had ended on Tuesday.

This was most perturbing, because it showed every indication of not having ended at all.

She'd awoken with the memory of a past which had no longer happened – and it made things no better that it seemed that she was the one responsible for it.

Sitting up in bed, she'd tried to conjure a flicker of the Endarkenment – just a tiny black spark from the tip of one finger. But there'd been nothing at all. Nothing but the utter certainty that she was now somewhere around the scuffed knee of the wrong leg of the trousers of time.

What do you do, with knowledge like that? It seems all

numinous and exciting as a concept, but when the sun is streaming in on a room decked out in heavy metal posters, and your mum is shouting something about breakfast from downstairs, it's easier just to let the auto-pilot of the brain do its thing.

She brushed her teeth, and wrangled her unruly hair, and almost put on her school uniform before she saw the neat set of black clothes laid out on her chair, by the computer desk.

That's right. Oh. They were going to bury him today, weren't they? And of course, Mister Mackleduff had given her the day off. Bereavement leave.

September tried to recall exactly what had happened to her great-great-granddad. There were memories there of a raging battle, and some kind of doublecross, and a beautiful, half-burned face collapsing into fear. Then, of course, there was the recollection of Miss Pennywhistle quietly summoning her to the front of the class, and handing her a little note. She remembered having to walk out into the corridor before the slap-shock of it turned to tears, and how they never came.

Because of some mad supposition that he'd beaten death already, and he'd made a plan, and he was...

Gone.

The world showed every indication of still not having ended as September went downstairs and had breakfast with her parents. They were dressed in sensible black, and her mum looked more than a little bit teary-eyed, for all that they'd tried to pretend that Septivarian Archimedes didn't exist for the past eighteen years. Both of them were wearing a curious lapel pin, of a big silver question mark.

Breakfast was toast and porridge. The conversation was brittle, forgettable, and unreal.

The town of Little-Mean-on-the-Average was stubbornly

undestroyed, as well.

September watched it slide by in reflection, out the back window of her dad's brown Austin Allegro, and saw the scars which weren't there. The gaping hole in the King's Toes pub, where Anubis had fallen. The burned-out tanks on the memorial bridge. The wrecked helicopters on Monkston's Green. They were just ghosts in her memory, but they were real. The fact of it sat there in September's mind, like the hole left by a missing tooth.

What replaced them were fresh facades of clean red brick, gaps in the ivy which spilled down old stone walls, and new patches of asphalt. The library was untouched, but she could see where smoke stains had been power-washed off the concrete. Anders' Veg was built, and was open for business behind a barricade of brassicas and spuds in paper sacks. A flapping neon banner screamed UNDER NEW MANAGEMENT.

The trousers of time, thought September. *They were down the wrong leg, and the fabric had become all tie-dyed with a different history. They were probably entering the bell-bottom of entropy, or something similar.*

If the temporal weirdness of Little Mean was strange, the funeral of Professor Septivarian Archimedes was even stranger. The allegro crunched its way up the gravel driveway of Wrinkly Acres between rows of weird super-vehicles, all of them finned and bubble-domed and blazoned with famous logos. The Septic Seven's Septic Tank crouched on rusty treads. The Confectioner's Voiture d'Eclair sparkled candy pink, and next to it was the Defenestration-copter, and Captain Captain's pirate-themed Harley-Davidson trike.

Government types had turned up, too – there were several long black armoured limos, and a couple of military off-roaders. It seemed that everyone had turned out to farewell September's great-great-granddad, despite having been quietly mortified about everything he'd ever done for decades.

Even her parents were weirdly supportive.

"It's OK to cry, you know," said September's mum, who had deployed a wad of handkerchiefs big enough to parachute into occupied Normandy with. Like many middle-aged respectable ladies, she thought that trying to cram this expanse of damp fabric up one cardigan sleeve made it physically vanish. "I know you're very brave, and he was rather odd, but he would have wanted us to grieve like a family."

September bit back any kind of comment on how Septivarian had actually gone out – as a disembodied spirit luring the Prince of Darkness into a death-trap. Instead, she meekly accepted an unprecedented maternal hug. Her mum smelled of lavender and rosewater.

"Come on. They're starting," said her dad. "Oooh, I hope they don't ask for a speech. I'm rubbish at public speaking."

A lone piper began to play, up on top of the marble stairs. There was no coffin to carry, but an honour guard, made up of Stoatman, the Red Mobster, Medusa Oblongata (and a notable moving absence which could only have been the Invisible Prince) carried one of his signature mortarboards on a black velvet cushion. The Confectioner gave a signal to Candy Caine, who activated a big pink machine off in the rockery. A cloud of grey cotton candy wisped out of it, and began raining sugary drizzle over a six-foot hole cut into the turf by the croquet lawn.

"They promised you this, didn't they?" said a voice in her right ear. A hand fell on her shoulder at the same time – not hard, but with the kind of weight and purpose which indicated that shrugging it off was not an option.

The second voice was a little more familiar.

"A lovely funeral? I suppose it is. In his own, weird way, of course. But you know what *really* happened, Miss Normalsson. And so do we. We think you'd better come with us."

September looked left and right, expecting to see a pair of grey-faced Elvis Presleys, but that wasn't who had accosted her at all.

"And if I think I shouldn't come with you? Stranger danger, and all that?" she asked the two black-suited white men. One had dark curly hair and a pair of Ray Ban wayfarers. The other was a stubbled, shaggy blonde, in gold-rimmed aviators.

"I think she knows *exactly* how this works, Mister Morrison," said the blonde, opening his coat just a little to show a flash of nickel-plated weaponry.

"I think she's testing us, to see if we're as dumb as the old model, Mister Cobain," said the dark-haired one, who, it appeared, had paired his suit jacket, tie and white linen shirt with black leather trousers.

The funeral went on around them as September shrugged.

"You know what I did to the last ones, gentlemen. Take me to your leader, then. But I'll be leaving as soon as you bore me with any big villainous monologues."

It wasn't far to a big black low-slung limousine. There were a few of them dotted around the parking lot and driveway, but this one seemed excessively fat and sleek, riding low on its shocks as if it weighed as much as a tank.

Mister Cobain held the door open, and Mister Morrison gestured for September to get inside. The interior of the car smelled of burning fuse wire, leather polish, and dry concrete basements. It was set up like a little office, with two bench seats facing each other over a walnut-burl table. Across the other side was Margaret Thatcher.

"September Normalsson," said Mrs Marjorie Goosegarden. "I'll dispense with the niceties, because I'm not very nice. We know that there was a Critical Reality Disconnect Event[40] here, in Little Mean, two days ago. We know that there's unsecured threads thrashing around in the time-stream, and some very bad sutures indeed. One example of note – London's chief police inspector is convinced that we need an anti-vampire squad. Then there's the fact that all of the 'special attaches' who used to look like Elvis are suddenly other dead musicians. Care to elaborate?"

"I couldn't possibly comment."

Mother Goose clicked and whirred in exasperation.

"Regular human minds will gloss it all over, but we know you did something. *You*, personally. Oversight says we should kill you, the Things Beyond say we should banish you, and the government has no idea what all this means. So we're here to offer you a job."

This was not entirely what September had expected. But she wasn't about to be wrong-footed, just because she'd been abducted for a corporate interview by what was almost certainly a robot version of the former Prime Minister.

"Thanks for the offer, but I really have to finish school first. Qualification are so important in today's modern..."

The automaton held up one hand and cut her off.

"I'm sure you think that some negotiations are in order, but they're not. We are aware of the Endarkenment, and the legacy of dear old Septivarian. One of the loose threads you left un-stitched was Silas Rosewood, who has very much vanished from history. We'd like you to replace him."

"As what?"

---

40. She pronounced all of the capital letters, just like Alan Rickman would have.

"Science advisor to the Bureau Innominandum. The pay is quite staggering, but of course, we don't collect all of those taxes for nothing."

"Ma'am, I'm seventeen and a bit years old. I'm not ready for a career in weird super-science."

The robot thatcher chuckled, with a sound like a terminally ill gearbox.

"Come on, girl! You think we don't do our research? You're not one of *them*. The average people. The cattle. The plebeian herd. You're one of *us*. You're from the weird side of the tracks, and you belong in more rarefied company."

"My parents gave up a lot to give me a shot at a normal life, Ma'am."

"Your parents will think you've gotten an internship with the Ministry of Oddly-Named Fish. They turned their backs on power. You're not that kind of fool."

September considered, for a moment, what might happen if she left, right now, and followed in the path her great-great-granddad had forged. The one which had led him to loathe and fear the government. The one that had made him a super-villain.

"I'm sorry. The answer is no," she said. "Now, if you don't mind..."

Mother Goose sighed, and shook her head.

"Oh, dear, dear girl. The thing is... we rather do."

Her hands came up again, this time with the skin peeling back in long ribbons, and the metal underneath folding and screwing apart. Fingers retracted, and wrists locked, as Margaret Thatcher's palms irised open, into the muzzles of twin plasma cannons.

September tried to call up the Endarkenment, but all she managed was a feeble black spark, sizzling between her fingertips.

"See? You don't even know that there's a delay, after a

reality shear that powerful! That kind of ignorance could hurt a lot of people, September. That's why it's either take the job, fall in line, or be obliterated."

She didn't snarl it as a threat. Instead it was a sad, certain statement of fact.

For a long moment, September stared into the twin cobalt throats of those plasma cannons. *If I scream, she thought, they probably won't even hear me. Two hundred super-powered pensioners out there, and not one of them will come to save me...*

But someone did.

There was a knock on the limo door, and it clicked open, swinging wide just as the boneless remains of Mister Morrison slid to the ground. That wasn't a metaphor; he'd disintegrated to a very familiar foul-smelling black slurry.

"I hope it's not a bad time," said Cedric Welbourne, slipping into the seat next to September. "Though I'm afraid it usually is, whenever I turn up."

He was dressed in a black tailored suit, of some material so fine that there was no discernible weave to it. He wore a massive silver chain around his neck, over a tie embroidered with cheerful skulls, and at its end swung the Tarot of Death.

"She's got diplomatic immunity," said Cedric, and his voice had a kind of confidence that September didn't recall. Not from this timeline, or the last. "Put the guns away, Mrs Goosegarden, or I might be forced to remember that putting your consciousness in a robot body counts as cheating death. And that's a bit personal, all things considered."

The plasma cannons dipped. Metal slid and locked, folding that blue glow away.

"*You?* They chose you? Another loose end, or at least that's what our army witches skryed. By what clause of the

Unmanifest Accords do you claim immunity for her?"

Cedric shrugged.

"I don't. I'm here to propose a few new ones. Recent events have proven that the Aught needs to be in contact with certain other powers. It's like the situation with the Things, now. Septivarian proved that you can meddle with us, and frankly, you don't want a war with the dead. Fiction might well come out on our side, too, and the Baal Shem would be... tetchy."

"But... *you?* It was your first day!"

Cedric smiled.

"Even the Azraeon had a first day, Mrs Goosegarden. And you're right. The old guard, the bureaucrats, the departmental heads, they don't like it. But the big fella picked me, not them. *I* was the one who held Dante's rubric together, according to the story they choose to believe. So I'm winging it. But I know who really helped. So... I'm appointing September Normalsson as ambassador to the Aught. I expect her to have a place around the table."

September went to speak, but Mother Goose cut her off.

"We were just offering her the same thing."

"At gunpoint! How novel!"

"That's not the point! We need her to replace Doctor Rosewood as our weird science advisor."

"And *I'd* prefer that she wasn't conveniently under your thumb. I owe her one."

"Hey!"

September slapped the table, and this time a crackle of Endarkenment slithered across its surface.

"This is all very flattering, and it's nice to see you, too, Cedric. But I'm getting out of this car, now. I'm going to attend my great-great-granddad's funeral. I'm going to have a piece of cake, and a cup of tea, and then go and have a bit of a cry, and then, tomorrow, I'm going back to school. I'll deal with the future when it gets here."

They both looked at her, then – the boy with the vintage face and the cold, haughty robot. They saw something that made them pause.

"Are you sure?" asked Cedric. "We've got lots of work to do, rebuilding Uncarnadine. Penny's taken over transit, and there's a whole city to improve. I know what you did. I kind of hoped you'd want to be with us. Your friends."

Mother Goose snorted.

"*Friends?* Be sensible, girl. We're offering you money, and power!"

"No. I don't think so. But I'll tell you both what. I'm going to find out who I am, separate from Septivarian Archimedes, and Dante's Magician, and all of that. I'm going to grow into it. And when I'm done with university, and maybe a gap year, I'll come and see you. I might have learned enough by then to do both, without becoming the job and not September Hyacinth Normalsson."

"Preposterous!" hissed the robot Thatcher. "You're too dangerous! And what are we to do, for five long years, not knowing how you'll shift the balance of power?"

Cedric smiled. It was a long, slow smile; utterly his own, with absolutely nothing of a grinning skull about it.

"I suppose we'll have to talk, Mrs G. And I can guarantee you this much, September. Until you're ready, you're welcome to visit my side of the veil, without even dying." He held up a hand, and a tiny scythe, only the size of a ballpoint pen, flashed into existence between his fingers.

"I'll do this for you, too. Any power, or potentate, or agency which tries to mess with you, for every minute you want to spend discovering yourself, will have the full weight of death itself to deal with. There will be no dimension dark enough, no dungeon deep enough, no conspiracy dire enough to protect them. We always get our man, Mrs Goosegarden. You might want to tell the other signatories to the Accords."

The robotic Margaret Thatcher reached under the limo seat, and produced a big black book of regulations. It was astonishingly thick.

"About that. The intervention of the Aughtic Nation of Death in diplomatic concordance means that we will have to ratify several new statutes regarding inter-reality communication protocols. I'll direct you to section nine, paragraph two, sub-clause twelve, on page three hundred and two..."

September didn't stick around. She reached over and gave Cedric's knee a squeeze, then popped open the door and stepped outside.

The air smelled of freshly turned earth and icing sugar, and the wind carried a hint of autumn. Across the lawn, Stoatman was giving a speech from a set of yellowed little cards, and the flowers in the garden plots all bent under the breeze. September could see her parents there, her dad with his arm around her mum's shoulders. She closed the door and walked away, felling curiously light, and absolutely, self-assuredly real.

There would be plenty of time for madness. It was pretty much inevitable, even if you weren't the successor to a super-scientist supervillain.

But now was for now.

And just for now, it was quite right to be part of it.

~~THE END~~
THE BEGINNING
OF SOMETHING ELSE

We hope you enjoyed this book.
If you did then please consider leaving a review or a
rating at Amazon – it would mean a lot to us all

The Threads Which Bind Us

Anna's life is falling apart. She's missing college lectures, lost touch with her friends and can't face her family. She wakes to find the ghost of a young man in her room. He has no memory of his past life nor any clue as to why he has appeared here.

In the beginning, she fights to get rid of him, but something about his glass-like sensuality fascinates her as he is drawn towards the only person in his world that can hear him, see him, touch him.

As they work to find out who he is, how he died and what is keeping him in the realm of the living, Anna's own recent and tragic past surfaces.

The Wolf Inside Us

Puppy love quickly turns to something altogether more serious in Darian Hart's werewolf romance novel.

The story touches on the crippling disabilities of agoraphobia, self-doubt and body dysmorphia.

Kat is able to accept Jake for all he is, and even what he has now become. Her feelings for the reclusive artist blossom when he suddenly goes missing from his penthouse apartment. But stranger still, why did he leave a tiny puppy behind, all alone, and where did he get it?

In this sensual but light-hearted paranormal romance. Life, and a mysterious other force throw all they have at this young woman and her dog.

The Calico Golem

Emily's teenage years had been marred by bullies because she was different. It wasn't just about how she looked, or that she preferred girls to boys. Mads – tall, athletic and delightfully strange too found herself entranced by Emily after a chance encounter in the school shower room and from there the deepest love blossomed.

But troubles pile upon troubles and things seem to happen around Emily that she just can't explain.

Now, living together in a high-rise flat deep in the crumbling concrete estates, an attack by an ancient and mysterious woman leaves the girls for dead in a cold, dark alley.

Emily believes her beloved Mads to have died in the blast, but the appearance of a sinister creature in the darkness suggests otherwise.

What follows is a struggle to cheat death itself and restore life and justice along with some outlandish alliances.

Into Dust

Ryan Malin had made a name for himself as the author of a very successful series of guidebooks on supposedly haunted houses. But there was always one that had been off-limits to him – Hewitson Cottage.

That was until he was approached by the alluring Kelley Stranack. She and her fellow university lecturer promised a whole weekend of exclusive access, all expenses paid. Naturally, he jumped at the chance.

Of course none of the places he'd written about were actually haunted, but this place... well, it had a history worth investigating.

But why had a cash-strapped university chosen HIM, paid all his expenses and who had paid for the cottage to be refurbished for their trip?

This delightfully spooky tale sits neatly in our paranormal series and meshes cunningly with the other stories whichever order you read them in.

9 781910 779484